"Ms. Zimlich is . . . stellar! 4 1/2 stars!"
—Romantic Times on *Heart's Prey*

A WEDDING SURPRISE

A soft gasp of surprise escaped Alexandra's throat as her new husband's mouth followed the downward course of his fingers. For a timeless moment, she reveled in the flow of sensations and allowed his tender ministrations to continue, although she knew it was insanity to do so. She jerked away suddenly. This man's soft lips and gentle fingers weren't going to stop her from reaching her goal. She wouldn't spend the rest of her days tied to a man such as him—or to any man for that matter.

She pushed Lucien onto his back with a suddenness that startled them both, then rolled, maneuvering herself so that she was stretched full-length atop him. Her braids fell forward, twining about his face and shoulders.

Lucien stared up at her in surprise and struggled to catch his breath. "Is something wrong?"

She smiled. They were near the head of the bed now, close enough for her to reach the small side table. "Absolutely nothing, husband." She shook her head so that more of her thick braids draped around his face, veiling his view. Unseen, her hand crept across the coverlet until her fingers found something heavy. Her teeth flashed white against her olive skin. "At least, not anymore."

THE BLACK ROSE

JAN ZIMLICH

LOVE SPELL BOOKS   NEW YORK CITY

*For my parents, Jim and Helen Nelson,
who taught me all about heroes and heroines.*

A LOVE SPELL BOOK®

June 2000

Published by

Dorchester Publishing Co., Inc.
276 Fifth Avenue
New York, NY 10001

ISBN 0-505-52384-1

THE BLACK ROSE

Chapter One

"To us." The soft tinkle of crystal striking crystal echoed briefly in the cavernous drawing room. Theodore Fallon lifted the gold-rimmed glass to his lips and gulped down the sparkling blue wine, then signaled a lackey to pour him more. He raised his goblet toward Charbonneau Castle's bland gray ceiling. "And to the future. May their union produce fifty brats, all sons with strong limbs and courageous hearts."

Baron Renaud Charbonneau inclined his head in response and took a minuscule sip, allowing only a trace of wine to slip past his tongue. The mere taste caused the corners of his mouth to twitch in a grimace that he was careful to suppress. Wine and women were the root of all the evils that afflicted humankind, but it would be bad form not to join his guest in a celebratory toast.

He cleared his throat, more from a desire to cleanse himself of the sickening aftertaste than

7

Jan Zimlich

necessity, and gave his newfound ally a prim, manufactured smile. A smile was expected at times such as these, a meager price to pay considering the power the new alliance would soon bring his clan.

"Truly a momentous occasion," Charbonneau said quietly, the smile so firmly entrenched now that the flesh of his cheeks was beginning to ache. His clan was now permanently allied with the doltish Fallons, a merger purchased with trade concessions and an outrageous outlay of credit chits. But what he had gained today far outweighed the expense—and risk. And the treaty would soon be sealed in blood, a tradition practiced for over two thousand years among the Dominion clans. In a month's time, his bastard son would be wed to a minor member of the Fallon clan, sealing the alliance forever. Still a small part of him hoped he hadn't made a mistake.

His gaze flicked over the sheaf of parchment stacked so neatly at the center of the antique conference table, the thin paper a glaring yellow-white against the reddish hues of polished mahogany. The treaty had been signed, the cover page witnessed and stamped with the ornate seals of Clan Charbonneau and Clan Fallon. It was too late for either of them to back out now.

Charbonneau's eyes turned a deep, flinty gray as his gaze drifted over the nobleman seated across from him, searching for signs of deceit or treachery in every twitch, every tiny movement that Fallon made. But there was nothing. Nothing visible, at least. Theodore Fallon was a coarse-faced bear of a man, an arrogant brute with thickset shoulders and huge hands that would have been more comfortable clutching the stock of a laser rifle than the fragile stem of heirloom crystal. His robe was rumpled and

8

unkempt, and his gray-splotched hair was tied in a profusion of shoulder-length braids, an unsightly style favored on Lochlain, the Fallon homeworld. But such coarseness wasn't entirely unexpected. Through the centuries, the Fallons had made their mark as a warrior clan, fierce soldiers whose sword arms were available for hire to anyone who could meet their price.

Charbonneau's graying brows pulled together. There was something vaguely disquieting about Lord Fallon, a veiled slyness that seemed to glimmer beneath the dark surface of his eyes, much like a shoal-shark's fin flitting through muddy water.

Then again, many things within the Dominion were not exactly what they seemed, especially among the elite. The corners of Charbonneau's mouth lifted a fraction higher, and for one brief instant, his smile was almost eager, as close to genuine as he'd managed in many a year. His so-called son would be married off to Fallon's niece, and a miserable chapter of his life would finally be laid to an uneasy rest. Lucien would be the Fallons' problem thereafter, and Charbonneau would finally be free—free of the shame that had followed him through life like a malevolent shadow, the fear that someday, someone would discover the truth.

Charbonneau frowned suddenly. Of course, if the union remained unconsummated or failed to produce the required heir within a standard year, the alliance would automatically disintegrate. In that event, the treaty and the marriage would be annulled, and Lucien would become a thorn in his father's side once again. "Perhaps it would be wise if we discussed the treaty's full implementation before you depart, Lord Fallon."

Fallon's shoulders rose in a diffident shrug.

"What's left to discuss? The nuptial ceremony will take place in thirty standard days, as agreed, and the first stage of the treaty's implementation will follow immediately after."

Charbonneau remained silent, busying himself by clearing his throat and glancing around the empty expanse of his castle's austere drawing room.

The baron's nervous silence caused a niggle of doubt to inch its way through Fallon's wine-dulled brain. "Is there a problem I'm unaware of, Baron?"

Charbonneau reddened and cleared his throat again, then smoothed the starched white lace at the end of his sleeve. "I was speaking of a different kind of implementation. . . . The sort that might occur between man and wife after they are legally wed."

A flash of amusement passed through Fallon's eyes as he swigged down the contents of his glass. "I assumed that they'd just frack each other in the usual way."

Embarrassment stained Charbonneau's cheeks even redder. "I simply think we should agree beforehand whether their offspring are to be produced naturally or with some . . . assistance."

Fallon shrugged and motioned for the lackey to fill his glass again. "I am Alexandra's liege lord. She will agree either way because she will have no choice." His eyes narrowed suddenly, and he gave his newfound ally a suspicious look. "Your son's not a man-lover, is he?" Fallon spies had determined that Lucien Charbonneau was a bit effete, a frilly-clothed weakling who seemed to relish his position as a court hanger-on.

Charbonneau sniffed and tilted his chin to an indignant angle. "No, Lord Fallon. My son is *not* a man-lover," he insisted, hoping that what he said was true.

"Good." Fallon sipped his wine, and a dangerous glint entered his eyes.

"And your niece?" Charbonneau watched his face intently. "What of her?"

"I don't anticipate any problems with Alexandra." At the mention of his niece, Fallon swallowed, but otherwise he appeared calm.

"The girl will do what she's told."

"As will my son." Charbonneau lifted his gaze toward the ceiling and prayed that he wouldn't be damned to hell for uttering such a lie.

Chapter Two

The exterior of Charbonneau Castle was as uninspired and austere as its master, a dull gray edifice carved block by block from plain native stone less than fifty years before. No turrets or buttresses graced the upper reaches, no spires soared toward the thin shroud of clouds scudding across New France's midday sky. The castle was no more than a series of rectangular buildings sprawled atop a wind-whipped hill. Stark, uninviting, and broodingly ugly, it was one man's monument to himself.

Lucien Charbonneau paused at the base of the stone steps and stared at the wooden entry doors. This castle was home, the place where he'd been born. His mouth flattened, and his gaze turned hard. It was also the place where he had learned the true meaning of hatred.

And nothing had changed in the past five years, not in the castle's appearance or his feelings. The last time he'd seen the keep, the tall armored

doors had been tightly sealed, the windows
draped, preventing any trace of light or warmth
from the planet's suns from reaching the castle's
gloomy interior. It was still that way, just as his
father preferred.

He wondered absently why he had agreed to
come back to New France at all. Curiosity? To
witness firsthand what sort of toll the passage of
years had wrought upon his father? Or was it
simply a matter of filial obedience? Old habits
died hard, after all. His father had sent a message
ordering him to come home, and he had suc-
cumbed, regardless of the past or what awaited
him inside.

Beside him, Tay Molvan shifted slightly, more
an uneasy twitch of the shoulders than an actual
movement. Lucien understood his friend's reaction intuitively. The castle's glum facade was
enough to make a seasoned warrior shiver with
dread.

Lucien lifted a blond brow and threw Tay a
sidelong look. "So, what do you think?"

"Truthfully?" A line of gooseflesh rose along the
nape of Tay's massive neck. "I think I'd rather eat
a ground-toad than go in there." A chill ran up his
neck. How had Lucien survived childhood in a
place like this? "I've got a bad feeling, Lucien.
Why don't we just turn around and go back to the
transport ship before it's too late."

Lucien grasped Tay's arm lightly, mindful that
there were probably a dozen spies watching their
every move, and shook his head slowly. "I have to
see him, Tay, just long enough to find out what's
on his mind. An hour or so, no more. I owe him
that much, I suppose."

Tay nodded in acceptance and huffed out a
nervous breath. "Okay, just hurry it up so I can
get out of these ridiculous clothes." His hands

moved unconsciously to the folds of red material, smoothing and adjusting the long, heavy robe. "I look like a court fop."

Lucien eyed his friend in amusement. "Not quite." The robe was simple and unadorned. Serviceable, no more. He flicked at a bit of dust clinging to the sleeve of his own silken robe, the costly fabric rustling as he moved. "You look like the servant to a fop."

"Thanks a lot."

"Just remember to act the part. Stay three steps behind me at all times and keep your eyes on the floor. Wait outside the door while I have the interview with my father, and don't speak to anyone in the castle unless they speak to you first." His gaze bored into Tay's broad face for a long moment. "And if anything goes wrong, get off the planet any way you can and follow the prearranged plan."

"Okay."

"Let's go then." Lucien climbed the staircase slowly, lifting the hem of his robe high to avoid mussing the delicate blue material. The castle doors swung inward as he reached the top, Tay the required three steps behind.

"Master Lucien." A sour-faced servant dipped his head slightly, the only show of respect due the baron's bastard son.

"Ah, Ludwig, how good it is to see you again. It's been quite a while, hasn't it?" Lucien fussed with the line of jeweled buttons running down the front of his robe, repositioning the one at his waist several times. "Would you be so kind as to inform my father that I have arrived?"

Ludwig dipped his head forward, again just the barest of movements, then moved deeper into the shadowy entry hall. "The baron has been expecting you for more than two weeks."

The gloomy twilight of the place, settled over them as Lucien followed the servant down a corridor, the only sounds the hushed tap of their footsteps against the bare stone floors. Memories from his childhood drifted down the corridor, whispering to him like musty ghosts flitting through the castle's shadows as he passed a familiar door or room: the words of half-forgotten conversations, the squeal of childish laughter. Happy times. Times that had been buried along with his mother.

Lucien's fists clenched as he paused for a split second and stared at a familiar section of wall. The portrait of his mother was long gone, burned, most probably. The only sign that it had ever existed was the darkened outline of the frame against the blank gray stone.

The servant pushed open a dark wood door, and Lucien stepped inside, ghostlike memories shouting a warning as he entered his father's domain. The musty-smelling room his father used as a study was just as he remembered: dark, dreary, and threatening. The drapes were tightly drawn against the warmth of New France's twin suns. A trail of dust motes crawled along a weak shaft of sunlight that had found its way through the draperies, the only trace of natural light to penetrate the gloom.

Lucien sucked in a breath to steady himself and forced his fingers to unclench. The thin line of sunlight faded into nothingness just shy of his father's simple wooden desk, as though it lacked the courage to intrude upon the black-robed man seated there.

The door clicked shut, and Renaud glanced up from the stack of parchment spread before him, his steel-hard gaze drifting over the lanky young man standing directly in front of his desk.

Renaud studied him for long seconds, his mouth a tight white line as he glanced at his third-born son's extravagant attire. "You're late," he said gruffly. "I expected you to answer my summons weeks ago."

Lucien took another breath, fighting the urge to turn and walk out of the room, to walk away from New France forever. His father's stony eyes were riveted on him, their cold gray depths filled with hatred and contempt. Five years had wrought no discernible change, either in his father's somber appearance or his chilly demeanor. "Did you think that I wouldn't come?"

"The thought crossed my mind." A jeweled button winked in the half-light, and the set to the baron's mouth hardened even more. Lucien's buttons alone must have cost at least a thousand chits. "But then I discarded the notion. If you hadn't come, you knew I would cut off your funds, and then who would pay for those costly robes?"

For a tiny instant, a flash of anger lit Lucien's eyes, but the moment passed, and his rage vanished as swiftly as it had risen. His body went still, very still, the lack of movement veiling the hostility he kept hidden inside. "Is there a point to this interview, Father?" He forced his lips to curl in an indifferent smile. "If not, I think I'll be on my way. I'm days overdue for a revel at the archduke's summer castle."

Renaud's expression darkened. "You will stay until you are granted permission to leave. We have important matters to discuss, your future uppermost." Lucien still had the look of his mother about him, from the sculpted lines of his face to the pale blond hair that fell carelessly to his shoulders. But in the past five years, he had changed from a gawky boy to a striking young man. There were other differences as well—nothing Renaud could put his finger on exactly, but they were there nonetheless, changes that reminded him even more of Lucien's mother.

A sudden frown crossed the baron's features, and his tight-lipped expression darkened even more. Save for the gray of Lucien's eyes, there was nothing of the Charbonneaus about him. Nothing at all. "I fear you will miss the archduke's so-called revel completely." The timbre of his voice roughened, grew thick with hostility. "Your days as a court wastrel are over. Since you haven't seen fit to make plans for your future, I have been forced to make arrangements for you."

Lucien's body finally moved: a stiffening of his shoulders, a twitch in his fingers as his hands knotted into hard fists. How like his father to try to impose such demands. "What sort of arrangements?" he asked in a mild tone, burying all trace of emotion deep inside lest his father use it against him.

The baron lifted his chin and gazed at his son through narrowed eyes, like a watchful predator who'd caught sight of his prey. "I have recently signed a blood-compact allying us with Clan Fallon. Your marriage to a Fallon will permanently seal the treaty and the alliance."

"My what?" Lucien's voice boomed through the room, ringing in the hollow silence. He had expected his father to demand that he return home, or order him to find gainful employment, but this . . . ? Lucien stepped forward and gaped at him incredulously, his hands gripping the edge of his father's austere desk. "Marriage? How dare you agree to such a thing without my approval! You don't have the right!"

"Don't I?" The baron lifted his chin slightly higher, his eyes and mouth thinning even more. He gave his son a disdainful glare. "In case you've forgotten, I do not need the approval of my bastard son for any decision I make as head of this Clan. I am your liege lord, and under Dominion law, you are legally bound to abide by any agreement I enter into on your behalf. You have no rights in this matter."

"And if I refuse?" The challenge hung between them, cold and dangerous.

"You will be cut off without a chit," the baron snapped matter-of-factly. "Stripped of the right to use the Charbonneau name and banished from Dominion territory forever. Or if I choose, I can petition the High Council to imprison you for the rest of your days. That is *my* right."

Lucien tried to breathe steadily, to still the tide of fury rising inside him. The fact that his father had only spoken truth made him angrier still. He had no rights under Dominion law, no hope that anyone would intercede on his behalf. Children were simply property within the Dominion, to be disposed of as the head of their clan so chose. The injustice of Dominion law was a festering wound, one that would someday lead to the government's downfall. But at this juncture, he could ill-afford a confrontation with the baron; it would be a war of wills and words that would undoubtedly lead to his own destruction instead.

"Please reconsider, Father," he said in a calmer tone, trying to quell his anger. "I cannot in good conscience marry a woman I have never met."

The baron waved a hand dismissively. "I will brook no further protests," he said tightly. "You are legally bound to marry a woman of Fallon blood in accordance with the provisions of the alliance. The ceremony will take place in three days' time on Lochlain, the Fallon homeworld. You will have ample opportunity to meet the woman there."

Lucien forced his hands to relax until his palms were stretched flat against the polished desk, but his fingers still trembled from the force of his rage. Though it galled him to do so, he had no choice but to comply with his father's decree. But a day of reckoning would come. Soon, he hoped. Lucien dipped his head slowly, grudgingly. "As you wish."

The corners of the baron's mouth lifted in a small, triumphant smile. The spineless whelp had caved in, just as he'd known he would. "Comm your regrets to the archduke. I fear you've attended your last revel for a long, long while."

Lucien stepped away from the desk, out of the room's wan light. The shadows enveloped his face and veiled his stiff expression. In three days' time he would be married off to a woman he had never met, never seen, a decision made by a father who loathed the very sight of him. He would be married off to a Fallon, no less, a member of one of the most disreputable clans within the Dominion. "Might I ask the name of my future bride?" There was a bitter edge to his voice, one he didn't bother to disguise.

The baron picked up the parchments stacked in front of him and rustled through the pages until he found what he sought. "Alexandra is her name, third niece of Lord Theodore Fallon." Charbonneau peered into the gloom, searching for signs of defiance. "It's a suitable match, and the best any bastard could hope for."

The quiet scuff of a boot heel scraping stone warned of the sentry's approach long before his

Jan Zimlich

shadow loomed like a grotesque insect along the corridor wall. Alexandra Fallon clutched her travel bag tighter and slipped into a night-darkened alcove, flattening herself into a dank puddle of darkness behind a crumbling column. She bit down on her lower lip as the sentry scuffled past, his heels clicking on the stone in a distinct rhythm she'd heard her entire life. Judging by the sound of the shuffling gait, the sentry was old Fomus, a permanent fixture around Fallon Keep since before she was born. The crotchety soldier dragged one foot behind him, the result of some long-forgotten battle of decades ago.

Time and distance finally extinguished the soldier's footsteps, and Alexandra pushed out a sigh of relief. Fomus was a meddling old fool, and would have no doubt screamed a warning if he'd caught sight of her slipping through the castle's shadows, travel bag in hand.

She waited another half minute, then another for good measure. When she was certain the darkness and winter quiet had resettled around Fallon Keep, she hiked the cumbersome robe up to her knees and inched down the corridor wall to a servants' staircase, feeling her way down the spiral steps by the touch of her toes against chilled stone.

As she neared the bottom floor, the darkness enfolding her turned an odd greenish gray, a signal that dawn was well on its way. Alexandra quickened her footsteps. Time was of the essence. She had to be far from the keep before full light, at least a mile or more away before her uncle discovered she'd gone missing again.

A sudden breath of sound drifted toward her from the shadows, a whisper of movement from the darkened steps beneath her. Alexandra stifled

20

a scream and gathered her robe to flee back up the winding staircase.

"Lady Alexa!" a hushed voice called out to her. "It's only me."

At the sound of the familiar voice, Alexandra halted in midstep and touched a hand to her chest. Her palms were damp, and her heart was pounding loudly enough to alert the guards. "Loran . . ." she whispered furiously. "You scared the wits out of me!" She peered into the green-tinted darkness shrouding the steps beneath her, trying to separate her handmaid's outline from the surrounding shadows. "What are you doing here?" Alexandra said in exasperation.

"Did you think me a fool?" The older woman climbed the steps until she was almost even with her charge. "I knew you'd make another run for it tonight, and you're not leaving me behind this time."

Alexandra sighed. She should have known. "Loran, you understand what Uncle Theodore will do if he discovers you played any part in my escape."

A haze of tears welled in the servant's eyes. "I don't care. I've been with you since you were a girl of five—close to eighteen years." Loran gripped the strap of her ragged travel bag tighter, "You can't get rid of me now. I won't let you."

Alexandra stared down at her for a long moment, then nodded and squeezed the servant's hand. "All right, then. If you insist. But don't say I didn't warn you."

They tiptoed down the remaining steps, careful to keep to the shadows. The metal latch on Loran's fabric carryall scraped against the stone wall as they finally reached the landing, the sound seeming to treble in volume as it echoed up the staircase. Alexandra held her breath, waiting for a guard to shout or an alarm to sound, but nothing out of the ordinary occurred. The keep was still locked in the spell of night.

The women shared a relieved grin, then eased into an unlit corridor, one used exclusively by the servants to move between the keep's vast kitchens and storage pantries. Alexandra paused and motioned toward a heavy wood door with rusted hinges. She brushed a coating of silvery cobwebs away. The doorway had once been used for the comings and goings of the keep's army of servants, but the entrance had fallen out of favor some generations ago and eventually been sealed shut. It had taken Alexandra several stolen hours of painstaking work to pick the frozen lock and oil the hinges back into working order, all the while terrified that some servant would spy her activities and report to her uncle.

Loran frowned at the sight of the creaky old door. "It's going to squeak," she whispered.

Alexandra smiled grimly and tugged on the latch. "Not a chance." The door opened smoothly beneath her fingers, so quietly not even the guard hounds would have heard.

As she stepped outside, a chilly breath of winter air brushed across her face. Alexandra could smell the scent of fresh snow riding on the night wind, and with it came a heady sense of exhilaration, the sure knowledge that freedom was finally at hand. Her heartbeat accelerated. She was free of Fallon Keep, free to make a run for the waiting ship and a future far different from the one her uncle envisioned.

Torches flared in the darkness, a score of orange-white flames. In the light she could see a long line of Fallon soldiers positioned in a half-moon twenty steps from the keep and door, guarding every avenue of escape. Flanked by her two other uncles, Theodore Fallon stood at the center of that line, directly ahead of Alexandra and Loran. Torchlight played across Theodore's coarse features, illuminating his fury for all to see.

Alexandra's heart sank. Beside her, Loran whimpered in fear and clutched at her mistress's arm and robe. A soldier chuckled at their predicament, and the others quickly joined in. They lifted the torches high in triumph and let loose a string of derisive hoots. Embers danced and swirled on the dawn wind as their torches bounced up and down, punctuating the soldiers' shouts.

Heat crawled up Alexandra's cheeks and stained her face with red. To humiliate her, her uncles were allowing the impromptu celebration to continue, their silence encouraging it to last for an unseemly amount of time. She suffered the embarrassment in stony silence, consoling herself with the knowledge that she could best each of the laughing soldiers with a weapon of their choosing. And if truth were known, they probably laughed and hooted because they knew it, too.

When the shouts of victory finally dwindled, Theodore Fallon folded massive arms across his chest and glowered at his wayward niece. "Do you think us dull-wits, girl?" he yelled angrily. "We knew you'd make another run for it—tonight of all nights."

She returned his glare measure for measure. "I don't think you a dull-wit, Uncle." *A fool, maybe, but not dull-witted* He was crude, coarse, and overbearing, a towering beast of a man who could probably kill her with a single swat of his hand. But he was no better or worse than Augustus and Stefan, his younger brothers. Yet at the same time, he was as different as night from day to Jarron—his other sibling and Alexa's dead father. "You're as sharp as a blade when the mood strikes, Uncle Theodore," she purred in a voice sure to mollify the man. Inwardly, Alexandra cursed herself soundly. She should have realized that if Loran could figure out her intentions, so could her uncles.

Theodore smiled slightly, pleased despite himself by the halfhearted compliment, even though he knew she was trying to manipulate him once again. Still, he'd always had a soft spot for his brother's only child. Alexandra was smart, courageous, pleasing to look upon, and as cunning as any man—everything his own brats were not.

He strode closer to his niece, his heavy battle armor clanking and creaking as he moved. "I've won and you've lost, Alexandra. It's too late to escape now. The ceremony is set to begin in just a few hours, so be a good girl and give up your resistance."

Her chin tilted in defiance, the dark profusion of braids in her hair falling around her shoulders. "I won't do it, Uncle!" she said in a belligerent tone. "You're my guardian, not my master. I will *not* allow you to sell me off like an old chair!"

Beside her, Loran stiffened in terror, the fingers clutching at Alexandra's arm trembling with fear. "My lady . . . please," Loran whispered. "Don't anger him further."

Theodore's expression turned dark and deadly, a thundercloud of rage directed at the rebellious girl. "I've already sold you," he shouted back. "And for a handsome sum of credit chits, I might add. So don't tell me what I can and cannot do! It's already done!"

Alexandra shook off her handmaid's clinging hand and marched forward, halting scant inches from her uncle's towering form. She glared up at him. "You would force me into a loveless marriage?" Her voice had fallen now, dropped to a dangerous whisper. "Condemn me to live with some simpering court peacock for the rest of my days . . . just to line your pockets with a few extra chits? What of your promise to my father?"

A muscle spasmed along the broad curve of Theodore's jaw, and his huge hands curled into fists. "Your father's dead, girl, dead and buried. I'm the head of this clan, and you'll do what you're told."

He snapped his fingers, signaling the watching soldiers to form into ranks. "Take Lady Alexandra to her rooms and see that she stays there," Theodore ordered. "Don't let her out until the ceremony is set to begin." His gaze drifted behind his niece, to where Loran was cowering in the shadows. "If she refuses to cooperate, have her serving woman flogged immediately. Ten lashes with a pain-stick to the back."

Alexandra gasped. "You wouldn't dare."

"Won't I?" Theodore grabbed a handful of her braids, twisting and pulling her dark hair around his fingers. He gave her braids another yank, forcing her to lift her face even higher.

A rush of tears filled her eyes, but she bit down on her lower lip to keep from crying out. She wouldn't give him the satisfaction.

"You've pushed me too far this time, Alexandra," Theodore grated between clenched teeth. "I'll do whatever is necessary to protect this clan . . . and that includes marrying you off to some snot-nosed aristocrat!" He loosened his grip slightly. "Think, girl, think what this alliance will mean to us!" A dreamy, faraway look crept into Theodore's eyes. "He may be a bastard but he's blood kin of the head of one of the most powerful clans in the Dominion. With this alliance will come power, prestige, and chits like no Fallon has ever known before! We won't have to survive on the crumbs left by the big clans anymore. We'll be able to stand toe-to-toe with them and claim our rightful share! So don't think I won't have your serving wench whipped if I have to. I'll beat the sass out of you as well, if that's what it takes to make you walk into that chapel with a smile on your face."

Alexandra glared. "Then I guess you'll just have to beat me."

His gaze thinned suddenly and focused on Alexandra's face, his dark eyes carrying a promise of swift retribution. "You ruin this opportunity for us and I swear on your father's grave that I'll send you to join him."

Chapter Three

Alexandra stared straight ahead, her shoulders stiff and unbending, her face as stark and forbidding as the slick black wood of Fallon Keep's chapel doors. She stared at the doors in silence, ignoring the mad rush of last-minute activity swirling around her. The keep's central corridor was awash with people waiting for the ceremony to begin, from the squadron of soldiers ordered to guard her to a host of servants and Fallon cousins. No one was bold enough to approach her, though; it was as if they had drawn an invisible circle around her and didn't dare to step inside.

Only faithful Loran had the gumption to stand by her side, either out of an exaggerated sense of duty, or, quite possibly, in search of continued protection from Theodore's wrath. Probably both, Alexandra decided. In the end, she had taken the promised lashing herself in Loran's stead, the sharp bite of the pain-stick still fresh each time she moved.

"One of the kitchen girls saw him," Loran said quietly, trying desperately to lift Alexandra's somber mood. She bent slightly and fussed with the folds of Alexa's best winter robe, smoothing the dark green velvet into fluid lines. "She said he looked quite striking."

Alexandra turned her head slightly, her dark blue eyes alight with a sudden glint of curiosity. The only thing she knew about her future husband was his name—Lucien Charbonneau—and that his manner of dress was both extravagant and effete. "What did the girl say?"

Loran hid a sigh of relief. It was the first time Alexandra had spoken in hours, ever since the beating she'd received from her uncle at dawn. "She said he's clad in a golden robe that seems to shimmer when he moves, and that the robe is trimmed with real jewels." She couldn't prevent a trace of wonder from creeping into her voice. "Arkanon rubies, green diamonds, and all manner of precious stones. She swore it looked like something out of a fairy tale!"

The vivid description caused a grimace to twist across Alexandra's lips. No man she had ever known would be caught dead in such attire. "How wonderful for him." She glanced down at her plain green robe, knowing he would think her backward and crude when he caught a glimpse of her. The robe was clean and fairly new, but her best would pale in comparison to this strutting peacock who glittered like a rising sun.

A red flush crawled up her neck and stained her cheeks with color. Hadn't she suffered enough humiliation for one day?

Loran sensed her mistress's sudden discomfort and shifted her attention from the robe to the cascade of thick black braids streaming down Alexandra's back. "Perhaps he won't be as bad as you think, my lady," she said in a reassuring tone as she lifted several braids to rearrange them, letting them fall willy-nilly across Alexandra's shoulders. "I've heard of many an arranged marriage that grew into a love match."

Alexandra snorted in disgust but held her tongue. Now was not the time to disabuse Loran of her belief in fairy tales.

A bevy of tray-laden servants scattered like birds as Theodore Fallon bullied his way through the crowd to Alexandra's side, a formal cloak of red-and-black plaid billowing about his thick shoulders.

Loran squeezed her hand gently, then scuttled well out of his reach. Alexandra simply glared at her uncle, the blue of her eyes deepening with renewed hostility. Her own blood kin was selling her off, trading her life for one of comfort for himself. "I hope the gods roast your spirit on a spit for all eternity," she said to him in a hiss.

Theodore laughed and grabbed her hand, tucking it securely beneath his arm. She tugged against him, trying to get away, but he tightened his grip to hold her in place. "After today I'll have enough chits to buy my way out of hell."

Two footmen clad in formal livery pushed the chapel doors open, their red ceremonial finery smelling of must and decades of disuse. Theodore half dragged, half pulled her inside the doors.

The acrid taste of bile rose in Alexandra's throat as she stepped through. The keep's ancient chapel was all but empty, the only people allowed entry to the signing ceremony a few aides and witnesses, as well as immediate family. Her spineless uncles Stefan and Augustus, clad in Fallon armor and tartan cloaks, were stationed to

Jan Zimlich

the left in the chapel, their droll-faced wives in attendance. To the right, the Charbonneaus waited. Her gaze skimmed over them curiously. Aides mostly, as well as a servant or two, all clustered near a gray-haired man dressed in a somber black robe. Baron Charbonneau, Alexandra surmised, her mouth puckering with distaste. He had the haughty, high-nosed air of a nobleman about him, which was common enough for someone of his station, but there was something about his pinched expression that set her teeth on edge. The baron's sour look appeared to be perpetual, and it had ridged his timeworn face with disdainful lines.

A splotch of gold touched the outer reaches of her vision, and Alexandra finally shifted her attention to her husband-to-be, who was standing well away from the other members of his clan. For a moment, her eyes were so dazzled by the shimmering gold that all she could do was gape in wonder at his outrageous attire. The kitchen maid hadn't exaggerated at all: Lucien Charbonneau did look like something out of a fairy tale—or a terrible nightmare.

"Close your mouth, girl!" Theodore snarled in her ear, then continued pulling her down the center aisle to the front of the chapel.

Her jaw snapped shut.

"You're gaping at him like he's something you just spied beneath a rock."

"He probably is," Alexandra grated back. She finally managed to force her gaze to Lucien Charbonneau's face, but it was an effort to do so. The shimmering robe was distracting, to say the least. She studied him openly, surprised to find that his face was quite pleasing to the eye. In her mind she had conjured him as some horrid troll with a fleshy body and cold, cruel eyes. Instead, Lucien Charbonneau's features were lean and clearly drawn, as if they had been sculpted from a fine piece of marble by a master's hand. His hair looked thick and well tended, the pale strands pulled into a tidy queue at the base of his neck. But his hair was blond, so pale it was almost colorless, just like his skin, and his body was far too lean and lanky to suit her tastes.

She suppressed a sigh. Charbonneau was definitely not the tall, dark adventurer she fantasized about, the bold, broad-shouldered man who could outwit and outfight her crude uncle and carry her to freedom. But at least he wasn't the troll-like mutant of a husband whom she'd feared these past few weeks. That was a mark in his favor, she supposed.

As the baron took his place beside his son, Theodore ground to a halt and forced Alexandra to follow suit, positioning her between himself and her future husband. He placed a hand firmly against her back and exerted enough pressure to cause her pain if she tried to flee.

Alexandra threw a sharp glance at her uncle, then focused her full attention on the young man standing so quietly to her right. Their eyes met, and her heart gave a surprised little thump. She hadn't expected to find him studying her as closely as she was studying him. His sharp gray eyes were regarding her intently, their brooding depths the same color as a stormy sky.

She returned his stare for a moment, watching, appraising, pleased despite herself that he was not fat and ugly after all. Still, those gray eyes were a bit too cool and jaded, his mouth so generous that it added a touch of femininity to the sculpted lines of his face.

Jan Zimlich

He bowed slightly, more a swift lowering of his eyes than an actual movement, then took her hand in his, the first touch of his flesh to hers giving her a peculiar jolt. Alexandra blinked in surprise. His pale skin was abnormally cool and far too soft to belong to any man.

A trace of disdain crept over her face. This strutting peacock was a wastrel after all, a golden weakling with soft skin and womanly lips.

She broke eye contact with him, glancing instead at the small sheaf of parchment stacked on an oval writing table directly in front of them. The marriage contract looked to be about ten pages in length, clause after clause of confusing legalese that had been agreed upon after days of intense negotiations. If she signed the compact, her marriage to Lucien Charbonneau would automatically become a matter of law, permanently binding her to the stranger at her side—for the rest of her life.

She took a half step backwards, her progress halted by a sharp jab from Theodore in the small of her back. She swung around to face her uncle, pleading with her eyes.

"You're supposed to sign first," Theodore said, his acid tone making his words both an order and a threat. He stuffed a quill-tipped scriber between her fingers and guided her hand to the papers.

Alexandra couldn't seem to gather the strength to tighten her hold. The scriber simply hung there, balanced between fingers that had suddenly gone numb, its long white feather quivering with her uncertainty. The waiting parchment blurred beneath her vision, the precise scribing on the page vanishing into a web of nonsensical scrawls.

A murmur ran through the waiting guests. Baron Charbonneau coughed discreetly and scowled. Witnesses shifted, straining to see the cause of the delay.

A tide of color and heat crawled up Theodore's neck. He jammed an elbow into the little twit's ribs. "Sign it!" he spat quietly, his breath hot and heavy against her ear.

Alexandra threw him a freezing glance. Well, if she signed the damned thing, at least she would have to answer to her husband, not him. Her fingers closed so tightly about the scriber that she risked breaking it in two. "All right," Alexandra snapped. She scrawled her name across the appropriate space, then flung the scriber toward Charbonneau's hands, throwing him a vicious glare for good measure.

Startled, Lucien fumbled for the instrument, managed to catch it without losing his dignity, and stared at the girl in complete surprise. Until his future wife hesitated and Lord Fallon jabbed her in the ribs, he hadn't realized that she was an unwilling participant in the ceremony as well. And until he'd caught his first glimpse of her, he hadn't realized that his bride-to-be was a raven-haired temptress. He had fully expected some great cow of a woman to come lumbering through the chapel doors. Instead he now found himself face-to-face with one of the most delectable morsels he'd seen in many a year. Luck of the draw, Lucien surmised, because his prudish father would never have knowingly chosen a beautiful woman to be his bride. He arched a single brow. This was an interesting development, to say the least.

He inclined his head in salute to her show of temper, then took a deep breath and signed his own name to the parchment with a dramatic flourish. For better or worse, it was done. Lucien blew out the breath he'd been holding. This

Jan Zimlich

young woman with dark blue eyes, a temptingly curved body, and a wild array of ebony braids was now his wife. In name only, of course.

Nervous laughter and a scattering of applause rippled through the witnesses. Glad that the perfunctory ceremony had ended, the assemblage began moving toward the doors, eager for the wedding feast to begin.

In less than a minute, the chapel had emptied, save for a few slow-moving guests and an aide who scooped up the signed contract and hurried out a side entrance. The door slammed shut behind him, the unexpected noise echoing briefly in the awkward silence. The newly wedded couple was alone.

Lucien straightened his shoulders and folded his hands behind his back, uncertain of what he should say or do. The sullen-faced woman standing beside him had yet to move or speak. Her attention seemed to be riveted on a section of bare stone wall, as if she were deep within some private pout and the marriage ceremony hadn't occurred at all. He cleared his throat and frowned slightly. He didn't have a bit of experience in dealing with a truculent wife. "I hate to intrude upon your reverie, my dear, but would you be so kind as to tell what is expected of us now?" Lucien lifted his voice a notch. "I fear I'm rather new at this marriage thing."

Alexandra turned slowly, the corners of her mouth curling downward in distaste. *Gods*. Even his voice annoyed her. There was a lilting, haughty cadence to his speech that she found revolting in the extreme. "There's to be a banquet in our honor," Alexandra said in a disparaging tone. "We're expected to put in an appearance."

"I see." He fussed with the folds of his elaborate robe, adjusting and readjusting the golden

34

fabric until it hung in perfect lines. "And after the banquet?" he asked in an innocent voice, turning his attention to the robe's voluminous sleeves.

Alexandra watched in dismay as he continued to preen, then sighed audibly and closed her eyes. She didn't want to think about what would happen after the banquet. In the small hours of the morning, her uncle and the baron would escort her alleged husband to her suite of rooms, then lock him inside and post a guard at the door. In keeping with Dominion tradition, she and her husband would be forced to stay there, alone and uninterrupted, for however long it took to consummate the marriage.

Her lids flew open and a sudden sly thought came to her. The coming night might very well prove to be the answer to her prayers. Of course, much would depend on Loran's cooperation, and her own ability to manipulate her fool of a husband.

She wrapped a possessive hand around her husband's arm and gave him a sudden, dazzling smile, then lifted herself on tiptoe until her mouth was almost even with his ear. "After the banquet, we'll have ample time to get to know each other . . . intimately," she said in a silky whisper. "After all, we are husband and wife now."

Her abrupt shift in mood caused Lucien to clear his throat uneasily. What was her game? One moment she acted as if she despised the very sight of him, but now . . . now she had positioned herself so close to him that one lush breast was perched atop the crook of his arm, begging to be fondled. To make matters worse, her mouth was lingering a scant inch from the lobe of his ear, each husky breath she expelled a torturous treat.

His neck and shoulders stiffened abruptly, and

he took a step away from her, far enough to remove her lithe body from close proximity to his arm and ear. "Though we are indeed man and wife, for appearance's sake I would suggest that you refrain from public displays of intimacy." Lucien sniffed to show his displeasure and folded his arms primly. "Such behavior is considered crude among the court elite."

Alexandra's cheeks reddened and her eyes narrowed to an angry glare. *Crude?* She bit down hard on her lower lip and clenched her fist to keep from punching him in the face. Manipulating the prissy peacock was going to be harder than she'd thought. It might even be an impossible feat. "Forgive me . . . *husband*. It will be an effort to do so, but in the future I'll try to restrain myself."

Lucien winced inwardly. *Husband*. She'd spit the term at him as if she were describing some loathsome thing stuck to the bottom of her shoe. And at the moment, that was exactly how he felt.

Chapter Four

The sound of music and ribald laughter drifted in Lucien's wake, a crescendo of noise that flowed through Fallon Keep's night-dark corridors like a rising tide. The wedding feast had ended hours before, but the celebration continued unabated, and from what Lucien could gather, it would last well into the small hours of the morning. But at this late hour only the foolhardy remained—Fallon soldiers and family who'd imbibed far too much potent Logo wine.

As for himself, what he longed for most was a soft mattress and a few blissful hours of uninterrupted sleep. The events of the past few days had happened too swiftly to guard against. As a result, the stress and strain had begun to tax his body and addle his wits. Worse still, the copious amount of wine he'd consumed at the banquet had served only to dull his brain even further, not a very intelligent move on his part when he was surrounded by potential foes. But if the smolder-

Jan Zimlich

ing, come-hither looks his mercurial wife had given him during the course of the banquet were any indication, sleep would be a long time coming this night, if at all.

Lucien suppressed a sudden smile, and his steps became a bit more eager as his entourage wound its way through the keep's shadowy corridors, moving inexorably closer to his wife's bedchamber. A single night's sleep was a small exchange for hours of bliss wrapped in a beautiful woman's arms. Besides, it was his duty to bed her. His prudish father had even told him so, much to Lucien's amusement. For duty, honor, and clan, he had to do it. The smile he'd managed to suppress finally broke free, lifting the corners of his mouth for a moment before he managed to get his expression back under control.

He lengthened his stride as he followed Lord Fallon and two sentries deeper into the bowels of the decrepit keep, the older of the guards dragging a foot that made an annoying sound as his boot scraped across stone. Beside Lucien, his stone-faced sire walked in silence, cold and aloof as always, compelled by tradition alone to join the party escorting his son to his raven-haired bride. Lucien didn't bother trying to make small talk with his distant father. Since leaving New France three days before, Renaud Charbonneau had uttered no more than a few stiff sentences to him, enough to make it uncomfortably clear that he was happy to be well rid of his bastard son.

And since there was nothing left to be said between them, Lucien spent the time glancing curiously at his surroundings. No carpets or padding warmed Fallon Keep's cold stone floors, and only a few dim sconces lit their way. The corridor itself smelled of old age, creeping dampness, and the musty odor of decay. A frown touched his forehead. Clan Fallon obviously held no power in the Dominion, so why had his father sought out such an alliance? What did he hope to gain, other than ridding himself of his troublesome son?

It was clear to see why Lord Fallon had seized upon the opportunity for an alliance. His father had sold him for a princely sum of chits, an amount sure to appeal to the impoverished lord of the Fallon Clan. Which would of course make it far more difficult to escape the man's clutches when an opportunity to leave Lochlain arose. According to the provisions of the treaty, he was obliged to remain on Lochlain for one full year or until his bride conceived. And if conception didn't occur during that time, the treaty would be annulled and Lord Fallon would be forced to return his newfound wealth. But Lucien didn't have any intention of spending the next year with Alexandra Fallon, no matter how tempting the prospect. A few days maybe, a week at the most, but then he'd have to be on his way, treaty or not.

"Not much farther now," Theodore announced, swaying slightly as he threw a drunken leer over his shoulder. "Your blushing bride should be abed now, awaiting your arrival." The lord of Fallon Keep downed the last dregs of wine from the bottom of his goblet and slung the metal chalice to the floor, forcing Lucien to step over it.

As they turned down an even dimmer corridor, Theodore prattled on about Lochlain, his brigades of soldiers, his many sons, as well as the ancient keep that had been built by his forefathers over a thousand years before. But he never spoke a word about his dark-haired niece or the mother of those sons, as if the female members of his clan were beneath his concern.

Lucien made polite sounds when forced to, but

other than that he didn't respond. He had no more to say to Theodore Fallon than to his own father.

The sentries stopped abruptly, and Theodore pounded on a wooden door, using both meaty fists like battering rams. "Alexandra! Open up!" His hammering echoed down the deserted corridor. "I've brought your husband to your bed!"

Theodore turned and smirked suggestively. "You gotta learn to ignore her sulks, boy," he advised, eliciting a snicker from the listening guards. "When that door opens, you just march right in there and give the little bitch a good fracking. That's all she needs."

Renaud Charbonneau reddened, the pinched expression he wore tightening until his mouth formed a thin, puritanical line. "Thank you for your hospitality, Lord Fallon. I shall be leaving now."

Theodore frowned and swung his gaze around. "What? Leaving? We still have many details of the alliance to discuss."

"My ship is waiting. I depart for New France within the hour." The baron's icy gaze moved in Lucien's direction, lingering for a split second on his son; then he spun on his heel and backtracked down the dim corridor, his boots smacking against stone in a hurried, precise rhythm.

Theodore stared after him, blinking. "What a cold bastard he is," he blurted in a slurred voice.

Lucien watched as his father disappeared from view. "Colder than you'll ever know," he murmured beneath his breath.

The door opened, flooding the corridor with a haze of yellow light. A blondish woman clad in servant's garb stepped forward and bowed to Theodore, her face pale and frightened in the rush of light. "Lady Alexandra is waiting, my lord."

Theodore wrapped a massive arm around Lucien's shoulders. "You do what I said, boy. Go in there and give it to her good." He propelled Lucien through the door, giving him one last slap of encouragement as he shoved him inside. "If she gives you any trouble, call the guards."

The door slammed shut and the lock slid home, latched by the guards to seal them inside. Lucien looked around the small sitting room curiously. Bookshelves lined the far wall, all stacked high with an endless number of data disks, as well as leather-bound tomes that probably dated back to ancient Earth. He glanced over the well-worn spines and was surprised to find that most were scientific texts. The books' subject matter varied, but most seemed to fall into the general categories of archaeology, anthropology, and planetary studies. Fallon Keep's entire scientific collection, most likely. Did his bride actually have a brain to go with that tempting body?

But other than the shelves of books, the room held little more than reading sconces and a threadbare couch and chaise. No warm rugs were scattered around the stone floor, and no feminine bric-a-brac cluttered the wooden table set before the couch. His gaze moved right, and he lifted a curious brow when he spotted several razor-sharp swords and ornate fighting daggers hanging in places of honor on the wall. Were the weapons simply for decoration, or did his temptress wife know how to wield such lethal weaponry?

The servant cleared her throat, distracting him from his perusal of his new wife's possessions. "Wine, my lord?" she asked in a tremulous voice.

"Lady Alexandra said that I was to offer you a cup as soon as you arrived."

Lucien turned. The wide-eyed woman was holding a filled goblet in an outstretched hand. "Thank you." He took a polite sip of the sweet blue liquid and hid a grimace behind the rim. He'd had more than enough wine for one day. "And who might you be?" The plump little woman looked pleasant enough, with deep brown eyes and blondish braids wrapped tightly about her head.

"Loran, my lord." Her owlish gaze moved up and down his attire, then to the goblet. "I'm Lady Alexa's. . . . your wife's handmaid."

"Ah, I see." Lucien pursed his lips.

"Is the wine not to your liking, my lord? I can have more brought if you want."

"No." Lucien shook his head. Definitely no more wine. "I've had my fill," he told her, and pushed the goblet back into her hands, though she seemed almost reluctant to take it.

"Are you sure?"

"Quite sure." He glanced at the collection of weapons again. "Where might I find your mistress, Loran?"

Spots of crimson grew on Loran's cheeks. She pointed to an arched doorway in the center of the bookshelves. "Lady Alexa is in her sleeping chamber." The stain on her cheeks darkened even more. "She's waiting for you there."

Lucien straightened his shoulders, and his mouth curved into an unconscious smile. "Well, I suppose I'll have to join her, won't I?" There were worse things in the universe than being forced to bed a beautiful wife. Far, far worse. "Duty calls."

Loran tried and failed to give him an answering smile. "Good night, my lord. I'll be out here for the rest of the night if you have need of me."

He inclined his head politely, then walked to the closed door and knocked three times. Discreetly, of course. Not at all like the battering Theodore had given the outer door.

"Come . . ."

A shudder of anticipation rushed through his body. The single word had been spoken in a low, throaty voice, a sultry invitation to attend an intimate revel for two. Lucien took a deep breath to prepare himself, trying to purge his mind and body of weariness and wine. If ever there was a time when he needed all his wits about him, it was now.

Lucien pushed the door open slowly. When he saw her, his mouth went dry and he made a small sound of pleasure deep in his throat. Alexandra Fallon was draped across the soft expanse of a white-covered bed, her chin cupped in a palm, the lush contours of her body visible beneath a thin silken underrobe. She smiled suggestively, and her sapphire eyes smoldered with that come-hither look that had made him yearn for more.

She patted the bed, enticing him to join her. "Rest yourself, husband. I'm sure you're weary from the day's events." She pushed at the dark braids falling over her bare shoulder, but they simply fell forward again, snaking about her neck and arm like thick black vines. "It's time you and I got to know each other," she said huskily.

He clenched his jaw and swallowed hard, fighting an almost irresistible urge to leap atop her and do exactly what her uncle had advised. For a fraction of a second, he considered throwing caution to the wind; then his mind cleared and the ramifications of such an act struck him full force. If Lucien Charbonneau, court favorite and boon companion of the Dominion archduke, was to survive this night with his position intact, he

43

couldn't step out of character for a single instant. Much as it pained him, he would have to allow his wife to play the role of seducer and he the innocent victim.

He closed the door behind him, then stood frozen with uncertainty near the foot of the bed—as if for the life of him, he didn't know how to proceed.

"Don't be shy, husband." She shifted languidly, positioning herself so that the underrobe slipped a bit lower, enough to reveal the tempting chasm between her breasts. "Come and sit on the bed."

Lucien complied, perching himself primly on the side of the bed. He had to let her do the work, cajole him into doing what he wanted most.

Her weight shifted on the mattress, and he knew she had moved, easing onto her knees behind his back. He sucked in a sharp breath as she loosened the ribbon holding his queue, her slender fingers sliding sensuously through his unbound hair.

"Relax," she whispered in his ear, her breath a warm shiver along the nape of his neck. "There's nothing to be tense about." Her hands roamed to his shoulders, rhythmically kneading the fatigue from his muscles. The golden fabric rasped beneath her fingertips. "Why don't you take off that heavy robe, husband? I'm sure you'd be far more comfortable."

He had to force himself not to rip the thing from his body. "All right," he whispered back, desperately trying to sound ambivalent about it all. "Perhaps I would be more comfortable." He could feel the swell of her breasts pressed against his back now, a torturous sensation that aroused him to a fever pitch. His fingers flew to the jew-eled buttons, clawed at the first two until they gave way; then he slowed his downward progress to a more normal pace. It wouldn't do to show unseemly haste.

Alexandra pushed the shimmering robe off his shoulders, allowing the fabric to fall in a rustling puddle around his waist; then she lay down slowly, drawing him with her as she moved. She pulled on him gently until they were face-to-face, stretched across the width of the bed. "Now isn't that better?" she said in a throaty voice.

"Much." Her heart-shaped face was scant inches from his, so close that if he wanted, he could count the dark lashes fringing those deep blue eyes. His rapt gaze traveled over lush, rosy lips, a finely chiseled chin, then moved lower, touching briefly on the full young breasts threatening to spill from the front of her underrobe.

She kissed him then, her lips gently grazing his own. The beat of his heart accelerated, pounding so hard and fast that he thought it would surely crash through his ribs. Her fingertips began moving along his neck again, the nails sliding and scraping across his bare skin.

Alexandra kissed him once more, a feather-soft joining of lips, then wrapped her arms about his neck and snuggled closer. "Does my touch please you, husband?" she asked quietly.

Lucien blinked in the near darkness. Please him? Gods, it was all he could do not to force himself upon her. "Yes," he answered hoarsely. "Your touch pleases me greatly."

"I'm glad." She sighed happily, her long lashes fanning downward to veil her eyes. "Perhaps another cup of wine would help you relax even more. There's a goblet waiting on the table beside the bed."

He shook his head slightly, his thoughts still held prisoner by the slow rise and fall of her chest when she sighed. "No more wine." He pressed his lips against the lobe of her ear and nibbled gently, the temptation so great he could no longer resist. "I had my fill at the banquet."

For a single moment, the fingers sliding along his shoulders went completely still. "What of the cup Loran gave you? It is much better wine than at the feast."

He lifted one shoulder in a half shrug. "I took a sip, no more."

"Oh," she said softly, "I see."

Alexandra bit down on her lower lip until she tasted a salty gush of blood, but that was far better than screaming the litany of curses that was frozen on the tip of her tongue. He'd had only a sip! Now what was she supposed to do?

She glared into the darkness behind his head, the elaborate plan she'd concocted in complete disarray. Her so-called husband had refused to drink the wine, and with it the drug that would send him into a long, oblivious sleep. "Are you sure you're not tired, husband?" she managed to ask in a breathy voice. Perhaps one sip would be enough.

"Not anymore," he whispered against her. His lips trailed down the front of her neck, pausing for a moment at the thready pulse at the base of her throat, then dipped lower, pressing gently against the curve of her breasts.

Alexandra rolled her eyes toward the ceiling. *Wonderful, absolutely wonderful.* She'd thought she'd been so clever. Now she was trapped half-naked in her own bed, wrapped in the arms of a complete stranger, one she had been far too successful in arousing. And judging by his increasingly ardent caresses, he had no intention of ending the night without a consummation of their marriage.

Lucien moved against her, trying to pull her

closer to his hips, his hands and lips gently exploring the ripe mounds of flesh peeping through the satiny underrobe. He nuzzled the soft hollow between her breasts, and his fingers crept beneath the edge of the underrobe.

A soft gasp of surprise escaped Alexandra's throat as his mouth followed the downward course of his fingers. For a timeless moment, she reveled in the flow of sensations and allowed his tender ministrations to continue, although she knew it was insanity to do such a thing. Yet those soft lips and gentle fingers were heating fiery little trails across her flesh, arousing her as she had done to him.

She frowned. Why was she even responding to his touch? He was vain and prissy, and the gods only knew what else. Lucien Charbonneau wasn't the sort she was attracted to at all, so why was she enjoying the feel of those soft lips and magical fingers?

Her mouth suddenly flattened into a resolute line. The fact that she found Charbonneau in some way attractive wasn't going to stop her from reaching her goal. She wouldn't spend the rest of her days tied to a man such as him—or to any man, for that matter. If she wanted her own life— the future she had dreamed of since before her father's death—she had to get away from Lucien Charbonneau at once. And desperate situations called for equally desperate measures.

She pushed him onto his back with a suddenness that startled them both, then rolled with him, maneuvering herself so that she was stretched full-length atop him. Her braids fell forward, twining about his face and shoulders.

Lucien stared up at her in surprise and struggled to catch his breath. She was smiling sweetly, but there was a peculiar glint in her eyes, some-

Jan Zimlich

thing he didn't quite recognize. The look reminded him of one she had given him in the chapel, a loathing look that was totally at odds with her licentious behavior of the past few hours. "Is something wrong?"

The corners of her mouth lifted higher. They were near the head of the bed now, close enough for her to reach the small side table. "Absolutely nothing, husband." She shook her head so that more of her thick braids draped around his face, veiling his view from side to side. Unseen, her hand crept across the coverlet until her fingers found the wine goblet sitting atop a heavy pewter tray. She smiled seductively as she moved the goblet off the tray, then grabbed the wide handle and eased the platter onto the bed.

Lucien continued to watch her eyes, his senses warning him that there was something amiss. But then she kissed him again, an eager, demanding exploration that muddled his senses and made him think he'd been imagining things.

Her lips pulled away from his abruptly, and she shifted her weight onto an arm, lifting her chest and shoulders from atop his own. Lucien frowned as her eyes turned a chilly, icy blue. "Are you sure there's nothing wrong?"

Her teeth flashed white against her olive skin. "Not anymore."

A blur descended from above, and something large, heavy, and painful made a ringing sound as it collided with his skull. Lucien blinked to focus his eyes, to try to figure out what had happened, but the effort was in vain. His vision swam, and with it the heart-shaped face poised above him. Then he felt and heard a second crash, and his world turned black and still.

For several seconds, Alexandra simply stared at the trickle of blood leaking from his forehead, terrified that she might have actually done him in. But then she felt his chest rise beneath her and heaved a sigh of relief. She'd wanted him unconscious, not dead.

The tray slid from her fingers, and she scrambled from the bed, feeling a twinge of guilt for what she'd done. It was brief, though, and that was a tiny price to pay for the freedom she'd just won.

She raced to the door and threw it open. "Loran! Quick!"

"Alexandra?" The pale-faced handmaid scuttled toward the open door. "Are you all right? I heard a crash."

She wagged an admonishing finger. "I'm fine, no thanks to you."

Tears welled in Loran's dark eyes. "I'm sorry, my lady, but he refused to drink it. What was I supposed to do?"

Alexandra shook her head and waved a hand in dismissal. "Never mind that now. I handled the situation as best I could, but I'm going to need your help."

"With what?" Looking puzzled, Loran stepped into the dimly lit bedroom and gasped when she saw the bed. The nobleman was sprawled atop the coverlet, his golden robe half-on, half-off, his slender body as still and pale as a corpse. Worse still, there was a tiny stream of blood coursing down his forehead. "Oh, gods, you killed him!" The tears gushed down her cheeks in earnest. Theodore Fallon was going to flay the flesh from their bones, then hoist what was left of their hides atop twenty-foot pikes. "What's going to happen to us now?" Her voice came out in a terrified squeak.

Alexandra made a disgusted face. "For heaven's sake, Loran, I didn't kill him. I just beat him over

Jan Zimlich

the head with a serving tray. He'll wake up in an hour or two, but we'll be long gone by then."

She blinked the wetness from her eyes. "We will?"

"Yes." Alexandra threw the velvet robe over her head and hurriedly dressed. "Now go find me something I can use to tie him up."

Loran looked around helplessly. "What? There's no rope or twine in your rooms."

She pointed toward the huge pile of luggage sitting in a corner. "Look through his things. The peacock probably has dozens of sashes in his travel bags."

While Loran rifled through his luggage, Alexandra finished buttoning her robe and slipped on a black travel cloak, snugging the hood down low to hide her face.

"I found some!" Loran crowed in triumph. Alexandra had been right: at least a score of the decorative sashes were tucked into his accessory bag. She unfolded an armful and raced back to the bed.

"Good." Alexandra grabbed a sturdy length of red satin. "I'll take his hands; you tie his feet. And do it tightly, Loran. I want him to stay tied at least till morning." She felt another stab of guilt as she flopped her husband onto his side and pulled his arms behind his back, then wound the sash about his wrists.

A few moments later Loran stepped back to observe her handiwork and frowned at the sight of the bound and bleeding nobleman lying atop her mistress's bed. "I guess I'm done." She pulled the top of his robe back up as well as she could to cover his bare chest. The night air was cool, and she didn't want him to catch a chill.

"Good. Get our bags ready, Loran."

"All right." The serving woman hurried into the sitting room.

Alexandra yanked on the material to test the knots binding his ankles and wrists, then used a third sash to fetter his hands and feet together behind his back. A grim, self-satisfied smile lit her features. It would take him hours to free himself from his bonds. "Sorry to disappoint you, husband," she whispered to him, "but I was never a willing party to this so-called marriage." On impulse, she dabbed the blood from the cut on his forehead with the end of the coverlet. "I've got better things to do with my life than play nursemaid to an aristocratic peacock."

She plumped a pillow and eased it under his head, then wadded the last of the sashes and stuffed it into his mouth. Judging by the size of the knot on his forehead, he'd have a nasty headache when he awoke, but he'd survive. His dignity and ego might not escape unscathed, though.

"Sorry about this, too," Alexandra said quietly, then proceeded to pluck the jeweled buttons from the front of his robe. "But I need them more than you do."

Her arms laden with heavy travel bags, Loran walked through the doorway and froze. She gaped in horror as her mistress stripped off her husband's jeweled buttons one by one and dropped them into a pocket of her robe. First she'd nearly killed him; now she was robbing him! "Alexandra! Have you lost your senses?"

Alexandra jerked the last button, which tore the costly fabric when it finally popped loose. The luminescent diamond glowed a faint greenish color as she cupped it in a palm. "We *are* husband and wife," she offered in explanation. "What's his

51

is mine." The green diamond disappeared inside her pocket. "So now his buttons legally belong to me."

Loran sighed and closed her eyes. They were doomed. If Lord Fallon didn't hunt them down like animals, Alexandra's outraged husband would.

Alexandra cast one final look at the hapless nobleman, then took her bags from Loran and strode into the sitting room. She locked the bedroom door and gave her nervous handmaid a confident smile. "Think about it, Loran. Those jewels are our salvation. We were going to have to travel in steerage and work our way to the borderworlds. Now we can buy supplies and first-class passage anywhere we want to go! Just one tiny jewel will see us all the way to Thasia!"

Loran frowned uncertainly. Taking the jewels didn't sound at all like thievery when Alexandra explained it. Still . . . "Are you sure it's legal?"

"Of course." She squeezed Loran's shoulder to boost her resolve. "Let's go. We still have to steal a scad-about to reach the settlement and bribe our way onto a ship, but that shouldn't pose much of a problem. Now's the perfect time to make a run for it. Every guard in the keep is either passed out or slack-faced drunk by now, my loving relatives as well. They're so busy celebrating their victory they'll never notice we're gone."

Alexandra stopped and felt along the edge of the bookcase for the key to her room that she'd stolen from old Fomus years before. As her fingers closed around the strip of metal, she had a sudden, unnerving thought. She threw Loran a swift look. "I hope you had more success giving the guards the wine than you did with my husband."

Loran nodded; it was her turn to give her mistress needed reassurance. "It didn't take much convincing. They were both peeved that they were stuck up here guarding you while everyone else celebrated. The fools swilled every drop I gave them and begged for more."

Alexandra blew out a relieved breath, then walked to the door. She slipped the key into the lock, turning it quietly in case the guards were not yet asleep. She cracked the door open slowly and peered outside, grinning triumphantly when she spotted the sleeping sentries. Old Fomus was sitting beside the door snoring loudly, his mouth wide open and his head propped against the door frame. Across the corridor, the second guard was passed out on the stone floor, drool running from his mouth and his limp arms and legs splayed impotently.

She waved for Loran to follow, relocked the door behind them, and sifted through Fomus's pockets until she found his key to her rooms. Without a key, the guards' discovery of her absence would be delayed a few moments longer, affording her and Loran extra time to see themselves safely away. She motioned to Loran, then lifted the hem of her robe and tiptoed past the snoring guards. Alexandra couldn't stop grinning as they scurried through the dark bowels of Fallon Keep. No one would catch them this time. No one was sober enough even to try.

Lucien awoke to a clatter of noise, unsure which sound was louder—the painful pounding inside his head, or the equally painful shouts and hammering coming from somewhere else.

As the hammering grew louder, he cracked his eyes open and blinked, trying to figure out where he was and why his head felt as if it were about to explode. Something had hit him. Someone . . . He

lifted a hand to rub his forehead but found that
he couldn't move his arms. Or his legs, for that
matter. And there was a strange taste and feel in
his mouth, as though it was stuffed with wet fabric.

His eyes opened wide, then narrowed with cold
fury as his memories of the night before came
back in a mind-numbing rush. Alexandra Fallon
had done this to him. His *wife*. She'd taunted and
tantalized him with her body until he'd been fool
enough let down his guard, then beat him over
the head and trussed him like a fat tree-hen being
roasted for a holiday meal.

The distant hammering trebled in volume until
it sounded like a barrage of thunder. There were
other sounds now, too, voices raised in supplica-
tion, as well as Theodore Fallon's angry roar.

"Break the damn thing down, you miserable
oafs!" Theodore shouted. "And be glad I don't
skin you alive! You were supposed to be guarding
the door, not getting so sotted that you passed out
on the floor!"

Lucien struggled to push the wad of silk from
his mouth but managed only to dislodge a portion of the gag. Theodore and his soldiers were in
the sitting room now, the renewed burst of
pounding their attempt to break down the bedroom door. He squirmed around the bed to try to
free himself, twisting and jerking on the cords
that bound his hands and feet. But his contortions were in vain. In the end he might have managed to loosen his feet a bit, but his hands were
still tightly bound. So well bound in fact, that it
made him wonder anew about his alleged wife's
abilities.

The door finally splintered, and a guard came
crashing through.

Lucien braced himself. It was embarrassing

enough to be found fettered and gagged, even more so that a woman was the cause of his ignoble state.

Theodore shoved a guard and the door's remains from his path and barged into his niece's bedroom, his jaw falling open in horror when he saw the angry-faced nobleman trussed on the bed. "Oh, gods!" he yelled in dismay. "What's the little bitch done now?"

Chapter Five

As the clouds suddenly parted, a wan stream of sunlight crawled across the narrow alleyway, throwing the grimy stone walls into shadow. Alexandra pulled her cloak tight about her face as a fierce gust of wind blew down the garbage-strewn alleyway, sending a storm of trash and debris spiraling across the cobbled paving. She wrinkled her nose and quickened her footsteps as the stench of rotting garbage began overpowering the cold, dusty wind. At least she hoped it was garbage and not a dead body putrefying in a shadowy corner somewhere.

She threw a suspicious glance at a smelly shadow to her right. The discovery of a decaying corpse wouldn't exactly surprise her. Not here. Thasia was a seedy little borderworld along the Dominion frontier, a dirty, grubby settlement on the fringes of civilized space where smugglers and cutthroats seemed to have free reign to ply their respective trades. Since their arrival two days before, Alexandra had learned more than once that dead bodies lying about weren't at all uncommon.

Beside her, Loran sniffed at a current of wind and grimaced. "What's that smell?" she asked fearfully.

"Garbage, I think." Alexandra realized that Loran's thoughts had obviously been traveling down the same path as hers. "It's not what you're thinking it is." A renewed gust of wind tugged at their cloaks, tangling the heavy material about their legs.

"I hope you're right." Loran flinched as a bit of paper sailed past her face, clung to the alley wall a moment, then blew out of sight.

"Of course I am." Alexandra lifted her hem high and stepped over a pile of papery debris and broken glass.

Loran's grip on Alexandra's arm tightened at the sound of distant shouts, drunken sounds that seemed to echo and grow as they turned another corner. "Are you sure this is the way to the landing field?" Loran asked in a tremulous voice.

"That's what the man at the hotel said," Alexandra told her confidently, although the deeper they moved into the maze of alleys, the less sure of herself she began to feel. Maybe the man had lied. Maybe he was lurking around the next turn waiting to rob them. That wouldn't surprise her either. Not on Thasia. She brushed a hand across her waist, reassuring herself that the stiletto she'd secreted beneath her cloak was still there. "He said the alley ends directly opposite the landing field."

"I hope you're right," Loran said. She glanced at their dismal surroundings fearfully, her fingers digging deeper into her mistress's arm. "It'll be dark soon. I'd hate to be lost in these alleys at night."

Alexandra surveyed the deepening shadows with an equal amount of trepidation. Nothing she'd ever experienced had prepared her for the grim reality of life on a lawless borderworld. She had fled Lochlain with the sense that she was embarking on a grand adventure, and it had been for a while. Two weeks in a first-class cabin on a five-star passenger ship, excellent meals, witty, urbane dinner companions—every amenity of civilized life that could be bought with her husband's pilfered jewels. But those much-enjoyed creature comforts had ended abruptly when the liner reached Thasia, its final port of call.

Alexandra had planned to hire a small ship after their arrival to smuggle them across the Dominion border to the Denault system, leaving Thasia behind as swiftly as possible. But her plan had gone awry right away, and what should have been a simple procedure had quickly turned into a hellish, two-day ordeal. The hotel was a dingy dungheap, their room even worse. And the smugglers she'd planned on hiring had refused to talk to her, many turning her away at the point of a pulse gun as soon as she mentioned booking passage. Even her attempts at bribery had failed to achieve anything other than a drastic lightening of her purse. The trip to the landing field itself was her final gambit. If she didn't find a smuggler willing to talk to her there, they would have to backtrack to a more civilized world in hopes of arranging a different mode of transport to the Denault system.

The alley suddenly widened, the high walls

stretching outward so far that it could now be loosely defined as a narrow roadway of sorts. Ahead, she could see where the walls ended abruptly, and the alley opened onto what looked to be a flat plane of cracked concrete and hard-packed dirt. Surprisingly, the hotel's desk clerk hadn't lied after all.

As they reached the alley's mouth, a cloud of grit and yellowish dust gusted across the settlement's small landing field. Alexandra lifted a hand to shield her eyes and surveyed the area. About forty ships of various shapes and design were scattered across the field. A few were nothing more than rusty derelicts, abandoned to the ravages of time and thieves years before, but there were obviously functioning ships as well. Cargo ramps were extended from two disreputable-looking ships, and a bevy of equally disreputable-looking workers were busy loading and off-loading an assortment of boxes and metal shipping containers. The workmen looked hard and weather-beaten, their grubby jumpsuits as worn as their faces.

Alexandra smiled grimly. She was in no position to quibble about the smugglers' appearance. Beggars couldn't afford to be choosers.

"You there!" Alexandra shouted. "I'd like to speak to your captain."

Her words were greeted by a series of hostile stares. A thin man whose face was a labyrinth of wrinkles eyed her for a moment, spit, then slung a box over his shoulder and went back to work.

Alexandra grumbled to herself and then moved on to the next ship, where they were greeted with more hostile stares.

"I don't think they want to talk to us, either," Loran said. She tried to bite back the whine that had crept into her voice. "Maybe we should just go back to the hotel, my lady," she suggested, though the idea of walking back through the alleyways terrified her anew.

"Not yet." Alexandra shook her head vehemently, her gaze sweeping over an elegantly designed ship sitting well away from the others. The sleek little bird with backswept wings was obviously well maintained and painted a glossy night black. Not big enough to draw unwanted attention, yet not so small and cramped that the voyage would be uncomfortable, it was perfectly suited for her needs. "Let's try that one," she said, pointing, and strode off in that direction. She would bang on the hatch if she had to.

As they neared the vacant gangway, a workman suddenly climbed from the shadows beneath the belly of the ship. Alexandra paused in midstep, and Loran gave a little squeak of surprise. The man was impossibly huge, a great beast of a fellow with long, brownish hair and massive shoulders and arms that could easily squeeze the life from the likes of even her brawny Uncle Theodore.

He put a tool down on the gangway and eyed them. "Yes?" There was suspicion in his voice, and a hint of a threat buried beneath the single word.

Alexandra swallowed the sudden dryness from her throat. His dark gaze was drifting over them curiously, lingering for a tad too long on Loran's plump form to suit Alexandra. Their experiences in the past two days had taught them that the men on Thasia had a penchant for overly endowed women. A more slender build was obviously held in disfavor, which was perfectly fine with Alexandra.

"I'd like to speak with you about chartering

your ship," Alexandra announced in a rush, more to distract him from his perusal of Loran's body than to hurry things along. "I can pay."

His gaze traveled down the length of Loran's body again, then moved down Alexandra's, as if he were assessing the cost of her attire. "I'm sure you can." His huge shoulders lifted in a dismissive shrug. "But this ship is not for hire. Try somewhere else."

This time Alexandra wasn't willing to give in so easily. "I'll pay top chits. A bonus as well if we can lift off by dawn tomorrow."

A glint of impatience flickered in his eyes. "I already said no. Now move on." He turned to leave, but Alexandra belayed him by grabbing his burly forearm—a dangerous move on her part, but she was desperate enough to try just about anything.

He swung back around angrily.

"Look," Alexandra began, staring up at him, "I've tried everyone else, but they won't even talk to me. All I want to do is hire a ship for a week or so to take us across the border and back. If you won't do it, at least direct me to someone who might. If we don't find a ship soon, we'll have to backtrack to another planet and lose weeks, so I'm willing to pay well." Alexandra held out her hand palm up, displaying two of the jeweled buttons from her stolen cache. The green diamond and large, square-cut ruby glinted in the waning light. She knew she was taking a risk by displaying the gold-rimmed buttons to a possible criminal, but she'd run out of options. If they didn't get off Thasia soon, either her uncle or her husband would hunt them down.

He glanced at the contents of her out stretched hand, his eyes widening then thinning slightly as he studied the jeweled buttons nestled in her palm. He blinked once, a curious, almost wondering smile lifting the corners of his mouth. "I'm not the captain, lady," he said slowly. "I think it would be best if you put your proposal directly to him. Considering the circumstances, I think he might just be interested."

Alexandra smiled inwardly, gratified by his reaction. His entire attitude had changed when he spotted the jewels, just as she'd expected. Greed was a great motivator. "Where can I find your captain?"

The man stared at her curiously. "I'll set up a meeting."

A thick haze of yellow dust curled along the domed ceiling, windblown eddies of sand and grit driven through the bar's thin plastic walls by a sandstorm gusting out of the Thasian hills.

Lucien slouched back in his dust-coated chair and slugged down the remains of his wine, his mood as bleak and dismal as the interior of Trader Vor's. A room-length translucent bar ran down the far wall, and a scattering of rickety chairs and tables were clustered here and there across the dusty stone floor. Beyond that, there wasn't much to see. Trader Vor's was identical in look and feel to a hundred other seedy taverns he'd visited in the past few years, a dingy, drab-hued hole frequented by the most miserable lowlifes the Dominion had to offer. Lowlifes like his alter ego, Damion Flynn.

Lucien tipped the rim of his battered wine cup in a mock salute to himself. In the past few years he'd grown so comfortable in the guise of Damion Flynn that at times he wondered which parts of the smuggler's persona he'd created, and which were actually him. He'd grown far too comfortable in places like Trader Vor's, so much so that he often wondered who he really was anymore. Was he still Lucien Charbonneau, the bastard son of Baron Renaud Charbonneau? Or had he in fact become Damion Flynn, the notorious smuggler who somehow managed to stay a step ahead of Dominion law?

The thought brought a brooding scowl to his face, a disagreeable expression that fit in well with his mood and surroundings. He'd been questioning himself far too much of late, a newfound trait that had begun three weeks before, an event that suspiciously coincided with his fiasco of a wedding night. His treacherous bride had played him a fool, and he had fallen headlong into her seductive trap, an unpleasant fact that neither Lucien Charbonneau nor Damion Flynn could quite accept.

Lucien cast a quick glance at his chronometer, idly wondering what was keeping Tay. He was an hour late already. If his friend didn't arrive soon, he'd have to go out searching for him. Even a man as large as Tay wasn't immune to the perils of Thasia at night.

He traced the rim of his empty cup with the back of a thumb, cursing himself for ever agreeing to Tay's suggestion that they stop over for a few days on a hellhole like Thasia. He should have picked up his cargo and immediately moved on. The busier he was, the less time he had to think about Alexandra Fallon.

In truth, he should be grateful to her in a perverted sort of way. By beating him over the head and absconding with his jewels, she'd managed to free him from the more troublesome aspects of his arranged marriage. He'd been able to escape from Lochlain far earlier than he'd expected and return to his double

Jan Zimlich

life—without the nettlesome encumbrance of an unwanted wife. Still, once word of his marital travails spread among the Dominion elite, the accompanying gossip had brought unwanted attention to Lucien Charbonneau. Within days of his being discovered bound and gagged in his wife's bed, his friends and enemies alike had gotten wind of the indignities the pitiable son of Baron Charbonneau had suffered at the hands of Alexandra Fallon, making him the subject of much tittering and amused speculation.

The embarrassing situation had given Lucien Charbonneau just cause to disappear for a while, though. While everyone believed the jilted husband was off licking the wounds to his bloodied ego, Damion Flynn was free to come and go as he pleased.

The only problem was, Damion Flynn was licking his wounds as well.

"Still brooding?"

Lucien glanced up at Tay, chagrined that his thoughts had been so transparent. He forced the corners of his mouth to rise in a nonchalant smile, but the gesture felt contrived, even to himself. "About what?"

Tay shook a layer of dust from his cloak and lowered his bulk into a spindly chair across the table. Lucien's carefree grin wasn't fooling him in the least. "I thought a few days to yourself might put you in a better frame of mind." He shrugged his shoulders. "I guess I was wrong."

Lucien dismissed his concern with a wave of his hand. "I'm fine, Tay. Don't worry about me."

"Oh, yeah, right. I can tell." He signaled the barmaid to bring them a cup of wine, then stared pointedly at a long hank of light hair falling to his friend's shoulder. Lucien was fortunate that it was fairly dark inside the bar. "You're slipping again, my friend," he said quietly. He jerked a thumb toward Lucien's head. "Damion Flynn doesn't have blond steaks in his hair. One of your eyebrows looks a little lighter than the other as well."

Lucien winced in surprise, then squeezed his eyes tightly shut, willing himself to concentrate on his appearance. He pushed the telltale hair from his shoulders with a slow, almost leisurely movement, masking the transformation taking place beneath his palms. When his hands finally fell away, the blond streaks had vanished, and his hair had turned a deep, almost uniform shade of black. Damion Flynn's color.

He lifted two jet brows in a wordless gesture of apology. "Better?" Slips like that could get them both killed, or imprisoned for a very long time.

"Much." Tay gave him a long, probing look. "That's the third time in the past week, Lucien. You've got to be more careful."

Lucien silently cursed himself, angry and embarrassed that he'd been so preoccupied that he'd allowed his concentration to slip yet again. It wasn't just his and Tay's lives that hung in the balance either. Innocents could die as well.

His fingertips began tapping an impatient beat along the edge of the knife-scarred table. It was time to quit dwelling on how Alexandra Fallon had gotten the best of him, time to leave thoughts of her behind and get on with his life.

"Has the cargo been loaded on the *Nightwind* yet?" Lucien asked abruptly, surveying the bar's other patrons with wary eyes. An assortment of smugglers, freebooters, and nervous clan spies were huddled in quiet little knots around the bar's sticky tables, but no one seemed to be casting

65

overly curious glances his way. A suspicious pair was seated off to themselves in a corner, though. The two men—one large and thin with a somewhat pointed face, the other small and compact—just didn't quite fit in with Trader Vor's usual clientele, and seemed a tad too interested in the bar's goings-on. Dominion security, by the looks of them, probably some of General Thigg's minions. But if he was lucky, his lapse had passed unnoticed.

"The shipment is loaded and ready," Tay replied quietly. "Several cases more than we expected."

Lucien nodded in approval. "The more the better."

The red-haired barmaid scuttled up, dropped two fresh mugs of wine on the table, and paused long enough to give Lucien a smile. Tay sighed. A month ago, Damion Flynn would have responded to the pretty barmaid's silent invitation in the blink of an eye, but tonight he didn't even acknowledge her presence, or seem to notice her at all. When Lucien continued to ignore her, the woman grabbed the chit Tay tossed her in payment and marched off in a huff. "We can lift off whenever you want."

"Good." Even though their cargo wasn't scheduled for delivery for more than a week, Lucien was quite ready to leave Thasia far behind. "Let's leave before dawn. We'll be less likely to draw unwanted attention from customs." He glanced covertly toward the corner of the bar, where the two agents appeared to be surreptitiously watching him. If they lifted off before sunrise, their departure would also be less likely to draw attention from Dominion security.

An uncertain look moved over Tay's roughhewn features, and he shifted in the too-small chair nervously. "Before we leave, there is one thing. . . ." He hesitated for a few seconds, reluctant to relate his news. Considering Lucien's recent frame of mind, he wasn't sure how his friend would react. "There's someone here who insists on talking to you right away," he finally blurted.

"Who?" Lucien lifted an expectant brow.

Tay cleared his throat, a nervous, strained sound. "A woman—a noblewoman, judging by the looks of her." He drained the rest of his mug. "She says she wants to charter your ship for a week or so."

Lucien snorted and shook his head in disbelief. "A charter? I hope you set her straight."

"I did. But she wouldn't take no for an answer."

"Tell her again."

"You tell her. I promised her a personal meeting. She'll be here any minute."

Lucien scowled. "Now why would you go and do something like that?"

"I've got my reasons." Tay hesitated again, vacillating over whether he should continue. He still had time to change his mind and drop the whole thing. He could simply change the topic of conversation and forget he'd ever laid eyes on the woman—or the jeweled buttons. "You need to see her for yourself." He eyed his friend carefully. "I think she just might be Lucien Charbonneau's wife."

"What?" Lucien stared at him for a long moment, dumbstruck by the very notion that Alexandra Fallon might actually be on Thasia. Tay had never even seen her, so how could he know that this woman was his wife? He shook his head firmly, denying the very possibility. "Come on, Tay. It can't be her. Not here. Lochlain is a hundred light-years away."

Jan Zimlich

Tay lifted his shoulders in a halfhearted shrug and lowered his voice to a near whisper. "Well, whoever the hell she is, she's got two of the jeweled buttons from your formal robe. She offered to pay for the charter with them. I've seen those buttons often enough through the years to recognize them anywhere."

A sudden, deadly smile danced across Lucien's lips. Was it truly possible? Could Alexandra Fallon be here? If so, the Fates had finally taken pity on him and dealt him a winning hand.

The door to Trader Vor's swung open and two black-cloaked figures entered the bar, pausing uncertainly as they glanced around the gloomy interior. The taller of the pair brushed at the dust clinging to her cloak and pushed a heavy cowl from her head, revealing a wild cascade of thick black braids.

Lucien watched her for a moment, then leaned back slowly and laced his hands behind his head, a sudden sense of triumph causing his smile to turn sly. "Well, well." His gray eyes narrowed dangerously. "Looks like you were right after all, Tay." His gaze roamed over Alexandra Fallon's familiar form, a slow, downward appraisal that began with the line of her brow and ended with a tantalizing glimpse of ankle visible beneath her cumbersome robe. "The universe is full of happy surprises."

Tay swung a wary look over his shoulder. The woman spotted him instantly and started across the bar, the pretty blond a few steps behind. "Now what?" Tay asked quietly, wishing he'd been wrong about the woman's identity. The calculating look on Lucien's face was unsettling in the extreme.

Lucien grinned, a flash of white against olive

skin. "She wants to meet Damion Flynn, and I plan to oblige."

"That's what I was afraid of," Tay said somberly.

Lucien's grin widened further. He watched as Alexandra Fallon paused a few tables away and angrily swatted at a hand that reached out to grope her companion, the plump little handmaid who'd offered him wine that night in his wife's rooms. He forced himself to look away as the women approached his table, a difficult task since his gaze seemed determined to linger on his wife.

Alexandra ground to a sudden stop and inclined her head politely to the giant she'd talked to at the landing field. "Mr. Molvan." She threw a quick glance at the dark-haired man seated across from him and found herself staring into a pair of chilly gray eyes. She drew a breath to steady herself. Those cool eyes were regarding her with a strange, almost unnerving intensity, as though he were searching her features for signs of . . . what? Treachery? Or something else? She lifted her chin a fraction, a trace of red crawling up her cheekbones in response to his unwanted scrutiny. Whatever the man's look signified, it didn't bode well for her chances of hiring him. "I assume you must be Captain Flynn," she began in a prim, officious voice.

He smiled back lazily. "In the flesh." His gaze traveled over the lines of her face again, lingering for a long second on the curve of her mouth, then moving back to those magnetic blue eyes. "And you are?"

Alexandra considered lying about her identity, then dropped the idea. If he agreed to the charter, it would be hard to keep up a pretense for days on end. "Alexandra Fallon." She motioned toward Loran, who was watching the exchange with wide, fearful eyes. "And this is my friend, Loran Pahs."

Damion Flynn nodded absently at Loran and turned his full attention back to Alexandra. His gaze burned into her with laserlike intensity.

Alexandra's heart gave a little thud of surprise, and a current of awareness rippled along the ends of her nerves. Flynn's cool stare had suddenly turned seductive, his smile equally so, as if the smuggler thought that he was devastatingly handsome and was letting her know. Even worse, he actually was, a fact that her senses were warning her of in no uncertain terms. Damion Flynn was outrageously attractive, with a bold-cut, dark face, wide-set shoulders, and a powerfully built body that would attract women like tree-moths to a candle flame. The air of coiled strength about him served only to add an element of danger to his darkly handsome looks.

She cleared the sudden dryness from her throat and pursed her lips, steeling herself against reacting to his overt sexuality in any way. She wasn't like most women, and would simply not respond to him like a silly tree-moth, even though in looks Damion Flynn nearly equaled the handsome adventurer she'd conjured in her fanciful imagining. There was a vast sea of difference between fantasy and reality, though. "Did Mr. Molvan tell you why I wanted to see you, Captain?" Despite her best efforts, her voice cracked, and Alexandra cursed herself inwardly for being such a weakling. She had to keep her wits about her and not allow him to see that his presence was affecting her in any way. This was a business proposition, nothing more, one she was entering into with a known smuggler, a black-hearted rogue who would probably steal her jewels and betray her to her uncle without a single trace of conscience or regret.

"As a matter of fact, he did."

When he failed to elaborate, Alexandra motioned toward a chair. "May we sit?"

Flynn was still staring at her with a smug, almost gleeful look that caused a prickle of uneasiness to touch the nape of her neck.

"By all means." Lucien watched her carefully, searching for the slightest trace of recognition in her face or voice, some little telltale signal that would reveal that she knew he was actually Lucien Charbonneau. But there was nothing, and that made him even more gleeful than he'd been before.

Alexandra pulled out a vacant chair and motioned for Loran to do the same. She sat down warily. "I want to hire your ship, Captain Flynn. Just a short flight across the border to the Denault system, then back. A week, no more."

He unlaced his hands and folded his arms atop the table. The Denault system was days away, a barren, uninhabited star system light-years from any trace of civilization. No one in her right mind would want to go there, not willingly at least. To his knowledge, there was nothing there but a couple of dead worlds and a few rocky moons. "Why the Denault system, Miss Fallon?" He stared at her intently, searching for clues in her wooden expression. "Or is it Mrs. Fallon?"

Impatience darkened the hue of her eyes. This man was impudent. She was trying to book passage on a ship, not appearing before a board of inquiry. "My marital status and my reasons for going to the Denault system are none of your concern," Alexandra snapped back haughtily.

"It is if you want to book passage on *my* ship." His voice was just as flat as hers, just as inflexible. "So I suggest you tell me, or climb out of that chair and leave now." His expression hardened. "The choice is yours. It makes no difference to me."

Tay glanced from one to the other but held his tongue. The current of animosity flowing between them was almost tangible, a sudden arc of electricity so powerful that he felt the urge to leave the table before he got burned.

Alexandra glared at Flynn as she considered her options, and finally decided that she had no other alternative but to comply with his demands. To some extent at least. He didn't need to know the whole truth, just enough to end his inquisition. And any lie was more easily swallowed if it was seasoned with a touch of truth. "All right," she said in a resigned voice. "If you really must know, it's *Miss* Fallon, formerly of the planet Lochlain, the ancestral home of my clan."

Tay coughed and glanced away.

Lucien stared at her long and hard, his face devoid of any detectable expression. The woman was a consummate liar, as well as a thief. At least her pale-faced handmaid had the decency to appear horrified by her mistress's conniving and falsehoods. "Do go on, *Miss* Fallon."

"As to why I want to go to the Denault system, I happen to be a planetary archeologist," she explained. "Some years ago archeological artifacts were found on one of the moons that piqued my professional interest." She shrugged slightly.

"I'm simply writing a paper on those artifacts, and I need to visit the site myself before publication to verify the discoveries."

A disbelieving frown crawled across Lucien's brow. "I see." He doubted if Alexandra Fallon would know the truth if it bit her on the backside. Still, there had been hundreds of books on archeology and planetary studies stacked on the shelves in her sitting room, so her story might actually contain a smidgen of truth. Just a smidgen, though.

Then his annoyance was overcome by skeptical curiosity. Not that he actually believed her, but he did want to know what she was really up to. After all, she was legally his wife. He had a right to know what she was doing. Lucien chewed on his lower lip a moment, considering. Alexandra Fallon had also stolen his jewels and cheated him out of the pleasures of her body on their wedding night. It was past time he reclaimed both and exacted his own peculiar form of retribution. Even if he had to do so in the guise of Damion Flynn.

His head moved up and down in a slow nod. "Tay mentioned some jewels . . . ?" He lifted his brows inquiringly.

Alexandra suppressed a tiny smile as she slid her hand into a pocket in her cloak. Greed always won out in the end. "Here." She reached across the table and allowed two jewels to fall into his waiting hand, watching silently as he dropped them into his own pocket without so much as a cursory glance. "Aren't you going to check to see if they're real?" she asked curiously.

He shrugged leisurely. "What for? You don't appear to be a woman who's prone to acts of stupidity, Miss Fallon. If I discover the jewels aren't real, I'll simply shove you out an air lock and be on my way. I think you know that already."

Alexandra shrugged in return, mimicking his leisurely gesture in every detail. "I don't think you're prone to stupidity, either, Mr. Flynn. If you try to cheat me in any way, I'll hunt you down like a sand-snake and carve out your worm-eaten heart." She gave him a dazzling smile. "And don't make the mistake of thinking that I'm not capable of following through on any threat. I am a Fallon, after all. Anyone with a functioning brain is well aware of my clan's peculiar fondness for weapons and warfare."

Lucien grinned back. She would make good on her threat; of that he was certain. He could still picture the collection of knives and throwing weapons hanging on her wall. He wouldn't make the mistake of underestimating his wife again. "Then we understand each other."

"Perfectly," Alexandra said brightly.

"There's one added condition," Lucien said as a sudden thought occurred to him. The very idea was imminently satisfying. "You and Miss Pahs will be expected to perform minor housekeeping duties while you're aboard my ship."

Alexandra's gaze thinned, and her expression turned suspicious. "Such as?"

"Cooking, cleaning, that sort of thing."

Her cheeks flooded with angry color. "I'm an archeologist, not a scullery maid, Captain Flynn. I won't do busy work just because it amuses you."

He shrugged and glanced at his chronometer. "It's your decision. We lift off at dawn, not a minute past. If you want transport, I suggest you and your companion be aboard . . . on my terms."

He knew she'd cave in because she had no choice. Lucien motioned to Tay, then climbed from the chair abruptly and sauntered toward the door. The next week was going to be interesting, to say the least.

Chapter Six

Sentries clad in the scarlet uniforms of the archduke's bodyguards ushered the baron into an
opulent drawing room, then discreetly slid the
doors shut. Renaud Charbonneau's lips pursed
even tighter than usual as he glanced around his
grandiose surroundings. High above, elaborate
frescoes of past Dominion monarchs stared down
at him from a domed ceiling lavishly decorated
with gold trim, the golden scrollwork illuminated
by a bank of arched windows that glittered like
jewels in the light of Primus's afternoon sun.

Outside the mullioned windows, the fortress's
manicured gardens stretched toward the horizon
in a profusion of geometric patterns and brilliant
colors. Inside, costly antique furniture and dark-
hued rugs were scattered about the white marble
floor, all bearing the unmistakable designs of Old
Earth craftsmen. Thousands of years old then,
possibly more. Renaud's solemn features pinched
into a disdainful grimace. Priceless pieces the

likes of which he'd never seen. But of course he should have expected such an unseemly display of wealth and waste by an effete wastrel like the Dominion archduke.

Unaccustomed to such fierce daylight, Renaud squinted slightly as he walked toward the solitary figure reclining on a white-clad chaise. A pack of small doglike creatures sprang to attention at his approach, mewling sharp, high-pitched sounds to express their dismay. The baron suppressed a disgusted shudder. At least ten of the white-furred beasts were skittering around his feet, their dark eyes, ringed tails, and upright ears far too large for such small, pointed faces. Several snapped at the hem of his robe, their tiny, pointed teeth and sharp claws threatening to tear the material.

"Children! Refrain from such behavior immediately," Archduke Luc Davies admonished, and clapped his hands together to drive his point home. "Your rudeness to our esteemed guest has displeased us greatly."

The creatures backed away instantly, scuttling back to surround the chaise longue and their cherub-faced master. "Ah, Baron Charbonneau, please do have a seat," the archduke said lightly, "and please forgive our beloved companions for their cloddish behavior. We see few strangers here within the walls of our fortress."

Charbonneau settled himself into a fragile wooden chair and smoothed the lines of his somber black robe. He cleared his throat and clasped his hands in his lap. "Thank you for granting me a private audience on such short notice, your grace."

Luc Davies stared at his unexpected guest intently. To his knowledge, no head of the Charbonneau clan had ever requested such an audience before, so the request had come as an utter

Jan Zimlich

surprise. In fact, to his knowledge, this was only the baron's second trip off his homeworld of New France since the unfortunate death of Ariell, his concubine and Lucien's mother. His other departure had been for Lucien's rather impromptu wedding ceremony, an event that was rumored to have gone terribly wrong. "We admit to curiosity about why you've come to Primus, Baron. You have never graced our castle or the court with your presence before, although we do see our dear friend Lucien quite often." A trace of sadness moved through the archduke's pale eyes. "Though not as often of late. We miss his charming company immensely."

The baron leaned forward slightly, his knotted hands working back and forth. Had he heard a note of censure in the archduke's voice? "I've come to beg a favor, your grace, for myself and my clan."

"We see," Luc intoned quietly. Another first on a day of firsts. "And the favor?"

"You are aware of my son's recent marriage?"

"Yes," the archduke said carefully. He was aware of many things, including the ongoing animosity between Lucien and his puritanical father. Lucien had never once divulged the reason for that animosity, but its existence was clear to anyone who dared broach the subject of Lucien's birth or background. "We have also been apprised of the unhappy events that preceded the nuptials."

"Then you know also that this Fallon girl cast aside her legal vows and fled before the marriage could be consummated."

"We are aware of that, too." Luc Davies lifted a pale brow in silent question, his equally pale ringlets shifting slightly as he moved his head.

Renaud cleared his throat noisily. Now that the

78

moment had come, he was loath to actually give voice to his plea. "The girl *must* be found and the marriage consummated; otherwise the blood compact I've entered into with the Fallon clan will legally disintegrate. I need this alliance, your grace. Clan Charbonneau's territory lies in a remote sector of the Dominion, far from your brigades of soldiers and close to the outlying borders. Those damnable rebels have actually had the temerity to make forays into the heart of Charbonneau space of late, encroaching on my right of absolute sovereignty. The rebels have also been actively inciting my subjects to rise against the Dominion, exhorting them to overthrow our system of government. Worse still, they are smuggling arms to those foolish enough to join their cause."

The baron paused to draw a short breath, his anger at his situation apparent in his eyes and face. "If I am to have any success at all in driving these subversive elements from my territory, I must have the assistance of my Fallon allies. The addition of Fallon brigades to my own will at least halt the rebels' momentum. And, the gods willing, we shall send their vile leader to a well-deserved death in the process. Surely their spy's death would be a great boon to you as well. He has masterminded the escapes of hundreds of political prisoners from your own dungeons."

"Ah, yes . . . this so-called Black Rose. We have been kept abreast of his exploits." The archduke frowned thoughtfully. No one knew who the Black Rose was, but on occasion it had been rumored that the criminal had access to the Dominion court itself. How else to explain the fact that rebel prisoners had been freed from Security Force prisons almost immediately after their capture? "We have also heard of his practice

Jan Zimlich

of leaving a single black rose behind once he completes a mission to mark his successful comings and goings. Such impudence. A rose has even been found within the walls of this fortress, as if the blackguard is actually taunting the Security Force." When the flower had been found within the fortress, General Thigg had gone on a tantrumlike rampage, conducting endless interrogations of the enormous staff and the archduke's own bodyguards. Thigg had discovered nothing, however.

"The Black Rose taunts me as well, your grace. His blasted roses have been found from one end of my territory to the other, like a hound leaving his despicable scent." Charbonneau's eyes sharpened, and so did his voice. "He and his rebels must be stopped, before he brings down both my clan and the Dominion itself."

The archduke idly stroked the soft head of one of his pets, his slender fingers easing through the docat's silky fur. Baron Charbonneau's motivation for requesting aid sounded noble and, oh, so altruistic on the surface, but things were not always what they seemed. Not one mention had been made of his son, or the embarrassment and humiliation suffered by Clan Charbonneau once the Fallon girl's perfidy had become public knowledge. The father's only concern seemed to be of the thwarting of his own plans for an alliance. "And if the girl is found and returned to her husband's side, your plans will go forward and this conundrum brought to an end?"

"Yes, your grace." Renaud suppressed a sigh of relief. At least the wastrel had the intelligence to grasp the direness of his situation. "Unless the rebels gain even more weaponry and allies in the interim."

80

Luc Davies fiddled with the folds of his elaborate robe for a moment, adjusting the golden train that trailed from the chaise onto the floor. He had another conundrum to worry about as well. Though the rebels were still a small but vocal minority, with each successful venture their numbers and influence increased. Public discourse about governmental reform had recently grown from angry whispering to belligerent shouts, the calls for democracy becoming so loud and fervent that many clan nobles had begun to fear those rebellious voices might be the vanguard of a political movement that would sweep them from power. Those same nobles, in turn, were now demanding that he take action to permanently silence the malcontents, and threatening that if he didn't, they might very well decide that *he* was the problem and silence him instead.

There lay the crux of his dilemma. If he answered the public's growing calls for democratic reforms, he would surely alienate his nobles and quite possibly jeopardize his life. But if he didn't, he risked alienating the public at large. Which was the more dangerous course of action?

The archduke made one final adjustment to his train and lifted a regal brow. Perhaps if he granted Baron Charbonneau's favor, then let it be known that he had generously come to the aid of an aristocrat imperiled by the rebels, he could at least fend off criticism from his nobles for a while.

"The favor is hereby granted," Luc Davies said magnanimously. "We shall instruct General Thigg of Dominion Security that the Charbonneau-Fallon alliance is of strategic importance to all the Dominion, and to find Lucien's errant bride posthaste so that the alliance may proceed. He is to spare no effort to accomplish this feat."

Charbonneau suddenly looked more nervous than before. "And in return . . . ?" He allowed the question to dangle between them, unanswered. A favor for a favor. It was the way of their culture, of the Dominion itself. A favor granted was always returned.

The archduke lifted a manicured hand and waved his bejeweled fingers in dismissal. "Our intercession on your behalf carries no price this time, Baron. We shall act upon your request out of sincere fondness and compassion for our dear friend Lucien. This young woman is legally bound to fulfill her duties as Lucien's spouse. We intend to see that she does."

The door to Trader Vor's swung inward and collided with the bar's thin wall with a penetrating crack akin to a small explosion. Conversation ceased, and the bar's disreputable patrons and several barmaids jerked their gazes toward the discordant sound, worried that trouble was coming. A dozen hands eased toward weapons secreted inside cloaks, sleeves, and hidden pockets, but retreated quickly when a line of heavily armed soldiers rushed through the open doorway, their armor-clad shapes sweeping left and right to take up sentry positions along the walls. A barmaid screeched in alarm as a score of pulse guns, fighting swords, and laser rifles glinted in the artificial light, but the most frightening sights of all were the shoulder-length braids and tartan cloaks worn by the armored invaders. *Fallons*.

Cutthroats, spies, and smugglers alike froze completely, and a thick, fearful silence descended over the dusty interior of the bar.

A mammoth-sized man ducked his braided head under the doorway and strolled inside Trader Vor's, a meaty hand swatting at the dust clinging to the folds of his red and black cloak. His eyes, fierce, lethal, and dark, swept across each of the bar's patrons in turn, lingering for a second here and there to take the measure of anyone in the path of his chilly gaze.

His chin suddenly rose to an imposing angle, and his gray-mottled braids swung to the back of his head. "Do you know who I am?" he bellowed to his captive audience.

A few heads nodded in frightened assent, but most of the bar's clientele simply stared in mute silence. But all knew exactly who the fierce intruder was, and were well aware of his clan's reputation.

"I am Theodore Fallon, warlord of the Fallon clan, overgeneral of all the Fallon brigades!" Theodore shouted, daring anyone to try to stand against him or his soldiers. He strode closer to the tables, his hand easing toward the leather scabbard strapped at his waist. "I have come to this dungpit of a world in search of information!" He pulled his sword free of its scabbard and swung it in a swift downward arc with enough force to decapitate a fully grown man. Instead, he bisected a wooden chair, which collapsed in a heap of splintered sticks. Several men jumped in response, and a frightened barmaid dropped the serving tray she'd been holding. A chorus of metallic clicks followed as a dozen Fallon laser rifles were primed and aimed.

The pale-faced patrons stared at the Fallon warlord with wide, fearful eyes.

Now that he had their complete attention, Theodore smiled, a skull-like stretching of his lips that let them know in no uncertain terms that if he didn't get what he wanted, their heads would be next. "And I must tell you that I don't have any intention of leaving this place until I get what I want."

He paced several steps to the right, then back left, making sure that all eyes were following his every move. As he walked, a small cloud of yellowish dust drifted around him, falling toward the stone floor from his travel-stained cloak and knee-high boots. "I'm hunting for a woman . . . a runaway with dark braids and blue eyes. She arrived here on a passenger liner five days ago, accompanied by a mousy little handmaid. This woman is my blood kin, and I am her liege lord." His voice hardened. "She has no right to run away . . . no rights at all that I don't grant her, so do not think to protect her or lie about her whereabouts."

When no one spoke up, Theodore's gaze grew sharper, thinner, and he lifted a triangular credit chit high over his head, displaying the coin for all to see. Fear hadn't worked as yet, so maybe greed would motivate them to loosen their tongues. "A hundred credits to the man or woman who tells me where to find her!"

A thin, sun-beaten man wearing a grubby jumpsuit eyed the chit held aloft in the Fallon warlord's hand for a few seconds.

"I saw her, your lordship," he said in a small voice. "About two or three days ago. The woman you described was out at the landing field trying to harass her way into chartering a ship. Another woman was with her." He fell quiet for a moment, his rapt eyes still fastened on the promised credit chit. "That's all I know."

Theodore nodded in grim satisfaction. *Finally.* He tossed the man the chit, then lifted another. "Who else would like to earn a hundred credits?"

He watched their expressions carefully, his hard glance sliding over one face, then another, then stilling on a comely red-haired barmaid who refused to meet his eyes head-on. "You!" Theodore pointed the hand holding the chit in her direction. "Barmaid! You know something, don't you?" he shouted, intimidating her with his eyes and voice. "What do you know of the woman I seek?"

The barmaid took a step backward and clutched a metal serving tray to her chest like a shield. Her eyes widened with abject terror, and her mouth opened and shut several times, as if she were having a difficult time forming the necessary words.

Theodore was certain now that she knew something and tossed the chit to the floor at her feet. "Speak up, girl, or face my wrath!"

Her mouth trembled slightly, and a slow flush spread over her pale cheeks. "I . . . my lord . . ."

"Speak up!" Theodore roared.

"She was here," the barmaid said in a rush, "in the bar." She gripped the tray tighter. "She met with Captain Flynn . . . Damion Flynn. I think she arranged passage on his ship."

Theodore's graying brows pulled downward in a frown. "And just who is this Damion Flynn?"

"He . . . he's a smuggler, your lordship. His ship is the *Nightwind*. He moves cargo on and off of Thasia every few months. He left two days ago, and I haven't seen the woman since."

The Fallon warlord's frown settled into an angry glower. The little fool had really done it now. If this barmaid was to be believed, the blushing bride was off gallivanting around the galaxy with a strange man—a known smuggler to boot. And everyone knew the sort of reputations smugglers had where women were concerned; he seriously doubted if this Damion Flynn was an exception to that unpleasant rule. Theodore stroked his bearded chin a moment, thinking. What would her husband do if damaged goods were returned to him?

Even more important, how would Baron Charbonneau react? The man was priggish in the extreme, and had already been humiliated by Alexandra's foolish stunt. If it became known that his son's wife had abandoned her nuptial bed, then freely consorted with a known criminal . . . Theodore tried and failed to blink away that horrible thought. Needless to say, the Charbonneau clan would jettison the new alliance like so much garbage, and *he* would be forced to return the settlement and dowry, hundreds of thousands of glorious credit chits. His mouth hardened. Never, not in his lifetime would that happen. They were his chits now. His.

So he would just have to make certain that Alexandra was found and returned to her rightful place. Quickly—before some smarmy, conniving criminal had a chance to make off with her maidenhood. And the only way to do that was to up the ante.

Theodore sheathed his sword and strode to a wooden column along the wall to his right, then reached into a pocket of his cloak, withdrawing a scriber, a folded slip of parchment, and an intricately wrought dagger. He smoothed the fresh parchment and held it up against the column, then, before he had a chance to change his mind about the chits, stabbed the parchment firmly to the wood with the tip of his ornate dagger. The knife point held a picture of Alexandra Fallon in place, her magnetic eyes and darkly beautiful face enlarged so much they were almost life-size. But the writing beneath that picture would cause far more of a stir than Alexandra's looks. The words inscribed beneath the picture advised any and all of the reward being offered by Lord Theodore Fallon in exchange for the safe and prompt return of Alexandra Fallon to Lochlain, her homeworld.

Theodore took a deep breath and pressed the scriber to the parchment, adding a string of zeroes to the amount of the reward he'd planned on offering. When he was done, he turned back to the bar full of ruffians. "Pass the word," Theodore announced gruffly, knowing that within minutes every thief, cutthroat, and stinking spy within three star systems would know of the huge bounty he'd placed on Alexandra's head. "On this day, the Fallon warlord has sworn to pay a ten-thousand-chit reward for the safe and swift return of his blood kin, Alexandra Fallon." He scraped the pad of his thumb across the dagger's sharp underside, slicing open a sliver of flesh. A spurt of blood dribbled down his finger to his palm and wrist. Theodore waited until more blood accumulated, then pressed his thumb firmly against the bottom of the parchment, sealing his vow with a bloody thumbprint. No one within the Dominion would doubt the truthfulness of a warlord's blood oath. "And I also vow a thousand extra credits if she is found and returned to Lochlain within the week."

Theodore saw the naked avarice glinting in a dozen pairs of eyes and knew he'd made the right decision. They would pass the word, all right, to a thousand others, and they to a thousand more, and they would all hunt Alexandra and Flynn down like a pack of rabid hounds. He smiled slyly. With every miserable scalawag in the Dominion hot on her trail, Alexandra would soon be found and returned to the bosom of her family. Then he would take every single chit he'd spent on the bounty out of her pretty hide, flaying the flesh from her treacherous bones inch by painful inch.

Chapter Seven

The *Nightwind*'s intercom emitted a birdlike chirp, and Alexandra's eyes thinned to sullen slits. "Him again, no doubt." Wanting something else. Her mouth curled downward in a disgusted grimace.

"Bring me a cup of coffee right away, *Miss* Fallon," Damion Flynn ordered, his deep voice echoing around the ship's small galley. "I'm in my cabin."

His voice faded into nothingness, but Alexandra could still hear his latest demand echoing through her mind. She slung a cooking spoon to the metal deck in protest. "Ohwww! Gods, how I hate that man!" she railed to Loran. She'd been trapped on his ship for two days now, two long days of endless "housekeeping duties" that always involved her waiting on the miserable oaf hand and foot. In fact, he seemed to relish dreaming up new and demeaning ways to make her wait on him, which usually consisted of manual labor and much sweat on her part. "'Do this, Miss Fallon, do that. . . . Get down on your hands and knees and scrub that corridor until it shines!' He's nothing more than a wart on the hind end of a ground-toad! A despicable, low-life cretin who's amusing himself by watching me sweat like a dung-pig!"

Loran sighed quietly. She'd listened to different variations of this same tirade over and over again since they'd left Thasia. But Alexandra was right about one thing—Captain Flynn was clearly taking advantage of the opportunity to bend a beautiful young noblewoman to his will, and seemed to be enjoying himself immensely in the process. It crossed Loran's mind to remind Alexandra that the journey—and the choice of transport—had been her own idea, and thus she'd inflicted Damion Flynn on herself. But to bring that forgotten point to the forefront would undoubtedly increase the volume and intensity of her mistress's current outburst. "It will all be over soon, my lady," Loran said in a soothing voice, and hopefully it would. Another few days and they would be off the *Nightwind* forever. "You won't have to wait on him much longer. And there is one saving grace . . . at least it's not your uncle ordering you about."

"I'd much rather deal with Uncle Theodore any day," Alexandra retorted. "At least I know what sort of treachery to expect from him." Her lips thinned in irritation. "Flynn's another matter altogether. I loathe the man, Loran, utterly loathe him with every bone in my body. He's absolutely infuriating! What manner of man would force his paying passengers to act as his scullery maids?"

She snatched a mug from a cupboard

mounted atop the small cookstove, then waved it around the cramped confines of the galley in an all-encompassing gesture. "Just look at this galley. It's positively archaic! Like something out of an Old Earth history text. He actually expects us to stand in here for hours every single day pounding and chopping foodstuffs like we're some sort of neolithic cavewomen! Doesn't the buffoon know anything about prepackaged foodstuffs and replication technology?"

"Perhaps he simply believes in a more organic approach to edibles," Loran said, still trying to defuse Alexandra's anger. "Many believe a more natural approach is healthier for the body."

"Healthier for whom? Him?" Alexandra slammed the coffee mug against a metal countertop. "Well, since he seems to prefer organic food, I'll be more than glad to slice and stew *him* up for dinner! Although I'm sure the taste of him would be about as foul as a roasted scum-mole." The corners of her mouth suddenly lifted, and she cast a surreptitious glance at the small vials of exotic spices lining a shelf in the cupboard.

"Alexandra . . ." Loran didn't like the sudden glint of mischief shining in her mistress's eyes. She'd seen that look often enough through the years, and it always boded ill. Alexandra was playing with fire. She was about to do something very, very foolish, and Captain Flynn was not the sort to trifle with. "I'll be glad to take Captain Flynn his coffee," she offered quickly, hoping to belay whatever it was that Alexandra had in mind.

"No, no." Alexandra shook her head vehemently. "You know the ogre expects me to do it. He'll probably force us both to scrub the neces-

sity room again if I don't." She held out the
mug and waited while Loran poured the steaming brownish green liquid from a large carafe.
"Why don't you take this mug to Mr. Molvan?"
Alexandra prodded sweetly. "Unlike his captain,
he's been very nice to both of us, and he has
been at the helm for hours now. I'm sure he'd
appreciate some coffee. I'll pour Captain Flynn
another."

Loran hesitated, and a wave of heat flushed her
cheeks. She would enjoy the opportunity to visit
Mr. Molvan for a few moments, but still . . .

Alexandra grabbed the carafe from her hands
and replaced it with the filled mug. "Oh, go on,
Loran, do it. I've seen the way he looks at you
when he thinks no one is watching. I think Mr.
Molvan is quite taken with you."

The heat spread over Loran's pale face in
earnest. Tay Molvan had been genuinely kind to
her since they'd left Thasia, so solicitous that on
more than one occasion she had dared to consider the idea that he might actually be attracted
to her. And he was such a huge, personable man,
a friendly giant who made her feel small and pro-
tected when he was around. "Do you really think
he might be taken with me?" The very prospect
was terrifying but made her feel giddy in the
extreme.

Alexandra pushed her toward the doorway. "Of
course he is. Now go take him that coffee." After a
momentary hesitation, Loran disappeared down
the metal-walled corridor, and a devious smile
tugged at the corners of Alexandra's mouth. Tay
Molvan did seem quite taken with shy Loran, so it
wasn't exactly a lie. More of a distraction, of
sorts.

She grabbed another mug from the tiny cupboard, then glanced over the array of spices

neatly arranged on the middle shelf until she spotted a small vial of amber tement sauce, an extract made from a plant that grew only on the planet Andwillia. Once a year, when the plant was in full bloom, maggotlike insects burrowed down to feast on the plant's tubular roots, leaving behind a sticky, sugary substance that was often added to chilled desserts to sweeten the taste. Alexandra laughed quietly. Tement sauce was wonderful on chilled foods, but if added to anything hot, it transformed into something unspeakably vile.

She hummed to herself as she poured the demanding clod his coffee, then added a healthy dose of sauce to the mug. After a second's hesitation, she added more, emptying the vial of its peculiar contents. She glanced inside the mug, sniffed at the liquid, and shrugged. The steaming coffee looked and smelled the same. It was still an uninviting brownish green, maybe a bit darker than before, and the scent was a little acrid, but not enough to truly be noticeable. "Well, Captain Flynn," she whispered to herself, "I doubt if you'll be demanding coffee from me again anytime soon."

Clutching the mug carefully, Alexandra sauntered down the ship's tubelike central corridor, still humming and smiling to herself. If nothing else, she would finally get to see the inside of the slime-pig's cabin, which had been completely off-limits to both her and Loran from the moment they'd had the misfortune to board his ship. Why they'd been barred, she didn't know, but it was a relief in a twisted sort of way—Flynn's cabin and the cargo bay were the only places on the entire ship that she hadn't been forced to clean in the past two days. She snorted in disgust. And to think she'd paid Flynn handsomely for the privilege of working her fingers to bony nubs.

She had to admit that she was a tad curious about the inside of his cabin, though. Some said that the eyes were windows to the human soul, but Alexandra had always found that a person's most cherished possessions revealed far more about them than their eyes. She smiled grimly. If the saying were actually true, then Flynn's cabin would be empty and bleak, as stark and miserable as his worm-eaten heart. Unfortunately, the exterior of the man himself was another matter altogether. The evil rogue's attractiveness was a rather unpleasant reality that she'd been reminded of several times in the past two days. Whenever he'd walked into her line of sight, her heart had immediately given little thuds of warning for her to get away.

But on such a small ship, avoiding any contact with Flynn was virtually impossible. He seemed to be there beside her each time she turned, in the galley, the ship's short central corridor, and a dozen other places, often so close that their bodies would brush as they passed. It hadn't taken her long to realize that all those chance meetings weren't chance at all. At times he simply lurked about with his arms folded over his chest, watching silently and giving her dark, knowing smiles as she scrubbed at this or that, as if he knew that her heart beat faster whenever he was around. He was like an Ornian spider as it sat in its web, waiting for the perfect moment to devour its mate.

She shivered inwardly. Worse, despite his constant watchfulness, ceaseless demands, and overbearing manner, she always seemed to feel like some adolescent fool whenever Flynn was around: awkward, acutely aware of his maleness, and very angry at herself that her mind and body would respond in such a way.

She paused outside his door and pushed a wayward braid from her forehead, steeling herself for the unpleasant encounter that would surely come. She planned to beard the beast in his own lair, after all, and she doubted if he'd take kindly to that. After taking a deep breath, Alexandra slammed a closed fist against the frame to announce her arrival, and his door slid open in prompt response.

"It's about time," Flynn said in an offhand voice. He was seated at a small desk, his gaze focused on a sheaf of parchment in his hands. "Come in."

As Alexandra stepped inside the semidark cabin, her mouth fell open in surprise. She'd expected Flynn's lair to be sterile, cold, and devoid of any grace or sense of style. But this . . . His cabin was far larger than the little closet she and Loran had been forced to share, roomy enough to accommodate a sitting area as well as a large and comfortable-looking bed.

Her gaze flicked left, away from the disconcerting sight of that satin-covered bed. She concentrated on the other furnishings instead. Several pieces of ornately carved furniture of a quality rarely seen outside museums stood in strategic spots about the tidy cabin. Two plump chairs upholstered in a soft blue silk that matched an oriental-inspired wall hanging were arranged against the wall to her left. The silk painting was of a single black flower set against pale blue fabric, a stark yet graceful design that held the eyes captive because of its compelling simplicity. As for the owner of that hanging, he was seated at an elegant wooden desk with its legs carved in the shape of animal legs, his own boot-clad feet stretched languidly beneath.

But behind him was the cabin's crowning glory, a sight so painfully beautiful that Alexandra had to suppress a wondering gasp. A curved viewing window ran the length of the outer bulkhead and the width of the cabin, a plethora of stars both young and old visible through the thick transparency. Light-years away, she could even see the cloudy pink hues of a distant nebula, a pale and spidery veil of light glowing against an ebony backdrop.

She forced herself to look away from the breathtaking sight and concentrate on the cabin's interior once again, an overall assessment that would give her some measure of Damion Flynn the man. His cabin and furnishings were indeed stark, just as she'd suspected earlier, but sterile, no. *Elegant* and *understated* were far better descriptions. Her gaze moved over him curiously. The room was not at all what she had expected. Of course, he'd probably stolen it all.

Lucien glanced up from the parchment and found himself staring into Alexandra Fallon's jewel-blue eyes. His wife was still standing near the doorway, a curious expression passing over her face as she studied him and the interior of his cabin at long length. A small smile touched the corners of his mouth. *Good.* Damion Flynn had managed to surprise her, although he wasn't exactly sure why that should matter to him. He rose from the desk and bent at the waist in a sweeping bow. "Welcome to my cabin, *Miss* Fallon." She looked particularly fetching today in a dark red robe that clung to the delectable curves of her torso, her only ornaments those glorious braids tipped with strips of ribbon in a matching red.

Alexandra lifted a dark brow. Flynn's bow had been court perfect, fluid and graceful, yet it bore no hint of the inherent foppishness that usually accompanied the archaic gesture. How had a thieving smuggler learned such a thing? And why did the man always insist on putting so much emphasis on the word *miss* when he addressed her?

A flicker of suspicion passed through her. Flynn was clad in dark trousers, the high boots polished to a glossy black, and a soft, half-fastened tunic that was hanging open down the expanse of his broad chest to reveal a smooth swath of well-muscled flesh. Casual attire. Fairly ordinary, as a matter of fact, and yet there was something not quite right about his appearance, something a bit out of place that had triggered a flash of suspicion when she'd seen him bow.

"Well?" Lucien said to break her intense perusal. She was still watching him a bit too carefully to suit his taste. The courtly bow had been an impulsive thing, an innocuous gesture on his part, but it had obviously raised a flurry of questions in her mind. He'd have to be more careful in the future. His loving wife might be a bit naive, but she had a quick and agile mind—devious as well. "Are you just going to stand there until my coffee chills?"

Her suspicion faded, replaced by a sour expression. "Here's your coffee . . . *Master.*" Two could play at his emphasis game. She walked stiffly to the desk and handed him the mug, flinching slightly when his fingertips grazed across the top of her hand. The jolt of awareness spiraled downward from her hand to her toes. She took a sudden step backward, out of his reach, though her gaze remained fastened on his roguish features and the strip of bare flesh running down his chest. "Will there be anything else?" she said in a nasty tone, wishing the man would cover his chest.

Lucien cleared his throat and broke contact with those deep eyes, moving away from her as well. He set the mug on his desk and fiddled with the parchment for something to do. He had been ordering her about for the past two days out of a desire for revenge, playing her for a fool instead of her playing him. Yet the inadvertent touch of his flesh on hers had affected him far more than he cared to admit, as much as it had on Lochlain all those weeks ago. And judging by her startled expression, she had felt the same twinge of passion as well. "No, not at the moment." He distanced himself further by moving toward one of the wing chairs, masking his sudden nervousness with a nonchalant air. "But we do need to discuss tomorrow. That's why I asked you here."

Alexandra blinked herself back to reality, trying to tamp out the tiny flame of desire still flickering deep within her brain. She would not allow herself to be attracted to a lowlife such as Flynn. She could not allow such a thing. "Tomorrow?"

Lucien frowned. Perhaps her mind wasn't as agile as he'd thought. "Have you forgotten the reason for this journey so soon? We've already crossed the Dominion border and will reach the Denault system in less than a standard day."

"Oh." Her cheeks heated with embarrassment. How could she have forgotten the most important moment of her life? The single-minded goal she'd worked toward all these years, in less than a week? "Of course I remember," she snapped back.

"Well?"

She was angry now, her cheeks turning a flaming red. She didn't care for his tone of voice or his condescending manner, and she liked the fact that he'd caught her memory lapse even less. "Well what?"

"Would you mind giving me some inkling of what I'm supposed to do when we get there? It is my ship, after all, and it would be a great help to at least know *where* we're going."

Her body stiffened and her chin tilted defiantly. The man was an arrogant snake. How could she have ever thought that she might be attracted to the despicable cretin? "The northern polar region of the fourth moon of the third planet. I'll give you the exact coordinates when we enter the atmosphere, not a minute before."

Lucien gave her a skeptical look. What was she up to, and what could possibly be of such interest to her on a dead moon in the Denault system? He'd had his fun ordering her about, but now she might be putting his ship at risk, and he wouldn't stand for that at all. "You'll give them to me now or I'll turn this ship around and head back to the border."

"No." Her lips compressed in a stubborn line, and her chin lifted a fraction higher.

"Then you leave me no choice." His voice and expression were just as sharp as hers, just as determined. "I won't risk my ship or our lives for something as silly and addle-brained as your stubbornness."

"Silly and addle-brained?" Alexandra crossed in three angry strides to where he stood and glared up at him furiously. "Did it ever occur to you that I'm being stubborn because I don't trust you, Flynn? You're a known smuggler and probably a common thief as well! People in your line of work don't exactly have the best of reputations." The blue of her eyes deepened to a chilly, angry hue, and her chest heaved in and out with the force of her rage. "I am *not* going to risk my father's life's work—and my own—by placing my trust in the likes of you. Do you think me that big a fool?"

"A fool, no," Lucien said evenly, his gaze riveted on the quick rise and fall of her chest as he remembered with sudden clarity how she'd looked half-dressed in a thin underrobe. But that memory triggered some rather unpleasant ones as well—memories of serving trays and foul-tasting gags. "But you're definitely a devious little bitch. I guess you come by it naturally, though, considering your background."

Utterly speechless, Alexandra stared up at him, her face growing paler and paler with fury and shock. A common thief had just had the audacity to insult her and her clan to her face. How dare he say such a thing! "Why, you vile-mannered dung-pig." Alexandra reacted instinctively, her closed fist arcing out and up, connecting with his jaw with enough force to snap his head back several inches. She gave him a smug, self-satisfied look, the fist still curled in readiness at her side. No one ever insulted a Fallon twice.

Dumbfounded, Lucien flexed the pain from his jaw and stared at his vengeful wife. He couldn't believe that she'd had the temerity to punch him in the face, and not a womanly punch at that. Her slug had been lightning fast and equal in strength to a man's, and just as painful, too.

"That was just a reminder, Captain. . . . We Fallons don't take kindly to insults."

Lucien's eyes turned an ice-filled shade of gray. He'd lowered his guard and somehow managed to underestimate his darling wife again. So far she had beaten him over the head, gagged, robbed, and hog-tied him, and now she'd punched him in the face. Quite an impressive tally for a slip of a woman who barely reached his shoulder. She was obviously living proof that the wild tales about her clan's fighting abilities were based in truth, not legend. Someone, her Uncle Theodore probably, had taught her very well indeed.

But that bit of unexpected insight didn't solve his immediate problem. Lucien rubbed at the tender spot on his lower jaw. One way or another, the stubborn little witch wasn't leaving his cabin without turning over those coordinates. He couldn't beat them out of her either, so he'd just have to cajole her some other way.

A slow, calculating smile spread over his lips. He would cajole her, all right, in his own special way, and teach his bratty wife a lesson at the same time. "We 'vile-mannered dung-pigs' don't take kindly to insults either, *Miss* Fallon. And we certainly don't take kindly to being punched in the face. In fact, we often react quite strongly . . . like the common street thieves that we are." His smile turned dark and boldly suggestive. Her full lips, usually so sullen and pouty, were moist and parted, as if they were poised and waiting to be kissed, a kiss he'd waited weeks now for the chance to give. A kiss she owed him. "Thievery takes many forms, you know, some quite unexpected."

Alexandra's eyes widened when she began to suspect his meaning, and she took a half step backwards. She didn't like that smile on his face one whit. It was too smug, far too sensual. Both hands curled into protective fists. "Don't even think about it, Flynn."

"Too late, I already have." He was ready for her this time, expertly dancing to the left to dodge the balled fist she aimed at his nose. As she flailed at empty air, Lucien twisted back and grabbed her by the shoulders, his hands snaking downward to imprison her upper arms. She managed to land a sharp kick to his shin as Lucien lifted her from the floor and threw her squirming body across his shoulder.

The air rushed from Alexandra's lungs as her chest collided with his shoulder blade. "Put me down, Flynn!" She tried to kick him again, but her foot tangled in the hem of her voluminous robe. "I'm warning you . . . put me down!"

In three quick strides Lucien made it to the bed. "Fine." He tossed her atop the plump mattress and crashed down beside her, locking her flailing form inside a tight embrace.

Alexandra struggled in vain to free herself, but the oaf was too large, too powerful simply to push aside. In the blink of an eye he'd managed to pin her arms and legs with his own and twine one hand around several long braids, holding her head to the mattress as well. He shifted a leg slightly, forcing their bodies even closer, and Alexandra's heart raced in her chest. She gritted her teeth and glared, unnerved by the intimate contact. "Let me go, Flynn. Now." Her voice came out thinner than usual, sounding more like a plea than a command, and that infuriated her all the more.

Lucien grinned back. For once he had her exactly where he wanted her. Her cool eyes, glittering a little less fiercely than normal, were following his every move, watching him expectantly. Warily. He took a deep breath, enjoying the moment, the sweet scent of her drifting around him. He'd almost forgotten how good she'd smelled on their wedding night: sweet, yet tangy in a sultry way, like a field full of flowers on a stormy day. "Not yet, love . . . not until you give me those landing coordinates."

Her eyes blazed. "Why, you despicable worm!" She tried to pull away from him, but his fingertips tightened around her braids. "Ouch! That hurts!"

"Not nearly as much as my jaw." Lucien loosened his grip on her hair a fraction, but not enough to allow her to escape. Her jet braids were scattered around her shoulders and chest, drawing his gaze lower, to the rhythmic rise of her breasts beneath the silky fabric of her scarlet robe. He watched raptly, as aroused by her nearness as he'd been on their ill-fated wedding night. He twirled the end of a braid around and around his fingers, marveling at the silken texture. The peculiar hairstyle was very becoming, but he really wished that he could see her just once with all that wonderful hair unbound. There was something vaguely disquieting about all those snakelike braids.

"I'm still waiting," he told her in a low voice. He dragged the feathery end of a braid across the base of her neck, then slowly followed that course with his fingertips, tracing the outline of the hollow of her throat.

"I already told you . . . no," Alexandra said adamantly. "It's a very simple word." She pulled as far away from his wandering fingers as she could, which only amounted to an inch or two. It was better than nothing, though. "What about it don't you understand?"

Lucien smothered a smile. He had to admit, the vexing witch was completely indomitable. A virtual stranger had her pinned to his bed, yet she still had the strength to oppose him. "Oh, I think you can be convinced." His fingertips moved lower, across the curve of her breast, then upward again, following the delicate line of her throat to her chin and jaw. "That is, if the right person is doing the convincing."

Alexandra swallowed the nervous knot that had wedged somewhere between her heart and her throat. His fingers were burning fiery little pathways along the side of her neck, and his torso and legs were pressing into hers in places that she didn't dare contemplate. "And of course you think you're the right person?"

"Of course," Lucien said matter-of-factly. Who better than her husband? He touched the end of a nail to her lower lip, teasing it slowly along the line of her mouth.

"You really are an arrogant, black-hearted worm, Flynn." A pulse quickened at the base of her throat as his fingertip moved across her cheek.

Lucien smiled darkly. "Maybe, but like always finds like. Your heart is just as black as mine, love." His mouth suddenly descended and captured hers. It was more of a slow caress than a kiss.

Alexandra's heart hammered against her rib cage, pounding so fast and furiously that she thought she might faint. He was kissing her, slowly, gently, his lips exploring hers with a thoroughness that was unsettling in the extreme. Unsettling but oh, so enjoyable. She knew she should fight him, either wrench her arms free or somehow give him the ball of her knee, but a languid heat had begun to spread through her limbs, dulling her senses into submission. His words echoed in her chaotic thoughts. *Like always finds like. . . . Your heart is just as black as mine.* And at the moment, she thought it might actually be true. Only a woman with a very black heart would reject the attentions of a noble-born husband to find pleasure in the arms of a scoundrel like Flynn.

His kiss suddenly deepened, the once-gentle exploration becoming insistent, demanding, his sensuous mouth caressing her in a way that no man had ever done before. Alexandra made a little sound in the back of her throat, a sigh of pleasure that seemed to heighten the urgency of his kiss. Her lips moved against his of their own accord, tentatively at first, tasting and exploring just as he had done. Black-hearted or not, she was enjoying his ministrations intensely.

Lucien suppressed a groan as she responded to his kiss, her lush mouth beginning to move against his with an ardor that nearly equaled his own. He felt her supple body relax beneath him, the tension melting from her limbs with each second that passed, and he responded in kind by relaxing his grip on her forearms. Somehow her hand immediately wound itself through his hair, then came to rest on his cheekbone, her palm sliding gently along the outline of his jaw.

She made that little sound of pleasure again, and this time Lucien groaned aloud, low and primal. Once again Alexandra Fallon had managed to surprise him. He had expected her to react to his advances like some coy virgin trying desperately to stave off a threat to her maidenhood. Instead she'd proven that she was a woman in full passionate bloom, eager and ready to seek pleasure in the arms of a blackguard like Damion Flynn. His other self, in the guise of Lucien Charbonneau, had known only a fleeting foretaste of the woman's passionate nature, and that quick sampling had left him reeling for weeks. But Charbonneau's misfortune would soon be Flynn's windfall; of that he was certain, because he was now bound and determined to plumb the depths of desire that lay hidden inside his wife.

As he deepened his kiss even more, he wanted to smile. How insane that thought had sounded, even to himself, as if he were in direct competition with his alter ego for his wife's sexual favors. His hand moved lower, boldly following the ripe curve of her waist to her hip, drawing her closer, the silk of her robe rasping deliciously against the skin on his chest. In this contest, Damion Flynn was going to win hands down. He always did.

He pushed at the shoulders of his tunic, trying to free his torso from the clingy fabric, eager to feel the touch of her soft flesh pressed solidly against his own. After a dogged effort, he managed to free one arm and pulled her tight to his chest once more, his hand moving swiftly to the intricate fasteners running down the front of her robe.

The first of the fasteners gave way, and Alexandra's body stiffened when he moved on to the next. She blinked the haze of desire from her thoughts and concentrated on Flynn's sudden contortions instead of the feel and taste of his lips. Comprehension slowly inched its way through her passion-dulled brain. Somehow he'd managed to rid himself of his shirt, and he was now systematically unfastening the front of her robe with the practiced ease of a man all too familiar with such things.

"Flynn . . . I . . ." There was something uncomfortably familiar about the entire situation, something curious about the glint in those silvery eyes that plucked at a thread in her memory. But for the life of her, she couldn't remember what it was. "Stop." What had possessed her to allow the worm to take such liberties?

Lucien gave her a decadent smile and continued his downward progress. "Don't worry, love," he murmured in a silky voice, "I'll have it off in a few seconds." His eyes turned a hot, smoky gray when the material gaped open, revealing the lush outline of her breasts beneath a scanty white underrobe. He pulled in a needed breath of air. "Oh, gods, you have a magnificent body."

Horrified, Alexandra grabbed at his hand and pushed it away, then pulled the gaping material together and began the task of refastening her robe. "No, Flynn," she said as forcefully as she could. In mere seconds the bold worm had managed to undo five of the difficult fasteners, an arduous chore that would have taken either her or Loran twice that amount of time. Her fingers trembled as she struggled to push the last two buttons back into place. "This was a mistake. A tremendous mistake."

Lucien leaned back on an elbow and cocked a dark eyebrow, bemused by his mercurial wife's sudden change of heart and his own change in fortune. "The word *no* is for the timid, love, and you are most definitely not the timid sort." He ran a hand down the outside of her thigh, the liquid silk shivering and shifting beneath his fingertips. He'd ignited her passions once and could do so again.

For a pleasurable moment, Alexandra felt the languid heat flowing through her limbs once again; then she bolted upright and scrambled to the edge of the bed, her pulse thundering protests in her ears. Her senses were shouting at her to stay, to simply lie back and let him have his way, but her mind kept carping for her to flee. She finally climbed free of the bed to stand on uncertain feet, the finale of a hard-fought battle won by her brain. The outcome of that internal battle had been close, though—far too close to ignore. If there was a next time, the result might not be the same. She was horrified at what she'd learned, but the cold, unvarnished truth was that she apparently was a wanton, fickle woman with a heart as black as his.

Lucien watched a series of conflicting emotions chase across her features. He saw regret in her shadowed eyes, as well as a touch of pity and self-loathing, so at least she wasn't abandoning him this time without a trace of regret. She hadn't banged him on the head with anything, either, a definite improvement. "Just where do you think you're going?" he asked in a casual voice, though at the moment *casual* was the last thing he felt.

"I'm leaving," she said without elaborating. She tidied her rumpled robe and tried to gather her scattered wits.

His hand snaked out and latched onto her wrist. "Not without giving me those coordinates."

Her eyes narrowed in sudden anger. What a manipulative cretin he was! For her the events of the past few minutes had erased all thoughts of the Denault system, as well as those of his demand. Flynn, on the other hand, hadn't forgotten a thing. She turned toward him and stared. He was still sprawled across the soft bed, leaning indolently on an elbow, his long hair slightly mussed and falling in dark waves to his bare shoulders. It was so dark and silky that in the cabin's dim light, she could see a trace of silver-white glinting in the ebony strands.

A knot of awareness wedged in her chest again. If she didn't get out of his cabin now, at this very instant, her mind and senses would do battle once more, and this time her desire would win. She rushed to the desk, grabbed up a scriber, and scribbled a string of numbers on a slip of parchment. "Here are your damn coordinates." She flung the piece of parchment toward the bed, then turned on her heel and fled to the door, hurrying away before a victorious grin could spread across his chiseled face.

"Wait!" Lucien called out, but the door had already opened and she had taken flight. The slip of paper drifted to a stop atop the bed. He sat up on the edge of the bed and pushed a strand of tousled hair from his face, a bit nonplussed that she'd beaten such a hasty and unexpected retreat. "Well, this may take more work than I imagined," he whispered to himself, then laughed aloud. Seducing his beautiful young wife was turning out to be a formidable task indeed.

Lucien climbed to his feet and retrieved his discarded tunic, pushing his arms back into the sleeves as he returned to the desk, retrieved the sheaf of parchment, and resumed decoding the text. His forgotten mug of coffee beckoned, a few wisps of steam still drifting upward from the insulated container. But at least it would still be warm and semidrinkable. Lucien sighed happily and took an unwitting sip, his features contorting with shock and fury as the tainted liquid spread over his tongue.

His outraged scream was long and impossibly loud, reverberating throughout the metal-walled ship. Alexandra froze when she heard his furious shout and visibly winced at the vile storm of invectives echoing down the narrow corridor from his cabin. "Uh-oh," she told herself in a quavering voice. "He actually drank it."

The stream of shouted oaths continued unabated, and Alexandra finally lifted a hand to hide the triumphant smirk threatening to sneak across her face. Her footsteps quickened. She could gloat later, when the storm had passed. Right now she needed a safe place to hide.

Chapter Eight

Pale light from the Denault system's aging yellow sun streamed across the surface of the pockmarked moon, a bland, insignificant sphere orbiting high above a long-dead world. Three smaller moons were visible in the distance, odd-shaped rocky cousins of the larger, fourth moon that was the *Nightwind*'s ultimate destination.

Alexandra squeezed past Loran to get a better view through the cramped control deck's small viewport. She rested an elbow atop Flynn's high-backed helm chair and stared raptly, doing her best to ignore the man himself. A difficult task, that, considering the hateful looks he'd been throwing her way since the day before. If she had known he'd get that furious about the tement sauce, she might not have added it to his mug. He'd even accused her of trying to kill him . . . again—as if she were solely responsible for every tragedy that had befallen him in his entire miserable life. She shrugged inwardly and bit back an amused smile. No matter. The oaf would get over it eventually. And her tactic, though somewhat dirty, had been a complete success. Flynn hadn't dared demand that she scrub, cook, clean, or bring coffee to him since.

As she continued to gaze at the moon's stark surface, a tiny thrill of excitement began to sweep through her blood. After all the years of planning, study, and scheming, she was finally here, within hours of finally proving or disproving her father's long-derided theories once and for all. She bit down hard on her lower lip. The evidence had to be there. It had to be.

"Hurry up and land, Flynn," she ordered, an edgy note of impatience leaking into her voice. "I want to get down there right away."

Lucien glanced over his shoulder and gave her an ice-cold glare. The woman was an absolute menace. "If you hadn't tried to poison the pilot, we might have landed already."

Alexandra rolled her eyes in exasperation. "Good grief, Flynn. It was just a little tement sauce. If I'd really wanted to poison you, you'd be cold and dead."

"I don't doubt it," Lucien said tersely. Her carryall was probably stuffed full of poisons, ropes, and throwing knives. "I should have hired a food taster before I let you aboard my ship."

Tay snorted and exchanged a swift look with Loran, but kept his thoughts to himself.

"Cheer up, Flynn." Alexandra chopped a hand toward the moonscape speeding beneath them. "You'll be rid of me in a few days."

"Good," he muttered, and fell silent, suddenly uncertain how he actually felt about being rid of her. His darling wife was maddening—and dangerous—at least to his own physical health, but, he admitted to himself, she was also the most

exciting woman he had ever met. For a millisec-
ond, a chagrined smile curled along the edges of
his mouth. She was also quite possibly one of the
most seductive women he'd ever seen, an alluring
siren whose looks were a feast for the senses, but
an utter menace to anyone fool enough to answer
her call. Even now, after all that she'd done to
him, he still wanted her in the worst sort of way.
Maybe even more than before. And that was a
self-inflicted disease being rid of her would never
cure.

Pushing thoughts of her and what else she
might do to him from his mind, Lucien slowed
their speed and eased the ship into a low orbit
above the moon's northern pole. He frowned as
he studied the distant surface. Though dimpled
with age and thousands of meteor hits, geologi-
cally the polar region looked more like an inhab-
itable planet than a dry and frozen moon.
Mountain ridges soared upward for a thousand
feet or so, the cliffs and towering crags eventually
giving way to smooth plains that could have once
been an inland sea. Stranger still, the formations
bore the unmistakable signs of erosion from
water and wind. If so, the dead moon must have
once had an active atmosphere. *Odd.* He'd never
heard or read anything about the Denault system
ever being capable of supporting life. He glanced
sideways. "What do you have on sensors, Tay?"

Tay bent low over a console, studying the col-
lection of data streaming down a readout screen.
He squinted suddenly and leaned closer.
"Hmmm . . . That's strange."

"What?" Alexandra said sharply, her nerves
strung so tightly she felt as though she might leap
free of her skin.

"The moon has a surface gravity of about
three-fourths planet norm, and traces of an oxy-

gen atmosphere." Tay checked another monitor, the screen's blue light throwing a ghostly shadow over his rugged face. "At some point in time there was surface water, too."

A rush of adrenaline surged through Alexandra's blood. Her father had been right all along. This moon had been inhabited at one time. She could taste it, feel the knowledge creeping through her bones. "And now?"

Tay shook his head. "Nothing. Just faint traces. Some water—ice a few feet beneath the crust a little north of your coordinates. There's still enough gravity to walk around down there with weighted boots if you're careful, but you'll definitely need a breather suit."

She nervously clutched at the top of Flynn's chair, her fingers digging deep into the leathery material. "Do you have any idea how many years it's been since there was a true atmosphere?"

Tay puzzled over the data for a few more seconds, thinking. "I'm not sure. A few thousand, maybe."

A few thousand. The tempo of her heartbeat lurched to an erratic rate. Humans had inhabited this region of space for only a short span of time, around two thousand years, to be exact. And in all those centuries, ever since humans had left the solar system and moved out among the stars, colonizing their way deeper toward the Milky Way's starry core, no evidence of recent sentient inhabitants had been found. The scant number of indigenous artifacts that had been discovered were far older than a measly few thousand years, more on the order of a hundred thousand or so. Some were even more ancient than that. Given the lack of evidence to the contrary, the scientific community had always believed that if an alien species had once thrived in or near Dominion space, they had long since moved on to unknown destinations.

But her father had never subscribed to that particular theory, always insisting that, for whatever reason, closed-minded Dominion scientists simply refused to consider the possibility that their assumptions might be wrong. And after a decade of grueling research and many archaeological digs, Jarron Fallon had published a paper claiming to have found credible evidence of more recent habitation by an unknown sentient race in the region that encompassed the lowly Denault system. The theory was laughingly derided and ridiculed by his peers within the scientific community. No one had believed him, and much of his data, as well as several small artifacts discovered on the fourth moon, had promptly and mysteriously vanished. With no proof and little data to back up his claim, her father had been subjected to public humiliation, followed by the Dominion government's withdrawal of all funding for his research. He'd soon been forced to abandon his digs and return to Lochlain in disgrace. Her father had died less than a year later, his professional reputation in tatters. But in the months before his death, and after careful review of his remaining data, her father had identified a series of caves in the polar region of the fourth moon as the most likely area to explore in search of additional proof. Alexandra, after studying all of her father's data, had confirmed his conclusions.

Soon she would fulfill the solemn vow she'd made to her father on his deathbed. Soon she would be able to stand proudly and announce to the entire Dominion that the much-maligned Jarron Fallon had been right after all. A race of sentient beings *had* once lived and thrived on this little moon-world, a living, breathing, intelligent race that had vanished not long before the arrival of humans only two thousand years ago. Only then would she feel that she'd kept her vow to her father.

The ship angled downward suddenly, and Alexandra grabbed the back of Flynn's chair tightly to keep her feet. The moon's surface rushed past the viewport, growing larger and more vivid with each second that passed. She stared out the viewport, transfixed by the sight. The pale mountains and craggy ridges looked close enough to touch.

Lucien dumped more speed and leveled off his descent as he approached the coordinates she'd provided, his frown growing more pronounced as the ship passed above one of the many craters. It was an impact crater, all right, but the edges were too concentric, too smooth and uniform to be from any meteor or asteroid fragment.

His troubled eyes cut toward Tay, who was seated in the chair beside him, his own dark gaze fixed intently on the wide crater as well. "What do you think?" Lucien asked him in a hushed voice.

Tay nodded once, a puzzled frown digging across his broad forehead. "The same as you," he said just as quietly.

Alexandra heard their enigmatic comments and tapped Flynn's shoulder, her nervousness increasing to a fever pitch. "What?" she demanded. "What did you mean by that?"

Another crater rushed past the viewport, the smooth, perfect hole bored in the moon's surface appearing to be no more than a couple of thousand years old. Lucien threw her a quick, probing glance. Her heart-shaped face was alive with excitement, her blue eyes glittering with so much anxiety that it bordered on fear.

What exactly did she think she knew about this strange little moon? "Those are impact craters, but they weren't made by meteors or asteroid hits."

Alexandra's features pulled into a confused frown. "I don't understand."

The *Nightwind*'s forward momentum stopped completely, and the small ship began dropping toward the surface. "They're weapons craters," Lucien said in an ominous tone, "probably from laser cannon."

A sudden chill swept down Alexandra's spine. Could it be true? And if so, what did the revelation mean? "Are you sure?"

Lucien nodded shortly. "I'm sure." An audible thud shuddered through the bulkheads as the landing gear settled onto the surface, the thrusters lifting so much of the surface's fine, powdery dust that the view through the transparent window faded into a thick cloak of gray. He switched off the thrusters, and the roar of the engines slowly faded into an expectant silence.

As the cloud of dust began to curl and drift away, he swung his chair toward Alexandra and folded his arms, his expression just as ominous as his tone had been a moment before. "Now, suppose you tell me exactly what we're doing here and why this moon is pocked from cannon fire."

Alexandra shook her head helplessly, her braids swinging gently across her shoulders. "I already told you why I wanted to come here. As for the other, I haven't a clue. My father's data didn't mention a thing about any battles." Could her father have not known? It was possible, she supposed. From a distance the craters looked natural to her, and maybe they had to him as well. Her Uncle Theodore might have recognized the telltale signs, just as Flynn had, but Jarron Fallon would not. "My father was a scholar, not a soldier. He might not have known what he was seeing."

Lucien rubbed a thumb across his chin as he considered her explanation, finally accepting what she'd said with an exasperated sigh. It was entirely possible, he decided. Outside the military, few ever saw the devastation left in the wake of a battle with laser cannon. Now he just had to get his secretive wife to reveal exactly what she expected to find on this moon. "So what is it that we're hunting for here? You mentioned archaeological artifacts back on Thasia. What sort, and why here, of all places?"

Alexandra blew out a regretful sigh. She couldn't put Flynn off any longer, though she wished she could forever. If her search did indeed prove fruitful, she would have to bring her find back aboard a smuggler's ship, a priceless cargo a thieving rogue like Flynn might find irresistible. "I'm hunting for concrete evidence of a sentient species that might have inhabited this star system not long before humans arrived. My father was certain this race once existed, and I'm quite certain of it, too." She pointed to the view outside the window, to the ridge line that sloped downward to butt against a flat, open plain. "There's a series of caves in that ridge. That's where I want to search. The three small pieces of statuary my father discovered were found deep inside one of the caves."

A niggle of suspicion slipped wraithlike through Lucien's thoughts, but he discarded his apprehension as absurd. All archaeological evidence of alien cultures that had ever been found was at least a hundred thousand years old, so ancient that the finds were considered museum pieces, nothing more. If there was indeed anything inside those caves, it would simply be more of the same. "All right then." He climbed from the helm chair abruptly. "Let's get going."

A flash of anger sparked in her eyes. "What do you mean, 'let's get going' "? Her expression hardened, wary and determined. "You're not going anywhere with me."

Lucien grinned back at her, unperturbed by her animosity and her unwillingness to have him around. "Sorry, love, where you go, I go. I trust you about as much as a shoal-shark, so I'm not about to allow you to go gallivanting around those caves by yourself. There's no telling what sort of mischief you'd get into."

"*Allow* me?" Her mouth flattened into a colorless line. The man was insufferable! "This wasn't part of our deal, Flynn!" she huffed angrily.

He walked toward the hatch leading to the corridor, then turned back slowly, a hint of amusement showing around the corners of his eyes. "It is now, so you can either accept the fact that I'm coming with you or forget about searching those caves." His amused look grew. She was so furious her mouth was working up and down but no words came out. "I've got the breather suits, remember? If you push me too hard I might just forget where they're stored."

Alexandra's cheeks flushed to a violent shade of red, and her jaw snapped closed. She really should have poisoned him, not simply sneaked a vile dose of tement sauce into his coffee. A golden opportunity had vanished into thin air. "Worm!" she said in a hiss between tightly clenched teeth, and stalked past him into the corridor. If she had killed him, she would have done the entire universe a very great favor.

A jumbled forest of stalagmites rose from the floor of the cave, soaring to needle-sharp points a few feet shy of a cathedral-high ceiling. Tay played the light from his hand torch over the arched cave roof, the wide beam of brilliant white doing little to pierce the smothering darkness that seemed to stretch into infinity beyond.

He sidestepped a dark stalagmite and moved deeper into the bowels of the cavern, a quick perusal with the torch revealing a thickening maze of the odd-shaped formations, so many he would be hard-pressed to squeeze between them wearing the breather suit, especially with Loran hanging on to the back of his utility belt like an additional appendage. She'd been hanging on to him for dear life for most of the day, her grip growing more viselike the deeper they moved into each cave.

"I think this is as far as we can go," he told Loran, his quiet voice sounding like a shout inside the confines of her glassy helmet.

Loran's sigh of relief sounded like an airy explosion through the suit mike. "Thank goodness," she said in a shuddery tone. "I've never done anything like this before, and I hope I never do again."

Tay smiled down at her tenderly, his broad face awash in the shadowy light reflecting off the helmet's visor. He patted her shoulder with a gloved hand. The poor little thing had been terrified from the moment she'd donned the breather suit and stepped off the ship, even more so when they'd searched the first few caves, but she'd put on a brave face and soldiered on. "I'm not too fond of caves myself," he admitted to her, "and I'm seriously beginning to wonder if your mistress has us all wandering around down here on some sort of fool's errand."

Loran gazed up at him, forgetting for a short

moment that she'd been scared out of her wits for the past day and a half, her fear of the cloying dark of the caves and of smothering inside the suit increasing with each step from the safety of the ship. The only saving grace about it all was that the four of them had divided up into teams of two to search the endless caves, with her paired with Tay Molvan. Alone. The two of them had been together for long, blissful hours each day. A shiver of awareness tingled down her spine. Fortune had truly smiled down on her, and his name was Tay Molvan.

"I don't think we're on a fool's errand," Loran explained in a hushed voice. "I knew Alexandra's father. He was a brilliant, driven man, and if he thought there was something in these caves, I'm sure it's true." A trace of anxiety touched her dark eyes. For Alexandra's sake, she hoped so. Her young mistress would be shattered if she discovered the nay-sayers had been right about her father all along.

Tay's hand moved to her shoulder again and lingered there. She was so short that the top of her helmeted head barely reached his chest. His appreciative gaze roamed down the length of her silvery breather suit, pausing for long seconds on the plush outline of her hips visible through the thick fabric. Loran was alluringly plump, like a pleasantly ripe fruit beckoning to be picked. "How long have you been with your mistress?"

"Since she was little more than five—over eighteen years now, ever since the death of her mother, but I've been in service to the Fallon clan even longer."

Tay swallowed the sudden dryness from his mouth, nervous about asking the pointed question that had been wedged in his throat all day. If

121

he wanted an answer, he had to ask. "Loran, have you ever thought about doing something else with your life?"

Loran tilted the helmet backward in order to see his shadowy face. She felt light-headed suddenly and hoped it wasn't from lack of air. "At times," she said slowly. "Lady Alexa and I are more friends now than mistress and handmaid. I came along on this quest of hers because I didn't want her to leave Lochlain alone . . . and I didn't want to be there when the head of the clan discovered she was gone. Her Uncle Theodore can be, well, a bit of an ogre at times, and Alexandra can be just as pigheaded as him when the mood strikes."

Tay's brownish eyebrows went up. "Oh? Do you mean the two of you ran away?"

Loran swallowed nervously. Had she said too much? "In a manner of speaking," she admitted, but refused to take the subject any further than that. "What about you, Tay? How long have you been with Captain Flynn?"

"About five years now."

"Have you ever thought of doing something besides smuggling?" she asked worriedly. The thought of his being captured and thrown into some dank dungeon had been preying on her mind.

"Occasionally, I guess," he confessed. The notion had rolled around his thoughts a good number of times of late. In his true line of work, a person was either successful or ended up very dead, and fortune couldn't favor him forever. Someone would eventually find out and unmask both him and Lucien as rebel agents. The Black Rose was playing a dangerous game of deception, one that made their lives as smugglers seem quite tame in comparison. Tay just hoped the day of discovery came later rather than sooner. "I've often thought about finding a quiet little world with lots of trees and grass and becoming a farmer, maybe raise krulls for a living."

Loran puzzled over the word a moment, then nodded. Krulls were towering three-toed beasts used for transport on many remote worlds within the Dominion, much like the horse had been utilized on ancient Earth. "I think that's a fine idea, Tay." It was a safe, secure occupation that didn't require a person to wear breather suits, tromp around in caves, or get thrown into dark dungeons. "A very fine idea."

He smiled and took her gloved hand in his, then began the slow journey back to the entrance of the cave. That grassy little planet was beginning to sound better and better. "So tell me more about your mistress," Tay prodded gently, curious about the strong-willed woman who had married his reluctant friend. "The two of you are so different I find it hard to believe you've stayed with her all these years."

Loran sighed and shook her head, her helmet moving stiffly from side to side. "Alexandra is stubborn, willful, impulsive, and exasperatingly manipulative, but she's also kind, loving, and generous to a fault." A small smile played across Loran's round face. "I love her dearly, and I think she'll make a fine wife for the right man someday, if she takes the time to give the poor fellow half a chance." She had hoped that the elegant Lucien Charbonneau might be the right man for Alexandra, but her hopes had been dashed. Alexandra wanted no part of the handsome blond nobleman, and had been scheming to shed herself of him and the marriage before they ever met.

A disbelieving look cut across Tay's features as he led Loran around yet another of the massive stalagmites. He'd seen no hint of the kind and loving nature Loran had described. Alexandra Fallon was a vengeful shrew, pure and simple. A beautiful one, maybe, but a horrible shrew nonetheless. She'd been fighting with Lucien since the night she'd first boarded the ship, spitting venom at a man who had supposedly taken her on board as a favor. Of course, Lucien had brought much of that upon himself by goading the woman into fits of rage. Tay supposed his friend felt some need for revenge.

Whenever the two were together, though, an animosity arced between them like an electrical charge, throwing off hot, violent sparks that threatened at any time to explode and burn them both.

Alexandra Fallon was giving as good as she got, and had even managed to best him a time or two at his own twisted game. He'd never seen Lucien so out of sorts before over any woman, so bound and utterly determined to . . . Tay's frown was deep and sudden. Then too, was his smile.

Whether Lucien admitted it or not, he was falling fast and hard for his wife. And Tay knew that the current that arced between them was charged both ways. It burned at both ends equally.

He stifled an amused snort. If he was right, what would Alexandra Fallon do if and when she discovered that Damion Flynn was in fact the husband she had fled?

He checked the readout on his suit's air supply and picked up his pace a bit, leading Loran toward a glimmer of sunlight leaking through the mouth of the cave. "Let's head back to the ship. Both of us could stand a break."

"What about Alexandra and Captain Flynn?" Loran asked in a worry-filled tone. They'd been separated for hours now, exploring a different string of caves.

"Oh, don't worry about them, Loran," Tay told her confidently. "I'm sure they're just fine. If they haven't killed each other yet."

Lucien squeezed his suit through the narrow fissure Alexandra had disappeared into, one side of his helmet scraping and banging against a slab of rock jutting down from above. "She really is trying to kill me," he muttered as he wedged his body through an even smaller opening, the sound of his voice echoing back to him through his breather suit's transceiver.

Alexandra halted her progress through the niche and directed the fierce light from her hand torch onto the front of his visor. "What did you say, Flynn?"

He winced and lifted a gloved hand to shield his eyes. Now she was trying to blind him, too. "Nothing . . . Absolutely nothing." He'd been stumbling around in the pitch blackness, crawling through fissures and dodging holes in the cavern floors for the better part of two days now, cursing himself soundly with each perilous step he took for insisting on accompanying her.

He blew out a weary breath and double-checked his air sensor. Only forty minutes left, thank the gods. "We have to head back to the ship soon," he announced gleefully. "We've got only forty minutes of air left, and only one recharge left for the suits." He also had cargo to deliver. Soon. "Your next expedition will have to be the last."

Alexandra grunted a reluctant acknowledgment and pushed onward, determined to put the remains of her dwindling air supply to full use. She slid through a small crevice on her stomach

Jan Zimlich

to reach yet another of the cave's small rooms, tons of dark rock poised mere inches above her head as she wriggled through. Moving her head from side to side, she played her helmet light over the uneven walls, hoping against hope that this cave would be the one. Her hope vanished. Nothing but dirt and rock and stalagmites again.

Tears of frustration sprang from the corners of her eyes, the salty moisture threatening to spill down her cheeks. Almost two days of searching and she'd found nothing at all, not even a sliver of evidence that would encourage her to search on. "Don't try to follow me, Flynn," she yelled back through the opening, the words sounding crestfallen even to her. "I'm coming back." She started pushing her body backward, squirming to free herself from the rockbound crevice. A shower of dust and gravel drifted downward from the overhang, the thick cloud of debris nearly floating in the thin atmosphere and gravity. Alexandra wiggled back and forth, inching her way slowly back through the tight cleft and drifting debris.

Lucien bent low and grabbed her weighted boots, dragging her backward through the small opening none too gently. Her muttered oath and the sound of her visor screeching across rock brought a self-satisfied grin to his face. She deserved a little manhandling for all she'd put him through. After he pulled her free, he rapped the back of her helmet with his hand torch to catch her attention. "Come on. Your time's up. We'll need at least fifteen minutes of air to make it back to the ship."

Alexandra maneuvered into a sitting position and simply stared at him, the shower of drifting dirt impairing her vision. A lone tear slipped free and trickled down her cheek, leaving a thin trail of moisture down to her jaw. She blinked the salty remains away but another tear soon followed its downward path. At least the haze of dust had obscured her visor and blocked Flynn from witnessing her moment of weakness. No man had ever seen her cry.

To Lucien's surprise, she didn't complain, argue, or berate him about pressing to go back to the ship. Uncharacteristically, she wasn't doing much of anything but sitting there, her arms folded over drawn knees. A sudden knot of worry lodged in his chest. Her helmet was pointed in his direction, but dust still veiled her face. "Are you all right?"

"I'm fine," she reassured him, but her voice sounded flat and eerily calm. Too calm.

Lucien offered a hand to help her rise but she swatted it away and struggled to stand upright on her own. "Are you sure?"

"Yes." She heard the quaver of weakness in the single word, and that made her want to cry all the more.

Lucien took a few steps backward and shone the torch on her dusty suit and helmet, hunting for rips or some other damage that might account for her odd behavior. He batted at the drifting debris, fanning the cloud away from the front of her visor. But as the dust finally cleared, she jerked her head sideways and down, obscuring the faceplate once again.

It was then that he heard a little sniffle, followed closely by an ill-disguised sob. Lucien blinked in amazement. The witch-queen was actually crying, sniffling and snuffling back miserable sobs as if she were about to flood the inside of her helmet with a torrent of tears. A big mistake when she was trapped inside a breather suit. There was no way to wipe one's nose or smear away errant tears.

He cleared his throat noisily, the muffled sobs like knife pricks to his conscience. "I, ah . . . well, I don't think that's a very good idea . . . what you're doing." He took a step toward her, drawn by guilt and the sense that he was responsible in some way. "You can't take off a breather helmet to blow your nose down here."

Alexandra wanted nothing more than to sink through the cavern floor. The toad knew. "Oh, shut up," she snapped, embarrassment stinging her cheeks as much as the salt in her eyes. "Just leave me alone!" She choked back a frustrated sob and sucked in a deep breath to calm herself.

"Well . . ." Lucien said and lapsed into an awkward silence, cursing himself mentally for his nonexistent response. Dealing with emotional females had never been his forte. He'd learned through experience that the correct reaction to a woman's tears was to run the other way. But this was not just any woman. Whether she knew it or not, this was his wife.

He stepped toward her slowly, deciding to ignore the admonition to leave her alone, but froze abruptly when he felt a spot of the cavern floor give beneath his heel. Lucien glanced downward warily. The rock felt loamy and soft, as though the surface had been magically transformed into something other than solid stone. Worry tore through him as the top of his boots sank deeper, vanishing into a spongy morass of pebbles and powdery rock.

A creaking, cracking sound suddenly vibrated through the cavern, like a string of bones rattling in a gust of wind. His gaze lifted to Alexandra, who was glancing around the cave with a panicked expression, obviously wondering where the odd sound had come from as well. "Don't move!" he ordered quietly. "Don't argue; don't even breathe."

The creaking sound increased to a dull, deep rumble emanating from somewhere within the dark bowels of the cave. He peered into the pitch blackness beyond the glow of their torches. Below them, maybe. Or somewhere to the rear. It was hard to determine in the suffocating darkness. They were surrounded by the cave's deep-throated groan now, the low noise reverberating from a thousand places at once. A crackling sound welled up from near Lucien's feet, and his gaze flew downward again, a sudden rush of adrenaline stealing through his blood when he realized that his boots had vanished completely and he'd sunk to his shins.

As the sound grew in intensity to a rumbling roar, Alexandra's eyes widened, and a shudder of fear spiraled down the length of her spine. Flynn was sinking downward, his legs melting swiftly into what had been solid stone just a few minutes before. Her heart pounded against her rib cage, an internal roar that rivaled the grumbling of the cave. "Shouldn't we run?" she managed to shout over the onrush of sound.

A fissure cracked open near Lucien's legs, a snake-thin fracture that wound and rippled across the stony surface. He tried to pull a leg free of the disintegrating rock, but instead sank up to his knees. *Gods.* He was being swallowed alive by the carvern floor. "Go!" he yelled at her. "Make a run for it!"

Alexandra couldn't move, couldn't breathe, her arms and legs suddenly watery and limp. A few feet away a stalagmite vanished, crashing downward with a thunderous roar. Another of the cone-shaped formations disappeared, then a third, falling into yawning blackness beneath the crumbling floor. Flynn was mired up to his hips now, struggling against the sucking rock and gesturing with his arms for her to flee.

She shook her helmet vigorously, its circular light beam careening wildly off the surrounding walls. "No!" she shouted above the din, her jaw firming with determination. No one deserved to die like this, not even Flynn. Alexandra scuttled to the edge of the narrow fissure and stretched out an arm, then leaned her body forward as much as she could. "Take my hand!" she yelled at him, her gloved fingers within inches of reaching his outstretched hand.

Relief welled inside her as Flynn leaned toward her and grabbed tight; then a split second later she found herself clutching at empty air. Alexandra gaped in horror. Flynn was gone, vanishing into nothingness just like the stalagmites. As the cavern's dull roar vanished as well, she peered into the newly formed abyss that he'd disappeared into. "Flynn?" she called shakily, her chest heaving in and out at a frantic pace. "Flynn!"

The slab of rock beneath her suddenly tilted, angling downward at a mind-numbing speed. Alexandra fell onto her backside and started sliding, unable to stop her descent into the heart of the fissure that had swallowed Flynn whole. She screamed as she slid over the edge and tumbled into the darkness, squeezing her eyes shut tightly to block any sight of what awaited her below. Terrifying images flashed like lightning through her mind, images of her own crushed and mangled body lying among the dark and rocks, of a slow and torturous death from lack of air. Her lids squeezing tighter, she gritted her teeth and waited for the end, praying the final impact wouldn't hurt too much.

She was falling feet-first now, the thick, weighted boots directing the rest of her body where to go. Any second she was going to die. Any second . . . Behind the faceplate, she suddenly knitted her brow in confusion. Shouldn't she have splattered against the rocks long before now?

Alexandra cracked her eyes open a fraction to take a terrified peek and gasped in surprise. She was *gliding*, not falling, in a slow, almost leisurely descent to the bottom of the abyss, all due to the moon's thin gravity. Dust particles danced and drifted through the narrow swath of darkness illuminated by the light on the top of her helmet. She was coasting toward the floor of an entirely new cavern, much the same as all the others, but this one was larger, grander in scale and scope, the ever-present stalagmites soaring upward for perhaps two hundred feet or so. Far below, she could see the unmoving glow of Flynn's hand torch. And every place the light touched rock, crystals glittered like iridescent jewels in the dark.

The bottom of her boots thumped against the dark hulk of a shattered stalagmite, and Alexandra's knees bent to absorb the impact. Then her body started tumbling again, bouncing end over end down a huge pile of rocky debris that angled inward to the bottom of the cavern floor.

The air rasped out of her lungs when she finally touched down, landing helmet to helmet atop Damion Flynn. Their visors banged, and Alexandra found herself staring into Flynn's startled gray eyes. She pulled in a noisy, needed breath. He was still alive, obviously, although whether that was fortuitous was still a question left open to debate. "Flynn!" she said hoarsely, her voice and wits still in the cavern above. "I thought we were both dead!"

Lucien gave her a darkly suggestive smile, his gloved hands winding around the back of her breather suit. "Did you miss me, love?" In truth, he'd thought they were both dead, too. Him, at least.

"No," she said sourly, and pushed his roving hands away. "Just how do you propose we get out of here?"

A shadowy grin played over his features. "Simple. Just take the weights off your boots and leap back up."

"Easier said than done." Alexandra pulled up onto her elbows and looked around, searching for an easy route back through the rubble to the cavern above. A surprised gasp suddenly slipped from her throat, and her face went pale, very pale. "Oh, my gods," she said softly, and jammed an elbow into his chest as she bolted to her feet and shone her hand torch along the cavern floor. The light danced back and forth at dizzying speed.

Her eyes widened, and the hand gripping the slender torch trembled with shock as the reality of what she'd found hit her full force. Relics of a vanished race littered the cavern floor, ornamental carvings made of polished wood or textured stone tossed about as if they were playthings discarded by an unruly child. A large urn inlaid with gold and geometric etchings lay overturned near Flynn's head, a plethora of bronzed medallions, and odd knickknacks spilling from its oblong mouth.

Lucien climbed to his feet and followed the direction of her wondering gaze, frowning uneasily when he spotted the urn and a small, three-sided statue lying close to his feet. The designs were hauntingly familiar. He shone his torch on several other artifacts, a deathly sense of foreboding beginning to inch through his veins.

"Flynn, look!" Alexandra cried out. Tears stung the corners of her eyes again, but they were tears of joy this time, not frustration. The artifacts that she'd seen so far were remarkably well preserved, with no hint of the deterioration expected in any antiquity that dated back an eon or more, which meant the articles had been forged far more recently than that. "I can't believe it . . . I've actually found proof! These artifacts look to be only a few thousand years old at the most!" She turned toward him and gave him a joyous smile. "Just think . . . if you hadn't fallen through that floor I would have never known!"

She bent low and scooped a thin medallion of metal into the palm of her glove, studying the strange line of glyphs inscribed on the slick surface. She brushed at a thick layer of clinging dust to get a better look. A perfect hole had been cut into the center of the disk, and the odd symbols marched in a tight arc around its rim. Her heart thudded painfully. The bold tracings were hieroglyphs of some kind, like none she'd ever seen before. "I think it's writing," she whispered in excitement, her gaze flitting back to the debris-strewn floor, where she spotted more of the disks half-buried in the dirt and debris. "There's dozens of them here!"

Her light played over the urn again, illuminating the assortment of objects that had spilled from its mouth. She frowned and dropped to her knees to study the odd little knickknacks more carefully, pushing the layers of dust aside with the fingers of her glove. A small, doll-like object made from a rubbery substance came into view, its painted surface worn and faded with the passage of years. But enough of the shape and coloring were still present to know that the effigy had been humanoid in appearance, or nearly so, though there did seem to be several faces painted onto the small head. She squeezed the soft figure, her frown deepening. The object cradled in her hand *was* a child's doll, or something similar, which meant some of the other artifacts from the urn could be children's toys as well.

She closed her eyes a moment, disquieted by the notion that she might be rifling through the cherished possessions of an alien child who'd died thousands of years before. Even more disturbing was the possibility that she might have discovered the artifacts only because their owner had been forced to take refuge within the cave to escape the calamity that had devastated the surface of the crater-studded moon.

Her thoughts still preoccupied by the doll's owner, Alexandra directed her light over the interior of the ornate urn and drew in a sharp breath when she saw several rolls of ancient parchment tucked inside. She laid the doll down gently then reached inside the urn, carefully removing a sheaf of the delicate paper.

"What is it?" Lucien asked in a somber tone, moving closer to glance over her shoulder.

"I don't know yet." She unwound the roll as carefully as possible, her eyes widening in amazement when her efforts revealed several child-like doodlings of stalagmites and the cavern's interior. "I think the items in the urn might have belonged to a child," she said in a reverent voice, then turned her attention back to her discoveries. The crumbling piece of parchment at the bottom of the stack was different from the others, containing row after row of the same hieroglyphs she'd seen on the disk. But there were other tracings on the paper as well, a second, partial column of childish scribing that seemed to correspond to some of the mysterious glyphs. Scribing that looked vaguely familiar. . . .

Alexandra gasped aloud and sank to the cavern floor, her knees suddenly too weak to hold her anymore. "Oh, gods," she said in a hushed voice. The scribing running down a section of the parchment hadn't been written in some exotic, alien language. Though the alphabetic lettering was only partial and rudimentary, it was clearly written in a language that Alexandra knew all too well. "This isn't possible!" It was the *human* alphabet. "It just can't be!"

Lucien peered over her shoulder, frowning when he saw the writing on the parchment. His sense of foreboding grew. "What's not possible?"

Her gloved finger pointed toward the crude lettering to the right of the glyphs. "This column is written in Anglish . . . I'm sure of it." She shook her head in disbelief. Could the piece of parchment actually be a translation key? Some sort of primer that had been used to teach Anglish writing to that long-dead child? "It's the damn alphabet."

She turned toward him, a flash of excitement glittering in her eyes. "Do you know what this means, Flynn?"

Lucien shook his helmet from side to side and tried to swallow the sudden knot of dryness from his throat. He was afraid he knew exactly what it meant.

Alexandra held the parchment high, light from her handtorch dancing across the thin paper. "It means that an alien race inhabited the Denault System at the same time humans were colonizing the Dominion! They must have actually coexisted for a time. There's no other explanation for the primer! It also means that I'll be able to decipher the hieroglyphs eventually. Then I'll have all the evidence I need. This parchment is the key!"

His troubled gaze refocused on the small marble statue resting near the toe of his boot, his expression growing darker and more worried with each quick beat of his heart. The statue had three faces, each distinct from the other, all different perspectives of the same head of a youthful male. "I'm sure you will," he said in a quiet voice. There was no mistaking the design of the statue. And no mistaking the hieroglyphs or the origin of the other artifacts she had found.

Lucien didn't doubt for a moment that she would decipher the writing, just as she'd said. Alexandra had her evidence now, but evidence of what? That the parchment and artifacts had been created by Arulian hands? His gaze shifted then stilled on Alexandra Fallon's determined movements. If she found proof of the Arulians and their secret, how long would it be until someone unmasked the Black Rose?

Chapter Nine

A contingent of the archduke's personal body-guards snapped to full attention, the heels of their polished dress boots striking with a sharp click that coincided with crisp salutes.

Hands folded behind his back, General Helford Thigg nodded imperceptibly and swept past the platoon of scarlet-clad guards, the high collar of his simple uniform tunic as stiff and rigid as his wooden expression.

A young lieutenant rushed to open an arched doorway before Thigg was forced to break his stride. The general marched through at a brisk pace and strode into the archduke's latest construction, a massive atrium with a glass ceiling that soared to a delicate point hundreds of feet above.

His upper lip curled in disapproval at the sight of scores of workmen bustling about in a frenzy of activity, hanging from scaffolds and planting trees and delicate vines down an intricate set of footpaths that angled outward from the arched double doors. If the archduke had seen fit to dedicate only a portion of the chits he'd spent on creating this costly atrium toward capturing the Black Rose, the rebel movement would have already been crushed and their spymaster's bones moldering in a very deep grave.

Thigg's gaze swept left, to a small, mossy clearing free of workmen and the bustle of activity. The archduke was there, observing the work in progress from a high, thronelike chair that dwarfed him, so much so that he looked like a pale, frail child seated in a giant's oversize chair. A platoon of richly robed courtiers was clustered nearby, favored clan lords and highly placed bureaucrats who graveled and fawned over the archduke on a permanent basis, squabbling among themselves for the dubious honor of catering to his every whim.

The general's lip curled even more. The archduke's horrid little docats were there as well, annoying fluffs of white scurrying and snuffling around their master. The thought crossed Thigg's mind that the courtiers weren't that much different from the irritating little beasts. Both breeds were equally irksome, and loyal to a fault.

The mossy grass softened the thud of his boots as he marched across the clearing, then halted in front of the monarch's throne. Thigg bowed low because such a gesture was expected of him, but nowhere near as deep as the fawning courtiers would have done. He straightened slowly, his dispassionate gaze settling on the small nobleman perched in his immense chair.

"Good morning, your grace," Thigg intoned, his voice as bland and dispassionate as his solemn expression. His sharp eyes fixed on Luc

Davies's moon-shaped face, focusing on the nobleman with zealous intensity.

The archduke's rosy lips pinched into an amused smile. The general of his armies was such a gloomy little autocrat, always brooding about one thing or another. He was the sort who was forever prophesying doom and destruction— if he were not allowed free rein to defeat the forces of darkness, of course.

Thigg's outward appearance more than equaled his gloomy persona as well. His dark hair was fastidiously kept, slicked back in a bland nonstyle that revealed a balding pate for all to see. His black moustache was equally fastidious, trimmed and manicured to such a level of perfection that the archduke had never seen a single hair mussed or out of place. And as always, the general was garbed in the drab black uniform of the Dominion Security Force, his tunic stiff and inflexible, the carefully pleated trousers disappearing inside knee-high boots polished to a blindingly glossy shine. The only spots of color on his uniform at all were the small gold epaulets that heralded his rank, and the twin triangles on either side of his collar that contained the golden letters DSF, branding him as part of the feared Dominion Security Force.

The archduke frowned as a sudden thought occurred to him. In over twenty years, he couldn't recall ever seeing Thigg attired in anything but his uniform. Perhaps he didn't even possess any civilian garb. He shrugged off the wayward thought. No matter. Thigg was simply a shining example of the negative effects of living a military life. Spending every waking hour obsessing over conspiracies, plots, spies, and counterspies had to have a profound effect on the psyche, he supposed.

"Ah, General Thigg," the archduke finally intoned. "What evil tidings do you bring us this fine day?"

Thigg suppressed a grimace of distaste. Two millennia of Dominion tradition dictated that the archduke always refer to himself in the royal plural, but that particular anachronism deserved to die a long-overdue death. "An update, your grace, on the hunt for the Black Rose." His suspicious gaze fell on first one, then another of the archduke's foppish courtiers. Experience had taught him that the Black Rose had eyes and ears even within the confines of the archduke's private fortress. In fact, it seemed no planet in the Dominion was entirely free of the spy's ever-growing web of influence. "May we speak privately?" Thigg queried, though his request held more demand than plea.

The archduke expelled an exasperated sigh and flicked a dismissive hand toward his cluster of courtiers. As they retreated out of earshot, his hand fell downward to stroke the silky head of one of his pets. He inclined his head toward the general in acquiescence, the pale ringlets of his hair bobbing gently as he moved. "You have our full attention, General."

Thigg cleared his throat, and his shoulders stiffened slightly. Had he heard a note of sarcasm in the archduke's cultured voice? He touched a pad on his wrist-com, and a sheen of gold shimmered into existence, sealing him, the archduke, and the vexing docats inside a high-level privacy field that even the most advanced listening devices would be hard-pressed to penetrate.

The archduke suppressed his amusement as his gaze trailed over the delicate bubble of energy that now enclosed them within a thin web of shimmering gold. Thigg was apparently feeling a touch of paranoia today. "You feel the need for such a technological device within the walls of our own fortress, General?"

He stared at the archduke steadily. "As a matter of fact, I do, your grace. You'd do well to remember that the Black Rose has already managed to breach fortress security—undetected—to free a rebel prisoner from your own dungeon." His glance fell upon the gaggle of court peacocks strutting around at the edge of the clearing, watching and whispering among themselves. "Remember, too, that your courtiers and hangers-on are not above suspicion."

Luc Davies laughed aloud, a gentle, rolling sound that rose to a crescendo, then trailed into a mirth-filled silence. Surely Thigg jested. He couldn't truly suspect a member of the Dominion court of being the notorious spy. "General, do you actually believe that one of our own courtiers might be, in fact, the Black Rose?" he asked incredulously.

Thigg's shoulders stiffened even more, and he reflexively brushed at a bit of lint marring the front of his uniform. "The words *impossible* and *improbable* carry far different connotations, your grace. When the plausible has been ruled out, all that's left to explore is the implausible."

"And you have already exhausted the plausible?" he asked in a petulant tone. He wouldn't suffer Thigg and his Security Force running about the fortress investigating the Dominion courtiers. That wouldn't do at all. The heads of the clans would be outraged, and justifiably so.

Determination etched small lines that angled outward from the corners of Thigg's eyes. "I must fully investigate every possibility, your grace, even the implausible. Everyone is suspect until this matter is laid to rest once and for all—including those of the court." His expression turned hard and inflexible. "It is my duty, after all."

The archduke sighed. "So it is." Thigg was relentless when it came to his perceived sense of duty, like a pugnacious hound snuffling after a meaty bone. And the Black Rose was the meatiest bone around. "Do what you must, but try not to tarry overlong on the implausible." He would let the dog have his bone for a while, long enough to placate the man's sense of duty. He could not, without minions such as Thigg, retain his throne and he knew it. "Your report . . . what news does it contain about our adversary's recent activities?"

Thigg folded his hands behind his back and squared his shoulders, a habitual gesture that did little to put others at ease in his presence. "My spies report that there has been a significant increase in rebel activity along the border of sector seventeen, near the holdings of Clan Charbonneau and Clan McConnell. Rebel troop movements have been noted, as well as an exponential increase in suspected arms shipments into that area. I suspect a large-scale foray across the border into Dominion territory is in the making. Within weeks, I believe—a month at the outside. Clan McConnell will stand firm against such an organized assault, but without the aid of their Fallon allies, Clan Charbonneau will surely be overrun."

Luc Davies nodded sagely. Baron Charbonneau's ruminations on his tenuous tactical situation had been far more astute than the archduke first thought. According to Thigg, the Charbonneau clan would fall without the military aid of the Fallon brigades, just as the baron had intimated in their interview a week before. "We requested some days ago that you devote your resources to resolving the problems that have sidetracked the Charbonneau-Fallon alliance. Have you done so, General?"

"Of course, your grace," Thigg said archly. "Charbonneau's bride was tracked to the planet Thasia. From there she bought passage aboard a smuggling ship, which we think has illegally crossed into the Denault system."

"The Denault system?" A shadow moved across the archduke's cherubic face. Like father like daughter? Was it possible? Or was he simply exploring the realm of the implausible, as his general so often did? "How very odd." He would have to send someone to investigate. Someone trusted. "Noble-born women don't often consort with smugglers and the like."

"My spies thought it peculiar, too, especially since the ship Alexandra Fallon boarded is owned by a suspected weapons smuggler named Damion Flynn . . . a name that has been high on my list of possible rebel sympathizers for a very long time."

The archduke's pale eyes narrowed slightly. Had that been a smug note he'd heard in Thigg's carefully modulated voice? "Ah, we see. And you suspect this Damion Flynn of being far more than a mere sympathizer?"

The general allowed himself a tiny smile. "Exactly, your grace. We'd been tracking Flynn's movements for quite a while, but until we started delving into his activities in order to trace Miss Fallon, it simply hadn't occurred to anyone that Flynn's past whereabouts seem to have a strange habit of coinciding with the known movements of the Black Rose." He leaned forward slightly and lowered his voice to a conspiratorial whisper, even though their conversation was shielded from casual listeners. "Think about it, your grace . . . Given the buildup of rebel forces in sector seventeen, just who would benefit most from a disruption of the Fallon-Charbonneau alliance?"

The Dominion archduke sat back in his chair abruptly, his elegant hands folding around its wide gilded arms. If the Fallon brigades didn't come to the aid of their Charbonneau allies, the Black Rose and his followers would be free to sweep across Charbonneau territory into the heart of Dominion space, only days from Primus, the seat of government, and his fortress itself. "Well, it would seem that the task of finding the Fallon girl has neatly dovetailed with your own hunt for the spy, General." This bit of news was indeed worthy of the privacy field the general had insisted upon. "Do you have any hard evidence that this smuggler is in truth the Black Rose?"

Thigg's mouth compressed. "Circumstantial only, based mainly on coincidence and speculation, but if there is any concrete proof, I'll soon find it. And I'll find Alexandra Fallon as well."

"See that you do," Luc Davies ordered. "Our own fleets must be held in reserve at all costs, not wasted in a futile defense of Clan Charbonneau against a rebel onslaught. If Alexandra Fallon is promptly returned to her husband and family, the Fallon-Charbonneau alliance will go forward as planned. The Fallons will then be forced to come to the Charbonneaus' aid, not the Dominion Security Force."

"I understand." Thigg kept his glee carefully hidden. *Perfect.* The archduke had given him virtual carte blanche in handling the situation; he was free to act as he pleased. "I have already instituted measures to that end, your grace. A picket line of Security Force ships will soon be positioned along the border near the Denault system to intercept the smuggler's ship when he tries to recross. We'll have Damion Flynn shortly—as well as Alexandra Fallon."

A glint of triumph stole into his dark eyes. "And I've taken the liberty of ordering battle plans drawn for a massive counterassault against the insurgents. The Fallons and Charbonneaus will fight the rebels first, taking the brunt of the initial assault; then once the cannon fire fades, our own forces will move in to sweep the battlefield clean of any remaining rebels." The general's lower lip curled upward, a movement all but hidden beneath the ends of his fastidious mustache. "You and our forces will be the ultimate victors in the coming battle—and the rebels will be defeated once and for all."

The archduke smiled primly and lifted a pale brow in silent approval. The machinations of General Thigg's mind were quite often a wonder to behold. The counterassault would catch the doomed rebels in a tactical pincer between the remainder of the Fallon and Charbonneau brigades—and his own fresh troops. Once the second battle was done, there would be no rebels left to threaten the throne. "An inspired plan of action, General. Truly inspired."

Lucien rubbed at the headache building behind his forehead and stared out the command deck's viewport, his thoughts as chaotic as the dense profusion of stars sweeping by. Ever since the *Nightwind* had lifted off from the Denault moon, Alexandra had been ensconced in her cabin, gleaning, perusing, and analyzing whatever nuggets of information she could from the treasure trove of discoveries she'd brought back to his ship. A crateful, to be exact, containing dozens of various artifacts she'd scurried around collecting from the debris on the cavern floor.

He snorted audibly. How she'd collected so much in such a short period of time was beyond him. If not for the lack of recharge packs for the breather suits, that single crate would have multiplied into more—many, many more. In fact, she'd already been chattering about plans for a return expedition before they'd even lifted free of the moon's surface. She planned to scour every inch of every single cave.

A dark scowl moved over his face. Time was running out. They would recross the Dominion border within minutes, and his shipment was scheduled for delivery on Janus Three no later than tomorrow. Alexandra Fallon would then be gone, both her and the artifacts out of his reach. Possibly forever. He'd be thrilled if he never had to lay eyes on those artifacts again, but Alexandra was another matter altogether. The woman was his wife, a tempting siren who could make his blood burn with a single look, despite her petulant nature and a stubborn streak that ran clear to her toes. But short of blowing up the crate and holding her prisoner, what could he do? She didn't even know who he was.

He checked the sensor array and set the ship on a new heading favored by smugglers, one that would take the *Nightwind* across the border on a circuitous course to evade detection by the spy beacons positioned along the fringes of Dominion space.

As the ship skirted the rings of a glowing gas giant, the door to the control deck slid open and Tay maneuvered his bulky frame into the copilot's seat. Lucien threw him a sideways glance as the door slid home and locked. "Ten minutes to the border. We've already reached the outer perimeter." His gaze dropped to the small proximity sensor, which was blissfully free of any contacts. "No sign of trouble yet. Better get the weapons array up and primed, though . . . just in case."

Tay nodded mutely and tapped a pad to bring the weapons system on-line. He checked and rechecked every system and subsystem, finally leaning back in the seat with a satisfied sigh. "Weapons at the ready."

"Good." Lucien gave him a quick, expectant look. "What about our passengers?"

"Loran is in the galley cooking up something that smells absolutely wonderful," Tay told him, "and your wife is still locked inside her cabin with all that stuff she dragged back from the cave." He shook his head in amazement. "She was actually singing to herself when I passed by the cabin door a minute ago."

Lucien closed his eyes, the throbbing in his forehead building. No doubt about it: she would decipher the glyphs, probably in record time.

Tay frowned in concern. "You've been in a black mood ever since the two of you climbed out of that cave. Are you ready to tell me why?"

He kneaded the ache in his temples with the pads of his thumbs. Tay had a right to know. He needed to know. "The artifacts are Arulian," he announced in a bleak, flat tone.

Tay's jaw sagged open in shock. "Aw, frack."

"My sentiments exactly."

Tay had a sinking sensation deep in his gut. The woman planned to analyze her find, then bellow her conclusions to the entire universe. If she did, everything they had worked for would be thrown into jeopardy. Everything. "Are you sure?"

"I wish I weren't."

"What are you going to do?"

Lucien sighed, long and deep. "I'm open to suggestions."

Tay fell silent for a long moment. "What do you think she'll do if she discovers the truth?"

"When she discovers that a race of aliens has been masquerading as humans for over two thousand years?" Lucien laughed once, a short, cynical sound that contained no mirth at all. "When she finds out that the few Arulians left have managed to insinuate themselves into human culture? What do *you* think she'll do?"

Tay met his gaze steadily. "Well, she could do what I did and befriend one of them."

He managed to give Tay a small, wry smile. "Point taken, my friend, but you're the exception to the rule. She's bound and determined to make what she finds public knowledge, just to restore her father's reputation." He shook his head helplessly. How had things gone so wrong so swiftly? "And when she does, humans will react just as they did two thousand years ago.... The few Arulians left will be hunted down and exterminated the same as before."

"Not all humans are xenophobic fanatics, Lucien. You of all people should know that."

"Some of them are," he whispered hoarsely. "Far too many." The color of his eyes deepened to a pain-filled gray as memories of his mother surfaced unbidden. He could still remember the look of utter horror and shock on his father's face when Renaud had walked through a castle door unannounced and caught Lucien's shape-shifting mother unawares. He also remembered what had happened next, how his father's shock had been transformed into a cold, deadly fury, and how his beloved mother had been unceremoniously tossed into a dark, dank dungeon by the man she loved. There she had remained, alone and afraid, her changeable face hidden from all until her death a year later, just to save Renaud Charbonneau from the shame of admitting that the woman he'd professed to love, the mother of his young son, wasn't human.

Renaud Charbonneau had never spoken Ariell's name again, or even mentioned her in passing, not even to her terrified son, who the baron had soon begun to treat like an embarrassing pariah as well. The son whose birth was tainted by the blood of his Arulian mother.

Lucien forced the memories into the depths of his mind, back into the past where they belonged. He had to focus his thoughts on the here and now and concentrate on the problem at hand. As Tay had said, not all humans were xenophobes, fearing anyone and anything different from themselves. But the fanatical few would sway the rest, in much the same way as they had so long ago when the first human colonists had discovered that they weren't alone. If the existence of his mother's people was revealed by Alexandra Fallon, the Dominion would erupt in violence once again.

His chiseled features hardened with resolve. "I can't let her do it, Tay. I've got to stop her somehow. The woman actually has a brain in her head. If she deciphers those glyphs, she might eventually figure out everything. Who knows what's on those disks? And she'll definitely determine the meaning of the Arulian statuary. Even if we do stop her from going public, I could slip up somehow like I did back on Thasia, and she'll start to put things together about me. Or at least about Damion Flynn." He shook his head slowly. "If she

149

does, Damion Flynn will have no other choice but to permanently disappear."

Tay thought for a few seconds. "We could just tie her up and turn her back over to her clan. Let them deal with her."

Lucien snorted. "Oh, that's an excellent idea. Her uncle would just hand her right back to me, and we're back where we started. I'm not perfect, Tay. Lucien Charbonneau is just as prone to slip up as Damion Flynn."

Tay thought a few more seconds, then lifted his hands in a shrug. "Well, if that won't work, why don't we just steal the artifacts from her instead? She might suspect us, but without proof, she can't do a blasted thing."

A slow, sly smile curved over Lucien's mouth. Why hadn't he thought of that? Damion Flynn could simply live up to his reputation as a thieving smuggler. Of course, if he stole the artifacts and she discovered his involvement, Alexandra would see it as the ultimate betrayal and forever loathe the very sight of him—not that she harbored much fondness for him anyway. But there were hundreds of other identities that she'd yet to meet, different guises that he'd used through the years. Surely one of them would suit her fancy. Given time, the effeminate Lucien might even grow on his youthful wife. And if worse came to worst, he could always invent an entirely new persona, one designed especially for her. Besides, Damion Flynn couldn't stay around forever. At some point he'd fall under suspicion, and be forced to vanish anyway. He'd just rather that happened later instead of sooner.

He clapped his friend on the shoulder and laughed. "You have a devious mind, Tay. We'll steal the crate after we land on Janus Three. She did say that her father's notes and evidence mysteriously disappeared. If we're careful, she may blame the entire episode on whoever that culprit was. She may never suspect us."

Tay grinned. "Glad I could be of help."

Lucien grinned back, the first true smile that had crossed his lips since leaving the Denault moon. All wasn't lost. Things were definitely looking up.

The proximity alarm sounded, a high-pitched klaxon that warned them that the *Nightwind* was no longer alone.

Lucien's startled gaze flew to the readout screen, quickly assessing the number of sensor contacts, and their positions and identities. His throat tightened. Dominion Security ships, four of them, positioned at close intervals directly in their path. Waiting. Smugglers obviously were no longer the only ones aware of the circuitous course through the security net. "Four stationary contacts dead ahead." Lucien increased speed and altered course to evade them. "They're DSF border patrol."

He hit a button to activate the shipwide intercom system. "Alexandra," he almost yelled into the speaker. "Stay in your cabin and strap yourself into your bunk! The acceleration harnesses are in compartments along the rails. Loran, get back to the cabin and do the same. *Now*," he ordered.

Alexandra's bewildered voice came back over the speaker. "What's wrong?" she demanded.

Lucien began strapping himself into his own seat while Tay did the same. "Don't ask questions; just do as you're told!" he snapped back at her, then hit the switch to cut off the intercom.

Tay glanced at him worriedly as the four war-

151

ships began maneuvering to intercept the *Nightwind*. "Think they were waiting for us?"

Lucien gave a troubled frown. Maybe Damion Flynn had already outlived his usefulness. "It certainly looks that way."

Chapter Ten

The *Nightwind* hurtled toward a small, dead world, skimming across the upper reaches of the planet's thin atmosphere. The thick layer of thermal shielding on the ship's underbelly glowed white-hot from friction as Lucien increased velocity, skipping along the edges of the atmosphere on a course that would slingshot them around to the planet's far side.

"The lead ship will have a weapons lock any second now," Tay announced, his eyes transfixed on the proximity scanner. The Dominion warships were accelerating, daggering toward them on an intercept course.

Lucien punched up their own speed a notch more, listening intently as the sound of the ship's engines increased to a roar of complaint. If he could reach the far side a few moments ahead of the Dominion ships, he might be able to find somewhere to hide the *Nightwind* until the warships passed them by. Navigation charts had indicated a large asteroid field in the area, rocky debris orbiting through the star system from impacts long ago.

"They're firing."

A bolt of blue energy sizzled across the ship's curved port wing. The craft shivered but held firm.

"Minimal damage," Tay intoned in a clipped voice. "Firing again."

The ship's bulkheads shuddered violently as two more bursts of pulse fire found their targets. The fierce impacts pitched Tay and Lucien sideways in their seats, despite their restraining harnesses. Metal groaned in protest, and an alarm sounded on the control deck.

Lucien hammered at the helm controls to alter their course, causing them to slingshot away from the atmosphere and around the curve of the planet's surface. A treacherous field of odd-shaped rocks began tumbling across the viewscreen, the hulking remains of ancient asteroids hurtling through the darkness in orbits around the system's small blue sun. "Where did they hit us?"

Tay swung his seat toward another bank of monitors to check the ship's systems. "Minor damage to the aft thrusters, but we've taken a direct hit on the cargo bay." He bent closer to the readout, his brows drawing downward in a worried frown. "There's still life support in the bay, but we've lost hull integrity, and microfractures are forming in the starboard bulkhead."

Lucien jerked his harness loose. The fractures had to be sealed before the entire bulkhead blew out. "Take the helm, Tay, and find someplace to hide the ship quick. Rig for silence and play dead. If we're lucky, the Dominion ships won't pick us up on sensors and will fly right by."

Tay nodded and slowed their forward speed, aiming the ship toward a tumbling, egg-shaped rock with hundreds of holes and crevices criss-crossing its barren surface. "What about you? That bulkhead could go any moment. If I cut power you'll be trapped in the cargo bay."

He gave Tay a swift look, but remained silent.

Alexandra ripped the harness from her torso and leaped from the narrow bunk, her mouth forming a determined line. Flynn wasn't answering the intercom, so there was no other way to find out what was going on. The ship was under attack, obviously, but from who? Dominion forces or other smugglers? Or had her Uncle Theodore finally tracked her down? She shivered at that prospect, and her mouth compressed even more.

"My lady!" Loran called out when she realized Alexandra had unstrapped herself. "What are you doing?"

"I'm going to find out what's going on," she said in a voice as resolute as her expression. "I'll not lie trussed in that bunk waiting for the end while someone's shooting at us."

"But, my lady—"

"Don't worry about me, Loran. Just stay put and you'll be fine." She hurried to the cabin door, her eyes narrowing with anger when she noticed that one of her precious statues had shattered during the attack. It was one of her favorites, too, a multisided figurine of a woman with three dif-ferent faces. She glowered at the broken pieces for a second, then opened the cabin door. Flynn would have to explain the reason for the attack and answer for the damage done to her statue.

She stepped into the corridor cautiously, then jerked back abruptly to avoid colliding with Flynn as he barreled past, running headlong toward the tail of the ship and the cargo bay doors.

A tiny rush of fear swept through her blood. Alexandra called after him. He'd looked worried as he sped past. Very worried. Deep lines had etched themselves around his eyes and mouth, and he was hugging a large tool pack to his chest.

"Get back in your cabin!" he shouted over his shoulder. Breathing heavily, he came to a stop and hammered the entry code into the cargo bay lock.

Ignoring his order, Alexandra followed, arriving just as the bay doors slid open.

He threw her a dark look. "I don't have time to worry about you now," he said harshly. "Just get back to your cabin and strap yourself in."

"No." She pushed past him into the ship's cavernous cargo bay, squinting to see in the dim half-light. The bay's emergency lights had cut in, throwing a faint blue glow across the shadowy interior. A hodgepodge of crates was strewn about the floor, their hazy outlines adding to the number of shadows crisscrossing the darkened bay. The attack had knocked row after row of metal shipping containers loose from the cargo nets holding them in place, tossing them about the bay.

"Alexandra!" Flynn barked impatiently.

She turned to look at him and waved an impatient hand. When would the confounded man quit trying to order her around? "Look, Flynn, there's obviously something very wrong in here. You might need my help."

He stared back at her for a long moment, considering. If the bulkhead went, she wouldn't be much safer in her cabin than here. And another pair of hands might make all the difference in the end. "Can you operate a laser welder?"

"Yes." She cocked her head confidently. "I learned as a child." Growing up on Lochlain did have some advantages.

Lucien tossed the tool pack atop an overturned crate and popped the lid open. "Let's get to work then." He threw her a rectangular welder, grabbed a breach detector and a second welder for himself, then pointed toward the starboard bulkhead. "We've lost hull integrity, and we've got microfractures in the inner bulkhead."

Alexandra's eyes widened. The hull had been breached? Fractures in the bulkhead? The pressure could cause the entire wall of the cargo bay to blow out at any second. She swallowed down a rush of fear and nodded woodenly, watching in silence as he quickly reclosed the airtight bay doors, sealing them off from the rest of the ship. If the bulkhead actually went, Tay and Loran might stand a chance. Possibly. But with the bay doors sealed tightly shut, their own fates were another matter altogether.

She wet lips that had suddenly gone dry and switched on the welder, quickly familiarizing herself with the control pad. There would be no time for a rescue attempt, no chance at all for them to survive. If the fractures widened into a full-fledged breach, she and Flynn would be sucked through the opening into the cold, dark vacuum of space, their lungs rupturing almost instantly, their veins and organs seconds later. The dryness spread from her mouth to her tongue and throat. If they were sucked into a vacuum, death would be a welcome release.

Lucien shoved an overturned crate out of his way and ran his detector down the damaged bulkhead, frowning in concern as the zigzag lines of the microfractures showed up on the tiny screen. He ran a finger down the length of one of the fractures. "Start here at the top and work your way down," he ordered quietly. His laser welder flared blue-white in the near darkness as he set to work on the line farthest to the right.

Alexandra closed her mind to the possibilities and did as instructed, slowly running the narrow beam down the length of the fracture. She stopped after an inch or so to recheck the detector, then ran the tip of a finger along the next portion of the crack, jerking her hand back in surprise and fear when she realized the metal bulkhead felt like ice against her skin. Sweat gathered along her hairline. The inner bulkhead was all that separated them from the numbing cold of space itself.

Her finger still burning from the painful cold, she redoubled her efforts, the welder moving more swiftly down the course of the fracture. Beside her, she could hear the hum of Flynn's welder, but she wasted no time glancing his way.

A metallic creak rumbled through the bulkhead, and Alexandra's heart lurched to an accelerated beat. The metal bowed inward slightly, then eased back into place. "Flynn?" A knot of fear lodged in the base of her throat.

"Keep working," Lucien whispered hoarsely, his attention shifting to the shorter middle fracture. "Don't stop . . . no matter what."

Alexandra swallowed and tried to still the trembling in her hands as she bent back to her task. The bulkhead bowed inward again then relaxed, rasping in and out like lungs filling with air. She worked her way downward in silence, the short beam of the laser finally edging closer to the base of the microscopic crack. The sweat was beading on her forehead now, threatening to spill over her brows. Two inches to go. No more than that.

The seconds ticked past as they continued to

work. How many, Alexandra wasn't sure. Hours could have passed, for all she knew. She finally sealed the last of the fractures, then checked her handiwork with the detector, sagging in relief when it revealed that her seal was intact. "I'm finished," she told Flynn in a weak voice. "Do you need some help?"

He shook his head and aimed the beam at the bottom of the fracture. "I'll be finished in just a second. There's a roll of bulkhead patch in the tool pack. Bring it here."

Alexandra hurriedly made her way to the tool pack, fished inside, and withdrew a short roll of black metallic material, then rushed back to his side just as he completed his final weld.

Lucien switched off his welder, unrolled the tightly woven metal, and placed it against the section of bulkhead they'd repaired, adjusting it back and forth until he was satisfied that all of the seals were covered. He thumbed a pad at the bottom of the swath and the material bonded to the bulkhead magnetically. "That ought to hold us until we can make port for repairs."

Weak with relief, Alexandra allowed herself to sink atop a crate. She wiped the sweat from her forehead with a clammy hand and glanced at Flynn, who was busy checking and repacking the tools, swiftly placing them back in the tool kit. Despite the worry she'd seen on his face earlier, he seemed fairly unruffled by their brush with death. In fact, unlike her, he hadn't even broken a sweat. "I take it you've done this before," she said, her voice pitched a bit higher than normal with residual fear.

Lucien shrugged and snapped the lid of his tool pack shut. "A few times." He turned toward her and gave her a lazy smile. "Hazard of the business, I suppose."

Her brows arched, dark slashes set against her pale skin. He made such an occurrence sound like an everyday event. "Who attacked us?"

"Border patrol ships. I guess they figured out the course smugglers have been using to sneak through the security nets lately."

She suppressed a little sigh of relief. Not her Uncle Theodore then.

He picked up the pack and placed it under his arm. "Come on. We need to get out of here before—"

The emergency lights winked out completely, throwing the bay into utter darkness, then slowly came back on, dimmer and more ghostly blue than before.

Lucien muttered a curse. "Too late."

Alexandra glanced around wildly as the now familiar sound of the engines withered into an abrupt silence. Her heart slammed against her rib cage and her fear increased to a fever pitch. The sudden lack of background noise was like a sound itself, so loud and terrifying she could hear it pounding like a drum inside her ears. She bolted to her feet. "What's going on?" she managed to whisper.

Lucien dropped the tool pack and rushed to grab her before Tay powered down the rest of the ship's systems, but he didn't make it in time.

Alexandra's stomach lurched as a sudden wave of dizziness swept through her body. She felt wobbly and light-headed, disoriented by the strange sensation. As Flynn reached out to grab her arm, her feet suddenly lifted from the floor. She let out a little shriek of surprise. Shipping crates lifted into the air as well, drifting upward a foot or so. The sensation of falling grew stronger, and Alexandra struggled to stay upright, flailing her arms in an attempt to regain her footing. But her attempt had the opposite effect, sending her body into a stomach-churning tumble, her heavy robe drifting around her like an unfurled sail.

"Gods! Flynn, help me!" Her head and braids brushed the floor; then the rest of her body began rising again, spiraling upward in an out-of-control ascent toward the cargo bay's high ceiling. "Flynn!" Alexandra cried out in fear. She was gaining speed, her body spinning end over end in slow circles.

Lucien laughed in amusement, delighted that for once his determined young wife was in a situation that she couldn't hope to control. "Quit fighting it, Alexandra!" Still laughing, he aimed his body and launched himself upward to grab her before she hit the ceiling. "The more you flail around, the more you're going to tumble."

She ended her wild contortions instantly but kept spinning toward the high ceiling. "Make it stop, Flynn. I don't like this!" She squeezed her lids shut tightly. Up wasn't up anymore, and neither was down.

"Haven't you ever been weightless before?"

"No," she snapped back. "What happened to the gravity?"

A few feet shy of the ceiling, Lucien caught up with her and gently grabbed her ankle to stop her from tumbling. "Tay powered down the gravity generator." Lucien put out a hand and pushed off from the ceiling, a tiny shove that sent them on a slow course back toward the floor. "I told him to find someplace to hide the ship, then rig for silence and cut power so the border patrol can't pick us up on sensors. Unfortunately, we were still in here when he did it. The airtight doors are sealed shut until the systems come back on-line."

She gave him a sour look, but even that felt strange, as if she'd lost control of her facial muscles. "You mean we're stuck in here?" She was trapped with Flynn . . . alone? "Without gravity?"

Lucien glanced up at her and grinned. "I'm afraid so, love. Maybe for hours, or at least until the border patrol gives up the search for us and moves on."

"Oh, great." A sudden, dreadful thought occurred to her. "What about air?"

"Don't worry—life support's still up and running. We'll have oxygen and heat, but nothing else." His grin widened. "I guess there's nothing for us to do but relax and enjoy it." He released his hold on her ankle and folded his arms behind his head, drifting along beside her semihorizontally. Her thick braids had formed a bizarre halo around her head, and one side of her dark green robe was floating so high that he caught a tantalizing glimpse of her inner thigh.

Alexandra didn't like the look on his face one whit. She'd seen the sudden glint of desire flare to life in his gray eyes, and those determined eyes were on her now, watching her every move, studying every nuance of her expression—searching for a chink in her resolve.

A rush of awareness accelerated the beat of her heart. Why did the treacherous toad have to be so damnably attractive? She had managed to sidestep his previous advances by fleeing from his presence, but there would be no such escape this time. She was trapped here, alone with Damion Flynn, possibly for hours, a dangerous circumstance for any woman, much less one whose resolve was weakening fast.

"What should I relax and enjoy?" Alexandra said sharply, though she knew full well what he'd been trying to imply. Physical intimacy with a man like Flynn would be a monumental mistake, one she knew she would live to regret. Yet knowing that didn't stop the flutter of her heart, or still the blood pounding through her veins simply because he was near.

His cool gaze flicked over the sliver of her exposed flesh for a second, then moved back to her heart-shaped face. "Being weightless, of course. I sort of enjoy it myself."

She'd seen the trail his heated gaze had taken and returned his lazy smile with a chilly look. The man was bold, arrogant, and completely insufferable. "Don't get any ideas."

"About what?"

"I'm not stupid, Flynn." Her jet brows lowered. "I know what you're trying to do."

Lucien fought back an amused smile. "Oh, and what is that?"

Alexandra shook her head in frustration, a sudden motion that sent her body on a slow course toward the bulkhead. Did she have to spell it out for the man? "You're trying to seduce me."

He grabbed the toe of her shoe as she drifted past, allowing her momentum to pull him along. "Can't you think of it as a scientific experiment?"

A startled laugh slipped free of her throat. "Scientific experiment?" The man was totally outrageous.

"Of course." His hand slid up her calf to the back of her knee, then eased higher, caressing her velvety thigh. He smiled suggestively, his eyes turning a dark, cloudy gray. "Surely you're curious, aren't you?" he asked in a husky voice.

"No, I'm not," she said forcefully, but the quickening of her pulse belied her words. A wave of heat stole through her body. What would it be like to make love?

Her gaze moved over the hard planes of his face, lingering on the firm line of his mouth, the dark flicker of desire visible in his silvery eyes. He wanted her. She could see the naked need burning in his eyes, feel the heat from his smoldering gaze scorching her skin. The worst of it was, she wanted him, too, and nothing would change that one simple truth.

Her body collided with the bulkhead, then quickly rebounded, sending her on a course that took her directly back to Flynn. They bumped gently, his head grazing the swell of her breasts.

Lucien took swift advantage of the contact by wrapping his arms tight about her shoulders, holding her close to prevent her from spiraling away from him again. For a timeless moment, they simply drifted, their bodies joined from chest to hip. The back of her robe meandered upward, and a thick braid slid across his hand.

A renewed tide of desire washed over him. Her lips were only inches from his, her eyes wide and luminous in the blue-tinged darkness, fever-bright with burgeoning desire. And with each breath she took, her lush breasts moved against his chest, the closeness kindling a fire inside him that he knew he couldn't control, didn't want to control. His heartbeat accelerated. She was so close, and so utterly enticing.

His lips captured hers in a feather-soft kiss that teased the edges of her mouth, his exploration slow and gentle, questioning.

For the space of a single heartbeat, her mouth lay dormant beneath his; then she moaned low in her throat and moved against him, returning his kiss with an intensity that shocked his senses and left him breathless for more.

His kiss deepened in return, and Alexandra twined her fingers through his dark hair, drawing him closer, her sudden movement setting their bodies into motion once again. She could feel her resolve weakening, splintering, and falling around her like shattered glass, but she no longer cared.

All the desire and need and passion she had so carefully held in check came to a sudden, tumultuous boil. Nothing mattered anymore except the touch of those sensuously soft lips, the driving urgency to feel his hard-muscled flesh crushed against her own.

She pulled away from his demanding kiss and drew a needed breath of air, her gaze holding him captive. "Damion . . ." she whispered, the single word a silken caress. She stared at him expectantly. It was inevitable that they would end up like this, and had been since the very first moment she had set eyes on him. "I want you."

Those were the words he'd been waiting to hear, needed to hear. And yet . . . He gazed back at her uncertainly, damning himself for engaging in such a masquerade. His wife wanted to make love to Damion Flynn—not her husband, but an alter ego who didn't exist, a fantasy that had sprung fully formed from the mind of Lucien Charbonneau.

A veiled look of frustration clouded his features. As ludicrous as it seemed, he couldn't quite shake the feeling that his wife had just issued an illicit invitation to another man. A ridiculous notion, he knew, but the peculiar thought refused to go to its grave.

Her fingers moved from his hair to the line of his jaw, gliding lower until the tips of her nails drew a pathway down the sides of his neck. He inhaled sharply as a shudder of anticipation moved through his body.

"Ridiculous," he murmured to himself, his deft fingers closing around a fastener on her robe. He was her husband, as well as Damion Flynn, and it was past time that he claimed his alluring bride.

Jan Zimlich

She nuzzled the base of his throat, intoxicated by his nearness, the feel of his flesh beneath her lips. "What's ridiculous?" she whispered dreamily. She tugged at the top of his tunic, eager to undo his fasteners as well.

"Nothing, love," he whispered back. He felt as if he were drowning in her heady scent, falling headlong into those deep blue eyes. The first of her fasteners gave way, and he quickly dispatched several more, the heavy fabric gaping open to reveal ripe breasts spilling over the top of a thin underrobe.

The burning within him turned insistent, demanding, and his hands hungrily followed the direction of his eyes, closing around the satiny mounds possessively. His groan of pleasure was low and deep as his palms began moving in slow circles, her delicate flesh filling his hands completely.

At his touch, Alexandra gasped aloud and arched against his questing hands, an action that sent them tumbling end over end. The cargo bay began to spin slowly, the walls tilting and shifting until one was above her instead of the ceiling. A shoe came loose from her foot and spiraled away, and the back of her robe lifted higher, trying to climb over the top of her head. And all the while his strong hands remained firmly around her, kneading, caressing her sensitive flesh, evoking a scorching heat deep inside her that threatened to set her aflame.

She clawed at the fasteners on his tunic as they rotated, desperate to see and feel his body without the encumbrance of clothes. One by one the clasps finally fell away, and her hands slid inside his silky tunic, pushing and tugging until the material slipped from his shoulders, but the sleeves refused to budge lower than his forearms.

The Black Rose

Lucien released her reluctantly and tried to
help, but his contortions only managed to free a
single arm. The other sleeve was now caught at
his elbow, his tunic inside out and hanging
flaglike from his arm.

"Twine your legs around me," he whispered, his
mind clamoring for a way for them to somehow
shed their clothing without bumping into something or being drawn apart.

She squeezed her lids shut briefly as the ceiling
tilted beneath her, a disconcerting sight that left
her dizzy and weak. "Will that help?" she asked
hopefully.

"Can't hurt."

She did as instructed and wrapped her legs
around his tapered waist, hot shivers racing up
the center of her body as her loins settled against
his.

He sucked in a startled breath and pushed
against her instinctively. "Oh, gods," he said in a
tortured whisper, then redoubled his efforts, rip-
ping the sleeve off and sending the tunic floating
away. After a dogged effort, he finally managed to
tug off his high boots as well as her remaining
shoe, but his frenzied gymnastics made them
tumble even faster. He bit his lip in consternation, trying to think of a way to hold them in
place. The lack of gravity was presenting far more
of a physical challenge than he'd ever imagined.

The back of his head suddenly bumped against
a bulkhead, and his eyes widened in gleeful comprehension. He reached out and grabbed a cargo
net attached to the wall, clinging tightly with one
hand to prevent them from ricocheting away.
Their movement stopped abruptly, and his body
drifted outward, Alexandra's legs still wound
around his hips.

He snugged his hand through the rope more

167

Jan Zimlich

securely, and gave her a decadent smile. "You
hang on to me, and I'll hang on to the cargo net."
He touched the pulse beating at the base of her
throat with his free hand, his fingertips gliding
lower to follow the top of her underrobe. "Simple," he said huskily.

She lifted a dubious brow and smiled. *Simple?*
He truly was outrageous. "Well, we'll soon find
out, won't we?" Her hands brushed down his bare
chest and slipped between the two of them,
pulling at the fastener of his breeches.

He grinned back at her. "I thought I was an
arrogant worm."

Alexandra caught and held his smoky gaze, the
rapid tempo of her heartbeat building to an
explosive crescendo. "You are, but I want you
anyway." She unwound her legs and moved
lower, an arm wrapping around his chest to hold
her in place.

He moaned softly as the clasp came free and
she pushed the dark breeches past his hips. Using
her bare feet, she managed to ease them lower,
the soles of her feet slithering down the length of
his legs until the breeches came off completely. A
tremor moved through his body. All that separated him from her now was a few strips of fabric.

Working swiftly, he tugged the thin underrobe
down to her waist, freeing her abundant breasts
from their silken prison. He cupped her gently,
eager to feel her bare flesh beneath his hand.
Their eyes met for an interminable second; then
he pulled her weightless body toward him, his
mouth closing hungrily around the taut peak of a
nipple.

A sigh of pleasure escaped her throat as his lips
and tongue began moving in feverish circles, the
intimate embrace growing more frenzied. But

168

she wanted more, much more. She wanted to feel the hard proof of his desire surging inside of her.

She shoved at the heavy fabric gathered around her waist, anxious to free her lower body from the confines of her clothing. The robe and silky undergarment finally slipped off and she kicked them away.

A current of cool air prickled her naked skin as she pushed herself against him eagerly, her hand sliding down and down to cradle him gently.

Lucien sighed against her flesh and suckled her fiercely, the heat inside him turning into scalding flame as her hand began moving in a sensuously slow rhythm. He pulled his mouth from her abruptly, gasping for breath, and wove his feet through the webbing to secure himself more firmly.

His anguished eyes found hers. "I've got to have you," he said in a raw, tortured voice. "Now, Alexandra."

She stared into his smoldering eyes for a long second, then wound her arms about his chest to brace herself and eased her hips downward, slowly sliding down his body to embrace him with her warmth.

Lucien gasped and plunged inside her, pushing into her warm body in a gentle rhythm that matched her downward thrusts. As her mouth captured his in a searing kiss, his hand closed around her hips, pulling her down even more. Closer.

She whispered his name over and over again as he increased the tempo of his thrusts, her features knotting in exquisite pleasure as she surrendered herself to a torrent of heat and rapture.

Her shuddery tremors began to enfold him, and Lucien lost complete control, plunging deep inside her to find his own fevered release. A

Jan Zimlich

moment later, his fierce cry of joy echoed across the darkened bay.

Alexandra sighed and stretched languidly, reveling in the feel of his powerful arms wrapped so tightly about her body. Her slight movement set their intertwined bodies into gentle motion, like birds drifting on a current of air. Beside her, Damion still slept, his chest rising and falling against the curve of her breasts, one foot still tangled in the cargo net, preventing them from drifting too far. The scent of him surrounded her, a tangy, airy smell that somehow hinted of sunlight and fresh breezes.

She smiled. He'd been right, of course, about everything. The lack of gravity had added an unexpected element of levity to their lovemaking, a joyous sense of adventure that had increased the passion they'd shared all the more. Never in her life had she imagined that intimate encounters could be so pleasurable, so utterly satisfying both physically and mentally. And never had she known such a sense of sheer contentment. Damion Flynn was as bold, arrogant, and insufferable in his lovemaking as he was in everyday life. But he was also tender, sweet, and oh, so damn sensual that the mere memory of their antics brought a flush to her cheeks.

Her smile faded, and she suppressed a sudden urge to laugh, to cry, or both, contrary emotions that whittled away at the afterglow of their lovemaking and left a profound sense of sadness in their stead. She had finally found the dark, bold adventurer she'd conjured in her dreams, a man who truly equaled her girlish desires and passions—but he was a man who was wrong for her in every sense of the word.

The Black Rose

From the moment she first saw him on Thasia, she had fought hard to resist the irresistible because deep down she'd known instinctively that he was dead wrong for her, a figment of fantasy destined to live only in her dreams.

Her fingertips slid along the lines of his back, tracing over the smooth expanse of muscled flesh that she had explored so thoroughly and recently. Damion Flynn was a scoundrel and a thieving smuggler, the sort who would never understand the concept of permanence. Or love. Despite the intimacy they had just shared, she knew he would soon dump her on Janus Three without a backward glance, exiting her life as swiftly as he had entered it. No promises or plans for the future, no regrets. No pining for what might have been, could have been. He'd just be gone.

The thought of a life without him in it was suddenly a very lonely prospect. But at least she had a treasure trove of artifacts and research to occupy her in the coming weeks, perhaps years of meticulous study that would fill the empty hours, and in time make her forget that their paths had ever crossed. They each had their own lives to live. Separate lives.

Alexandra winced in the blue-tinged darkness when she remembered that part of her separate life included a gaggle of angry relatives and a husband, if a pathetic wastrel like Lucien Charbonneau could actually be termed such a thing. Sooner or later, she would have to deal with her so-called husband, as well as Theodore Fallon, but she didn't want to think about either of them now.

She wrapped her arms about Damion more tightly and nuzzled his neck, enjoying the moment, the last sweet taste of intimacy they would ever share. "Damion . . . ?" she whispered softly, a bit reluctant to wake him from such a deep slumber.

"Hmmmm?" Lucien's lids fluttered open, and he sighed deeply, a long, contented sound. They were drifting together, weightless, a few feet shy of the bay ceiling, their naked bodies still entangled from the most passionate and gloriously vigorous bout of lovemaking he'd ever experienced.

Erotic memories of the past hours flashed through his mind, and he made a small sound of pleasure low in his throat. The memories alone were enough to stoke the flames of his desire, fanning to life the embers left in the wake of their tumultuous encounter. Alexandra had managed to surprise him once again. In fact, he was utterly amazed. Though he had sensed the passion she carefully held in check, he'd been utterly astounded by her adventurous nature, and the physical strength coiled within her beautifully sculpted body. He'd also been astounded by his own primal response to their first encounter, an outrageously enjoyable session that had left him physically exhausted, and desperate for more of the same.

He smiled covertly and ran the pad of a thumb along the lush curves of her breasts. To think, his own wife had triggered such a heated response within him. Not many men could boast of such a thing. He pulled her close and kissed her greedily, the velvety feel of her lips crushed against his sending a renewed rush of desire spiraling through his blood.

Lucien reluctantly broke free of that soft mouth and gazed into her smoky blue eyes, his hands moving to caress her face and throat. "Has anyone ever told you just how delectable you are, love?"

She gave him a startled smile that was half-embarrassed, half-shy. "Not until now."

He gazed at her curiously. Could it be that unattached Fallon women were forced to live a celibate life? "Well, don't ever think otherwise." The notion hardly seemed credible, considering how hot-blooded she was. Perhaps she had simply scared most suitors away; very few men appreciated a woman who could best them in combat. Her Uncle Theodore and that viperish tongue of hers had surely been hindrances as well. Either could emasculate a man as swiftly and surely as the sharpest blade.

His finger traced the outline of her full lips. He was thankful she had not emasculated him with her tongue. Another rush of desire swept through his veins. But now that he had tasted the sweetness of her passion, he doubted if he could ever willingly let her go. Lucien Charbonneau was truly a fortunate man, if for no other reason than that he possessed the legal right to bed her whenever he wished, a right any other man would envy until the end of his days. "Your husband is a lucky man, Alexandra," he whispered against her ear.

He realized his mistake when she stiffened against him, her muscles drawing tight and still with suspicion. "That is, he will be. . . ." Lucien amended quickly. "If you ever decide to marry."

She untensed slowly, and so did he, but she remained uncharacteristically quiet for a long stretch of time. Certain that he'd roused her suspicions, Lucien cursed himself inwardly. He'd dropped his guard and made a foolish mistake, one that could cost him dearly in the long run.

Alexandra chewed on her lower lip thoughtfully. What had he meant by that? He'd recovered from his verbal misstep quickly enough, but had he misspoken, or did he know more than he claimed? She hadn't breathed a word about her ill-fated marriage to him or anyone else. Could Loran have spilled her secret to Tay, and he'd shared it with Flynn?

After a little thought, Alexandra shrugged off her anxiety. What did it matter anyway? Whether she was married or not would probably be irrelevant to Damion. The truth wouldn't matter to a man such as him, especially since she would be out of his life in less than a day. Besides, it might be quite interesting to see how he reacted to the news, to see if he had any perceptible reaction at all. None, more than likely, and that thought made her both angry and sad.

"I have a confession to make," Alexandra said slowly, her gaze focused intently on his features. Would he be jealous, angry, or utterly indifferent? "I'm already married."

Lucien blinked and cocked a startled brow. "Oh?" He didn't have to pretend astonishment at her revelation—he *was* astonished, mostly because she had admitted it at all. Especially now, as she lay naked in what she believed was another man's arms. "Anyone I know?"

Alexandra watched him carefully. "Probably not. It was an arranged marriage—in name only. He's . . . he's . . . well, let's just say he's not exactly my type."

He bit back an amused grin. Once again he seemed to be in direct competition with himself for his wife's affections. Charbonneau had obviously lost the battle if not the war—lost it miserably—but to some extent, he had won as well.

He frowned suddenly, an expression he camouflaged by burying his face among her drifting braids. In truth there was no real victor here.

Though she was bound to his Charbonneau persona, she neither liked nor wanted him as Lucien; as Damion, he would soon be held in the same regard if he were caught trying to steal the artifacts. That would be a betrayal she would never forgive. His mind raced over the possibilities, searching for a way to keep her in his life—in one of his lives. "And what exactly is your 'type'?" he prodded softly.

She lifted her shoulders in a small shrug. *You*, she wanted to say. But she didn't. Couldn't. He was curious, nothing more—not jealous or angry or anything else. And he was treading perilously close to forcing some sort of admission from her, one she was loath to give him or any man. "I've never really thought about such things," Alexandra lied.

Lucien sighed. Her curt tone of voice cut off any further discussion of the subject. If he pressed her now, he would surely rouse her suspicions again. He would just have to improvise, create a new persona or re-create an old one that might appeal to her. Of course, that would mean he would have to somehow entice her into his arms all over again.

His arms moved around her and he pulled her tight to his chest, their bodies turning slightly so that she ended up atop him, if such a term could be applied in weightlessness. He ran his hands through the fan of braids, drawing her face closer to his lips. "Your husband really is a lucky man," he said against her cheek. "Even if he's not exactly your type."

Alexandra pushed all thoughts of Lucien Charbonneau and the future from her mind, concentrating instead on the here and now. It was Damion Flynn she concentrated on, how his mus-

175

cled body was pressed along the length of hers, how those firm lips were trailing across her own, eliciting a familiar reaction deep inside her.

She moaned softly, a tortured sound that was matched by a similar sound from him. Alexandra clung to him tightly and reveled in the rush of sensations, the feel of his warm body and demanding lips crushed to hers once again. "Take me again, Damion," she whispered against his mouth, her eyes glazing with renewed passion.

The drumming of his heart quickened. She was so hot, so passionate. "Gladly, love," he whispered back.

The lights in the cargo bay came back on full force, a blinding rush of white that left brilliant after images behind their lids.

Lucien muttered a curse and threw an arm up to shield his eyes, pulling Alexandra's face into his chest to protect her as well. "Hell." Tay had damned lousy timing.

"What now?" Alexandra said in exasperation.

"Tay's powering back up." He twined his foot more firmly through the cargo net and desperately started maneuvering their bodies toward it. "Grab on to the net tightly. The gravity generator will come up next."

Her mouth fell open. They were at least twenty feet above the bay floor, and the only thing holding them in place was Damion's foot. Worse, they were still naked. "Oh, my gods!" Alexandra made a frantic grab for the net and a piece of her clothing that was drifting past. She caught the net but missed her underrobe, her movement sending the white material spiraling out of reach. A slipper hung suspended above her, and she made a grab for that, too, managing to grasp the heel for a moment before it squirted from her grip and flew away.

"Forget your clothes and hang on!" Lucien ordered. He wrapped the corded webbing about his hands and planted the soles of his feet in the ropes.

Alexandra's body suddenly felt heavy, very heavy, as if there were three people sitting atop her, crushing the life from her bones. The muscles in her arms and legs screamed in protest as she struggled to hang on to the ropes. She slipped slightly, and Damion's arm coiled tightly around her waist, supporting a portion of her body weight to keep her from falling. Her wayward slipper hurtled downward, as well as the remainder of their clothing and Damion's boots.

Beneath them, shipping crates crashed to the floor, sharp cracks of sound that did little to quell her anxiety. Containers tumbled atop each other and to the metal deck, some slamming with enough force to spring their lids and spill their contents across the metal floor.

Lucien peered downward and released a short bark of laughter. "Well, at least we didn't fall."

A wave of heat rode up her cheeks. In the glare of the lights, the reality of their situation returned in a rush. She was as naked as the day she'd been born, hanging from a net some twenty-odd feet from the floor, an equally naked man hanging beside her. The flush in her cheeks turning a hot, flaming red, she started climbing down the net at breakneck speed, descending so rapidly that she knew she'd given herself a rope burn in a decidedly uncomfortable place.

Ignoring the stinging on her chest, she leaped free of the net, her bare feet hitting the metal deck a few seconds before Damion reached the bottom. Alexandra scrambled around, retrieving her scattered clothing, managing to have her underrobe half-on by the time he dropped from the net.

She breathed a sigh of relief when she jerked her underclothing into place, shielding her body from those piercing gray eyes. She got her robe on next, her trembling fingers refastening the ornate buttons in what was surely record time.

Lucien pulled his trousers on slowly, bemused by her frantic efforts to veil her body from his view. What had happened to the passionate vixen he'd come to know just a short time ago?

Alexandra jammed a foot into one of her slippers, then started rummaging around the overturned crates in search of the other. She finally spotted the missing shoe near an upside-down shipping crate, the contents of the heavy metal box tossed in a jumbled pile across the floor.

She stared at the spilled cargo for a long moment, comprehension sliding slowly through her veins. Her eyes narrowed, and a sudden shiver crawled up her spine. The smooth metal barrels of a dozen new pulse rifles winked in the harsh white light, the latest and most efficient model on the market . . . the current weapon of choice for soldiers within the Dominion, her own clan included.

Her shoe forgotten, Alexandra turned toward Flynn slowly. She should have known, should have suspected *something*. She'd known he was a smuggler, but never imagined anything like this.

"You're a gunrunner," she said in a flat voice. Her instincts had been right about him all along.

Lucien blinked in surprise, his gaze speeding over the contents of the overturned crate, then moving back to Alexandra, stilling on her pale, angry face. *Damn.* "Sometimes," he answered slowly.

She bent down and picked up a small metallic

sphere sitting near her feet, the slick metal heavy and cool against the skin on her palm. A plasma grenade, one of the smallest she'd ever seen. She shook her head in disgust. Weapons smugglers were the scum of the galaxy, merchants of death who preyed on both sides of every conflict. And Damion Flynn, the man she'd given her body to, was one of them.

Distraught, Alexandra surveyed the interior of the bay. It was filled with box upon box of smuggled weapons, too many to count. "Who's this shipment for, Damion? Some warring clan? Maybe the Modalbeaus or the Lyseenes? I heard they have a nasty little war going right now," she said harshly.

Lucien stared at her for long seconds, debating the perils of revealing too much about his cargo or his life. The less she knew, the better—for him and for her. Yet there was something within him that made him want to tell her the truth, or as much of the truth as she could handle. Through their passion they might have temporarily found common ground between them, but politically he knew they were poles apart.

A muscle in his jaw worked back and forth as he slipped his arms back into the sleeves of his shirt. He held her angry gaze for a long space of time, then motioned toward the stacks of crates with a wave of his hand. "They're for the rebels." His fingers moved downward to refasten his shirt. "That's all I'm going to say . . . and I trust you'll keep that bit of information to yourself once we reach Janus Three."

She gaped at him in horror. She had assumed the weapons were destined for some interclan conflict, but had never dreamed that he might actually be supplying arms to the insurrectionists. "You're a *rebel?*" For all she knew Flynn might be allied with the notorious Black Rose himself, a man whose long-professed goal was to overthrow the Dominion government. Democracy was the dream these rebels allegedly espoused, but Alexandra knew anarchy would reign if their goal was ever attained.

"You're supplying weapons to those outlaws?" If the rebels won, Dominion culture would be utterly destroyed, the various clans stripped of the power and wealth accumulated over the past two thousand years. Her own clan was at risk, even Lochlain itself, everything her family held dear. "Have you lost your wits, Flynn?" Alexandra demanded. "You can't possibly subscribe to the rebels' ideology! They're trying to destroy our way of life!"

Lucien snorted. "Whose way of life, Alexandra? Yours? You *are* a noblewoman, after all. What of the billions who spend their entire lives as vassals in service to the heads of the clans, simply because they had the misfortune to be born on the wrong world?" Conviction darkened the hue of his eyes. "Even those fortunate enough to live on nonaligned worlds like Janus Three are forced to beg like dogs for the simplest favors from some hereditary warlord—one who may or may not throw a bone their way, depending on his mood."

Alexandra shook her head in disagreement, yet deep inside a niggle of uncertainty surfaced unbidden. Under Dominion law, her own uncle had the absolute right to force her into a loveless marriage, and to beat her into submission when she refused and tried to run away. Was it so wrong to rebel against such a government? By fleeing from her husband and Lochlain, in her own small way, she had herself rebelled against what it stood for. "It's tradition—"

"Tradition be damned," he said forcefully. "Dominion culture is corrupt, has been for countless centuries. The rebels simply want to cut away the corruption and begin anew."

"If you truly believe that, then you're a fool, Damion. Read your history texts. Democracies have never endured." She was an even bigger fool than he was. She'd fantasized about a lover like Flynn, whiled away the years on Lochlain with silly daydreams of finding her soul mate in a bold adventurer like the infamous Black Rose. Instead she'd found that lover, and his feet were made of clay; he was a man with skewed values and beliefs that would get him killed.

She was thankful she had discovered the truth now, before she wasted the coming months pining and dreaming of the day when she might meet him again. Damion Flynn would be out of her life on the morrow, and good riddance to him. Good riddance to her stupid dreams as well.

She fought back a sudden prickle of tears as she walked stiffly toward the cargo bay doors. He wouldn't see her cry again.

Chapter Eleven

New Chicago glittered like a pale jewel shimmering beneath a warm, early morning sun. Alexandra stood at the top of the *Nightwind*'s short gangway and took a breath of the clean, salt-tinged air, enjoying the sights and scents of a new day spreading across the surrounding mountains, setting the narrow spires aflame with bold hues of red and green. To her right, she could see the slick waters of a great inland sea, cool, foamy green beneath the newborn sun.

The city was by far the largest on Janus Three, which was the largest world in the Janusian system. It was a sparkling oasis of civility and culture nestled near the heart of Dominion space. After Thasia and the desolation of the Denault moons, the sight of the city and civilization was welcome indeed.

The central section of the city itself lay huddled in a crescent along the edge of that vast sea, then sprawled westward across a rolling valley encircled by the thin, snowcapped spires, like white-tipped fingers reaching for the bright morning sky. A profusion of stark white buildings made from native limestone dotted the landscape, their fluid lines and domed roofs rising and falling with the wide valley floor.

Behind her, Loran stood on tiptoe and peered over her mistress's shoulder, gasping aloud when she saw the city and landscape that awaited them. "My word!" Loran said in a reverent tone. "It's beautiful!"

Alexandra watched as the reds and brilliant greens faded from the tops of the mountain spires, replaced by the diamondlike glare of sunlight reflecting off a layer of snow. "It is, isn't it?" she answered absently. Almost too beautiful, as if she were about to walk into the throes of a waking dream.

She took another breath to steel herself and descended the gangway, her fingers brushing down the length of the metal handrail, the last time she would have to touch any part of Damion Flynn's ship. And it was his ship, even though it no longer looked the same at all. The night-black ship she'd spotted on the Thasian landing field had been transformed, the color of the hull now a dull gunmetal gray. A smuggler's trick, Tay had explained, electronic paint that could magically change hues at the touch of a button. The name and registry numbers had been transformed as well. The ship was now called the *Daystar*, an innocuous-looking vessel that seemed to blend in more readily with its new surroundings.

Her expression soured. Neither the *Nightwind* nor its captain were exactly what they seemed, a thought which filled her with anger and sadness all over again. Damion Flynn was a living, breathing lie, a political renegade who'd cleverly cloaked himself in the mantle of a simple smuggler. Her thoughts spun. She no longer knew the difference between reality and fiction where Flynn was concerned. What else about him was a sham? Worse still, had the intimacy they'd so recently shared been a farce as well?

She watched as a group of furtive-looking workmen bustled around the tail of the ship, hurriedly unloading Flynn's cargo of smuggled weaponry and whisking the crates away to unknown destinations, all in the name of politics. Maintenance techs were busy as well, rushing about in a frenzy of activity to weld and repair the breach in the ship's hull.

Within a matter of hours the cargo would be off-loaded, the repairs complete, and Flynn would be free to lift off and get on with his life. So would she.

Their travel bags were waiting, piled in a neat stack at the bottom of the ramp, along with a metal shipping container bearing her precious artifacts. The traitorous Flynn was waiting, too, standing near her bags, a brooding look etched across his hawkish face.

Alexandra paused and lifted her chin to a defiant angle. "We'll be on our way now, Captain Flynn." *Captain Flynn*. Even to her the formality sounded absurd. He'd been her lover less than a day ago; now she was referring to him as if he were a complete stranger. A *rebel* lover, she reminded herself. Her mouth curled in a grimace. "Don't worry," she said in a low voice, "I plan to keep your secret."

Lucien winced inwardly. He'd made yet another mistake, not the first in dealing with this truculent woman. Obviously, Alexandra Fallon hadn't been ready to handle the truth. "Well, for that I thank you." He met her eyes. "Good-bye,

The Black Rose

Alexandra," he said, purposefully using her first name in stark contrast to the way she'd addressed him. "I wish you well."

A young porter began stacking their possessions atop a luggage cart. As he worked, the brown-haired adolescent gave Lucien a quick, probing look. He nodded imperceptibly in return, ordering the youth to accompany the luggage and Alexandra to their destination.

Alexandra gave Flynn a primly polite smile. "I wish you the same . . . I just hope you stay alive long enough to enjoy your life."

A small smile touched his features. "Don't worry; I will. I plan to enjoy many things in the coming years. Who knows? I might even find someone who's my type and settle down one day." Lucien cocked a dark brow and bowed slightly, an informal gesture this time. "Until we meet again?" With that he was gone, vanishing up the gangway into the interior of his ship.

Alexandra stared after him for long seconds, pain rippling through her. His comment had been mocking, hurtful, a sarcastic replay of the words she'd spoken only yesterday. As if he were saying that he planned to settle down in the future, but with someone more to his liking than her, the woman he'd made such passionate love to only the day before.

Sensing the reason for her mistress's bleak expression, Loran laid a gentle hand on her arm and squeezed. "Come, my lady," she said softly. "The porter is waiting."

Alexandra blinked away the sudden haze that filled her eyes. "Must have gotten something in my eye," she muttered to her watchful handmaiden, then stalked off to catch up with the porter, who was waiting for them near an exit from the terminal.

185

He tipped his peaked cap as Alexandra approached. "Where to, my lady?"

Her brow furrowed. She didn't have the slightest idea where they were going, or even how long they'd be staying on this particular world. "Can you recommend an establishment where we might lease a suite of rooms for a month or so?"

The young man smiled shyly and pointed a finger toward the section of the city that abutted the water. "Gammon's, perhaps. They're quite pricey, but the food is good and the upper rooms have a pleasant view of the sea and mountains."

"Sounds wonderful." She would have to sell another of the jeweled buttons to pay for their lodging. "Would you be so kind as to direct us and carry our luggage there?"

"Of course, my lady. Just follow me." The wheels of the cart rumbled against the pavement as he pushed it onto a pedestrian walkway, turning eastward, toward the most congested part of the city and the glistening waters of the inland sea.

Alexandra and Loran ambled in his wake, enjoying the cool breeze and the sights of the city proper. Despite the early hour, the pathway was filled with pedestrians walking to and fro, some with bundles of goods or foodstuffs tucked beneath their arms. Though Janus Three was a nonaligned world, many among the crowd wore the uniforms or traditional garb of various clans, from the smaller and less affluent clans like her own to the coal-black uniforms of the all-powerful Vahntis, the wealthiest within the Dominion.

She frowned and touched a hand to her telltale braids. If she could pick out members of certain clans from their style of dress, so could others. Her braids would have to go temporarily, until she was certain her Uncle Theodore had given up trying to track her down. It wouldn't hurt to buy new clothing, either, robes cut in styles more common on other worlds. For Loran as well.

"After we find our lodgings and eat, I want to take my braids down. Then let's do a bit of shopping, Loran." All manner of shops lined the walkway, more than Alexandra had ever seen.

Loran glanced at her in surprise. "Take your braids down?"

"We need to blend in with the locals if we plan to stay here for a while." She tugged on the end of a coiled length of hair. "These don't exactly mark me as a local."

As if to prove her words, a pair of men heading in the opposite direction paused and gave Alexandra long, probing stares, their hard eyes seeming to linger a bit too long on her face and thick braids.

Loran took a protective step toward her mistress, her fingers moving unconsciously to the blond braids wrapped tight about her own head. "I see your point," she agreed quietly.

The men moved on, but Alexandra felt their eyes burning into her back long after they had passed. "Maybe we ought to take our hair down first thing," she whispered to Loran.

A cluster of ruffians loitering near a storefront seemed to be staring at her as well, hungry and boldly curious looks that set Alexandra's teeth on edge. Obviously slender women weren't eschewed by men on Janus Three as they were on Thasia, where a more voluptuous form had been held in such high regard.

She shivered and quickened her footsteps to catch up with the porter, tugging on Loran's arm to hurry her as well. New Chicago had suddenly lost some of its appeal.

* * *

Lucien adjusted the lighting in his cabin and stared into the mirror for long seconds, shifting his face this way and that as he scowled at Damion Flynn's reflection. The face and persona had served him well for the past few years, but Damion had attracted far too much attention of late. He scowled at himself. Unwelcome attention like the unexpected set-to with the Dominion border patrol. They would be on the lookout for him now, as well as the *Nightwind*, with General Thigg not far behind, hell-bent on discovering the identity of the Black Rose.

And if Flynn had become a suspect, it wouldn't be long until someone with half a brain rooted around and somehow connected him with the Black Rose. And from there the trail might even lead to Lucien Charbonneau. Damion Flynn would just have to disappear for a while, at least until the hounds lost that particular scent and moved on to other prey. It might be safer if Charbonneau continued to stay out of sight as well, at least for a while. He could ill-afford to bring suspicion down on his true name.

He snorted in amusement. *Poor Thigg.* So far the Black Rose had managed to stay one step ahead of the autocratic general, outmaneuvering and outwitting him by switching identities at the first hint of suspicion. Damion would simply leave on an extended journey. Soon. But not before the clandestine meeting arranged for tonight. Rebel commanders from across the Dominion were set to meet within hours to map out plans for a series of infiltrations into clan McConnell space, defensive measures to try to stop the mass executions of suspected rebels by that clan's despotic warlord. And Flynn was the rebel commanders' contact, the only face each of them recognized and trusted. Once the meeting began, he could give them a new password and warn that they would have a "different" contact in the future. But to do so, Damion Flynn had to make an appearance at the meeting tonight. Then after the meeting, he had to somehow slip into Alexandra's rooms and make off with her treasures before she found out the truth about Arulians and endangered all of his identities.

He sighed deeply. Alexandra and her archaeological discoveries were complications that he'd neither wanted nor expected, especially now, when he was actually making headway toward achieving his long-term goals. But the problem had to be dealt with—the sooner the better, so that he could get on with the business of the insurrection without further distractions. And once this business had been dealt with, perhaps he could make amends to her in some way, forge a lasting relationship between her and . . . *someone*.

Lucien closed his eyes a moment and experimented, allowing his features to shift a millimeter here, a more drastic change there. The bold, hawkish features of Damion Flynn slowly melted away, replaced by a face that was older, more refined and aristocratic, yet still thoroughly rakish in a softer sort of way.

He experimented a bit more, lightening his hair to a pale blond, then quickly darkening it to a rich shade of brown, though not nearly as dark as Flynn's had been. With the long blond hair he had looked too much like an older version of Charbonneau, enough so that his looks might arouse suspicion if a person were observant enough.

After long minutes, Lucien stepped away from the mirror and studied his new face with a critical eye. *Not bad at all*. His eyes were still gray, as always; they were the only features that he was unable to change. But their shape was a bit different, larger and more rounded, with fine age lines webbing toward his temples from the corners of his eyes. His jaw, chin, and mouth were fuller, less chiseled now, yet still bore a trace of Flynn's strong features, just more refined. He looked like a physically fit, middle-aged aristocrat used to getting his way.

"Perfect." Lucien grinned at himself, pleased with his handiwork. A bit of a combination of Charbonneau and Flynn, just older and more settled-looking than either of them, the sort of man who might even appeal to his mercurial wife.

He cocked a brownish brow and tilted his head, his mind ranging over possible identities for his new face. Through the years, he'd worked diligently to develop a score of different identities, ranging from the casual to intricately detailed guises backed up by identity cards, assets, and mounds of legal paperwork. One of those guises was needed now, a persona with a noble background and bonafides to prove his lofty station in life.

Lucien's thoughts stilled and he bowed mockingly to his new reflection. He'd never masqueraded as Vashlen Thackery before, though the guise had been developed long ago, waiting for the moment it would be needed and put to good use. "Lord Thackery, I presume?" he asked the stranger in the mirror.

It was indeed perfect. A nobleman would have instant access to the Dominion court on a level similar to his real self. And the name gave little cause for concern. The Thackerys were sympathetic to the rebels' goals, and had cooperated fully in the creation of a fictitious member of their clan, so he had nothing to fear in that regard.

Tay strolled through Lucien's cabin door and stopped cold when he saw a stranger peering at himself in the full-length mirror. Startled, he cleared his throat uneasily. "Lucien?"

Lucien turned toward his friend and grinned. "Were you expecting someone else in my cabin?"

"Of course not." Tay snorted and shook his head in disbelief. "You just startled me." No matter how many times he'd witnessed Lucien's chameleonlike transformations, he would never grow used to them. His friend could change his looks the way others changed their boots or shirts. "So who are you today?"

"Meet Lord Vashlen Thackery . . . Vash for short."

"Lord?" Tay's mouth turned downward. "Does that mean I have to brush off my livery and pose as your servant again?"

Lucien shrugged. "Possibly, but not right away."

"Good." He grimaced. "I hate dressing like that."

"Well, be prepared just in case." Lucien closed his eyes again and concentrated. Within seconds Damion Flynn reappeared. He double-checked his reflection to make sure he looked exactly as he should. "Has the cargo been off-loaded yet?"

Tay nodded. "Right on schedule. The shipment is already en route to our forces positioned near the McConnell border."

Lucien's expression turned solemn. The warlord of the McConnell clan had to be stopped, and soon. Over a hundred prisoners had been put to death so far, and even more were locked away in McConnell dungeons, simply because they were suspected of supporting the rebels. Even worse, many of those executed were complete innocents, with no involvement whatsoever in the insurrection. "Send a message to our forces. Their commanders will be returning shortly with plans for an offensive against the McConnells. For now, though, tell them to lie low and concentrate their efforts on freeing as many prisoners as possible, but to avoid open conflict if at all possible. They know the drill . . . free as many prisoners as they can and leave black roses in their wake for the clan authorities to find. The McConnells will be in a state of confusion. They'll think the Black Rose is in ten places at once, and report as much to General Thigg, who'll waste his time and resources searching for me in the wrong place as usual—while I'm right under his nose."

"They won't like having to lie low," Tay told him. "They're itching for a fight with the McConnells."

"I don't expect them to like it." Lucien paced across his cabin, then returned, his hands folded stiffly behind his back. He didn't like the cat-and-mouse game they'd been playing either, but there was no help for it right now. "It's too risky, Tay. If we take on the McConnells directly, the war might spread across their borders to neighboring clans, giving General Thigg and the Security Force an excuse to intervene." He shook his head slowly. "We're nowhere near being ready to take on Thigg and the DSF. Not yet."

Tay studied him for a long moment. McConnell territory adjoined Charbonneau space, so closely that his friend's father would surely be drawn into any hostilities that might erupt. "What of your father, Lucien?" he asked quietly. "If we're forced into a fight, he'll be drawn into it for sure."

Lucien frowned and rubbed his forehead. He

might despise his father for what he'd done, but he didn't truly want to be responsible for destroying either him or his clan. "My father has already chosen sides. If the shooting starts, there won't be anything I can do about it."

"And what about you, Lucien?" Tay asked even more quietly. His friend had been taking ever more dangerous risks in the past year. Now he was activating an entirely new guise, this Lord Thackery identity, which meant that he needed the cover of a nobleman to do whatever it was that he planned. Worse still, he'd said that he would be right under Thigg's nose . . . a very dangerous sign indeed. "Where will *you* be?"

Before he answered, Lucien glanced at the small painting of a black rose hanging on his cabin wall, one of the few items that he possessed that had belonged to his mother. "I think Vashlen Thackery just might pay a little visit to the Dominion court and nose around." The archduke's annual masquerade ball was scheduled to take place in less than a week—an appropriate place for the Black Rose to make an unexpected appearance. He turned back to Tay and produced a grim smile. "There's no telling what he might turn up."

From the small balcony, Alexandra watched the sun slowly descend over the water, a breathtaking explosion of yellow, red, and blue that seemed to merge with the foamy green of the sea for a few seconds, then fade into a pale, dusky rose that sent shadows riding across the mountaintops. In the street below, the pace of life in New Chicago seemed to be accelerating with the coming of night; laughing, gaily robed crowds hurried through the walkways in a flurry of movement, colors, and sound.

Jan Zimlich

She propped her elbows on the balcony's rail and continued to watch, her unbound hair drifting across her cheeks in the evening wind. It felt peculiar to have her hair brushing against her face—a simple thing for many, but for her it was a refreshing change. Her hair had been worn in the traditional Fallon braids for more years than she cared to remember, ever since she was a very young girl, usually with colorful beadwork intricately woven around and through every braid. She shook her head, luxuriating in the cascade of sensations the simple movement gave. Discarding the style was somehow very freeing, as though the change itself had brought with it a sense of exhilaration that she found hard to resist.

Behind her, soft white draperies billowed outward in the evening air, drifting around her body much like her long black hair. Alexandra sighed and closed her eyes, enjoying the sensations, the utter satisfaction she found in the place and moment. The suite of rooms she'd leased was sumptuous, soft and cozy and distinctly feminine, well worth the outrageous sum of chits Gammon's proprietor had demanded. She'd simply sold another of her jeweled buttons and paid without complaint, deciding that she and Loran deserved to live at least a few weeks in the comfort and splendor common to Dominion nobility.

She frowned slightly. *Comfort* and *splendor* were alien words on Lochlain, where such notions were dismissed out of hand and a spartan lifestyle held sway. Many a night she'd shivered herself to sleep, with no heat or energy allotted to warm her rooms in any way. Her Uncle Theodore's idea of frugality, that. *Waste not, want not*, he was fond of saying, an adage he insisted had originated on Old Earth. But Alexandra was certain he'd simply made that up to justify making all Fallons suffer. Besides, he had plenty of chits, a hoard he'd accumulated in the clan's name but refused to part with for anyone or anything.

So she had no qualms about living in comfort for a while, buying new robes for her and Loran and eating well for a change. She did feel a tiny pang of guilt, though, simply because it was Charbonneau's money that she was using to live so well. It would be far more just if she were spending part of Theodore's hoard instead.

Somehow she'd find a way to pay Charbonneau back, and to thank him for unwittingly giving her the opportunity to stay in this costly suite and continue her work. Without his jewels, she knew Theodore would have caught up with her long before now. She doubted if she would have even made it off of Lochlain on her wedding night, much less to the Denault system.

Thoughts of Charbonneau inflating her sense of guilt, she pushed him from her mind and refocused her attention on the scene playing out in the street below. The throng wandering past had definitely grown, a kaleidoscope of movement and sound that she found almost impossible to resist. She was antsy to join in, or to at least be part of the crush for a little while, to taste the pleasures of life others considered their due. On Lochlain, gatherings on such a large scale were reserved for funerals and feasts, not enjoyed nightly, as they seemed to be here.

She leaned out over the balcony even farther, straining to see down to the end of the street, and gasped in surprise when she saw a familiar head bobbing through the crowd. The steady thump of her heartbeat increased.

Flynn.

Her hands moved to grip the rail as she watched him weave his way toward Gammon's. She'd thought he'd gone already, that he had lifted free of Janus Three as soon as his ship was repaired. Instead he was still here. What did it mean?

She cursed herself inwardly as the pounding inside her seemed to double in strength. It wouldn't have mattered if it had been years, not hours, since she had seen him last. She would have known his gait, his powerful shoulders, and his darkly sensual face anywhere, anytime. Damion Flynn was a man no woman could easily forget, and despite her protestations to the contrary, she was no exception to that.

She watched raptly as he maneuvered through the surge of people and paused near the entrance to a dining house just a few doors from her residence. A young man with dark brown hair appeared at his elbow, talking and nodding near Damion's ear.

Alexandra's mouth tightened with suspicion when she recognized the youth. The porter, the friendly adolescent who had guided them here, was now laughing with Flynn as though they were friends. Her suspicions multiplied with viruslike speed. What was the connection between the two, and how did it relate to her? Had the porter sent them to Gammon's himself, or was it at Flynn's suggestion? And if so, why?

The beat of her heart slowed to a sudden crawl. *The artifacts*, her mind whispered, an insidious thought that kept slithering around her brain. Flynn was a known smuggler, after all, and a smuggler plus a crate of priceless artifacts equaled certain disaster. The value of her finds was incalculable, a fortune in black-market booty that any museum would salivate to possess.

Her gaze narrowed and slid down the side of the building to the ground below, searching for anything that might give Flynn entry to her rooms. Thick vines laden with blooms ran up the stucco on both sides of her balcony to the pitched roof, the gnarled wood looped and sturdy enough for hand- and footholds within the vines. A perfect ladder for the nimble, and Flynn was definitely that.

She pressed her lips together in dismay as Flynn and the porter entered the restaurant's wide double doors and disappeared. "Loran!" she called out impulsively. "I'm hungry. How about we go down the street for a bite to eat?"

Loran pushed the flowing draperies aside and eased up to the threshold of the balcony, focusing her gaze on Alexandra's face so she wouldn't have to look down. She had never liked heights, or edges of any kind. Caves either. "We just ate a few hours ago."

Alexandra's chin rose to a stubborn angle. "I'm hungry again. There looks to be a nice place just a few doors down from here. Let's try it."

Loran shrugged and pushed a final pin into her coiled hair. Her braids were gone, but she still had the blond strands wound about her head. "All right." She really wouldn't mind eating again anyway, especially if someone would be serving her for a change.

Alexandra brushed past her, eager to be on her way before Flynn could disappear. She paused inside and locked the balcony doors, then glanced around the elegant sitting room, double-checking that all was secure. The crate containing her artifacts was still closed and locked, shoved into an unobtrusive corner behind a plump wing chair. She would unpack the contents tomorrow, as well as begin to compile and catalog her notes. She would also buy new locks and proximity alarms to protect their rooms. For now, the crate was safe enough, or as safe as such valuables could ever be with someone like Flynn or his ilk hanging about.

Determined to find out what Flynn was up to, she grabbed her new blue cloak and hurried through the door. She had to know the real reason why Damion was still here, and just how long he planned to remain. Besides, her artifacts would be far safer while she had him in sight.

The street was as clogged with people as it had appeared from the balcony, a glorious assault of the senses that washed over Alexandra when she stepped through Gammon's door. Loran clung tightly to her arm, overwhelmed by the press of people, laughter, and sounds. Music wafted to Alexandra's ears as they made their way to the doorway that had swallowed Flynn, dodging this way and that along the sidewalk to avoid colliding with the sea of pedestrians. But even though the throng was so large, she sensed no danger on the street, saw no ruffians giving her hard-eyed stares as she had that morning.

Nighttime in this part of New Chicago was a thing to be savored, an experience unlike any she'd ever had before. Though full dark was nearly upon them, the shops lining the street were still open and doing a brisk trade in all manner of goods, from costly robes and slippers to curios and other oddities. One shop in particular grabbed her attention, and Alexandra hesitated a moment to glimpse inside. The unobtrusive green sign hanging above the front door said RARITIES & ANTIQUITIES, which served to make her linger a moment to peruse the glass. Old books made of paper graced the dark wood shelves, along with old and new bric-a-brac from dozens of worlds.

Alexandra made a mental note to visit the shop the next day, then continued on to the restaurant's entrance in the building next door.

Loran glanced at Banji House's simple white sign. "They serve banji steak," she said, a bit awed by the prospect. "I've never had it."

Alexandra wet her lips and tugged open the door. "I haven't either." The meat had been served at her own wedding feast, but her Uncle Theodore had made clear beforehand that no one could touch it except him and his special guests.

A dour-faced server clad in an elegant black robe greeted them inside the doors, his dark gaze moving down their clothing as if to calculate whether they could afford the meal. "May I be of service to you ladies?" he said in an officious voice.

Alexandra cocked a brow and tilted her head at a haughty angle. Obviously they had passed muster, though she doubted if they would have if they were still wearing their braids. "Two for dinner, if you please."

"Of course."

As he escorted them to a table near the rear of the building, Alexandra's gaze swept over the interior of the restaurant and the many stylish patrons seated at tables they passed. A wide stone staircase dominated the far corner of the restaurant, winding upward to the building's other floors. Were the upper floors another part of the restaurant or something else? She'd yet to see any sign of Flynn on the bottom floor, although she was positive she'd seen him enter. Still, judging from the establishment's ambience of restrained elegance, it was a bit puzzling that he'd come

Jan Zimlich

here at all. The Banji House wasn't exactly the sort of place he might frequent. TraderVor's was more his style.

The server seated them and bowed politely. "Enjoy." With that he was gone.

Loran cleared her throat uneasily. "What do we do now?" she whispered to her mistress. "I've never been in a place like this before."

Alexandra shrugged one shoulder and gave Loran's hand a gentle squeeze to help put her at ease. "Me either, Loran," she said in a whispery voice. "This will be a night of firsts for both of us."

A few seconds later another server appeared, a young woman clad in a plain gray robe. Wordlessly, she placed a tray containing breads and a variety of elk cheese on the table, then proceeded to pour them each a goblet of sparkling blue wine before backing away from the table without a word.

Alexandra took a small sip and relaxed into the comfort of the high-backed chair. "Ummm, Logo wine." She sampled the buttery cheese and soft bread. "I hate to think what the bill for this meal is going to be."

"Too much, I'm sure," Loran said, still intimidated by her costly surroundings. She watched as her mistress's gaze swept back and forth across the restaurant's other patrons, lingering on an occasional table for long seconds. Loran frowned. Alexandra's perusal was too thorough, too purposeful. "Are you going to tell me why you insisted on coming here?" she asked in a hushed tone.

Alexandra blinked and took a larger sip of wine. There were times when she wished Loran didn't know her so well. "While I was on the balcony, I saw Damion . . . Captain Flynn come in here."

A startled flush crawled up Loran's face. "Captain Flynn? Are you certain?" The flush on her face turned scarlet. "I thought they were leaving Janus Three this morning." If Damion Flynn was still here, Tay wouldn't be far away.

"Obviously not, because I saw him on the street." Alexandra didn't tell her about the porter, or her suspicions about what Flynn was up to. Loran worried over things enough as it was. "And yes, I'm very sure it was him." Her voice cracked as she said the words, trailing off to a miserable silence. She wished she'd never seen him on the street. Her suspicions about him and the porter were like knife blades twisting in her gut.

Loran gave her a long, penetrating look. Her mistress's bleak expression told her all she needed to know. She had expected as much ever since Alexandra and Captain Flynn had been trapped alone in the cargo bay for several hours. It also explained why they had seemed to go out of their way to avoid each other since then. The thought had occurred to Loran more than once that the pair were behaving like quarreling lovers. She really wasn't surprised, though. Damion Flynn was a handsome devil, the type she'd always known Alexandra would be drawn to if given the chance.

She would have reached out to Alexandra to offer consolation if she could, but Loran knew her mistress well enough to know that she would never stand for it. "I wonder if Mr. Molvan is still here," Loran pondered aloud.

Before Alexandra could answer, the serving woman returned bearing hot platters of steamed vegetables and banji tenderloins heaped atop dark beds of Andwillian rice. Her mouth watered. "I don't know . . . I saw only Captain Flynn."

She stabbed a piece of meat with her fork and bit into it reverently. The banji steak was even more delicious than she'd imagined it would be. "Oh, that's good." She tasted the fluffy black rice and each of the colorful vegetables in turn, then proceeded to devour the contents of her platter with unfettered zeal.

Loran picked at her food more slowly, anticipation that Tay might actually still be near diminishing her appetite. The costly meal was indeed a rare treat, but she would have been just as happy with simpler fare.

A young man strolled past a nearby table, and Alexandra's fork halted in midair. It was the porter. She smiled to herself and watched the youth proceed up the main staircase with a nonchalant air.

She laid her fork atop her platter slowly and dabbed at her mouth with a fine linen napkin. "I'll be back in a minute, Loran," she said abruptly.

"Where are you going?" Loran asked, hating the petulance in her voice. She was uncomfortable enough as it was. The thought of being left at the table alone was too disquieting. Besides, there was an odd glint in Alexandra's eyes that lifted her hackles.

"I'll be right back . . . I promise." Alexandra bolted from the table before Loran could object further, and sauntered toward the main staircase. She walked as if she knew exactly where she was going. She'd learned long ago that if she acted as if she knew what she was about, most people thought that she did.

She lifted the hem of her new velvet robe and started up the steps, careful to keep her pace ladylike, slow and measured. Once she'd moved out of sight of any casual observers, she quickened her footsteps, racing pell-mell up to the landing.

Alexandra stopped a moment to get her bearings and to smooth her robe back into place. A wide corridor ran toward the front of the building, with three closed doors on either side. She tiptoed past the first door, listening for sounds from within. Nothing at all. But as she neared the second door to her right, she heard the low hum of a conversation inside. Several voices were talking at once, one of them distinctly Damion Flynn's. Congratulating herself, she crept closer to the doorway and listened intently, but could make out little of the words being said.

"He's our new contact?" she heard a woman's voice say; then a man muttered something unintelligible, followed by a distinct "Yes" from Flynn.

A hand clamped onto her shoulder, and Alexandra let out a startled yelp as the grip tightened with painful force.

"What are you doing here?" a sharp voice demanded.

Alexandra swung her head to see who had a death grip on her shoulder. It was the gangly porter, but now he didn't look friendly or at all nonchalant. He didn't even look as young as he had that morning. "I, uh, I was hunting for the women's conveniences." Even to her the excuse sounded lame. "What are *you* doing here?" she demanded in just as sharp a voice. Often the best defense was a strident offense. "I thought you were a porter not a waiter."

Instead of arguing with her as she'd hoped, he simply shoved the door open and pushed her inside before she had a chance to react.

"I picked her up on a security lens listening at the door," he announced to the people in the room.

Five pairs of eyes turned toward the doorway, all registering varying amounts of shock and anger. But one pair, a deep, impenetrable shade of gray, was far more shocked and angry than the others. A red-haired woman grabbed a data disk from atop the short conference table and shoved it inside a pocket, while a small, furtive-looking man snatched a stack of papers from the tabletop and hurriedly left through a back door.

Lucien felt himself flush with rage, concern, and no small amount of desire. For a heartbeat, he hadn't even recognized the beautiful eaves-dropper as his wife. Clad in a stylishly cut robe made of soft blue velvet, Alexandra looked even more fetching than she had that morning when he'd said his good-byes. And her dark hair was finally unbound, cascading down her chest and shoulders in curling tendrils that made him long to reach out and run his fingers through the silky strands. At that moment, he wished for nothing more from life than the opportunity to slowly strip the robe away and bury his face in that glo-rious tumble of hair.

He clenched his hands and jaw tight and nar-rowed his eyes, forcing himself to concentrate on the here and now. His angry gaze stilled on his wayward wife. Was she trying to get them all killed? To get herself killed? "What are you doing here, Alexandra?" he asked harshly.

She met his chilly gaze measure for measure, but inwardly she was quaking—as well as cursing herself for being such a fool. Why had she come up here? The meeting she had unwittingly stum-bled into was obviously clandestine, and that meant it must have something to do with Flynn's double life. She'd been caught trying to eavesdrop on a nest of gunrunners, or worse—rebels. Putting a brave face on it all, she shook free of the porter's grasp and faced Flynn head-on.

"Answer me!" he ordered even more harshly.

She considered her options, few as they were, and finally decided that for once, the complete truth was the best course. "I saw you in the street and came here to find you. I thought you might have designs on my cargo and wanted to know if you were planning on stealing it."

His bark of laughter was short and harsh, mocking. Inwardly he couldn't help but wince. Her instincts obviously matched her intellect, although at this particular moment he wasn't sure she had a brain at all. She was lucky that these people hadn't killed her outright. "This has nothing to do with you, Alexandra, nothing at all."

A chagrined look passed over her features. "I see that now."

Lucien motioned for the others to depart. The meeting had been close to its conclusion anyway. Her interruption had ended it only a minute or two early. "I'll handle this."

The others filed out the second door, glancing over their shoulders to throw suspicious glances Alexandra's way. Only Aton, the porter, refused to budge. He was still standing in the doorway, hands folded across his chest, blocking any escape Alexandra might try to make.

"Aton," Lucien said, jerking his head toward the door. "Go on. Make sure no one followed her here." If Alexandra had been able to hunt him down, someone else could have, too.

Aton stood his ground for another few seconds,

then dipped his head in acknowledgment and moved into the corridor, pulling the door shut behind him.

His anger fading, Lucien massaged his temples wearily. As if he didn't have enough to deal with already. Now he had to worry about the possibility that he might be betrayed by his own wife. "What exactly did you overhear, Alexandra?"

She shrugged. "I heard a woman say, 'He's our new contact'; then you said, 'Yes.'" She threw up her arms in disgust. "That's it. I didn't hear any of your precious secrets . . . whatever they are."

He studied her face for a long time. He didn't think she was lying, but he'd learned the hard way not to underestimate her. Although she didn't understand the meaning of what she'd heard, it was enough to possibly get her killed if she were fool enough to repeat it to the wrong ears. "Is that the truth?" he finally asked.

Alexandra rolled her eyes and sighed. "Of course it is. You're the only reason I came here to begin with. I don't trust you, Flynn. I saw you in the street with that porter . . . Aton, and got suspicious. I thought the two of you might be planning something."

He rubbed at his temples again, feeling guiltier by the second. "Well, the feeling's mutual. I don't trust you either." Her intuition must be working double time. But there was no way he could admit that she'd had him pegged correctly. "For your own sake, don't ever involve yourself in my personal business again, Alexandra," he said in a threatening voice.

A flash of anger stole through her eyes. Who did he think he was? "Don't worry. I have no intention of *involving* myself in your life again." Her lids lowered until her eyes looked like twin blue slashes set into her face. "But you'd best stay out of mine as well."

She pitched her head high and stormed out the door, slamming it behind her, then flounced down the staircase back into the restaurant, her face red with indignation. *The worthless toad.* To think, she'd half convinced herself that she actually cared about him. "Never," she muttered to herself. *Good riddance to bad rubbish.*

Chapter Twelve

An hour later, Alexandra's cheeks were still stained an angry red when Gammon's lift-tube deposited them on the third floor. Without a word to Loran, she marched out of the tube and stalked down the plush corridor to the door to their rooms, jabbing her thumb against the identipad. She tapped her foot impatiently while she waited for the door lock, to release. "Miserable worm," she mumbled to herself, the tempo of her foot increasing to a furious beat. She'd wasted fifty chits and an evening of her life obsessing over Damion Flynn. But she wouldn't do that again. "No sane woman would be fool enough to *involve* herself in his life."

Loran caught up with her angry mistress just as the lock clicked and the door swung wide. "You shouldn't have gone upstairs," she pointed out for the third time since leaving the restaurant. In fact, she'd tried to discuss what had happened several times while they walked along the shore, but Alexandra would have none of it.

"You said that before, Loran, but it's beside the point," Alexandra shot back. "I had my reasons for going up there." She pushed the light pad inside the door and glowered into the darkness when the room remained black. She hit the pad harder, but the lights still didn't come on. "Oh, great, what now?"

"What's the matter?"

"The damn lights won't come on," Alexandra told her, and walked into the sitting room anyway, guided by the soft glow of the city lights creeping through the balcony drapes, as well as a dim rectangle of light flooding in from the hall. She fumbled toward the balcony, bumping her shin on a table as she passed. "Don't close the door until I open the drapes, Loran."

The door slammed shut behind her and the room turned night black.

"Loran!" Alexandra said impatiently.

Strong hands grabbed her from behind, digging painfully into her shoulder blades. Alexandra gasped and flailed wildly as utter darkness suddenly descended over her head, but she managed only to land a jab or two before muscular arms moved downward to trap her hands. She jerked her neck from side to side, trying in vain to dislodge her attacker and the suffocating layer of material that had been thrown over her head.

"Run, Loran!" she managed to yell through the hood, but she heard no answering footsteps, only a muted shout, scuffling, and a thud as something collided with the floor. *Loran?*

A surge of adrenaline rushed through her. At least two assailants had been hiding in their rooms, likely blackguards who'd come to steal the crateful of artifacts, just as she'd feared. And there was only one blackguard brazen enough to attempt such a thing. "Flynn, you worm, I swear I'm going to break your neck!"

A deep bark of laughter cut across the dark, a harsh, unfamiliar sound. "Sorry, lady. You'll have to stand in line. I plan to break Flynn's neck myself."

A chill sped down her spine. The voice and laugh weren't Damion's at all. Alexandra's eyes widened behind the hood and she started kicking backward with all her might. She twisted her arms, hoping desperately that her attackers grip would loosen for a second and she could reach the scabbard strapped to her knee.

She felt a hand move across her face and seized the opportunity by opening her mouth wide and biting down through the cloth into flesh, then clamping her jaws shut with all the strength she could muster.

The man howled in pain and tried to snatch his hand free. Alexandra bit down harder and rammed an elbow into his sternum, eliciting a gasplike explosion of air. She followed with a stomp to his instep, which generated a second, feeble howl.

"You little witch!" the man screeched near her ear. "You'll pay for that!" He tore his hand free and sent her careening in darkness across the room.

Alexandra winced as she slammed into a wall, then slid to the floor, stunned by the sudden impact. She blinked away the pain and floundered for the knife hidden beneath the voluminous robe, but before she could reach it, her assailant had her by the hair and dragged her to her feet.

"You'd best let me go!" Alexandra announced in

her haughtiest voice. "I'm Lady Alexandra Fallon of the Fallon clan, and my uncle won't take kindly to—"

"Shut up, girl," he snapped back. "We know exactly who you are."

That brought her up short. They knew who she was?

"Don't hurt her!" another voice commanded. "You know our orders. Just tie her up and be done with it! We've got to get her and be out of here quick!"

"I'm trying!" Her assailant made short work of binding her hands with a cord, then proceeded with some difficulty to do the same with her kicking feet.

Alexandra's mind raced as she struggled against the cords knotted around her wrists and feet. *Orders? Get her out of here?* She'd thought these men were thieves after the crate, but now she wasn't so sure. It almost sounded as if they had come to steal *her.* "You are making the worst mistake of your life!" she said in a rush. "I order you to take this hood off me and untie me now! If you do, you can just walk out the door and I won't press charges. Otherwise you'll have to deal with Lord Theodore Fallon, and he won't take kindly to your manhandling his beloved niece! He'll carve out your livers and serve them up for dinner—and if he doesn't, I promise you, I will!"

"Gods, shut her up, will you?" the second voice said in exasperation.

"I will!" He tied a strip of cloth around the hood to cover her mouth, knotting it none too gently about the back of her head.

"Roll her up in that carpet and let's get out of here!"

"What about the other one?"

He made a snuffling, snorting sound. "Leave

her. He said she's just a servant. She fainted dead when I grabbed her, anyway."

Alexandra squirmed as she felt herself being lifted into the air, then dumped unceremoniously atop one of the small plush rugs that decorated the sitting room. Who had told her attackers that Loran was her handmaid, and why would that matter to anyone? Her shoulders banged against the floor several times as her bound body was rolled inside the carpet. But at least she knew that Loran had simply fainted instead of being beaten or worse.

The air rushed from her lungs as she and the carpet were tossed over a burly shoulder. Alexandra screamed behind the suffocating hood and gag and twisted her bound legs in order to give the man carrying her a kick with her toes, but he retaliated by sticking his hand up the carpet and pinching her calf, squeezing unmercifully until her body stilled. Her eyes watered.

"Quit that or I'll really hurt you next time," he muttered angrily.

Alexandra redoubled her efforts. She wasn't going to allow them to haul her out of Gammon's like a lump of luggage. Not while she had a breath in her body.

Lucien stepped out of the shadows opposite the elegant hotel and studied the small third-story balcony. The streets of New Chicago were almost deserted now, with only a few stragglers wandering about as they made their way home. Gammon's was equally quiet. No light shone through the draperies of Alexandra's rooms, and the suite looked dark and peacefully still.

He studied the thick vines crawling up the side of the building on either side of the balcony, then turned to Tay. "Think those vines will support our weight?" he whispered to his friend.

Tay grimaced. "I suppose." The very thought of breaking into the suite to steal the artifacts had been bothering him all day, but he knew it had to be done—for all their sakes. Still . . . "You sure this is the only way?"

A tight frown swept across Lucien's brow. Tay didn't sound too happy about what they were about to do. Hell, he didn't like it either, but there was no other way. "Can you come up with a better idea?"

"No, I guess not." Tay sighed raggedly. The fear that Loran might discover his part in this was making him decidedly uneasy. He glanced up at the twin vines snaking up the stucco facade. The vines looked sturdy enough, and the thick, leafy foliage would shield them from casual view as well. "So what's the plan?"

"We each climb a vine to the balcony, break inside, and find the crate; then we unlock the door and sneak the crate downstairs in a lift-tube." Lucien lifted one shoulder in an offhand shrug. "Simple," he said confidently. "They might suspect us, but they'll never know for certain that it was us."

Tay snorted and gave him a disbelieving look. "Simple, sure." Loran would never forgive him if they were caught, and he didn't dare to contemplate what Alexandra might do. "Well, let's get it over with, then."

Lucien glanced both ways down the empty street, then sauntered to the front of the hotel, easing his way through flowering plants and a hedge of meticulously cut bushes to the vine on the left of the building's front door. At a nod from Lucien, Tay did the same, moving as quietly as

Jan Zimlich

his huge body would allow to take up position on the opposite side of the entrance.

After checking the gnarled wood for strength, Lucien started scaling his vine, climbing swiftly toward the distant balcony. Twice he was forced to stop when the twisted wood made a threatening creak, but both times he simply shifted his hand-and footholds and continued on his way, the only casualties of his upward trek a constant stream of flower petals drifting toward the ground.

Simple, just as he'd said.

Beneath him, the front door to Gammon's suddenly swung wide, throwing a bright beam of light across the darkened street. Lucien froze and flattened himself to the wall, while across from him Tay did the same.

Lucien glanced downward as two men scuttled out of the building's entrance, whispering back and forth as one struggled under the weight of a long bundle thrown across his shoulder. As he watched, the bundle seemed to flop around.

His eyes cut to the side, where Tay hung flat against the vine. His friend gave him a mystified look in return, obviously as perplexed as he was by the turn of events.

There was a sudden crash above them as Alexandra's balcony door banged open, startling Lucien so much that he nearly lost his grip. His glance sped upward, and his heart thundered against his ribs at the hair-raising sound of Loran's terrified scream.

Loran rushed to the edge of the balcony and bent over the rail, her once neatly coiffed hair hanging down in limp disarray. "Help! Thieves! Brigands! They've taken my lady!" She screamed again, louder and longer than Lucien thought possible from so small a woman.

The import of her words took root in his mind, twisting around and around his thoughts like the gnarled vine he clung to. Loran was screaming about someone taking her lady, and a man on the street beneath him was carrying a large bundle—one he'd seen move.

Lights flooded the windows of several of Gammon's rooms as Loran's panicked screaming roused tenants from their sleep. "Tay!" Lucien called. "See to Loran!" As Tay began moving upward again, Lucien backtracked down the vine faster than he had risen, unmindful of the risk to his body and limbs. The men below had sprinted off down the darkened street at the sound of Loran's hysterical shrieks, lugging the rolled-up carpet between them.

Lucien hit the ground and started running, his boots striking the pavement in a staccato rhythm that matched the accelerated tempo of his heart. A block from Gammon's, he caught a shadowy glimpse of his quarry rounding a corner, threading their way down a narrow alley that would eventually lead them to New Chicago's landing field and sprawling departure terminal.

The realization caused him to pick up speed. He could hear their footsteps now, hollow clacks that echoed loudly against the pavement. Burdened by the bundle they were trying to carry, Alexandra's kidnappers couldn't run as fast as he could. The alleyway twisted to the right, and Lucien followed as the sound of labored breathing reached his ears.

Lucien smiled darkly as he heard their panicked gasps. *Good.* They knew they were being chased and were getting scared. What they didn't know was that if they had hurt Alexandra, both would soon be very dead.

He was gaining ground now, closing on them

fast. The smaller of the pair glanced over his shoulder, his face pale and frightened in the glow of a passing street lamp. Lucien frowned. The moon-shaped face and compact body were naggingly familiar, but he couldn't remember where he'd seen them before.

Obviously unnerved by the idea of being caught, the round-faced assailant suddenly dropped his end of the rug and took off running, leaving his cohort to struggle with the bundle alone.

The taller of the pair made a feeble attempt to heft the carpet atop his shoulder, seemed to think better of the idea, then dropped it and ran in a different direction from his friend.

Lucien winced as he heard his wife's squirming body hit the street, but he didn't stop, even though he ached to reassure himself that Alexandra was indeed all right. He sprinted after the kidnappers. He had to find out who they were, and the only way to do that was to catch one of the men.

His prey suddenly stumbled and went down hard, muttering an oath as his knees collided with the pavement. Lucien was atop him a split second later, the tip of a stiletto he'd had hidden up his sleeve digging into the center of the man's back. The struggling ended instantly, but the kidnapper's chest was heaving in and out, wheezing for needed air.

He pressed the point of the knife through the material, just deep enough to nick bare skin. "Who are you?" Lucien demanded in a quiet, dangerous tone.

When he received no answer, Lucien flipped him onto his back, the blade moving up to prick at the soft layer of flesh directly over the jugular vein. A street lamp illuminated a long, thin face, so thin it appeared almost pointed. Recognition flared in Lucien's eyes, and he saw that same flash of awareness steal across his quarry's face. Now he remembered where he'd seen the smaller fellow before, and this one, too. And they both obviously knew exactly who *he* was, as well.

"I remember you," Lucien said darkly. "From Thasia. . . . you were in Trader Vor's." The pair had seemed out of place in Vor's, and he had halfway suspected them of being agents then—most probably General Thigg's minions. His grip on his knife tightened, the tip pushing a little deeper into the agent's flesh. "Now suppose we begin again. . . . Who are you and what's your interest in the Fallon girl?"

The man gasped as the blade drew blood, but he remained stubbornly silent, his terrified face white in the glow of the nearby street lamp.

Lucien's eyes thinned and he muttered an oath. Thigg had taught his men well. No matter, though. He used his free hand to rifle through his captive's pockets until he found a small black case containing an identibadge.

He held the case up to the dim light, one eyebrow canting upward as he read the neatly lettered badge. "Well, surprise, surprise . . . Special Agent Drammic Vos . . . Dominion Security Force."

The man's dark eyes grew round and wide, and his face turned even paler than before. "General Thigg will have your head for this, Flynn," he whispered hoarsely.

Lucien smiled grimly. The agents obviously knew him, which meant General Thigg suspected Damion Flynn of something. Unfortunately, that meant Flynn's usefulness had truly come to an end. But other than her brief association with Damion, what role did Alexandra play in Thigg's little game?

"You still haven't explained why you tried to take the girl," Lucien said, slowly dragging the blade across the agent's throat. His lips stretched in a death's-head smile. "Speak up . . . or forever hold your peace."

Vos swallowed hard. "I don't know, I swear!" he said quickly. "The general ordered us to take her, and to do it quietly . . . that's all I know!"

Lucien frowned. If Helford Thigg even suspected Alexandra of being involved with Damion Flynn, he wouldn't hesitate to use her as a pawn, probably to lure him into a trap. She had been seen with him on Thasia, after all, and she had left with him on the *Nightwind*, so such a speculation wasn't beyond plausibility. "*Where* were you supposed to take her?" Lucien demanded.

"To a freighter waiting at the terminal. From there, I don't know!"

There was a muffled sound somewhere behind him, a strangled, low-pitched wail. Lucien risked a quick glance over his shoulder. A short distance down the alleyway, the rug was rolling back and forth, emanating muffled shouts that were both angry and pleading. But the carpet's mad rocking let him know that Alexandra was still breathing, and as mad as a sand-snake that had been poked with a pain-stick.

Lucien suppressed a grin. His darling wife had received a large dose of her own humiliating medicine. Now she knew exactly how it felt to be bound and gagged. Too bad he couldn't remind her of what she'd done to him.

He turned back to the panicked agent, giving him a long, threatening glare, then eased the

218

knife away from his throat. Much as it pained him to do so, he would have to let Vos go, especially if he wanted to tweak Thigg's arrogant nose just a little bit more.

Lucien released a long, exaggerated sigh. "Well, Vos, I'm feeling a touch generous tonight, so I've decided to let you go, but only if you carry a message back to the general for me."

The agent nodded eagerly, relief washing over his lank features. "What's the message?"

He leaned close to the man's face, his eyes cold and threatening, his expression grim. "Tell him the Fallon girl isn't connected to me in any way. My intervention here tonight was purely by accident. Tell him that if he sends someone after her again that Damion Flynn won't come running to save her, but I *will* pay him a little visit someday when he least expects it—just to teach him the perils of meddling in people's lives. Understand?"

He grabbed the wide collar of the agent's robe and twisted the material tight around his neck, squeezing off his circulation for a moment to drive his point home. What he planned was risky in the extreme, but if his ploy worked, Thigg would focus his spy hunt on Damion Flynn, a search that would prove fruitless in the end, because after tonight Damion Flynn would never be seen again. "And I have a special, personal message for you to give him, too . . . just to let him know I mean business."

The agent gaped at his tormentor in terror. His eyes bulged as his airway squeezed shut.

Lucien released the material abruptly and slipped a short-stemmed flower into the agent's collar. Smiling thinly, he adjusted and fussed over the petals and stem. "Tell General Thigg that the Black Rose sends his warmest regards."

Jan Zimlich

Vos's gaze shifted downward. He gawked at the small black rose now adorning his collar, then glanced back up at Flynn in shock. His head seesawed up and down in terrified acknowledgment.

Lucien climbed to his feet, the cold length of metal glinting in his hand. "Then I suggest you get out of here, and you'd best pray to whatever gods you believe in that we never meet again."

The panicked agent scrambled to his feet, gaped in amazement at the man who'd just identified himself as the Black Rose, and bolted down the alley, leaving his identibadge in his haste to flee. Lucien flipped the case into the air, then deposited it in a pocket and sprinted back to free Alexandra from her prison of carpeting.

She was still wailing when he reached her, howling and pitching back and forth across the pavement. Lucien shook his head in amusement, then bent and grabbed the end of the carpet, rolling it out along with his wife. She immediately started squirming to sit up, her muffled wails more urgent and demanding.

Lucien laughed. "My, my, look what I've found lying in the street. Can't leave you for a minute, can I?"

Beneath the hood, Alexandra's eyes widened, then thinned to furious slits. *Flynn.* She'd known in her bones that he was involved in this, known it as surely as she knew that voice and deepthroated laugh.

He used his knife to cut away the strip of material binding her mouth, then slit the black hood from her head and torso, sitting back on his heels when the thick material fell from her sweatdampened face. Her delicate features were reddened and tight with fury, her angry eyes a blazing, arctic blue, hot enough to melt a block of solid stone. She glared at him, and Lucien grinned back. "Did you miss me, love?"

Her eyes flashed. "Cut me loose, Flynn," she said in a clipped, flat tone. "Right now."

He rocked back on his heels, still grinning. "You could at least say thank-you."

Alexandra let loose a string of invectives, colorful curses she'd learned from her clan's soldiers. "Thank you? For having me tied up and dragged across the city? I'll thank you, all right! I'll cut out your black heart and hand-feed it to a pit of worms!"

Lucien shook his head in mock sadness and gave her a pitying look. "That's all the thanks I get for rescuing a damsel in distress? Such ingratitude, and from a noble-born lady at that." He shook his head again. "I'm shocked ... utterly shocked."

Her mouth formed a thin, downward curve. "I know you had a part in this, Flynn, so quit pretending."

His grin faded, and he gave her a small smile instead. "Sorry, love. I can't claim credit for this. If you want to rip out a heart, I suggest you look to the Dominion Security Force instead of me." He pulled the identibadge from his pocket and displayed it for her to see. "Your would-be kidnappers were Security Force agents."

She stared at the badge blankly. "What do you mean?"

"Just what I said. For some reason, General Helford Thigg ordered them to take you, probably because you had the misfortune of being seen with me, so you'd best be on your guard in the coming days. I sort of discouraged them from trying anything like this again, but you never know. If General Thigg and his agents truly think you and I are involved, they might just decide to take the risk, and I won't be around to stop them next time."

She stared at him in suspicion. She didn't know whether to believe him or not, but his explanation made more sense than anything else. Her assailants had been interested in her, not her artifacts. Plus, the border patrol had been hot on his ship's tail just two days ago, and he did have a Security Force identibadge cradled in the palm of his hand. It could be fake, of course, but she really didn't think so.

She frowned. If Flynn was right, her life had gone from bad to worse since meeting him. Now the Dominion Security Force was after her, and suspected her of being involved with a rebel gunrunner. "Are you telling me that they attempted to kidnap me because they thought you and I were . . . well, we were . . ."

"On intimate terms?" he asked bluntly. Her shocked tone made the very notion sound ludicrous.

Her frown deepened, and her face turned scarlet. "Yes, I suppose that's what I mean."

Grinning, Lucien offered his hand and helped her to stand upright, grabbing her forearm to steady her when she faltered. "Don't worry, *Lady* Alexandra, my lips are sealed forever. If I'm captured and tortured, I'll just say that I ravished you when you weren't looking. They can rip out my fingernails one by one and I'll never tell them that you enjoyed being on intimate terms with a lout like me."

Alexandra glowered at him, her cheeks reddening even more. "Oh, shut up, Flynn. That's not what I meant." She jerked her arm free of his grasp and huffed off down the alleyway, hoping she'd chosen the right direction.

"Gammon's is this way," he called after her.

Alexandra cursed under her breath and did an about-face, marching past him in the opposite direction.

"Do you want me to bring your rug?"

She shook her head and kept walking, determined never to lay eyes on that suffocating piece of carpet again. If Gammon's put up a fuss about it, she'd just buy them a new rug, one that didn't smell like the inside of a pair of work boots.

Lucien fell into step beside her, throwing a speculative glance her way every now and then as they exited the alley and turned back onto a main street. Though she was still furious, and a touch more somber than usual, Alexandra appeared to have survived the ordeal relatively unfazed. "Remember what I said about being on your guard the next few days, Alexandra. I'm leaving here tonight, and won't be back. It might be a good time for you and Loran to think about going home. Your clan can protect you."

Her gaze cut toward him sharply. "That's not possible," she said in an emotionless voice. He was truly leaving this time, and she'd probably never see him again. Despite everything, despite knowing what sort of man he was, she still felt a pang of loss to hear him actually say the words.

"Why isn't it possible?"

"I've got my reasons." Deep down, a part of her was gladdened to hear that he was leaving, but another part felt achingly dispirited, as if she were about to lose something of incalculable value.

"What reasons?"

"They're none of your concern, Flynn."

Lucien shrugged and sighed. He'd known she wouldn't do it, but it never hurt to try. "All right, just watch your back." He'd be watching as well, at least for the next few days, but as Vashlen Thackery this time. Hopefully Thigg's efforts to find Damion Flynn would cause his interest in Alexandra to wane.

"We wouldn't have to watch our backs if it weren't for you," Alexandra accused. She snorted in disgust. If it weren't for Flynn, she'd be safe and secure in her bed right now, getting a comfortable night's sleep.

A thought suddenly occurred to her, one that made her heart stop a beat. She frowned. Much as she hated to admit it, if it weren't for Flynn's intervention, she would probably still be rolled up inside that stinking rug as well. Her frown deepened. The last time she'd seen him he'd been upstairs in the Banji House, yet he had appeared from nowhere to effect a timely rescue.

"Flynn," she prodded slowly. "How did you know they'd abducted me?" She watched his sculpted profile from the corner of her eye.

"Happenstance, love." He felt her suspicious gaze burning into the side of his face. "Tay and I just happened to be walking by Gammon's when Loran started screaming. I guess it was just your lucky day."

She chewed on her lower lip thoughtfully as they turned a corner. The discreet sign in front of Gammon's was visible now, glowing a soft blue beneath the haze of the streetlights. "I guess it was," she said quietly, her suspicions growing stronger with each second that passed. She didn't believe in coincidence—or happenstance. What was he up to? Had Flynn or one of his lackeys like that Aton fellow been watching her?

Two shadowy figures were standing on the landing in front of the quiet hotel, the smaller of the pair pacing up and down the flagstone walk leading to the leaded-glass doors.

Loran spotted her mistress and rushed down the walk, her slippers beating quickly against the stones. "Alexandra!" she cried in an anguished voice. "I've been worried sick!" Sobbing, she threw herself at Alexandra, enfolding her mistress in her arms. "What did they do to you?"

Alexandra returned the fierce embrace. "I'm fine, Loran," she said soothingly. "You can stop crying."

Loran pulled back finally, a torrent of fat tears still trailing down her cheeks. "When I woke up and found they'd taken you, I was so terrified I thought I'd lose my mind!" she said, sniffling back a new gush of salty tears. "Thank the gods Tay and Captain Flynn saw movement in our window and decided to climb up to investigate! When I screamed for help they were right beneath the balcony, and Captain Flynn was able to chase after them right away."

Alexandra's shoulders stiffened, and she swung her head in Flynn's direction, watching and waiting for yet another explanation, another lie. "Amazing, isn't it, Loran?" Her gaze burned into him, and her features froze in a sour expression. When would she learn? "Captain Flynn just happened to be scaling the vines to our balcony at the very moment we needed him. I guess it was just my lucky day," she echoed, but this time her voice had an acidic edge.

Lucien hid his wince behind a bland smile, then shot a pointed look at Tay, who lifted his huge shoulders in a sheepish shrug. "Well, I guess Tay and I will be on our way now," he said hastily.

"Not so fast, Flynn." Alexandra stepped so close their toes almost touched, and glared up at him coldly. "Now I understand how you made such a miraculous appearance. You worm, you *were* trying to steal my artifacts, weren't you?" She shook her head slowly, thoroughly disgusted. Besides being a thief, a gunrunner, and probably a spy, the cretin was also a consummate liar.

It was Tay's turn to bear the heat from her laserlike glare. She pitched her head back to glower at him and waggled an accusing finger. "And you!" Alexandra ranted, "I thought you were different from your captain! At least I hoped you were!"

Tay shrugged again and dipped his head slightly, refusing to meet her angry eyes. An awkward silence descended over the walkway.

Loran's bewildered glance shifted back and forth from one to the other. "Alexandra, what are you talking about?" she finally asked, her voice rising on a pleading note. Her mistress was wrong—had to be. "They saved your life!"

Alexandra gave her arm a gentle squeeze. "Happenstance, Loran . . . ? They were here to steal from me."

A new rush of tears stung Loran's eyes, and she stared at Tay with a wounded expression. "Is that true?" She asked quietly.

When his friend didn't respond, Lucien cleared his throat noisily and grabbed him by the elbow. "Come on, Tay. I think it's time for us to leave—before we're accused of an even worse perfidy for doing a good deed."

"Good-bye, Flynn," Alexandra snapped back harshly. "I hope I never see you again."

A grim, almost regretful look rode across his features. "Don't worry. Damion Flynn is out of your life as of tonight."

Alexandra watched in silence as they walked down the center of the street, following their movements until they turned the next corner and disappeared from view. Loran started bawling, and Alexandra blew out a troubled sigh, castigating herself soundly for ever getting involved with someone like Flynn. The Dominion was teeming with available men, millions upon millions of prospective mates who were far more suitable for her than Damion Flynn. Suitable and acceptable men who didn't thieve, run guns, or engage in some other skulduggery. Why couldn't she have been attracted to one of them? Or to her own husband, for that matter?

Chapter Thirteen

Afternoon sunlight streamed through the open balcony doors, flooding the sitting room with a haze of glaring white. The soft draperies weaved and danced on a current of air, a warm, salty breeze blowing inland from the distant reaches of the Janusian sea.

Her mood little improved from the night before, Alexandra dabbed at her sweatdampened face and tossed the parchment she'd been scribbling on aside, the heat sapping her ability to concentrate on the work at hand.

Her papers and books were strewn about the rectangular sitting room, littering every tabletop and parts of the tiled floor. The artifacts were in a state of disarray as well, perched or lying upon tables and chairs, grouped according to subject and size.

She tapped the scriber against her palm and cast a critical eye on the three-faced figurine resting on the table before her. Three distinct male faces stared back at her from the stone carving, each different, unique, and exquisitely perfect. Yet there was something vaguely familiar about all three faces, some little oddity that kept twining around the edges of her thoughts, a nagging sensation that she was missing something vitally important. One little tidbit of information that would solve the puzzle of the carvings' creators, allowing all of the archaeological pieces to fall magically into place.

She made a puzzled face. It wasn't just that single figurine that was bothering her, either. Almost every piece of statuary she'd retrieved from the Denault cave bore the three-sided images, all of humanlike men and women, both young and old, some handsome or breathtakingly beautiful, others plain or apallingly ugly. And yet that strange sense of familiarity remained firmly entrenched in her mind, refusing to be cast aside as speculative drivel.

The hieroglyphic lettering on the small disks she'd found had been nagging at her as well. Even with the aid of the parchment primer she'd found in the cave, she'd been able to decipher only five of the strange symbols so far. Unless she'd taken a mental wrong turn somewhere, a small row of the triangles, circles, and vertical squiggles found on one side of every disk translated into four letters of the alien alphabet, forming what she thought could be a single word.

"Arulia . . ." Alexandra muttered aloud, pronouncing the lettering in what she hoped was the proper sequence. She sighed and squeezed her lids shut wearily. *Arulia.* What did it mean? Was it a person or an object? A place?

She rapped the scriber against the wooden table in frustration. She was truly beginning to understand her father's obsession with solving the mystery, the single-minded determination that had led him to eschew the traditional life of a Fallon lord and leave Lochlain—as well as his young daughter—for years at a time while he scoured space for proof of his theories.

But had such an obsession been worth the price *she'd* been forced to pay? While Jarron Fallon was off gallivanting around the quadrant on quests for his personal grail, she, in turn, had been left to grow to adulthood in Theodore's draconian household, nurtured more by Loran and other clan servants than by her indifferent uncles and aunts. Even old Fomus, the keep's crippled guardian, had been more of a parent to her than her own father had been.

Perhaps that was why she had fallen so readily into the trap of continuing her father's work. She'd never really had a life of her own, never been allowed such a thing, and by fleeing from Lochlain to carry out her promise to him, she had severed her links with her family, husband, and past—all to forge a new life, excusing her behavior with the pretext that she did so in her father's name.

That particular thought brought a guilty grimace to her face. Tossing the scriber atop her notes, she climbed to her feet abruptly and stretched the kinks from her shoulders and neck. She would continue her quest for answers for as long as it took, but she would no longer allow herself to obsess over the research as Jarron Fallon had done. It was her life, after all, not his, and she wouldn't waste the rest of her days trying to set right all the wrongs in his life—and her own.

She glanced through the balcony doors, her gaze resting on the white-capped mountain peaks shimmering beneath a brilliant sun. *So beautiful.*

But since her arrival, she'd barely given the breathtaking scenery a second glance. Except for her brief sojourn around the city rolled inside the carpet, she'd hardly left the suite, and she'd seen very little of New Chicago or Janus Three. But that was one wrong she intended to immediately set right.

She didn't have to worry about Loran for a while. Her handmaid had left hours before to explore the city, a solo venture made at Alexandra's suggestion to take her mind off the events of the previous night. Loran had grown dispirited since learning that Tay Molvan was nothing but a common thief, depressed and weepy to the point that Alexandra had grown increasingly concerned.

Just thinking about what had transpired infuriated her all over again. "Lying worm," she mumbled hotly. At least Flynn was gone now, permanently out of her life, unless he'd lied about that, too. "Wouldn't surprise me," she mumbled again.

After smoothing her rumpled robe and unbound hair, Alexandra armed the proximity sensors she'd installed in the suite not long after first light. If anyone was fool enough to break into her suite again, the silent alarm would seal the rooms and bring both her and the city guard on the run.

Satisfied that her artifacts and notes would be safe for a while, Alexandra closed off the balcony and exited the suite, double-checking the alarm sensors once more just to be sure. She locked the door, then turned toward the lift-tube, flinching in surprise when she collided with a man leaving the next room.

Alexandra took a half step back, flustered by

the close physical contact with a complete stranger. They had bumped chest to chest, hard enough to push air from her lungs.

"Forgive me," he said in a deep, silky voice. "I had no idea you were there."

"Don't worry . . . I'm quite all right." Alexandra found herself gazing into a pair of deep gray eyes, a smoky, cloudy hue that seemed alive with intelligence and a glint of humor. And the gentle face that went with those eyes was equally appealing. Strong and aristocratic, yet surprisingly warm, it was as if its courtly, middle-aged owner had rejected much of the pomp and pretense of his noble birth to live life on his own terms. Rich brown hair framed his aristocratic features, the straight strands tied at the nape of his neck in a tidy queue that trailed down the back of a richly tailored brocade robe. "No permanent harm done," she managed to croak, nonplussed by his proximity and stately appearance.

Smiling warmly, he eased back toward his own door to give her more room, then bent his tall frame into a fluid bow, one hand cradling the head of an intricately wrought walking stick. "I would never intentionally put a frown on such an exquisitely beautiful face."

Normally, she would have snorted in distaste at such an obvious come-on, but she resisted that urge. Instead, she found herself smiling back at him. "You're very kind." Even more peculiar, her thoughts suddenly careened to Damion Flynn, the last place in the universe that she wanted them to go. Why couldn't she exorcise the cretin from her mind?

"Now I've managed to make it worse," he said regretfully.

A wave of heat rode up Alexandra's cheekbones, so hot she knew immediately that her

The Black Rose

blush was embarrassingly deep. "Sorry." She forbade herself to think about Flynn again. Ever. "If I frowned, you weren't the cause."

"Thank goodness." The smile he gave her was one of relief mixed with curiosity. "Since we do seem to be neighbors for a while, allow me to introduce myself." A warm smile slanted over his features again. "I am Lord Vashlen Thackery, and you are . . . ?"

"Alexandra," she offered in return. "Lady Alexandra Fallon." Now why had she gone and done that? She hardly ever admitted to having any sort of title, had never cared a whit about that sort of thing.

He immediately took her arm in his and placed a soft kiss on the back of her hand. "I'm delighted to meet you, Lady Fallon," he murmured against her flesh.

The feathery touch of his lips against her skin sent a tiny spark of heat spiraling up her arm. Her blush deepened. What was the matter with her? The man was an utter stranger. Attractive, yes, but no more so than millions of other men his age.

She gently pulled her hand free as soon as it was polite to do so. "Delighted to make your acquaintance as well, Lord Thackery," she said in return, berating herself as soon as the inane response slipped from her mouth. "Well, I'll be on my way now." She fled to the lift-tube and jammed her palm against the control pad.

As the doors whispered open, she hurried inside, intending to put a good measure of distance between herself and the disarming nobleman, but he followed her into the clear tube before the doors could close.

"Hope you don't mind that I joined you," he said smoothly. He moved into the center of the

233

Jan Zimlich

small tube, so close to her that his shoulder brushed against her unbraided hair.

"Of course not." A nervous lump gathered itself in her throat. What the devil was wrong with her? Why was this man's presence affecting her so?

"Fallon, you said?" he asked in an offhand tone. "You wouldn't be related to Lord Theodore Fallon, would you?"

A sensation akin to dread left a hollow feeling in the pit of her stomach. Why couldn't she have simply lied about her name? "Yes." She cleared the nervous lump from her throat. "Theodore is my uncle. Do you know him?" she asked, praying that he didn't.

An amused smile played over his lips. "Our paths have crossed once or twice." He watched her intently. "Quite a colorful character, I must say."

Alexandra winced inwardly. *Colorful. What an understatement.* But at least the man was polite enough not to elaborate on the subject. "He's that, all right."

The tube doors reopened and Alexandra exited, but the nobleman stood fast beside her, only inches from her shoulder as she made her way out the entry hall to Gammon's front landing.

A niggle of uncertainty ran through her. Lord Thackery appeared to be sticking to her like glue, and she wasn't quite certain how she felt about that. He was charming, engaging, and very attractive, yet some part of her was whispering a warning that something was amiss.

He studied her out of the corner of his eye as she paused on the landing, obviously unsure how to rid herself of his company. "It's such a beautiful afternoon for a stroll, and I loathe the notion of walking about the city alone." A plaintive note

234

crept into his voice. "Would you do me the honor of accompanying me, Lady Fallon? My mother was born here, so I've spent a great deal of time on Janus Three through the years. I would make an excellent guide."

She hesitated before answering, her curious gaze moving slowly over his features and plumbing the depths of his eyes. She saw no hidden motives or machinations in his gaze, only the warmth, kindness, and sincerity of a lonely man with a generous soul. Yet deep inside her, a tiny alarm was still sounding, telling her that Vashlen Thackery wasn't exactly what he seemed. "Sorry, but I have plans already," she said in a firm tone of voice. It was true, in a way. "Another time, perhaps?"

The nobleman lifted his shoulders in a regretful shrug. "Of course." He dipped his head politely. "Another time."

Alexandra watched him stroll off toward the seafront, the end of his walking stick tapping softly against the pavement. The stick appeared to be for effect, a fanciful accoutrement to his impeccably tailored robe. Though his gait was slow and carefully measured, he didn't look to be handicapped in any way, and he certainly didn't walk with the mincing gait often seen among the nobility. The only word that came to mind to describe him was . . . *intriguing*.

So why had her senses shrieked such a determined warning?

She continued to stare at the retreating lord for long seconds, a rueful half smile touching one corner of her mouth. It had been overreaction, obviously, one inspired by her experience with Flynn's chicanery. If Lord Thackery bothered to ask her for a stroll again, she would definitely agree. Anything to keep her mind from straying to that other rogue.

She turned in the opposite direction and headed immediately for the small shop she'd spied the day before. The small green sign still hung suspended above the glass door, proclaiming in neat lettering the shop's name, Rarities & Antiquities, as well as the proprietor's name, Kimren Baldasian.

Alexandra pushed the door open and stepped inside, hesitating a moment to give her eyes time to adjust to the store's diffuse light. The telltale scent of aging books and old wood flowed over her, a heavenly combination that made her eager to explore.

Row after row of rich wood shelving lined the back of the small store, each brimming with ancient tomes and newer handcrafted objects carefully displayed in order to pique a buyer's interest. Glass cases containing more valuable items sat here and there throughout the store, some containing only a single artifact, others displaying objects of interest from dozens of worlds.

An aged man appeared from behind a curio case, his thatch of unruly white hair a perfect counterbalance to his stark black robe. He folded his hands in front of his chest and dropped his head in a polite bow of greeting. "May I be of service, my lady?"

"Are you Mr. Baldasian?" she asked, remembering the name on the sign.

His head dipped again. "Please call me Kimren, my lady."

She smiled. "Only if you stop calling me 'my lady . . . ' Call me Alexandra instead."

"With pleasure. Now, what can I do for you?"

"I really just wanted to wander about a bit,

maybe find an artifact or book to add to my collections."

A spark of curiosity flared in his pale blue eyes. "I must admit, it isn't very often that a young lady such as yourself admits to an interest in antiquities. Are you a student of history, perhaps?"

"I suppose I am."

"Earth history or more recent?"

"Dominion history—archeology mostly, and I collect antique statuary." Her gaze skimmed over several glass cases and moved on. The objects they contained were mostly bric-a-brac, small carvings and everyday items with no historical significance. A few even looked to be brand-new. She glanced longingly at the leather-bound books lining the shelves. "Although I must admit I've acquired a taste for Old Earth's literature as well."

"Ah." The old man scuttled toward a small display case near the back of the store. "Perhaps I can satisfy at least one of your cravings today." He unsealed the glass and removed a small stone bowl, placing it gently atop the display case for her to see. "This is one of my favorite early Dominion pieces. Exquisitely wrought, isn't it?"

Alexandra stared, a sudden chill touching the back of her neck. She had to bite her tongue to suppress an excited gasp. The circular bowl was no more than eight inches in circumference, crafted from a single piece of pale green marble, with four intricately wrought faces carved in bas-relief around the edges of the bowl. Each of the marble faces was unique—and hauntingly familiar.

The tempo of her heart increased to a fever pitch. Although the form, age, and style of the bowl were far different from the statuary in her rooms, she was certain that they were related artistically. "May I touch it?" She asked quietly, trying desperately to keep her voice from quaking with excitement.

"Of course."

She trailed her fingertips across the small faces, then along the bowl's rim, searching in vain for any flaws or markings that might unmask the piece as an artistic fraud. The only flaw that she found was a small singed spot inside the bowl itself, as if the object had been scorched long ago. "Do you have reliable information on the bowl's age and origin?"

"I had it dated last year, as a matter of fact . . . very early Dominion. About two thousand years, ago around the time of the Great Clan Wars."

"And it's origin?" Alexandra asked curiously.

"Why, it's Janusian, of course." He sighed and gestured toward the other cases with a gnarled hand. "Most of my older artifacts are. The cost of imported antiquities has risen so much in the past few years that I can afford to bring in off-world artifacts only on consignment, and even then, only rarely."

Alexandra continued to stare at the bowl, her fingers freezing in place. The bowl was only two thousand years old, and Janusian? "Any idea where it was found?"

"On the shoreline about fifty miles south of here, buried in the sand. I purchased it from the father of the youth who discovered it."

She pulled her hand away slowly, more puzzled than ever. Janus Three was hundreds of light-years from the Denault system, yet she was certain that the objects found in both places were artistically similar. And the burn on the bowl caused her thoughts to veer instinctively to the scorched craters pockmarking the surface of the Denault moon. Two dissimilar places and events distanced by time and light-years of space. How could they possibly be artistionally connected? Unless . . .

"Kimren, do you know if any similar artifacts have been found here?"

The old man lifted a bent shoulder. "By accident occasionally, but only along the shorelines and underwater. The problem is, by order of the Dominion government most of the Janusian seas were declared off-limits to exploration and development not long after the Great Clan Wars."

A bewildered frown edged across her brow. "Why?"

"To give the oceans time to recover ecologically. Janus Three was the site of one of the largest battles of the Clan Wars, you know. It's said that the damage was so extensive that most of the seawater on the planet boiled away."

Alexandra gaped at him in astonishment. She'd never heard or read anything about a pitched clan battle being fought on Janus Three. "Gods," she whispered. "I never knew."

Kimren made his way to a shelf at the back of the shop, searching the rows until he found a slender leather-bound tome. "Time has a way of making even the historians forget, I'm afraid." He blew at a bit of dust clinging to the top off the yellowed pages, then handed the old textbook to her. "It's a book on Janusian history, a reprint of a text first published seventeen hundred years ago. This copy is only a few hundred years old, but it's far more accurate and complete than many modern history texts."

"Thank you." She cradled the book in her hands. "How much do I owe you—for the book and the bowl?" She smiled ruefully. "I'm afraid I can't leave here without that beautiful bowl. That is, if the price is right."

Jan Zimlich

Kimren nodded shortly, obviously pleased. "Two hundred chits for the bowl, and twenty-five for the book."

She wanted the bowl badly, and wasn't going to waste her time or his quibbling over chits. "Done." She dipped into a pocket of her robe and extracted a small velvet pouch, counting out the required amount from the hoard secreted inside.

The old man smiled and dropped the triangular coins into a pocket. "I'll wrap them up for you," he said quickly, and whisked the bowl from atop the case, making short work of sealing it and the history book inside an insulated packet. A hand strap appeared at the top of the package as he handed the case to Alexandra. "The packet is heavily insulated and shatterproof. Your bowl will be quite safe."

"Thank you, Kimren." Alexandra snugged the strap over her hand. "I enjoyed meeting you."

"My pleasure."

She waved a final good-bye and headed back onto the street, unable to prevent a triumphant grin. With the bowl and the book perhaps she could start to make sense of the archaeological puzzle, or at least find a trail of crumbs that would lead her to new clues.

Suddenly eager to share the news of her find, she bypassed he accomodations and set off toward the seaside in hopes of finding Loran. But even if she didn't find her handmaid, she would have a chance to take a good, hard look at the sandy shoreline that had entombed the marble bowl for so many centuries.

As she pressed her way down the crowded street toward the shore, she spotted a man to her right who seemed to be throwing one too many covert glances her way. Was he following her?

Alexandra slowed instantly, Flynn's words of the night before coming back to haunt her thoughts.

Watch your back, he warned.

She stared hard as the man slowed to match her pace. Bearded and grubby, he was clad in a cheap brown robe that looked as if it hadn't been cleaned in weeks. So did he, for that matter. Alexandra grimaced in distaste. He had the rumpled sullen look of the louts she'd caught watching her the day she arrived. He didn't look like a Security Force agent, although she wasn't too sure how they were supposed to look—especially since she'd never gotten a gander of her would-be kidnappers the night before.

Her grip on the hand strap of her bag tightened. A thief, maybe? One who'd seen her exit the shop and now scurried after her to steal her package? Whoever he was, he would get a rude awakening, because she was far more prepared this time. Her free hand moved to the pocket where she'd secreted a second knife, her fingers wrapping slowly about its hilt.

"Lady Fallon, what a lovely surprise!" a familiar voice said.

Alexandra's head snapped left, her startled gaze settling briefly on the nobleman who'd appeared at her elbow. Vashlen Thackery. Then her eyes cut back right, but the ruffian was nowhere to be found. She glanced at the surrounding pedestrians and shopfronts but found no trace of him. Thackery had obviously scared him off.

"Is something amiss?" the nobleman asked in concern. "You look worried."

She heaved out a relieved breath, her tight grip on her knife beginning to relax. "No, nothing's wrong. I am just preoccupied."

He motioned toward the packet strapped to her wrist. "I see you've done a bit of shopping."

"A bit." She smiled briefly and kept walking, glancing his way every now and again. A tiny worm of suspicion edged through her thoughts. Where had he come from so suddenly? "I hate to ask, but were you following me, Lord Thackery?"

He grinned disarmingly. "I suppose I was, in a way. I spied you leaving a shop a few blocks back and hurried to catch up." His grin broadened. "In case you haven't figured it out already, I don't respond very well to the word *no*, Lady Fallon. And I certainly don't intend to let the opportunity to spend a few hours with a beautiful woman slip away from me again."

She stared at him for a long moment, then laughed. "You're very blunt, Lord Thackery. I'm not quite certain how to take you."

"Vash. My friends call me Vash, and you may take me any way you wish." A playful, suggestive look darkened the gray of his eyes.

Alexandra laughed again. "All right, Vash, but you may get far more than you bargained for. We Fallons have an odious reputation, you know."

"No worse than my own reputation, I'm sure." He linked his arm through hers. "May I call you Alexandra?"

"Of course."

"Then where to, Alexandra?"

"The seashore . . . and a restaurant. I'm utterly famished."

"Your wish is my command, fair lady."

Chapter Fourteen

Bright shades of pink and violet spilled across the horizon as the setting sun eased toward twilight, the sky and sea merging in a breathtaking display of color. The snowcapped mountain peaks turned gray, then blue as the sunset deepened, throwing shadows and brilliant hues across the darkening landscape.

Alexandra leaned back in her chair and watched the transformation raptly, awed by the simple beauty of the dying sun. From her vantage point atop the restaurant's seaside terrace, she had a glorious view.

She took a sip of the sweet Janusian tea and gave her dinner companion a contented smile. Vashlen Thackery had turned out to be an expert guide and a charming host, so much so that she had begun to regret that their time together was swiftly coming to an end. The hours she had spent with him had been filled with camaraderie

Jan Zimlich

and lively conversation, a surprisingly pleasant interlude with a very attractive man. And the meal of sea clams, fresh maize, and eel tips they'd shared had sated her to the point where she found it difficult to move. All in all, it had been a very enjoyable afternoon.

She sighed happily and propped her elbows on the tabletop, the evening wind curling through her unbound hair. "We may be here for a while, Vash. I'm so full I don't think I can get out of this chair, much less back to the hotel."

Lucien fought off an amused smile as he glanced at the scraps and empty shells scattered across her plate. She'd eaten all of her meal and part of his. His wife definitely liked to eat, something he hadn't realized before now. "I'm in no rush," he told her hastily. "We can stay here until you recover, however long that takes. I'm enjoying the companionship."

And he *was* enjoying her company, far more than he ever dreamed possible. As Damion Flynn he had sparred and warred with her, and made wildly passionate love, but they had never truly been on what could be called friendly terms. They'd never really gotten to know each other without her viperish tongue, circumstance, or his own lust interfering in some way. But Lord Thackery seemed to have brought out a hidden side of Alexandra that he hadn't suspected, a warm and witty woman who loved to laugh and tease unmercifully. It was almost as if Alexandra Fallon possessed as many identities as he did, diverse and unexpected traits that would suddenly rise to the forefront of her personality and startle him anew.

He grinned at her across the table and took a drink of wine, careful to lift his glass with a lordly

244

air. One thing was certain—he would never grow bored with his ravishing wife.

Alexandra lifted a questioning brow. His secretive smile was almost gleeful. "What?"

"Nothing. I'm just glad I had an opportunity to spend some time with you." As Vashlen Thackery, he felt far freer to express his true thoughts to her. "I've thoroughly enjoyed getting to know you."

On impulse, she reached across the table and squeezed his hand. "Me, too, Vash. You're kind and endearingly sweet, and I've enjoyed every minute I've spent with you this afternoon."

A pained look passed over his features. "Endearingly sweet? Does that mean I'm doomed never to be more than a friend?"

It was her turn to look pained. "Vash, I told you, I just extricated myself from one relationship. Besides, we've known each other for only a day. By tomorrow you might despise the sight of me."

He laughed at the notion. Since their wedding night, his attraction to her had increased with each second spent in her company. "That's not very likely. I already feel as if I've known you much more than a single day."

A troubled shadow suddenly moved through her eyes. Oddly, she felt as if she had known him far longer than a day as well. It was as if she really knew him, as if she knew already how his tall, elegant body would look without his brocade robe, how his hands and lips would feel upon her skin. Even his laugh sounded hauntingly familiar, as if she had heard it somewhere before.

She shook her head slightly to ward off the peculiar thoughts. The sense of familiarity left her feeling rather as though she'd experienced déjà vu, as though her body and mind were trying to tell her that she'd known Vashlen Thackery long before now.

Her eyes wandered over his face, searching his aristocratic features for a clue of some kind, an explanation for the odd sensation. But her perusal revealed nothing more than a kindly nobleman slipping gracefully into middle age. He was forty-five, maybe fifty, but no more. Though a touch of silver-gray glinted at his temples, and a fine webbing of lines had begun to weave around his eyes, Vash still looked youthful, his shoulders and torso hinting of a powerful body that defied his years. He would always be handsome, she decided, even as a very old and settled man.

Her gaze moved to his eyes and stilled, the odd sensation of recognition returning full-force. There was something about his eyes that bothered her most of all—not the shape or size, exactly, or anything that she could truly grasp on to. Perhaps it was simply the hue. Their deep gray reminded her of the peculiar color of Damion's eyes. "Are you sure we haven't met somewhere before, Vash?" she asked suddenly. "You said you'd met my Uncle Theodore—could it have been on Lochlain?"

He cleared his throat noisily, then drained his wineglass. Was it simply instinct that prompted her question, he wondered, or had she seen something to make her suspicious? He focused his concentration on his appearance, making certain that he hadn't slipped in any way. He'd slipped up before, and could easily do so again if he didn't concentrate. "No, not that I can recall." He shook his head slowly. "And I know I'd remember if I'd ever been to Lochlain."

"Hmmm." She pursed her lips and frowned. "I

can't seem to shake the feeling that we already know each other."

"Perhaps we knew each other in a previous life," he said with a mischievous smile, hoping to divert her to another subject. Any subject. "Kindred souls destined to reunite."

She laughed and lifted one shoulder, trying to shrug off her eerie feeling of recognition. Yet for some reason, it continued to nag at her thoughts. "Maybe you're right."

He heard the uncertainty in her voice and decided to move the conversation on without delay. "You never did tell me what you bought earlier," he said, pointing to the package sitting on the side of the table.

"A marvelous antique bowl and a book on Janusian history. Quite a find. Both date back to the Great Clan Wars."

He blinked once but kept any other reaction carefully held in check. Inwardly, he cursed. "Ah," he said feebly. Of all the subjects he could have brought up, he'd had to choose her package.

She gave him a probing look. "Didn't you say that your mother was from Janus Three?" she asked intently.

"Yes." He cleared his throat again. The conversation was shifting to even more treacherous ground.

"Did she ever mention anything about a battle being fought here? Supposedly one of the greatest of the Clan Wars? I was told that the seas were even permanently closed to development to allow them to recover ecologically."

"She might have mentioned it once," he told her carefully. "But I don't remember many details." Forced back the pain. "She's been dead quite a while now."

Alexandra saw the flicker of grief in his eyes and could have kicked herself. "Vash, I'm so sorry. I wouldn't have mentioned your mother if I'd known."

He smiled slowly, though a trace of sadness touched his expression. "It's all right."

An awkward lull descended over their conversation. During the brief respite, Alexandra's thoughts kept returning to the tantalizing tidbits of Janusian history that she'd learned from Kimren. "Perhaps you can explain something to me about this planet's history that I don't quite understand. . . . If the clans were fighting over Janus Three, how did the planet end up being nonaligned? That doesn't make sense. Surely there was a clan that would have claimed this planet and star system as spoils of war."

He lifted his hands impotently. A pleasant afternoon was quickly spiraling into something else entirely. "Who knows? I'm not a student of history, I'm afraid." Gods, not only did he still need to make another try for her artifacts, he had to get rid of that book, too. The last thing she needed to be doing was reading about Janusian history. Her mind was too quick, too thorough and well trained. Even if she didn't quite know it yet, Alexandra was on the verge of putting it all together and ferreting out the truth.

Alexandra noticed Vash shifting uncomfortably in his chair, as if he were growing antsy. Perhaps her company was beginning to wear a bit thin. "Well, I think I can make it back to Gammon's now," she announced, and climbed to her feet, her fingers wrapping tightly about the strap on her package. "Thank you for a lovely afternoon, Vash. I can find my own way back if you have something else to do."

He tossed a small pile of chits atop the table and shook his head. "Something better than spending time with you?" He offered her his arm. "We'll take the long way back and see some of the sights. There's a wonderful little museum on a side street not far from here. They're open late, and their twenty-first-century Old Earth collection is one of the best I've ever seen. They even have a few articles of period clothing, as well as a vid of the first Mars base."

"Sounds wonderful," Alexandra said with an enthusiastic grin. She would get to spend another hour or so with him, an encouraging sign. "I love Earth history, even though we're so far removed from there I sometimes feel as if my ancestors were some sort of aliens."

He lifted a brow in amusement. "I've felt the same way at times."

They strolled along the beach boardwalk in companionable silence, pausing every now and again as Lucien pointed out examples of local flora and architecture. As they turned down a narrow side street near the museum, the soft gray of twilight melted away, replaced by a dim near-dark that heralded the arrival of the Janusian night. Streetlights flared to life along the quiet side street, and the flow of pedestrians thinned substantially, decreasing to a trickle of movement near the museum's canopied entrance.

Down the street, a small knot of men suddenly stepped from the shadows, casting furtive glances their way. Lucien stiffened instinctively. Four of them, all with cold, calculating eyes. Although they lacked the lithe grace of most trained agents, there was something threatening about their presence, especially so close on the heels of the events of the previous night. He watched intently as they formed a loose line, whispering and shifting like nervous scum-moles caught in a stream of light.

He lifted the tip of his cane from the pavement, holding it at the ready a few inches shy of his knee. Beside him, he felt Alexandra's arm tighten against his. "Don't be alarmed," he murmured to her, "but I do believe that our afternoon is about to come to an unpleasant end."

Her eyes narrowed and her fingers found the dagger tucked inside her pocket. The bearded, rumpled man on the far right was the same ruffian she'd caught following her earlier in the day. This time he'd brought along a few friends. "So I see." Her hand closed about the hilt of the throwing knife.

"Be prepared to run," he told her quickly. "I think they plan to rush us all at once."

"Don't worry over me, Vash," she whispered back, hoping the nobleman would be able to handle himself when the time came. For a split second, she found herself wishing that it was Damion at her side. "I'm a Fallon, remember?"

He shot her a startled look. She had eased her arm free of his and slipped the strap of her package up to the crook of her elbow, then shifted her body into a fighting stance. His wife didn't lack courage. From the determined look on her face, he knew she would attempt to take them all on single-handedly if need be.

There was a tiny sound somewhere behind them, like loose gravel ticking against the pavement. Lucien straightened and squared his shoulders. More than four, then. "Not good odds, even for a Fallon," he told her softly. He signaled with his eyes that there were more behind them. "Discretion is oftentimes the better part of valor."

A chill sped down her spine as she caught his meaning. The odds had definitely gotten worse.

The bearded ruffian edged toward them suddenly, but was careful to keep his distance. He eyed the elegantly dressed nobleman disdainfully. "We don't have any quarrel with you, your lordship!" he called out tersely. "Just turn around and go back the way you came! It's her we want." He shuffled in a pocket and produced a crumpled piece of parchment. "I knew it was her the first time I laid eyes on her, even with that hair." He held up a two-dimensional picture of a young woman with dark braids. "All we want is the girl . . . and the bounty."

Alexandra's jaw fell as she stared at her own image, one taken on Lochlain a couple of years before. *Theodore*. It had to be. Who else would have posted a reward? "Bounty? What are you talking about?"

The man refused to meet her startled eyes. Instead he fixed his watchful gaze on the nobleman at her side. "She's blood kin of the Fallon warlord, a runaway with a bounty on her head that we aim to collect. So just leave now and you won't get hurt. I swear by all that's holy in the universe that we won't harm the girl. Lord Fallon would skin us alive if we did."

Lucien stared in amazement. Had Theodore Fallon lost his wits? By posting a bounty on Alexandra's head, he had ensured that every greedy blackguard in the quadrant would be hot on her heels. "And if I refuse?"

He scratched at his beard for a moment, thinking. "Well, I guess we could cut you in for a share," he said slowly. The others muttered and nodded. "Or we could just kill you . . . your choice."

Jan Zimlich

"How much would my cut be?" Lucien asked in a matter-of-fact voice.

Alexandra's jaw fell further, and her cheeks turned a hot, flaming red. Was she doomed to be attracted to despicable men?

The man eyed his companions and wiped his palms on his grubby robe. "A thousand chits?"

"Hmmm," Lucien said, stalling for a time, "that's a lot of chits. Let me think about it a moment."

"Vash!" Alexandra said in a hiss. She didn't know who she wanted to throttle more, him or the guy with the bristly beard.

"Decide now! You're either with us or against us."

Lucien flashed Alexandra a rueful smile, but his eyes conveyed a different message entirely. "Discretion, remember?" he muttered beneath his breath.

As he turned back to face the group's self-appointed leader, his muscles tensed in readiness and his fingers tightened around the head of his walking stick. He shook his head and sighed. "Well, then, I guess I'll have to say that I'm against you."

Before anyone had a chance to react, Lucien lunged right and pivoted, using the cane to whack the head and shoulders of a burly man stationed behind him. A second attacker bulled toward him and flailed at him with meaty fists, but Lucien ducked low and kicked him in the gut before any of his wild punches found their mark. The man went down hard, clutching his stomach and heaving for air.

"Get them!" the bearded one shouted. The remaining four charged in a group, swarming toward them in a frenzy of movement and angry shouts.

Alexandra released her throwing knife before the first had a chance to reach her, eliciting an outraged howl from the cretin who'd been following her. A circle of red bloomed on his shoulder. Still bellowing, he fell to his knees, clawing desperately at the blade imbedded in his blood-soaked flesh. She jerked her hem up and slipped a second knife free of its scabbard, quickly raising her arm in preparation to throw.

Lucien belayed her from throwing again by grabbing hold of her arm. "Run!" he shouted, spinning her in a half-circle when she balked.

"Vash!" Alexandra tried to pull free but he refused to let go. "We can take them!"

"Forget it!" The pair he'd felled were on their feet now and obviously planned to rejoin the fray. He started running toward the end of the street, half dragging his reluctant wife by the arm. A hand reached out to snatch at her flying hair, but Lucien batted it away.

Alexandra gave up trying to pull herself free and sped along beside him, her thin shoes rapping across the cobbled pavement. They were not exactly the shoes to wear when running from a band of brigands. Behind her she could hear the rapid pounding of boot heels, grunts of exertion, and breathy curses. She lengthened her stride to pull abreast of Vash, lifting her hem high to keep from tripping over her cumbersome robe.

They barreled around a corner onto a main thoroughfare, startled pedestrians and shopfronts rushing past in a swirling kaleidoscope of light and color. Lucien's fingers clamped tight about her hand as he ran headlong down the busy street, dodging and weaving his way through knots of people blocking their path.

He threw a quick look over his shoulder, wincing as her heavy package smashed against his hip.

"They still there?" Alexandra called between gasps for air.

He nodded and kept running. Four were still chasing them, their faces sweaty and grimly determined, but they didn't appear to have gained much ground.

Lucien tugged on Alexandra's hand, directing her toward the right, deeper into the press of pedestrians clogging the busy street. He bypassed a street vendor's cart, narrowly avoiding a collision with a couple who'd paused on the curb. Gammon's was only a short distance away now, a defensible refuge where Alexandra could be deposited until he made arrangements to keep her safe.

A woman screamed somewhere behind them, the sound followed by a crash and a man's angry shout. He glanced back for a split second. A woman had been knocked to the ground, and the vendor's cart turned upside down, spilling sweetmeats and delicate pastries across the pavement. Lucien grinned. The outraged vendor and several witnesses were taking revenge for the carnage on two of the assailants, throttling the unfortunate pair with fists, feet, and damaged pastries.

A small scad-about appeared in the sky above, its emergency lights and City guard emblem winking a rapid blue in the evening light. The craft skimmed over rooftops, then hovered over the street, directing a search beam downward into the throng of people below.

Lucien glanced back in time to see their remaining pursuers slink away from the searchlight and vanish into the milling crowd. He slowed his breakneck pace to a jog as they rounded another corner and Gammon's came into view. "They're gone," he announced in satisfaction. "They ran off when the searchlight hit them."

Struggling to regain her breath, Alexandra slowed to match his pace, grateful that the pursuit had come to an end. She was winded, her feet hurt abominably, and sweat had dampened her face, robe, and hair. "Thank goodness," she said breathlessly. "I don't know how much longer I could have kept running."

She brushed a wild strand of hair from her face and glanced at her companion, frowning in consternation when she realized that he wasn't winded at all. In fact, he seemed fairly unmoved by what had happened. The man was obviously in excellent shape, especially for someone in middle age, while she, in turn, felt shaky from the run and was still pulling in great gulps of air.

As they walked up the short steps to Gammon's and through the door-way, she was grateful for his steadying arm. "You're not even sweating, Vash," she said in a wondering voice. He didn't look at all like a man who'd just been chased for blocks by a gaggle of bounty hunters. "You must keep yourself in good shape." Although his body appeared to be softening with maturity, he obviously had the strength and physical endurance of a much younger man.

He smiled sheepishly and kept her moving until they were inside the lift-tube, rising to the third floor. "I try." She was giving him a suspicious, slant-eyed look, as if she knew something was not quite right but couldn't lay a finger on the cause. He decided to subvert any further questions by asking some himself. "Now, my dear, would you be so kind as to explain what that set-to was all about?"

It was her turn to look sheepish. "I'm so sorry,

Vash." She dipped her head, unable to meet his probing gaze. Through no fault of his own, the nobleman had been caught in a treacherous web spun by her uncle, one that could have injured them both or possibly cost them their lives. He deserved the truth. If not for him, she would probably be on her way back to Lochlain right now. "I ran away from an arranged marriage," she told him in a resigned voice. "Obviously that didn't sit very well with my Uncle Theodore." She shook her head wearily. She should have suspected, should have realized the warlord might respond in such a fashion. "I didn't know . . . I never dreamed he'd be furious enough to post a bounty on my head."

The lift-tube popped open and Lucien stepped into the hallway, careful to check in both directions before guiding her toward the door of her room. He gave her a stern look, but inwardly he was gleeful. Her uncle had unwittingly given him the means to accomplish his goals. "You do realize that today was not the end of it, don't you? As long as you're here, they'll keep coming after you, probably in larger numbers as word of the bounty spreads. By now they probably know where you're staying. They'll be watching—and waiting. You won't be able to poke your head out your door without them trying to grab you again."

Alexandra bit down on her tongue. He was right, of course, but the realization left a sour taste in her mouth. She sighed deeply. What was she going to do? Remaining in New Chicago was out of the question now.

"As I see it you have two choices," Lucien said confidently. "You can either go back to Lochlain willingly, or you can leave with me tomorrow, just as soon as I can make arrangements to get you out of the city secretly. I have an oceanfront villa

on the opposite side of the planet at my disposal."
It was a workable solution. His mischievous wife
and the artifacts would be securely tucked away
on a secluded estate owned by one of his alter
egos, safely out of reach of spies, cutthroats, and
General Thigg. He could deposit her and Loran
there, spend a day or so with them, then leave for
Primus exactly as planned, secure in the knowledge that they would remain out of harm's way. "I
think you'll be safe there, at least for a while."

She frowned and shook her head firmly. "No,
Vash. You're far too generous for your own good.
I appreciate the offer, but my troubles aren't your
concern."

He waved a dismissive hand. "I won't take no
for an answer, Alexandra. And generosity has
nothing to do with my offer." He smiled slowly.
That was true enough. "My motivation is outrageously self-serving. It would give me a perfectly
acceptable excuse to spend a few days in the
company of a beautiful but unhappily married
woman with a price on her head. Quite an adventure for a staid and lackluster fellow like me."

Alexandra couldn't help but laugh. "*Staid* and
lackluster aren't terms I'd use to describe you,
Vash."

He could see in her eyes that she was vacillating. "So how would you describe me, then?"

"Irrepressible, perhaps." She gazed at him
fondly. In less than a day Vash had managed to
attach himself to her heart. Even if she never saw
him again, she would always consider him a
friend.

He pinched his features into a mock frown.
"Well, I suppose I can live with irrepressible." His
eyes held hers captive for a long moment. "Say
yes, Alexandra . . . please?"

"All right, Vash." She gave a small smile. "I'll

Jan Zimlich

go." Vashlen Thackery was a true gentleman: generous, polite, and kind to a fault. The sort of man every woman should dream of marrying, but rarely did. "How can I ever repay you?"

He gazed at her for a long moment. She was staring up at him with those sultry jewel-blue eyes, a gentle smile tilting the edges of her lush mouth. His heart rate accelerated in a familiar way. The look on her face was tender, inviting, and maddeningly sweet.

On impulse he kissed her, unable to resist the temptation her closeness engendered. His arms moved around her shoulders, drawing her closer, and his mouth captured hers in a slow and sensual kiss. For a moment she remained perfectly still, not responding to his touch or unexpected kiss. But then she suddenly sighed against his lips and moved closer, winding her own arms about his.

Alexandra lost herself in the moment, in the wild surge of desire that sprang to life inside her. Blood pounded through her veins in response to the feel of his hands, the touch of his lips, a brief joining of flesh that left her breathless for more. She felt as if she were falling, slipping backward in time to an encounter that had already occurred, a moment that had already burned itself into a memory she wanted to savor again and again.

Time lost all meaning as the past intruded on the present, the memory so sharp and passionately vivid that reality shifted and she was in Damion's arms once again. It was his strong arms wrapped around her, his lips crushed against hers. She could taste him on her tongue, feel his flesh beneath her fingertips, even smell his salty, stormy scent in the air around her.

"Damion. . . ." she said softly against his cheek.

Damion? His heart stilled and he cracked a single lid open in surprise, surveying her flushed features from beneath the safety of his lashes. But there was no outward sign that she'd used that name intentionally. On some instinctual level did she recognize him for who he was, what he was? Or even more startling—was it possible that she actually cared for Damion Flynn?

Alexandra suddenly realized what she'd said, and her lids flew open in horror. She broke the heated kiss slowly, pulling back to disentangle herself from Vash's embrace and her memories of Damion Flynn. Her cheeks flooded with embarrassed color. Had Vash heard her whisper another man's name? How had she done such a foolish, hurtful thing?

She stared at him for a long second, trying to determine whether he'd heard her odious blunder or not. But his face was devoid of clues save for a quick glint of some odd emotion that flickered briefly in the depths of his eyes. She became curious. Had it been amusement she'd seen there, or something else entirely? Satisfaction, perhaps? She shook herself mentally. That didn't make sense at all. "Vash . . . I'm sorry. I'm just not ready—"

He lifted a finger to her lips. "Shhh. There's no need to explain. I shouldn't have kissed you. That was presumptuous of me." His lips brushed the top of her forehead in a wordless apology. "Pack your things. We'll talk more once you're safely out of New Chicago."

She held his gaze for long seconds. A lesser man would have walked away in the face of such humiliation. "Are you sure, Vash?"

"Very. Now go. I need to make some arrangements."

She thumbed the identipad and the door

clicked open. "I'll be ready within the hour." She half turned toward the open door—and froze in place. A stranger was standing inside her suite, a black-clad man with dark hair and flint-hard eyes. Behind him she caught a glimpse of Loran seated in a wing chair, her eyes round and her face a frightened shade of white. Tears were trembling in the handmaid's eyes, and she was clutching her arms about her chest like a protective shield. Flanking her were several stone-faced soldiers, all armed with pulse rifles.

Instinctively, Alexandra took a half step backward, her heels bumping against the toes of her companion's shoes.

Lucien's body went rigid with shock as he glanced over the top of her head, but he kept his face expressionless.

"Ah, Lady Fallon." Helford Thigg cocked a brow in amusement, his chilly gaze locking on the woman's heart-shaped face, which had lost any trace of color when she opened the door. "How good of you to finally join us. And I see you've brought along a friend." His appraising glance flicked once over her companion's aristocratic face and costly robe, then returned to the woman, lingering overlong on her sensual curves. Somehow he hadn't expected her to be so utterly striking, or to be in the company of a nettlesome nobleman. No matter. He would dispense with her gentleman friend soon enough. "Pictures and holos don't do you justice, Lady Fallon. You're a very beautiful woman."

Alexandra finally found her voice. "Who are you?" she managed to croak, swallowing the lump of fear rising in her throat. Golden chevrons glinted on his stiff collar, surrounding the chilling letters *DSF*.

"Forgive me." He dipped his head slightly, then surreptitiously straightened the crisp hem of his dark uniform tunic. "I am General Helford Thigg, commander of the Dominion Security Force." He waved a dismissive hand in Loran's direction. "I've been patiently waiting for you to return for several hours now. I fear poor Miss Pahs was growing quite bored with my company."

Lucien cleared his throat, his thoughts racing over possible reasons for Thigg's presence. One thing was certain: it didn't bode well for either of them, but there didn't seem to be much he could do about it. He would just have to bluster through the encounter as Vashlen Thackery. "Would you be so kind as to explain your presence in Lady Fallon's suite . . . General?" he asked in a lordly, demanding voice.

A thin smile lifted the ends of Thigg's meticulously groomed mustache. Why did these nobles always think they could intimidate him with their rank and lineage? "And you are . . . ?" he asked disdainfully.

"Lord Vashlen Thackery."

"Ah . . . Thackery." His dark gaze sharpened. The odor of rebellion clung to the Thackery line, nothing he had ever been able to prove, but the stench was there nonetheless. Which brought to mind an interesting question—why was Thackery in New Chicago with, of all people, Alexandra Fallon? "I'm afraid that I'm here to place Lady Fallon under arrest."

Alexandra gasped. "What?" Distantly, she could hear the sound of Loran's sniffles and muted sobs.

Lucien glowered and placed his hands on her shoulders protectively. He tilted his chin high and glared at Thigg. "On what charge?"

The general motioned to his men, who lifted their pulse guns to a threatening angle. "High treason."

Loran's quiet weeping transformed into hiccuping howls.

Anger suffused Alexandra's face. "Treason!" She had thought this was simply more of Theodore's doings, but now . . . A shiver of dread spiraled down her spine. "That's outrageous!" she sputtered furiously.

Lucien clamped his fingers on her shoulders to offer reassurance and to still her now-trembling limbs. "There must be some mistake," he said haughtily, but the sinking feeling in the pit of his stomach told him there wasn't. Thigg was far bolder than he had ever dreamed—bolder and more determined. "What could this young woman have possibly done to warrant such a ludicrous charge?"

The general tucked his hands behind his back and smiled unctuously. "Consorting with known traitors, for a start."

Alexandra scowled and broke free of the hands gripping her shoulder blades. She stalked inside the suite, infuriated by the charge and the soldiers' presence in her rooms. "That's ridiculous! I'm a loyalist. I don't consort with traitors!" Even as she said the words an image of Damion flashed through her mind. She had all but called him a traitor herself.

Thigg pulled a small black flower free of his pocket and twirled the stem around and around in his fingers. He lifted the flower to his nose, sniffed, then began twirling it again. "Not even the Black Rose?" he asked in a quiet, probing tone.

She laughed incredulously, a nervous, high-pitched sound that filled the sitting room, then faded into a sudden, anxious silence. Her worried gaze moved over the tiny black rose trapped beneath his fingers. "Is this some sort of joke?" she asked in a belligerent voice. "If so, I'm not at all amused."

"Is the name Damion Flynn more familiar?"

All trace of color drained from her face, and a cold, deathly chill crept through her blood. Her eyes slowly widened at the accusation. No, it wasn't possible, she told herself. Damion Flynn was many things—a smuggler, gunrunner, rebel sympathizer, and all-around treacherous toad—but he wasn't—couldn't be—the Black Rose.

A doubt touched her suddenly, and she shook her head to try to stop the frown of uncertainty that had come unbidden to her lips. In truth, what did she really know about Damion? He was secretive, attended covert meetings like the one she'd stumbled on at the restaurant, and he was an admitted gunrunner and rebel sympathizer.

Her gaze fell on the dark blossom in Thigg's hand once again. Given Damion's checkered history, it wasn't much of a leap to suspect that he might actually be the infamous spy.

"I don't believe it," she said forcefully, though inwardly she was reeling from the possibility and its implications. "You're wrong . . . I know you are. Damion Flynn is not the Black Rose!"

Thigg shook his head reproachfully. "Your defense of him is admirable, my dear, but misplaced." He lifted the flower almost reverently. "Flynn himself placed this flower in the lapel of one of my agents, here in New Chicago. He then freely admitted to being the Black Rose. Of course you didn't hear his admission of guilt. You were otherwise engaged with a roll of carpet, I'm told."

Her mouth fell. She'd accused Damion of engineering her kidnapping when he'd actually been telling the truth. It really had been Security Force agents all along. Thigg's agents. "Why, you sniveling excuse for a human being! How dare you send those creatures to kidnap me!"

Thigg felt nothing but disgust for her outrage. If the Black Rose hadn't intervened, this woman would have already been on Primus by now, without all this fuss and bother. "You forget yourself, Lady Fallon." He tossed the flower to the floor and squared his shoulders, his fingers moving to adjust the golden insignia at the top of his collar. "I dare whatever I want."

"Now see here!" Lucien interjected as he moved to stand at Alexandra's side. The situation was swiftly spiraling out of control. The Black Rose and Thigg had been playing a high-stakes game of cat and mouse for years now, a standoff with no hope of a resolution while he remained free and Thigg was in power. But Alexandra's involvement had changed the rules. It was suddenly win or lose, with no further allowance for a draw. Lucien had no intention of losing, either Alexandra or the endgame. "I must protest your treatment of Lady Fallon."

The general's flinty eyes flickered on him briefly. "Stay out of this, Lord Thackery. Her situation doesn't concern you."

"Of course it does. I consider Lady Fallon a friend." His hand found hers and squeezed reassuringly. "It's my duty as a lord and a gentleman to protect her honor, which you, sir, have gone out of your way to impugn."

Thigg ignored the nobleman's blathering and fixed his gaze on the woman. "Do you deny knowing Damion Flynn?"

She glanced at Vash helplessly, then at Loran, whose terrified sobbing grew louder each time

Thigg opened his mouth. "I simply booked passage on a ship owned by a man named Damion Flynn." She glared at the pompous little general. "Does that make me a traitor?"

He smiled thinly. "Under Dominion law, quite frankly, yes. Or if not a traitor, then an abettor at the very least. That is a matter for a tribunal to decide."

Alexandra closed her eyes for a moment and shook her head in disbelief. This was an absolute nightmare, one from which she feared she would never awake. Her eyes reopened suddenly, then narrowed, lit from within by anger at the injustice of it all. Just knowing Damion Flynn had automatically subjected her to a charge of treason? If it was true, then the law was wrong and unjust. "This is an outrage, General. Under such a law, anyone who has ever *met* Damion Flynn is subject to arrest!"

"True," Thigg announced in a self-satisfied tone. It was a law he'd forced upon the High Council himself. They had resisted for a while, but they'd eventually caved in to his demands, hoping the suspension of individual rights would help preserve their positions and way of life. "Rest assured, Lady Fallon, you won't be the archduke's only guest in the fortress dungeons. We've rounded up quite a few of Flynn's compatriots in the past day. Janus Three was absolutely teeming with them. By week's end the majority will be in custody, perhaps even Flynn himself."

Alexandra curled her lips in disdain. "Flynn is gone—permanently—he told me himself that he was leaving. Beyond that, I don't know anything, so why waste your time on me?"

The general gave her a pitying look. Was the girl dull-witted? "First of all, I'd be a fool to believe you, and I assure you, I am not a fool.

Jan Zimlich

Secondly, my dear, my agents would have been searching for you even without your involvement with Flynn." The tips of his mustache lifted briefly. "Or is your memory so short that you've forgotten the little matter of the husband you left behind? Your little escapade has caused quite a stir among the Fallons and Charbonneaus, and jeopardized a political alliance the archduke considers to be of vital interest to the Dominion."

Alexandra bit down on her tongue until she felt a warm trickle of blood. She was either going to be imprisoned for treason, returned to her husband—or both.

"I must admit Lord Theodore made the job of finding you much easier," Thigg went on. "Although you and Flynn led my agents on a merry chase, once word of your uncle's bounty began to spread, my people simply sat back and waited for the bounty hunters to track you down. It didn't take long at all."

She dipped her head and stared at the tiled floor vacantly. What would become of her now? No one would dare come to her aid. She had alienated her clan, the Charbonneaus, her husband, and most frightening of all, the Dominion archduke.

"Don't be so downhearted, Lady Fallon," Thigg said in a cheerful tone. "You and I are going to have plenty of time to get to know each other in the coming days." The general motioned to his men. "I took the liberty of having your handmaid pack your things. I fear you'll be needing them. . . . Maybe they'll be all you have for quite a while."

Lucien eased in front of Alexandra reflexively. "General, I protest! You cannot simply walk into this woman's suite and take her into custody without formal charges and a writ of arrest!"

266

The barrels of two pulse rifles were leveled at his midsection.

Thigg shook his head in mock sadness. "Don't be foolish, Lord Thackery. If you interfere, my men will kill you where you stand. Save all that aristocratic bravado for someone who deserves it."

She applied firm pressure to his hand. "Vash, don't," she whispered quietly. "There's no use."

Lucien felt frustrated—and guilty. It was his fault she was in this predicament, and he couldn't do a thing to extricate her now without exposing himself. For a second he considered doing just that, but then he rejected the idea. If he was taken into custody now, Alexandra would appear guiltier than before. Worse, he would place untold lives at risk if Thigg had him chemically interrogated and extorted the truth. And if he were taken or killed, who would help free Alexandra from the archduke's dungeon?

"Alexandra . . ." His hands curled into impotent fists. Thigg would interrogate her endlessly; his reputation for cruelty to prisoners was legendary.

She shook her head vehemently and blinked back a glaze of tears. "No, please, stay out of this. Just see to Loran's welfare for me . . . and I suppose you should notify my clan of my arrest." She'd done nothing to endear herself to Theodore of late, but he was still blood kin. Maybe he would help.

"Lord Fallon has already been notified of your impending arrest," Thigg interjected, smiling icily. "There's the little matter of the bounty, you see. I may have been doing my duty by taking you into custody, but there's no reason why I can't line my robe with Fallon chits as well. I also sent a message to Clan Charbonneau. I'm sure your dear husband will be overjoyed to know you're alive and well . . . so overjoyed that he might pay a reward himself out of gratitude that this sordid business has finally come to an end."

Lucien forced himself not to react, but for a fraction of a second, he had to fight not to laugh. Thigg's own words had presented him with a plan of action.

At a nod from the general, one of the soldiers hefted Alexandra's stuffed carryall and headed toward the door.

She glanced wildly at the shipping crate standing to the side, her artifacts and research papers packed inside. "Wait! My artifacts and notes . . . please, I need them." She appealed to Thigg with her eyes, beseeching him to at least grant her this small favor.

He considered for a moment, then decided it would be in his best interest to capitulate. She would be indebted to him if he agreed to her request, and it was such a minor request. Besides, the woman had magnificent eyes and breasts, so enthralling that he felt an unexpected thrill of desire whenever he happened to gaze her way. Having her in his debt might prove advantageous for him in the end. He enjoyed the company of a woman far more when she didn't feel obliged to scream.

Thigg nodded brusquely. "Very well. Bring her crate." He appropriated the package she was carrying and threw it to a guard. "And this."

He grabbed Alexandra's forearm and directed her to the door, his grip growing more insistent when she tried to resist. "Come, along, Lady Fallon. My ship is waiting."

Loran leaped to her feet, the tears running fast and free down her damp cheeks. "Alexandra!"

The Black Rose

She glanced back at her friend. "Take care of yourself, Loran," she said in a shaky voice.

Loran nodded and bit back a frightened sob. Then she whispered, "I'll find someone to help you, Alexandra. Don't you worry."

Numb with shock, Alexandra gazed helplessly at Vash as Thigg forced her out the door. "Promise you'll take care of Loran for me, Vash," she said over her shoulder. "Don't send her back to Lochlain, under any circumstances!"

Grim faced, Lucien stared after her, his throat tightening with despair. "Don't lose hope, Alexandra, no matter what. . . . I'll do whatever I can to get you out of this. I swear it."

The door slammed and she was gone. A thick, heavy silence descended over the room, punctuated by a renewed burst of sobbing from Loran.

Lucien started pacing back and forth across the sitting room, his eyes turning a searing, pain-filled gray. It was his fault this had happened. His fault. He should never have agreed that she could buy her way onto his ship on Thasia. If not for him, she would be perfectly safe, but his pride and desire to retaliate had caused him to throw caution to the wind. He knew better than to involve himself in any woman's life for more than a few stolen hours—that was why he'd never wanted to be married—but Alexandra had some-how managed to burrow her way into his heart. He'd let his guard down and suddenly found that he didn't want them to be apart. He'd even plotted and schemed to remain an integral part of her life. Now they were both paying a steep, steep price.

His nails dug into the flesh of his palms. Thigg was using Alexandra as a pawn; he thought she would lure Damion Flynn into the merciless arms of waiting troops. He still had an edge, though, because it didn't have to be Damion who took the general's bait. But if he hoped to free his wife from Thigg's clutches, he had to work fast. And he *would* free her. He would not allow his wife to suffer the same fate as his mother, not while he had a breath in his body.

He paced to the balcony window, pulling the drapes back in time to see Thigg shove his wife inside a military scad-about. He watched as the vehicle lifted into the air, hovered for a moment, then sped off into the darkness, coasting over rooftops toward New Chicago's landing field.

His mouth flattened with grim determination as he turned back to Loran, who was still standing in the middle of the room, weeping quietly and staring at the closed door in shock.

"Loran," he said, and gently touched her arm to get her attention. "Don't worry: we'll get her back. Now calm down and tell me where you want to go. I'll make whatever arrangements you want. If you want to stay in New Chicago, that's fine. Just tell me now because I'm going to have to leave here soon. I also need you to tell me exactly what the general and his men said while you were alone with them . . . every word. Did any of them mention the planet Primus, or say anything else about Damion Flynn?"

She frowned and turned toward the unfamiliar nobleman, blinking away a lake of unshed tears. "Who *are* you?" Her mouth trembled, and she stared at him in confusion. "I know what Alexandra said, but I've never laid eyes on you before." A trace of suspicion crept into her voice. The man had come out of nowhere—just as that ogre Thigg had closed in on Alexandra. Had it been coincidence, or something more ominous? She took several steps away from him. "I'm not sure I trust you."

Loran edged toward her cloak, which was thrown over the back of a chair. She scrubbed at her cheeks with the back of a hand, her back stiffening with resolve. It was time to quit weeping and wailing and do something to help. If Alexandra was ever to be saved, she knew of only one man who had the will and the means to accomplish such a feat.

Puzzled, Lucien watched as she settled the heavy cloak over her shoulders, then started for the door. "Loran," he called. "Where do you think you're going?"

She paused but didn't turn back, snuffling back a few errant tears threatening to spill down her cheeks. "I'm sure you mean well, my lord," she said shortly, but the suspicion in her voice belied her words. "But there's only one man who can possibly help Alexandra now, and I'm going to try to find him."

He cleared his throat nervously. "Who?"

"Damion Flynn." She walked toward the door. She would try the landing field first. If she found Damion, she'd also find Tay.

"Wait! What makes you so sure this Flynn fellow will help you?" he asked in a rush, hoping to delay her departure for a moment or so.

Loran grasped the door handle. "Because I know he loves her. He'll do whatever he can to help."

He closed his eyes a moment, and his heart squeezed tight with despair. *Because I know he loves her,* Loran had said. Could that be true? Had Loran simply spoken words that he refused to admit to himself?

Yes, his mind suddenly whispered. He did love

her, with a depth and burning passion that he'd long thought himself incapable of, had refused to believe possible. Alexandra was in his blood, had been since the moment they met, an integral part of himself that he couldn't live without—wouldn't live without. He had to save her, no matter the risk.

He reopened his eyes slowly, mulling over the consequences of what he was about to do. Loran was about to leave, and that was something he couldn't allow, especially if she planned on wandering about in search of the nonexistent Flynn. Desperate times called for desperate measures, though, and right then, he was desperate to save his wife. "Loran," he called softly. "Turn around."

Impatient to be on her way, Loran turned back to the nobleman.

"There's no need to go out hunting Damion Flynn."

She blinked once, her round face turning a ghostly shade of white. Her mouth opened wide and closed, as if she were trying desperately to produce a scream. Then her eyes rolled back and she slid bonelessly to the floor.

Lucien sighed. Somehow he'd known that would happen.

Chapter Fifteen

As cells went, Alexandra supposed hers wasn't too bad, although she didn't exactly have any past experience to base her conclusion on.

For perhaps the thousandth time, she paced the confines of the bland little room. Ten steps to the side, ten steps back, the same exact distance no matter which direction she went. The high ceiling and thick stone walls were cut from smooth gray granite cubes. The only openings were the exit and a tiny doorway leading to the cell's conveniences.

No windows relieved the sterile sameness; no exterior view broke the monotony of the featureless room. Since her arrival on Primus six meals ago, she had seen nothing save the inside of this one little room.

For furnishings, she had only a narrow metal cot and a single wooden chair. The armored exit door was cut from granite also, heavy, thick, and immovable, with a small slot through which all her meals were served. Not much different from her spartan rooms on Lochlain, now that she thought about it. Of course Theodore had rarely locked her in. At least her cell was clean, though, not dire and dank like dungeons of lore.

She threw herself upon her cot in frustration and stared at the ceiling, counting the joints between the granite blocks. Had she been here two days now? Without a chronometer or the rise and fall of the sun, she wasn't sure if three meals equaled an entire day. Probably, but even though she was fed regularly, hunger never seemed far away. By the time her meals were served, her stomach was rumbling in complaint.

Alexandra glared at the ceiling, fantasizing about doing terrible things to General Thigg. The man was odious, a greedy speck of offal that she'd love to step on with her shoe. He was a liar, too, as evidenced by the fact that she hadn't been allowed to keep her crate and notes, despite his assurances that she could. Her precious artifacts had been confiscated as soon as they landed on Primus, taken away by a scarlet-clad platoon of soldiers, supposedly on orders from the Dominion archduke. Worse, they'd searched her and taken her last knife, too.

All she had left was the history book, which still lay atop the chair mostly unread. She'd skimmed the pages here and there, but didn't really have the stomach to give the tome a serious read. It was hard to concentrate on much of anything with her future so up in the air.

Since she'd been locked in the cell, the thought lay heavy on her mind that she might be left to rot here within the confines of this one small room for the rest of her natural days. Alone. Forgotten. Left to wither away by angry relatives and the husband she'd betrayed. She winced at the ceiling. She couldn't really blame them if they did.

Her tightfisted uncle would never intervene, especially since Thigg planned on submitting a claim for the reward. He would be furious, and leave her in prison to retaliate for the loss of his chits. And her husband . . . what would he want to do to her after their wedding night?

Her only hope was that Vash might actually be able to help, although she doubted very much that his efforts would lead anywhere. Besides, he owed her nothing. They were merely acquaintances, nothing more. Why should he involve himself in a muddle such as this?

That left only Damion to come to her aid—the man General Thigg insisted was the Black Rose, a wild notion that she still considered ludicrous. And yet . . .

She snorted loudly. Damion Flynn, a notorious spy? She mulled over her time with him, the little oddities that she'd noticed but not connected with anything, like the small picture hanging on a wall of his cabin—a painting of a single black rose. She hadn't given the painting more than a passing thought when she'd spotted it, but it seemed rather damning now. And she'd gotten the distinct impression that Damion was in charge of the meeting she'd stumbled upon above the restaurant. In charge of Aton, the porter, too.

The memories caused her heart to skip a sudden beat. It wasn't impossible, she decided. He'd surprised her before—about many things. In truth, he could very well be the Black Rose, the rebel spy reportedly able to move about the government's halls of power with seeming impunity, the man thought responsible for the escapes of hundreds of political prisoners throughout the Dominion.

She sighed deeply. Now she'd become a political prisoner herself, locked away in the bowels of the archduke's fortress for an interminable period of time. Would the Black Rose attempt to free *her?* And if Damion was indeed the Black Rose, did he even know that Thigg had taken her prisoner? Would it matter to him if he did?

Her eyes filled with the salty sting of unshed tears. Why should he care what happened to her? He was gone now, out of her life, just as she wanted, had even demanded. Yet a tiny part of her still clung desperately to a thread of hope. Despite everything, she had sensed that Damion might actually care about her, at least a tiny bit. He wouldn't leave her in a cell to rot away.

"He'll come for me," she whispered to herself. "I know he will."

The heavy door pushed inward and Alexandra bolted upright, her heart thundering with anticipation. But her hopes plummeted when General Thigg strolled through the open door.

Her mouth turned down. He looked the same as he had in New Chicago, with his crisp black uniform, slicked-back hair, and perfect moustache. Not a crease or wrinkle marked his tunic and pleated trousers: not a single hair had the temerity to be out of place. It was as if his clothing and hair always did exactly what he commanded.

The corners of her mouth turned down even more. There was something peculiar about her enemy that made the blood chill in her veins.

"Oh, it's you." She gave him a nasty look.

Thigg squared his shoulders until they were ramrod straight. "There will come a day when you'll be overjoyed to see my face."

She blew out a disgusted breath. "Not very likely."

The general clasped his hands behind his back. It was time to begin Lady Fallon's reeducation in earnest. "Not even if mine is the only face you ever see again?"

"Especially then."

"Such bravado, especially from a prisoner yet to be questioned." His gaze flicked downward, moving over the curve of her breasts, hovering for a moment on the ripe swell visible under the fabric of her robe. "I'm going to enjoy interrogating you."

Her eyes stilled on his face. She hadn't liked his tone of voice or the threat conveyed by his words. She didn't like the way he kept glancing down at her chest, either. There was something obsessive and lecherous about it. About him. "So what are you waiting for?" she said belligerently. "Interrogate me and be done with it."

A flush rose on his neck and face. "I'll question you when I'm good and ready!" he snapped. "Just be glad I haven't done it yet!"

She lifted a brow. Thigg had been nearly salivating at the prospect of interrogating her, so why the delay?

"Your time will be here soon enough," he said sharply, "and I assure you, it won't be a pleasant experience. I'm quite an expert in inflicting pain, so I always get what I want in the end." The flush in his face receded as he pulled his emotions back under control. "We've simply captured so many of your compatriots lately that our time schedule's a bit bogged down."

Alexandra climbed from the narrow cot and faced him head-on. "I'm beginning to understand why my 'Compatriots' all seem to have such a low opinion of you, General. It's no wonder the rebels have made so many gains in the past year. You and your ego have done more to advance their

277

cause than anything the Black Rose could have possibly done."

For a fraction of a second, she thought he might hit her. Instead his hand snaked out and latched on to her hair, his fingers winding around the long black strands. She stared back at him coolly.

"I warned you before," he said in a low, ugly tone, "don't mistake me for a fool." His fingers wrapped tighter, coiling toward her scalp and making her flinch. "Very soon the rebels and their cause will be relegated to a worthless chapter of history . . . Flynn included. Don't sacrifice yourself needlessly."

Alexandra winced but said nothing, did nothing more to reveal that she wanted to cry out or scream. She continued to stare at him coolly, refusing to give him the satisfaction of yowling in pain. For the first time she began to understand why the rebels had sacrificed everything—family, friends, their very lives—to try to topple a sadistic despot like Thigg from his lofty position of power. Humanity deserved more. "I'm not sacrificing myself. I don't know anything about the rebels or the Black Rose that you'd be interested in."

He eased the painful pressure on her scalp and hair, releasing his hold by slow degrees. "Oh, I think you do." His fingers began drifting through the silken strands, almost a caress. "And I think it's time you began to understand the reality of your situation."

He lifted an index finger to her face and trailed the end of the nail down the length of her cheekbone, smiling slightly when she flinched but held her ground. The woman had spirit, far too much for her own good. He would have to cure her of that. "I am your lord and master now, capable of giving you either pain or pleasure." His nail teased across her chin. "Please me, Alexandra, and all will be well between us. Defy me, and I'll make you suffer pain like you've never known before. The choice is yours."

Goose bumps sped down her arms. What was he implying? Alexandra schooled her face into a bland expression, but inwardly she felt as if a dank chill had blown through her soul. She had the distinct feeling that Thigg enjoyed giving pain far more than anything else. "What do you want from me?"

Thigg allowed himself to savor the moment. He was making progress. For just a moment he'd seen a vivid flash of fear in her eyes, a momentary glint that she'd quickly veiled. But it was enough to make him decide that a change in tactics was now in order. Time for the beneficent master to replace the evil inquisitor. Temporarily, of course.

"I want nothing from you . . . for the moment." He stepped away from her abruptly and moved to the heavy door, tapping for the guard to release the lock. "You have a visitor," he announced in a bland voice. "I'm feeling quite generous today. . . . I'll give you five minutes."

Alexandra stared at him in utter amazement. The man was certifiably mad, threatening her with torture one moment, then allowing her a visitor the next. "Who?"

He exited without another word. A moment later the door swung inward again and Vash appeared.

Stunned, Alexandra gaped at the nobleman, dumbstruck that he'd actually come.

"Well, aren't you going to at least say hello?" His eyes narrowed as he studied her pale face, searching for bruises or other signs of abuse. But there was nothing visible that he could see, no physical signs of torture. His wife looked as beautiful and appealing as ever, a sensual feast for the eyes and senses.

Alexandra finally shook herself out of her stupor. "Vash!" she cried happily, and threw herself into his arms, hugging him fiercely. "I'm so glad to see you!"

He fought the almost irresistible urge to kiss her, to fold her tightly inside his arms and never let go. Instead he clasped her hands in his and pressed her fingers to his lips in more of a brotherly gesture of concern.

"They wouldn't let me see you sooner, Alexandra." He studied the interior of the cell covertly, mindful of hidden security lenses. More than likely Thigg was observing their every move, watching and listening through a multitude of hidden devices. "I've been requesting permission to visit since yesterday, but I couldn't get past the general's aides to press my appeal. In fact, I'd just about decided that the general planned to leave me sitting in a vestibule forever."

She gave him a tremulous smile and squeezed his hands. The moment he touched her she'd experienced a sense of déjà vu again. Her legs felt weak, rubbery, as if they could barely support her weight. "You shouldn't have come at all, Vash."

He shook his head slowly and smiled in return. "Maybe not, but I had to, for the sake of our friendship if nothing else. My family does have a little influence at court. I thought I might be able to intervene in some way, but I'm afraid our influence appears to be less than I imagined. Even minor bureaucrats have refused to meet with me."

Her hopes for release dwindled into nothingness. She blinked away the threat of tears and tried to put on a stoic face. "Don't worry, Vash. I'll be fine. Thank you for trying, though."

Lucien searched his wife's anxious eyes. "Has anyone mistreated you?" he asked quietly.

"No." She laughed shortly. "I haven't even seen anyone else until Thigg waltzed in a few minutes ago." She frowned suddenly. "How long has it been since my arrest?"

"Four days."

"Oh." She'd lost two days somewhere. No wonder she'd been so hungry all the time. Obviously she couldn't mark the passage of time by the number of meals. "I thought it was two."

Concern washed over Lucien. She'd already lost her sense of time, which was a very bad sign. Thigg was trying to distort her body clock to keep her off balance, a common interrogation ploy designed to confuse and weaken a prisoner psychologically.

His expression turned grim. So that was why Thigg had suddenly relented and given permission for the visit. He was purposely allowing it to build up Alexandra's hopes, just so he could dash them again. After a few days of such highs and desperate lows, she would be far more vulnerable to his tactics, both mentally and emotionally.

Anger flared up inside him, hot and violent. He wanted to kill Thigg right now—before the man had a chance to interrogate her—to torture the general in ways the evil man himself had never imagined. But Lucien couldn't risk everything for the sake of vengeance. His plans had already been set into motion. Alexandra would have to survive on her own for another few days until the Black Rose could arrange her escape. She was strong and willful, a formidable foe for any man, even Thigg.

He tilted her chin upward, forcing her to meet his furious eyes. Their five minutes were winding down fast, and he had little time left to convey what he came to say. "You must be strong, Alexandra. Don't ever give up hope. I'm still your friend, and I don't plan to abandon you." His fury faded, replaced by tenderness and concern. "I have to leave Primus on business right away, but I'll never be far from you. And I'll continue appealing for leniency. Sooner or later someone with influence will grant me an audience."

Alexandra's mouth trembled slightly, but she refused to cry. A man she hardly knew had tried to come to her aid, had placed his security on the line to help her when no one else had dared. For a second, she lost herself in the depths of his cool gray eyes—eyes so hauntingly familiar that she felt as if she were tumbling through zero gravity once again, slipping backward in time to a particular moment engraved on her memory forever. She felt light-headed, disoriented, as if she were staring deep into Damion's eyes, not Vashlen Thackery's.

She shook off the wild notion abruptly. Was she losing her mind? The very idea was ridiculous. "Thank you, Vash," she said, forcing herself to concentrate on the man standing before her. "You're a good friend, but I don't want you to put yourself in jeopardy by trying to help me."

"Don't worry." He smiled to ease her fears. "I'm irrepressible, remember?"

She nodded slowly. "I remember." That night in Gammon's hallway seemed like ages ago now. "I have to know . . . is Loran safe?" she asked worriedly.

"Safe and well."

She blew out a relieved breath, but the cautionary look he gave her warned her not to ask more. "Good."

"Well, I suppose our time is about up," he said

carefully, then pulled her to his chest. "A good-bye hug is in order, I think."

He lowered his mouth close to her ear, masking the movement with a friendly peck on the cheek. "He has surveillance lenses everywhere within this fortress," he breathed against her, his words no louder than a sigh. "Keep your guard up at all times." His hand moved downward to her waist, delving in and out of her robe in one deft movement. "Don't let him break you . . . help will be here soon."

Alexandra forced herself not to react when she felt his fingers slide into her pocket and deposit something inside. Her heartbeat quickened as he pulled away from her. "Good-bye, Vash," she said calmly, though inwardly she was anything but. Whatever he'd given her was as light as a feather, but she could feel some small object pushing against the material of her robe. "Thank you again." Her gaze caught his, expressing silently what she couldn't say with words.

The nobleman bowed deeply, then turned and swept out of the cell. The lock clicked home a moment later, and Alexandra found herself alone once more.

Keep your guard up at all times, Vash had warned.

She wet her lips nervously and resisted the urge to dig into the pocket to find out what was there. She had to be careful. Very careful. If Thigg had observation devices planted throughout the fortress, surely there were plenty in her cell as well.

She blinked rapidly until her eyes filled with mock tears, not a difficult task, since she'd been on the verge of a monumental crying jag for days now. Once the tears started, they came unchecked. She sniffled a few times, then tilted her head toward the ceiling, giving any watching eyes a clear view of her angst-ridden face.

A stricken sob broke free of her throat, followed by a low wail of despair; then she tossed herself facedown atop the room's uncomfortable cot, her long hair tumbling around her as she wept into the mattress for dramatic effect. When she was certain that her hair would cloak her movements, she inched a hand downward into the pocket. Her fingers closed around something small and silky-soft, with a slender projection trailing from one end.

Realization dawned on her, and she was hard-pressed to keep up the flow of pretend tears. She wanted to laugh out loud, dance, and scream in joy. A tiny flower was nestled in her palm, and she knew instinctively that it was a rose.

Tears gushed down her face in earnest. *Damion.* It had to be. She mouthed his name between sobs, not daring to say it aloud. He had sent the rose through Vash to let her know that he was near, a signal from him that she would soon be freed.

She eased her hand upward, toward her chest and face, peering down at the contents of her palm just to reassure herself that she hadn't been mistaken. A pulse quickened at the base of her throat. A rose the color of midnight lay in the center of her palm, its tiny petals only now beginning to unfurl.

Her fingers closed tightly around the small, perfect flower. It was Damion's symbol, she reminded herself, the emblem of hope and courage spread near and far by the infamous Black Rose. She clung to the hope the rose represented, drew courage and comfort from its presence, just as she knew hundreds of others had before.

The corners of her mouth twitched upward. She hadn't been forgotten after all.

Deep down she'd known he would come for her, that he would never desert her in her time of need, but the knowledge that she'd been right all along brought with it a sudden stab of anxiety. What if something went wrong? If the Black Rose were captured while trying to free her, a gleeful Thigg wouldn't hesitate to have him tortured and killed. And Vash had taken a terrible risk by acting as a messenger. What if he were discovered, or Thigg forced her to reveal something incriminating during her interrogation?

Her jaw clenched with determination. Those were possibilities she couldn't abide. Damion's safety depended in part on how she handled herself in the next few days—Vash's, too, and she wouldn't let either of them down.

She frowned into the mattress, curious how Vash had come to be a messenger for Damion Flynn, unless . . . She shook herself. *Ridiculous.* Such a thing wasn't possible. Was it?

The harsh sound of stone grating against stone caused the thought to die half-born. Her hand clenched as tightly as her jaw, and her heart pounded. The door to her cell had opened again. For an instant she froze, the tell tale rose crushed inside her fist. *Thigg.* If he found it . . .

Terrified, she redoubled her mock sobbing, then quickly stuffed the evidence inside her mouth and began to chew, furiously grinding the flower into a pulp that she could choke down.

General Thigg swept through the cell door and, glancing at his grief-stricken prisoner, was pleased with himself that Thackery's visit had obviously inspired the desired effect. She had thrown herself atop her cot as soon as the visitor departed, her back heaving up and down as she wept.

He allowed a gratified smile to touch his austere features. She was ready for the first of her interrogation sessions now. Thackery's admission that he'd been unable to change her current state had caused whatever dim hopes she still harbored to crash around her, leaving her disheartened, miserable, and emotionally broken. Soon her spirit would be broken, too.

"Get up, Lady Fallon," he announced in a pleasant tone. "You and I have an appointment. The first of many."

Alexandra ignored him. She kept her face buried in the thin mattress and continued to chew, frantically swallowing mushy bits of petal as fast as she could. She fought back the urge to gag.

Thigg glowered and narrowed his eyes. She hadn't moved, and her wailing had died down to an occasional muffled sob—sobs that sounded almost manufactured. "I said get up!"

When she failed to respond to his order a second time, he grabbed her by the elbow and pulled her to a sitting position, forcing her to face him. "My orders are to be obeyed instantly!"

Alexandra swallowed hard, her heart slamming painfully against her ribs. She stared up at her enraged jailer with wide, nervous eyes. Bits of flower pulp still clung to the back of her tongue, and a dry bit was wedged inside her throat.

"Do you understand me?" Thigg demanded.

She nodded but didn't speak.

Thigg's gaze darkened with suspicion. She wasn't reacting at all as he'd expected. Though her face was pale and streaked with tears, he saw no fear there, none of the usual terror exhibited by prisoners on the verge of a formal interrogation. If anything, she appeared only uncomfortable, nervous at best.

He studied her more carefully, surveying her face and robe, then moved his attention to the cot she'd been lying upon. A spot of black on the coarse brown blanket caught his eye. Frowning, Thigg leaned down and picked it up.

For a split second, he didn't understand; then the dreadful reality solidified in his mind. He was holding a tiny flower petal between his fingers—the petal of a black rose.

His gaze stilled on her face, and he turned deathly cold, brimming with an anger as lethal and sharp as the tip of a blade. The Black Rose had managed to send a flower here, to a prisoner in his own dungeon? With him only steps away from the cell door?

Alexandra's face turned a ghostly shade of white. *Gods.* A flower petal had fallen onto the cot, and Thigg had found it.

He choked down a scream of rage and lashed out with a hand, his fingers digging into her forearm as he dragged her to her feet. "Your friend Thackery has made a monumental mistake, Lady Fallon! So have you!"

A cold chill sped through her body. Thigg's features were twisted with rage, distorted so much that he appeared crazed. But his eyes were even more frightening: dark, forbidding, and glittering with a malevolence that promised swift retribution.

"I had that flower before I ever arrived here," she hastily explained. She lifted her chin defiantly. "Your guards just weren't thorough when they searched me."

The blow to her face snapped her head sideways, then back. Alexandra stumbled slightly, then regained her footing, the pain in her cheek making her eyes water. She glared back at her jailer, her chin rising even higher. "I bought that flower myself on Janus Three."

Thigg shoved her back onto the cot. "Guards!" he shouted furiously.

A young soldier appeared in the doorway and snapped to attention.

"Find the man who just left this cell. Don't allow him to escape the fortress. I want him arrested immediately!"

"Right away, General." The wide-eyed soldier saluted crisply and hurried away, the pounding of his footsteps echoing down the stone corridor.

Thigg turned back to the girl and smiled malignantly. "Come along, Lady Fallon. I'm going to make you rue the day you ever met Damion Flynn."

A security alarm sounded as Lucien neared the fortress's columned entrance, causing a gaggle of curious courtiers and bureaucrats to pause uncertainly in the wide corridor, milling and glancing around in search of the reason for the discordant sound.

Comprehension flared in his eyes. The milling nobles were muttering and mumbling among themselves, speculating over what the unexpected ruckus could be about. But Lucien already knew the answer to that. The alarm was for him—for Vashlen Thackery, which meant Alexandra was in even graver danger than before. Thigg had somehow managed to discover the rose: he was sure of it.

Lucien cursed himself soundly for risking the visit, but he'd known no other means to give her a measure of hope and to assure himself that she hadn't been injured in any way.

Now he'd really bungled things. He closed his eyes for a fraction of a second, praying that his wife had the fortitude to survive Thigg's rage. Time was running out, far too swiftly for him to intervene in any effectual way. Only one man could hope to save her now, and it wasn't the Black Rose.

He slipped into the shadow of a column as a platoon of soldiers raced past, pushing their way toward the security posts positioned at the fortress's entrance. The security guards were forming up around the only exit, vigilantly checking the papers and faces of everyone who requested to pass through.

He put a bland smile on his face and minced his way through the crush of anxious nobles toward the waiting guards, his gait and manner confident, his expression sublimely unconcerned. The guards could spend the next week looking for Thackery, but in the end, the search would be in vain. It was Lucien Charbonneau who would exit the fortress doors.

Chapter Sixteen

A thick, unnatural silence fell over the drab hotel suite, an anonymous hideaway far from the arch-duke's citadel of power on the opposite side of the planet. Outside it was nearly daybreak, the pale shades of sunrise crowning the clouds with streaks of purple and red.

Time stretched as Lucien stared out the dingy window, his sense of guilt forcing replay after replay in his mind of the previous day. But no matter how many times he went over the scene in his head, the result was always the same: he was safe, but his wife was not. It was as simple as that.

Over fourteen hours had passed since the alarm sounded and he'd walked to safety through the fortress gates. Fourteen hours of hell for his wife.

He moved back to the small table and dropped into a rickety chair, his thumb tapping an impatient beat atop the wood. "I'm going back in," he announced abruptly. "Today. This morning."

Tay stared at him in shock. "Lucien, have you lost your mind?" he whispered furiously, then glanced toward the bedroom door to make sure Loran was still sleeping. It wasn't often that he dared to use his friend's true name. "You can't go back in there now! You barely got out alive yesterday. Think of the risk you'd be taking! Everything you've worked for—we've worked for. Your luck can't hold forever."

Lucien's brows pulled downward. "I have thought about it. A lot." He sighed and leaned back in his chair. Maybe his luck would hold one more time. "I can't stand by while Thigg does his worst to her, Tay. You know his reputation, and you've seen firsthand the results of what he's done to some of our people. She won't be able to hold out for long." His hands bunched into fists. "He's using her to get to me. I have to try to get her out of there. Even if I fail, I've got to try."

"Just what do you intend to do?" Tay demanded, worried sick that his friend wouldn't leave the fortress alive this time. How many times could he beard the jackal in his own den and live to tell the tale?

Lucien shrugged. "I guess I'll just walk back in."

Tay snorted in disbelief. "As who? The entire Dominion Security Force is out there looking for Thackery and Damion Flynn."

He smiled slyly. "As myself."

A chill crawled over the nape of Tay's neck. "You can't be serious! It's one thing to risk exposing a false identity like Damion Flynn, another thing entirely to risk your real self. Charbonneau's connection with the court is the rebellion's ace in the hole. Almost all of our information comes through you. If Charbonneau is exposed as a spy, the consequences will be disastrous! The rebellion itself might not even survive if you are caught."

Lucien sighed, and his eyes darkened with emotion. "The rebellion will go on, Tay, with or without Charbonneau the spy." What had all the years of subterfuge and deception truly accomplished? The Black Rose was still nothing more than a symbol of discontent, a mysterious figure both cheered and reviled for his efforts to free political prisoners. True, his work for the rebellion had made inroads in the public's perception of their cause, but they weren't much closer to a final victory than they'd been five years before. General Thigg was still the de facto ruler of the Dominion, while Luc Davies remained its puppet head. Not a single unjust law had been changed, and the feudal lords and warlords still held sway. Dissenting still meant a term in one of Thigg's prisons, and freedom of choice simply didn't exist. To the vast majority of humankind, democracy was nothing more than an out-of-reach dream.

And what had the past years gotten him personally? A life of loneliness? The sense that he was an actor in some sweeping play, onstage every moment of every day, fearing he might slip in some way? He was tired of standing center stage, tired of being alone.

"Maybe it's time Charbonneau took a few risks," Lucien said slowly. Some things were more important than politics. "Time for an endgame, winner take all." If he failed, then he'd be dead. But if by some miracle he succeeded, he would never be alone again.

Tay chewed on his lower lip and frowned, his mind ranging over the perils and possibilities of such a bold move. Suddenly his dream of raising krulls on a remote colony didn't sound so far-fetched. "How?" he asked quietly.

"We seize the initiative for a change instead of constantly being on the defensive. Thigg is gathering his forces and allies for an all-out assault against us. We know he plans to try to wipe us out, so why don't we attack him instead? We'll strike before he's ready instead of waging yet another defensive campaign."

"But we're not ready!" Tay protested. "You said it yourself! We don't have enough troops or arms to stand against brigades of seasoned soldiers!"

"We will if I can steal his battle plan in advance."

Tay blew out a shocked breath as the implications took root in his mind. Lucien just planned to walk into the devil's lair, free his wife from prison, and steal the Security Force's battle strategy, all in one fell swoop. His chances of success were slim to none. "Gods. You really are mad."

Lucien sighed and glanced at the drab gray ceiling, staring grimly at nothing, at everything. "Maybe."

"Even if you're successful, Charbonneau will eventually become a suspect. Think of what that will mean! They might even discover what you really are." He fell quiet for a long moment. "You won't be able to go back, Lucien. Ever. Not to Primus or your homeworld."

He nodded sadly. If he was successful, Alexandra would be his home . . . if she could find it in her heart to accept him for what he was. That was the one doubt that kept gnawing at him. Could she accept the fact that her husband wasn't quite human? That alien blood flowed through his veins? Could she give up everything and everyone she knew just for him? "I'll start all over with a new identity, and I'll find a new homeworld . . . with Alexandra, if she'll have me." His own father had never been able to accept or forgive. Could Alexandra?

"And if she won't?"

Lucien lifted his shoulders briefly. "Then I suppose I'll have to make a life without her somehow." His voice faded into silence, the possibility that she might reject him weighing heavily on his thoughts. His cool gaze lingered on his friend's face. "You understand it means the same for you if I do this, Tay. Someone will eventually recognize you and tie the two of us together—we've been lucky no one has before. You'll have to disappear before that happens."

Tay shifted guiltily in the straight-backed chair. His thoughts had been wandering in the same direction for quite a while, to the long-held dream of living an ordinary life. Maybe Lucien was right. Maybe it was time to take some risks. "I know." His glance cut to the door of the bedroom, where Loran lay sleeping, blissfully unaware of the goings-on in the next room. "I've been thinking about the future myself for some months now," he admitted, still staring at the door. "The idea of a farm on a quiet little colony world holds a lot of appeal." The idea of having Loran at his side was even more appealing.

Lucien followed the direction of his gaze and nodded to himself. He'd known Tay was growing weary of the life they led, had watched how his friend stared longingly at Loran whenever her back was turned. "Sounds good, Tay." Though he would never admit it, an idyllic little colony world had begun to sound appealing to him, too, a notion he would have rejected out of hand just a few months ago. But everything had changed since Alexandra came into his life. Everything.

"Sounds real good." Fate had grabbed him by the collar and flung him into a great, yawning chasm with countless twists and turns that would either lead him to happiness or despair.

Tay rubbed at his chin, thinking. "If we're actually foolish enough to go through with this, how do you propose we go about it?"

He pulled in a determined breath and exhaled slowly, forcing himself to concentrate on Tay's question. "The archduke's annual masque to mark the opening of the court season is in two days, and Lucien Charbonneau is invited. Hundreds of clan nobles will be in attendance—all wearing costumes. Can you think of a better opportunity? A masquerade ball will provide the perfect cover for me to steal Thigg's plans."

"And Alexandra?"

"I'll simply arrive a little early . . . and appeal for her release." His smile widened. A thousand things might go wrong in the interim, but at least he had some semblance of a plan. "How can the archduke refuse? After all, she is his good friend's wife. Even Thigg can't deny that."

Tay gave him a skeptical look. Lucien had an annoying habit of making the most convoluted plan sound almost simple. Too simple. "I think I should go with you."

He shook his head quickly. "Sorry. Not this time, Tay. Someone might have already connected you with Flynn. I think you can do me far more good on the outside by providing Thigg with some sort of distraction."

Tay raised a brow. "I'm listening."

"Our friend the general seems to have an obsessive interest in black roses." One side of his mouth lifted in a half a smile. "Why not scatter a few flowers around the planet for his troops to find? Taunt him a little to keep him occupied."

Tay threw his head back and laughed. Now, this was a mission he was going to enjoy. "I'll keep him distracted, all right. By the time I'm through with the general, he won't know which end is up." His merriment faded suddenly. "I'll have to find a safe house to leave Loran in while I'm gone."

"You're not leaving me anywhere, Tay Molvan!" Loran said forcefully.

Tay glanced toward the bedroom and winced. Loran was standing in the doorway, her arms folded tightly across her chest. How much had she heard? "Loran . . ."

She raised her chin in a defiant gesture that reminded Lucien of her strong-willed mistress.

"I'm going with you, Tay, and I don't want to hear any argument about it! Despite what you may think, I'm not some helpless female who needs protecting. I can help if you give me the chance."

"Loran," Lucien said quietly, "how much did you overhear?" She already knew Thackery was in fact Damion Flynn, but little else, and he preferred that it stay that way, for her sake.

"Enough to know that you're going to try to help Alexandra in some way, and that Tay is going to create a diversion."

He gave her a stern look. "You really shouldn't involve yourself in this, Loran. It could be dangerous."

She made an unladylike sound and turned her full attention to the dark-haired man she knew as Damion Flynn, studying him warily. She couldn't help but feel a little nervous in his presence, had felt that way ever since New Chicago, when he'd transformed himself before her eyes and she'd fainted dead away. At the moment he was

Damion Flynn, at least in looks—but appearances could be deceiving, as she'd so recently discovered. "I don't care if what you're doing is dangerous. I won't be left behind to twiddle my thumbs while the two of you go off to try to help Alexandra."

Lucien and Tay exchanged a glance. "All right, then," Lucien said in a resigned tone. "Go with Tay, if you insist. Just be careful. We can't afford for anyone else to be taken prisoner."

Loran's eyes were still riveted on him. Years of servitude had taught her never to pose too many questions, but one thing still bothered her enough that she felt compelled to ask. "What *are* you?"

"Just a man, Loran, and one who happens to be in love with his wife." The edges of his mouth curled in an enigmatic smile.

His hem whispered across the gleaming lapis floor, an endless expanse of glossy blue that eventually melted into walls cut from the same polished stone. Twin rows of graceful marble columns climbed from the lapis and marched toward a distant wall, like towering sentries standing at full attention. The columns soared upward for hundreds of feet to a concave ceiling adorned with ornate scrollwork and whimsical frescoes. And where the columns finally ended, the Dominion archduke sat upon a massive golden throne, its curved back sculpted in a brilliant sunburst that dwarfed his diminutive form.

Lucien forced himself to produce an indolent smile as a scarlet-clad guard ushered him through the throne-room doors, sweeping past a horde of supplicants who'd been clamoring for an audience in the corridor beyond.

Heads swiveled and bobbed as the jam of waiting people struggled to catch a glimpse of the favored noble who'd bypassed them all. The young lordling who swept past was tall and slender, lanky in an ungainly way. His fair hair was knotted in a fashionable queue at the nape of his neck, tied with a brocade strip that matched his shimmering robe. His lean face was almost as fair as his long hair, stylishly pale, his elegant features set in a half-bored, half-haughty expression that carried with it a faint trace of amused indifference. The robe he wore was jewel green, cut from a rich brocade pattern embossed with a flock of golden birds, their wings stretched out in flight. Trimmed in glossy black vinemon fur, the collar rose to chin level, an outrageous height for any self-respecting male.

"Look! It's Charbonneau!" a voice whispered in surprise.

A malicious titter weaved and danced through the crowd, yet a hundred pairs of eyes scrutinized his attire with meticulous care. Charbonneau might be a political lightweight, but everyone present knew he was the premiere trendsetter for fashions of the court.

"Wonder where his bride is!" a minor lord dared to say, causing the titter to swell in volume.

"Anyplace he's not!" another muttered, drawing a burst of scurrilous laughter.

Lucien sniffed and kept walking at an elegantly timed pace, his head lifting to a haughty angle to show his detractors that he'd heard their comments and didn't care. Charbonneau had been the butt of many a joke through the years, so many he'd grown quite immune to the verbal spears. Each time he heard such an insult, he took it as proof that his cover identity remained intact. Still, he couldn't help but feel a pang of discomfort this time, since the jibes made reference to his bride.

As he swept between the double row of columns to the crowd gathered near the archduke's throne, a knot of courtiers and clan hangers-on parted to let him pass. The whispers and titters began yet again, less strident this time, in deference to the archduke, who had made it clear time and again that Lucien Charbonneau was held in the highest regard.

One of the archduke's docats mewled in greeting and scurried down a short flight of steps to meet him, more of the ring-tailed creatures following close behind.

Luc Davies pulled himself out of his boredom and sat forward slightly, a brow canting in surprise as his gaily dressed friend approached, the docats skittering happily around Lucien's flowing robe. A pleased smile touched the archduke's round face. He had missed the young nobleman's company these past weeks—missed it greatly. Lucien had always kept him amused, planning an endless succession of entertainments that held the tedium of his station temporarily at bay.

His pale gaze moved over the droll crowd of courtiers, then rested on his friend. "Ah, Lucien, we are gratified to have you back with us again. We have grown bored without your company."

Lucien bent low in a perfect bow, then straightened slowly and gave the archduke an urbane smile. "Please forgive my absence, your grace. I had an urgent . . . personal matter that required my attention."

The admission caused the archduke's platinum brows to rise. Everyone present knew of Lucien's "personal matter" in scandalous detail, from his bride's wedding-night betrayal to the accusation that she had consorted with a criminal. They also knew that his mysterious bride was now an unwilling prisoner in the fortress dungeon, the subject of much gossip and renewed speculation.

"Your absence is forgiven," the archduke said magnanimously, "although we admit surprise that you have chosen to return now." Luc Davies had thought the gossip and humiliation would keep his friend in seclusion for quite a while, at least until the scandal dwindled a bit. Lucien's unexpected return, with the opening of the new court season only days away, would provide much fodder for the rumor mill among the Dominion elite. His friend must have a pressing reason to appear at such an injudicious time. "What has prompted your return to us, Lucien?"

"I've come to beg a favor, your grace."

The archduke settled himself more comfortably on his throne and studied the man carefully. Not once had Lucien ever pressed him for a favor of any kind, for which Luc Davies was eternally grateful. He was besieged by a steady stream of supplicants on a daily basis, so many that at times it seemed as if everyone in the galaxy wanted something from him. "Such as?" he prodded cautiously.

Lucien met his wary gaze steadily. "It's my wife, your grace . . . I'd like to have her back."

Gasps of shock rippled among the throng of listening courtiers, which the archduke silenced with a single look. He stared at his friend in dismay, bewildered by the unexpected request. The woman had scorned and abused him, made him the subject of public ridicule and derision throughout the Dominion. Why in the heavens would he want such a social albatross back? If anything, Lucien should demand that she be locked in the fortress dungeons forever. That was even his right under Dominion law. Of course, the law applied only if the marriage contract had been fully implemented, and implementation occurred only with consummation.

"Lucien," he said in an uncertain tone, "this woman has caused you public embarrassment. Would you subject yourself to more of the same?"

He cast his gaze downward in mock humiliation. "It is my duty, your grace, to my clan and my father. These are perilous times. The Charbonneau-Fallon alliance must move forward for the sake of both our clans, no matter the cost to my personal honor." Eyes still downcast, he slumped his shoulders in resignation, as if the weight of the universe had suddenly fallen upon him. "And if I do this," he said more quietly, "perhaps I'll be able to salvage my personal honor and lay this distasteful scandal to rest."

The archduke looked beneath the meaning of his words and nodded in sudden comprehension. Nothing was ever as it seemed within Dominion society, even the supposed motivations of his friend. If the marriage were consummated, the alliance would move forward, and Lucien would then have the legal right to demand changes to the contract—he could even have the marriage annulled, if the baron gave his permission. But until then, Lucien was mired in a legal limbo, not fully married, but no longer free to do as he pleased.

Still, Alexandra Fallon posed a significant threat to the Dominion and possibly his throne, perhaps even more of a danger than her father had represented. The archduke's pale blue eyes clouded with worry. The woman was trying to dig up all the old, ancient bones best left moldering, unseen and forgotten, in very deep graves.

For a brief second, Luc Davies considered the possibility that Lucien knew of his wife's intentions, might even be in league with her, but he quickly discarded the notion. His friend was many, many things, but never a fool. He simply wanted to extricate himself from the scandal created by his rebellious wife, and ingratiate himself with his estranged father.

As he pondered the ramifications of Lucien's request, the archduke smoothed his silky sleeves and adjusted his monogrammed train, pushing the shimmering material to the side of his throne. A hasty decision might prove disastrous for all concerned. Besides, he hated to make decisions on an empty stomach, especially ones with an uncertain outcome. Perhaps a delay was in order, a brief sojourn in which he'd have his feet massaged and a quiet meal. Broasted tree-hen, perhaps, served with pickled eel tips and a vegetable loaf. After that, it might be prudent to have a brief chat with the Fallon woman himself.

He rose from his throne abruptly and gazed at Lucien for a long moment. "We shall take your request under advisement. Please remain in the fortress until our decision is made. A suite of rooms will be set aside for your use."

Flanked by uniformed bodyguards, the archduke swept down the short flight of steps and exited the throne room through a door hidden in the lapis wall. A dozen docats scurried after him, their claws tapping furiously on the polished floor.

Lucien stared after the archduke, frowning worriedly. He had assumed Luc Davies would grant his request immediately, out of respect for their friendship if nothing else. A delay of any sort spelled trouble.

Helford Thigg's thin lips tightened with barely contained fury. He locked his hands behind his back and straightened his body, his shoulders stiff, his grim features flushing a deep, angry red. "I won't allow it," he said in a brittle voice. "Your interference in this matter is both unwarranted and unwise." His interrogation had broken the girl's will, but not her spirit. He had her exactly where he wanted her—defeated and as helpless as a mewling infant. Now was the perfect time to have his way with her, but the archduke's ill-conceived plan would preclude him from collecting his prize. "As general of the Security Force, it is my prerogative to deal with prisoners as I see fit. You have no right to intervene!"

The archduke's gaze sharpened, and twin spots of color appeared high on his cheekbones. How dare General Thigg criticize him in the presence of lackeys! His eyes cut right to the impassive bodyguards stationed at the doors of his private dining room, then to the liveried servants positioned on either side of the long, polished table. All wore the same wooden expression, their faces devoid of any visible reaction, yet their eyes contained a flaring of interest that infuriated the archduke.

He slammed a frail fist atop the mahogany table with enough force to rattle the fine china and an antique bowl. Until the arrogant general had chosen to speak to him in such a manner, Luc Davies had been vacillating over whether to grant Lucien's favor or not. Now Thigg had settled the matter for him. He would not back down in the face of such impudence.

"You will not *allow* it?" he snapped back furiously, his clipped words echoing briefly in the cavernous room. "You forget yourself, General. How dare you speak to us as if we were some lowly serving wench! We have made a request of you and demand that you comply! You would do well to remember that you serve solely at our pleasure. It is not within your prerogative to refuse a direct command from us!"

His eyes narrowed, the irises cold and lethally bright. The general of his forces was treading on perilous ground. To refuse the order was tantamount to mutiny. "Is it your desire that we inform the High Council that you have refused our order?"

Thigg swallowed hard, and his face reddened even more. Perhaps his anger had gotten the best of him and he'd stated his case too vehemently. Obviously the archduke was of a mind not to countenance any further objections about the girl, a decision Thigg would be a fool to resist. Luc Davies might be little more than the titular head of the Dominion, but he still wielded enormous influence and power. If the archduke were vindictive enough to bring the matter before the High Council, the clan nobles might very well rule in his favor, which would prove disastrous for Thigg's future plans.

He swallowed again, but this time it was his pride that slid down his throat. He dipped his head in a polite bow, though the gesture brought the taste of bile to his mouth. "Forgive me, your grace. I simply allowed my sense of duty to cloud my judgment for a moment. I defer to your wishes, as always."

A self-satisfied smile creased the archduke's cherubic face, but his pale eyes were still narrowed with anger. He'd known the general would back down in the end. His rank, position, and wealth meant far too much to him. "Your passion for capturing the Black Rose and his cohorts is commendable, General, but it has grown into a dangerous obsession in recent months, one you would be wise to temper before we decide your judgment has been dangerously impaired."

The subtle threat hung between them, a palpable cloud that weighted the air.

General Thigg notched his chin up and compulsively straightened the hem of his dark tunic. He would have to walk carefully in the coming days. Very carefully indeed. Although few actually knew the archduke intimately, it was widely known that the man never forgot a friend, a favor— or a slight.

"I understand, your grace," he said slowly, capitulating in the face of the veiled threat. Though the warning had been couched in careful terms, Luc Davies would have him stripped of his rank and power if he didn't comply. And that was something Thigg couldn't allow to happen. Not now, not when he was so close to reaching his goals. After his plans came to fruition, he would dispense with the nettlesome aristocrat. "The prisoner is yours to dispose of as you will."

"See to it," the archduke said sharply.

Thigg snapped his fingers, and a guard opened the doors. Two Security Force agents hustled a small figure inside the dining room, saluted smartly, then retreated out of view. The doors closed quietly behind them.

The archduke stared in dismay. The woman's neck was bent low, as if she feared to lift her head and look him full in the face. Her robe was rumpled, and a torrent of silky black hair fell in tumbling waves down her shoulders and back, shielding the planes of her face from direct view. But he could see enough of her delicate features to know that she looked weak, frightened, and pale. Deathly so.

His mouth set in a straight, tight line as he

focused his gaze on General Thigg. Shock and anger simmered in his eyes. No matter the crimes she was accused of perpetrating, Alexandra Fallon had been born of noble blood and deserved to be treated accordingly. "You may leave us, General," he said icily. His glance moved to the guards and silent servers. "All of you, leave!"

"Your grace, I don't think—" Thigg interjected.

"Out!" the archduke commanded in a shrill voice. "At once!"

Thigg masked his anger with an abrupt nod. "Very well." He spun on his heels and marched out the doors, the guards and frightened servants following at a rapid pace.

The doors reclosed, but with the sharp sound of wood slamming against wood this time. Thigg, the archduke surmised. No one else would have dared act with such temerity.

The prisoner had yet to make the slightest movement, even a twitch or gesture to show that she was still alive. She simply stood there, frozen like a frail sliver of glacial ice.

"Lady Fallon?" he said quietly.

She lifted her head in slow motion, the long veil of hair shifting and falling into new positions. She blinked several times and glanced around at her new surroundings, her heart-shaped face as frozen as her body had been. Her eyes finally found his, and Luc Davies forced himself not to gasp aloud.

Dark shadows formed half-moons beneath her eyes, purpled smudges of exhaustion and despair. But those haunted, sapphire eyes troubled him even more—they were like deep pools of grief and inconsolable pain. But despite her debilitated state, he could see that she was a strikingly beautiful woman, so much so that she could heat the blood of any man. Even himself. Perhaps Thigg's obsessive interest in her had more than one cause.

"Lady Fallon?" he said again.

A look of confusion rippled across Alexandra's features. Where was she now? The room was massive, with towering ceilings and a long, gleaming table surrounded by high-backed chairs. Statuary graced the tabletop, several small figurines and bowls. And at the end of the table sat a pale little man with a round face and silver-white ringlets in his hair. She gave him and the room a bewildered frown. Who was this, and why was she here? And where was her tormentor, Thigg?

The mere thought of the general caused a shudder to travel down her spine. Her palms grew damp and clammy, and the room receded, fading from sight until all she could see and hear was Thigg's rage-filled face and oppressive voice. *Tell me everything*, he had screamed at her over and over again. Then had come the pain, endless waves of unremitting agony until her nerve endings felt as if they'd been set aflame. And when that failed to loosen her tongue, he had resorted to mind-sifting drugs.

"I betrayed him," she whispered hoarsely. Dazed and shaken, she stared blankly at the top of a chair. "I didn't think I would, but in the end, I did . . . just like he said I would."

The archduke gave the closed doors a contemptuous glare. Was this how the general treated his noble prisoners? "Who did you betray, child?"

Alexandra bit down hard on her lower lip and shook herself mentally. Reality returned by slow degrees as the memories of Thigg's interrogation gradually lifted from her brain. The chemicals Thigg had given her were still in her blood, she reminded herself, forcing her tongue to give voice to her deepest thoughts. She had to be careful when she spoke, to concentrate hard before the words slipped free of her throat. "I betrayed no one," she said softly, wishing she could forget, wishing she could just lie down and sleep. Where didn't matter. She just needed to close her eyes—and cry. "No one at all."

He eased back in his chair, watching her anguished features carefully. She was swaying slightly, her body weaving from exhaustion. "Please sit down, Lady Fallon." He gestured toward a nearby chair with an elegant hand. "You appear to be a bit unsteady on your feet."

She shuffled to the chair obediently and slumped into it, sighing as her body relaxed into the plush upholstery. "Thank you."

For a brief second he gazed at her uncertainly, berating himself for being so hasty as to dismiss the servants out of hand. She was in dire need of refreshment of some kind, and wine would always do in a pinch. He climbed to his feet and carefully poured her a goblet of sparkling blue wine, feeling very daring for doing so on his own.

"Please . . . refresh yourself." He placed the golden goblet before her with a dramatic flourish.

Alexandra gazed at the goblet suspiciously. Did the blue liquid contain more mind-sifting chemicals? Was this just another part of Thigg's interrogation? She licked her lips thirstily. Her throat was parched, as dry as a desert plain. Thirst finally prevailed over suspicion, and she drank the wine greedily.

The liquid's warmth slid down her throat and curled through her stomach, bringing with it a sense of calm and well-being that she knew she shouldn't feel. When she'd emptied the goblet, she sighed and shut her eyes.

"When did you last sleep?" he asked her.

Her lids reopened. How long had it been since Thigg had taken her from her cell? "I don't remember," she said truthfully.

The archduke tapped his manicured nails on the gleaming tabletop, mulling over how to proceed. The side of his finger brushed the base of the antique bowl, a vivid reminder that Thigg's treatment of her was not the real reason he had insisted on this interview. She had been to the Denault system, digging up secrets that were none of her concern. "Do you remember this bowl?" he asked pointedly.

Frowning, Alexandra stared at the ornamental bowl resting near his hand. She blinked once, puzzled, then the fog of confusion suddenly cleared away. It was the Janusian bowl she'd bought in Kimren's shop ages ago. Her frown grew more pronounced. At least it felt like ages ago. "That's my bowl," she said, bewildered by its presence until she remembered that it had been confiscated when she arrived.

"Yes." Luc Davies trailed a finger along its marble rim, studying the four bas-relief faces with a critical eye. "Was it recovered with the other artifacts you found in the Denault system?" He had to find out how much she knew, how much she'd guessed. "It's similar yet quite different from the other objects you discovered."

Her brows lowered. Why was her bowl even here? "Who are you?" she asked hoarsely.

He sniffed and adjusted a jeweled fastener beneath his collar, the green diamond glinting in the light thrown by a massive chandelier. He'd never had occasion to introduce himself before. He wasn't even sure how it was properly done. "We are Luc Davies, archduke of all the Dominion clans."

Alexandra's eyes widened in shock. This pale

little man was the Dominion archduke? "I'm . . .
I'm sorry, your grace," she stammered in apology.
"I didn't know."

"Quite all right, considering the circumstances." He moved an index finger along the
light green marble. "We would be interested in
examining your research on this bowl, Lady Fallon."

She eyed him warily, more worried and curious
than before. When she'd spotted the marble bowl
in Kimren's shop she'd simply been struck by the
notion that it was amazingly similar to the artifacts found deep below the Denault moon's surface. Perhaps the bowl was more of a find than
she'd first thought. She was certain now that
those stylistic similarities went beyond mere
coincidence. Something more was going on here.
She was being grilled about the origins of the
Janusian bowl by the archduke himself.

"I've done no research as yet." *Careful*, she
warned herself. His methods weren't as crude
and painful as Thigg's had been, but she was
being interrogated all the same. She forced herself to concentrate, to shrug off the aftereffects of
Thigg's truth drugs and choose each word she
uttered with exquisite care. "I didn't have the
time, your grace. Your general interrupted my
research, and then the artifacts were confiscated
from me when I arrived here." She hadn't said
anything that could be construed as a lie. Not in a
literal sense. But at this juncture, it seemed prudent not to reveal the entire truth, at least until
she discovered what this was all about. "Are you a
collector of antiquities, your grace?" she asked
politely.

The archduke nodded slowly, not entirely satisfied with her previous answers, but uncertain

how to garner more information without revealing more than he wished. "In our own way."

A sudden thought occurred to him, and he pushed the bowl in her direction. "If you desire, you may examine it more fully now. It has been brought to our attention that you have inherited your father's interest in such things and are something of an expert."

Her eyes narrowed a fraction as she picked up the bowl and cradled it carefully, the marble cool and slick beneath her fingers. Why would the Dominion archduke know anything at all about her or her father? "You knew my father?" she said as casually as possible. She traced over the interior, noting once more the singed mark marring the surface, then shifted her attention to the row of small faces carved along the outside.

"We are aware of his work."

"Then you know that his theories were roundly rejected."

"We are aware of that as well."

She turned the bowl over leisurely and studied the bottom, which she'd never had time to do on Janus Three. Her heartbeat quickened. A series of triangles, circles, and vertical squiggles was etched into the flat surface, the exact same hieroglyphs she'd deciphered on the disks recovered from the cave. *Arulia*.

A rush of adrenaline pounded through her body, but she forced herself not to show any visible reaction to the discovery. The artifacts from the cave and the bowl weren't just similar—they were the same. Yet the Denault system and Janus Three were light-years distant from each other. How could the bowl have been discovered buried on a beach on Janus Three? Unless . . .

She pulled in a slow breath. Could the same

race that crafted the artifacts have once made its home in both places?

Yes, her mind whispered back. It made perfect sense.

Alexandra flipped the bowl upright immediately so she wouldn't appear overly interested. For whatever reason, the archduke was testing her, trying to make her reveal what she knew about its origins, and she understood instinctively that to do so might be dangerous in the extreme.

She stared at the interior of the bowl again, her impassive gaze moving over and then returning to the curious singe mark. According to Kimren, the bowl had most probably been damaged and buried during the clan battle on Janus Three two thousand years ago in a war so fierce that the seas had boiled away. And Damion had estimated that the cannon craters pocking the Denault moon had been gouged into the surface during the same time period. The two events had to be related, and if an alien race had indeed once inhabited both places, but vanished about the same time that humans arrived to colonize . . .

A sudden stab of guilt knifed its way through her thoughts. It didn't take a genius to figure out what her ancestors had done. Despite all they'd accomplished since the dawn of their species on distant earth, the human propensity for brutality and bigotry had often led to outbreaks of horrific violence.

"Do you subscribe to your father's theories, Lady Fallon?" the archduke asked abruptly, intent on every nuance of her expression, searching for any sign that she had come to any dangerous conclusions.

Alexandra shrugged slightly and met his probing gaze. "Not entirely, although I do believe my father was correct in asserting that a race of sentients inhabited this region long before humans." She watched him as carefully as he was watching her.

He broke eye contact with her and examined a fingernail. "If that alleged race did by chance actually exist, what do you suppose might have become of them?"

Alexandra lifted her shoulders in another shrug, a diffident gesture designed to hold his suspicions at bay. He *knew*. She was certain of it now. The archduke knew exactly what fate had befallen this alien race, and was trying to determine whether she knew it, too. But according to Dominion history, no evidence of nonhuman sentients had ever been found, anywhere—a two-thousand-year-old cover-up designed to hide the shameful truth.

"I fear that's a mystery that may never be resolved, your grace." *Careful*, she warned herself again. The truth had been suppressed for two thousand years. If the archduke had any inkling that she'd discovered the lie, she would never leave the fortress again. "My father never found an answer to the puzzle, and neither have I. Who knows? They may have been a spacefaring race and simply moved elsewhere, colonizing outward just as humans did."

Luc Davies nodded slowly. He was content with her answer as well as her demeanor, at least for now. Still, he couldn't quite shake the feeling that he might have just played a verbal match of chess and lost. But if she really did know anything, he would eventually ferret out the truth. If not, there was always General Thigg. She was an accused traitor, after all, and traitor's were at his mercy. In the meantime, he would grant Lucien his favor— until after the ball, at least. What harm could it do? The wagging tongues would be silenced, and the wrong she'd done poor Lucien would be publicly set right. Plus, she'd be forced to remain within the confines of the fortress, a pseudoprisoner trapped in a velvet-lined cell. An eminently suitable solution for all concerned. Except General Thigg, of course.

"You may keep the bowl," he said generously. "Consider it our welcome gift to you. As for the other artifacts, they have of course become the property of the throne."

She nodded in quiet acceptance because she was in no position to object, although doing so annoyed her immensely. How dared he simply claim her artifacts as his own? But if she put up a fuss about it, he might begin to suspect that something was amiss.

The archduke pushed his chair back and stood abruptly. "We have enjoyed our little conversation with you, Lady Fallon, but urgent matters of state require our attention." He had yet to have his feet massaged. "A servant will see you to the suite of rooms assigned to your husband."

Alexandra blinked. The conversation had shifted unexpectedly, to an even worse subject than the confiscation of her artifacts. "What?" she asked, her voice rising. Her *husband?*

A spark of amusement flared in the archduke's pale eyes. *Poor Lucien.* Better to lose his honor than spend his nights with a woman who seemed to loathe the very thought of him. "We have decided to return you to your estranged husband, Lady Fallon. Either that, or you may remain a guest of General Thigg. Which would you prefer?"

With that, he swept toward the doors, his long robe and train rustling across the granite floor.

An icy shiver of dread crawled through Alexandra's bones. Fool that she was, she hadn't thought her situation could possibly get any worse. "Oh, gods," she whispered to herself. After all these weeks, it seemed her life was about to come full circle.

Chapter Seventeen

The sprawling guest suite the archduke had placed at Lucien's disposal opened onto a long stone balcony overlooking the fortress's manicured gardens, an endless labyrinth of colors, shapes, and flowery scents that startled the senses and made visitors want to linger and stare. Streams of water jetted skyward from a hundred elaborate fountains, showering parts of the gardens with a fine mist that caught and refracted the sunlight in brilliant rainbow hues.

Lucien turned away from the mesmerizing vista and continued prowling the length of the oval-shaped sitting room, too nervous and worried simply to stare at anything for long. Luc Davies had yet to send word of his decision, and the day was swiftly winding to a close. The delay didn't bode well for his chances, not well at all.

A discreet rap was his only warning before a uniformed guard opened the suite's heavy wooden door. Lucien spun toward the sound and eyed the guard with no small amount of trepidation.

The guard officer dipped his head slightly, the scarlet cockade topping his helmet bending with him as he placed a carryall on the floor. He straightened and pushed the door open wider. "With the archduke's compliments, my lord."

Alexandra stepped through the opening, and the officer vanished, sealing them alone inside the borrowed rooms.

Lucien stared at his wife, his heart pounding madly with relief. Sunlight slanted through the balcony doors, throwing shadows and dappled light across her unmoving figure. For several worry-filled hours he'd thought he might have overplayed his hand, but the archduke had come through for him in the end.

"Alexandra . . ." He took a hasty step toward her, then stopped himself midway across the room. He was Charbonneau now, and had to act the part. A jilted husband wouldn't be in any sort of rush to sweep her back into his arms. And perhaps a bit of distance between them would be better for them both. Alexandra had almost recognized him in at least one of his various guises.

He forced his lips to pinch into a prim smile. "Welcome back, my dear," he said in a politely formal tone. "I had begun to despair of ever seeing your lovely face again." In truth she looked ghastly. She was bone pale, with bruiselike crescents darkening the flesh beneath her eyes. If Thigg were here now, Lucien would have squeezed the life from him with his bare hands. "I'm gratified to see that you appear to have survived your adventures relatively unscathed . . . although you do seem to have lost your braids somewhere along the way." He peered at her appraisingly. "The new look is quite becoming, though."

Alexandra closed her eyes a moment, wishing she had escaped "unscathed," as he'd so blithely termed it. The memories of those hours with Thigg would haunt her for the rest of her days. Even darker was the memory of how she'd betrayed Damion. "Yes, I guess you could say I survived." Her voice was dead.

"Well, it's all over now," Lucien said, "and we are together once again." He lifted an elegant hand and directed her toward a plush chair. "Please have a seat. We have several matters of import to discuss."

She sighed and picked up her carryall, eyeing her husband wearily. He was standing near the center of the room, his slender features pinched into petulant lines. Her tired gaze skimmed over his face and shimmering attire. He was dressed as outrageously as he'd been on their wedding day, perhaps even more so. Soaring golden birds decorated his brocaded robe, and his high collar was trimmed in costly fur.

"Is there something amiss?" Lucien asked, forcing himself not to smile at her look of dismay. "You're staring at me quite oddly. Don't you like my new robe?" He fussed with the heavy green material to keep her focused on his attire instead of on his face. "I had it made expressly for the new season here at court."

"How wonderful for you." Ignoring him as best she could, Alexandra walked slowly to a wing chair and tossed down her bag, then threw herself onto a matching settee a few feet away. She sighed again, deeper this time, and gazed at him expectantly. "All right. I'm sitting. What exactly did you want to discuss?" She sighed inwardly. As if she didn't know already.

The Black Rose

His features stiffened as he settled himself into a chair directly across from her and laid his hands atop the upholstered arms, one finger of each hand drumming against the silky material. He pursed his lips in annoyance and pitched his chin high. "My dear, dear wife, was the thought of marriage to me so odious that you felt you had to rob me and run away?"

Embarrassed, she glanced at a tapestry on the wall behind him and pretended to study the ornate design—anything to keep from looking at him. She hadn't expected him to discuss her actions quite so bluntly. But now that he had, how should she answer the peacock's question? With the truth or a comforting lie? The thought of being married to him *was* odious. He was an effete wastrel obsessed with his clothing and social position—everything she'd never wanted in a husband, and the exact opposite of Damion Flynn. She finally decided that silence was far more palatable than the truth or some pathetic lie. Still, it appeared she was stuck with him once more—perhaps it was time for her to try to make amends.

"Well?" Lucien prompted, still polite but more demanding. He tapped a foot against the plush carpet impatiently. "Have you nothing to say on the subject?"

"I'm very sorry for what I did to you," she blurted before she changed her mind, then fell silent, the awkwardness of the situation sharpening her sense of guilt. She continued her perusal of the tapestry, avoiding eye contact with him.

Lucien cocked a pale brow. Her halfhearted apology proved that Thigg hadn't broken her completely. His wife was as unrepentant as always. "Is that all?"

She threw him an exasperated glance. "What more do you want?"

He sniffed loudly. "I am your husband, Alexandra. I believe that entitles me to an explanation, at the very least. The scandal generated by your behavior has caused me no end of public humiliation."

That last part made her wince, especially since it was obviously her husband who'd managed to engineer her release. Not Damion, as she'd hoped and expected, or even Vash. And certainly not her family. Charbonneau appeared to have accomplished that remarkable feat all on his own, without any prodding from anyone. "It was never my intention to humiliate you, Lucien. As for robbing you, well, I'm sorry about that, too." She shrugged guiltily. "I'll give you back the remainder of your jewels. The rest I sold." Her expression turned somber. "I had to do it in order to keep a promise to my father. I used your jewels to travel to the Denault system so that I could recover some archaeological artifacts."

His gaze sharpened. He'd been so busy the past few days trying to secure her release, he hadn't given the damnable artifacts much thought. "This was all over some sort of archaeological expedition?" he said innocently.

She lifted her hands helplessly. "I'm too tired to fully explain it right now. Suffice it to say that it was all in vain. . . . The archduke has confiscated everything I found." He'd taken everything except the Janusian bowl, but without the other pieces, the bowl didn't prove much of anything. She had nothing left that could vindicate her father's reputation. Nothing at all.

"Oh?" He held himself very still, carefully masking his curiosity. What was Luc Davies up to now? There had to be a connection he wasn't aware of. "Well, I'm quite sure the archduke has his reasons. Perhaps it has something to do with this Damion Flynn character you became entangled with." He arched a brow and peered over at her. "I'm told this fellow is little more than a despicable pirate."

She was in no mood to talk about Damion with anyone, and especially not with her husband. "Please, I'm too tired to discuss this any further." She blinked several times to squelch a sudden urge to cry. "All I want to do right now is bathe and have a few hours of sleep."

His gaze softened with concern. He'd needled her and acted the part of the jilted husband long enough. She was dead on her feet and looked on the verge of tears. She probably still suffered from the aftereffects of Thigg's mind-sifting drugs as well.

"How thoughtless of me," he said solicitously. He pointed toward an arched doorway that led to a bedroom and the suite's facilities. "A long, hot soak often works wonders when I'm tired and overwrought. I'll order dinner brought up while you bathe. We'll dine here in the suite; then you can get a good night's sleep. You'll need it to prepare for the ball tomorrow evening."

"Ball?" Her brows drew together in a frown. "What are you talking about?"

"The annual masquerade marking the opening of the season of court. I thought you knew." He hoped she wouldn't fight him on this. Too much depended on her attending the fete as Charbonneau's wife. "It's the high point of the season. Everyone with any social standing at all will be in attendance. And the archduke paroled you for the express purpose of us attending as a couple. I've already made arrangements for your ball gown, so you have no worries on that score."

She gaped at him in complete astonishment. This was insane; he was insane. Mere hours ago she'd been a prisoner in the fortress dungeon, and now the archduke and her husband expected her to act the dutiful wife and go to a masked ball? Defiance glittered in her eyes. "You can't be serious!"

"Perfectly serious." He sighed inwardly. Did she always have to argue with him about every little thing? "We're to attend the celebration as a couple to help lay the scandal to rest . . . a scandal you created, I might add."

Alexandra shook her head vehemently. "That's silly. I won't do it. Let people talk all they want. I don't care!"

He rose from the chair abruptly, all pretense of proper decorum melting from his features. "But I do care, my dear. So does the archduke. You sullied my honor and the Charbonneau name with your selfish stunt, not to mention your own family and the alliance itself." This was one battle his rebellious wife couldn't be allowed to win. He gave her a withering look. "Your uncle and my father are dependent upon us to set matters right, and that is exactly what we shall do."

Alexandra stared at her reflection in the ornate mirror. The dark-haired woman who gazed back at her still looked weary, despite almost a full day's sleep, but the smudges beneath her eyes had for the most part faded away. Although she'd bathed, rested, and recuperated to some extent, her mood hadn't changed in the least. She felt leery, anxious, and resentful about the situation she now found herself in, even though her husband had yet to make any demands on her at all.

After their confrontation the day before, she had fully expected him to force himself upon her the moment she climbed into the suite's soft bed and stake his husbandly claim upon her body. She had girded herself for that moment, gritted her teeth and told herself that it was her duty to let him have his way this time. But she'd been thankful when the moment had never come. To her knowledge, he had never even entered the room where she slept.

Her lips tightened suddenly. The moment would come, though. That was a given. Tonight, maybe, or tomorrow, he would demand that their marriage be consummated. The alliance between their families wouldn't move forward until she submitted.

Sighing, she picked up an onyx comb from the top of the dresser and dragged it through her unbound hair, wincing as it caught in a tangled length of curl. She jerked the comb downward, only to catch the teeth in yet another tangle.

"Damnit all," she muttered to the mirror. When her hair was in braids she didn't have to worry about such things.

"Would you like me to do that for you?" a soft voice asked.

Alexandra flinched and glanced into the mirror, her startled gaze locking with Lucien Charbonneau's. He'd entered the room so stealthily that she hadn't heard a thing. She watched in nervous silence as he deposited several bundles and an expanse of shimmering fabric atop the bed, then walked to stand directly behind her.

"I didn't mean to scare you," Lucien explained, though in truth he'd been glad to catch her unawares. His alluring wife was sitting cross-legged atop a small ottoman in front of a dressing table, a loose-fitting white robe doing little to hide her body from view. The gauzy material barely concealed her breasts, and her shapely legs

323

were exposed from her ankles up to the tops of her satiny thighs.

He cleared the sudden dryness from his throat. The sight of her sitting there half-dressed was more than he could bear. "Your ball gown has arrived. It's on the bed."

He freed the dark comb from her fingers before she thought to decline and began at the top of her head, working the teeth down gently, his fingers sliding through the long strands to lift and separate the silky tendrils. The knot released, and he moved his attention to the top of her head again, dragging the comb downward in a sensuously slow movement.

"You have beautiful hair," he said in a low voice, and took a deep breath, reveling in the clean, sweet scent of her bounteous curls. Keeping his distance from her had proved to be an unmanageable feat, especially after the long hours he'd spent watching her sleep.

Alexandra continued to stare into the mirror, studying his face in silence as he gently worked the knots from her hair. She'd forgotten that her husband's eyes were gray, a soft, silvery hue that caused a momentary look of confusion to pass across her brow. Funny how she'd forgotten that, but then they really hadn't spent much time together on their wedding day. Now that she thought about it, she remembered that his eyes had been the exact same shade as those of his aloof father, Baron Charbonneau, so the color wasn't at all surprising.

A fingernail lightly grazed her scalp, causing her thoughts to leap back to the here and now. A curious tingle swept down her neck in response to her husband's touch, heating her cheeks with sudden awareness. No man had ever wended a comb through her hair, and despite her feelings about her husband, she found his gentle touch now oddly compelling.

Memories of their wedding night surfaced unbidden, how her body had responded to his touch even then. Other memories suddenly surfaced as well, recollections of another encounter, another man—a man she now knew she would never forget. She shook herself mentally. "Lucien . . . I . . ."

His eyes found hers in the mirror. "What, love?"

A stricken look settled over her features. *Love.* That was what Damion had called her, an endearment that had both enthralled and annoyed her, one she'd never hear from his lips again. "I need to tell you something," she whispered, wishing for the thousandth time that she'd had the good sense to tell Damion how she felt about him when she'd had the chance. Now it was too late—too late for many things. But she could set matters right between her and Charbonneau. Much as she wished it weren't so, he was her husband, and as such he had the right to know. Theirs might be an arranged marriage, but it was still a marriage, and any hope of intimacy between them shouldn't be darkened by the shadow of Damion Flynn. "It's something you have a right to know."

The comb paused midway down her back. "What?"

She cast her eyes downward. "I know I shouldn't be, but I'm in love with another man." She blew out her breath in a rush, relieved to finally give voice to the words. "I'm very sorry. I just can't seem to help myself where Damion's concerned."

Lucien stared at her reflection in astonishment, thrown off guard by the unexpected admission. For a fraction of a second, a trace of elation shone in his face and eyes; then he tamped down hard on his emotions, forcing them back into the nether reaches of his mind. "You mean that pirate?"

"Yes—I mean no!" Alexandra's features knotted in dismay. "He's not a pirate, Lucien . . . he's, well, he's a rebel spy . . . allegedly the Black Rose."

"The Black Rose?" He gave an outraged little sniff and folded his arms across his chest, the comb pointing outward like a dagger. "My *wife* has been consorting with that blackguard?"

She lowered her head in a slow nod. "Yes, but you don't have to worry. He's gone from my life now."

"Do I have your word on that?" he asked in a petulant voice. "I will not be scandalized further by sharing my wife with another man."

She closed her lids and kneaded the ache building behind her eyes. The man couldn't possibly be that shallow, could he? He seemed more concerned with the talk such a liaison would generate than anything else. "You have my word," she said tightly. "That hideous little man, Thigg, will see that I keep it. He's not going to give up his hunt for the Black Rose until Damion is either captured or killed. That's why he imprisoned me. He made me tell him everything I knew about Damion Flynn." She fought back tears. "I doubt very much if Damion survives the week."

"I see." Lucien busied himself by studying the tip of a fingernail, forcing himself not to react to her revelations. At the moment, he wanted nothing more from life than to toss his wife atop the massive bed and make wild love to her for hours on end, tell her the truth about himself and leave the future to fate.

He sighed regretfully and glanced at the lengthening shadows spilling through the open doorway. Unfortunately, the truth would have to wait a bit longer, and so would his fantasy. The archduke's ball would be beginning soon, and Charbonneau had much to accomplish before the evening was through. He had to keep up the guise within a guise for the rest of the night—be the oafish husband that Alexandra both reviled and despised.

"Well," he said lightly, "I suppose I forgive you." A glint of mischief flashed in the depths of his eyes. "At least you had the good taste to choose a legendary lover. Now that I think about it, the fact that my wife was indiscreet with the Black Rose might even serve to enhance my own reputation. After all, he has always been portrayed as quite the dashing figure, a dark and mysterious fellow rumored to make women swoon with uncontrolled passion. I wouldn't be too embarrassed to admit that he was once your lover. Especially since it's me you'll stay with." He adjusted the lines of his robe. "Why, I've always thought I was a little like the Black Rose myself. Don't you agree?"

Alexandra gaped at him in disbelief. Lucien? How could he even think of comparing himself to the Black Rose? She shook her head slowly. Without a doubt, he husband was the vainest, most shallow creature she'd ever known.

"I won't wear it," Alexandra said, her mouth setting in a stubborn line. She glared at the thing beneath Lucien's arm as the lift-tube hurtled downward to the fortress's ground floor. The flowing gown was bad enough, yards and yards of gauzy gold fabric that ballooned outward from her waist in the shape of a gargantuan bell. Now her husband expected her to wear an elaborate mask as well. "It's ridiculous." The animal-head mask was at least two feet tall, replete with curv-

Jan Zimlich

ing, slender horns and a long blue snout. Worse, it was an oort, and everyone knew about oorts.

Lucien glared back just as stubbornly. "The archduke chooses the theme for his masquerades. This year he's ordained that everyone dress in gold and wear an animal costume of some sort. I had nothing to do with his decision."

She glanced at her mask, then at his. The one he planned to wear was cradled beneath his other arm, a sleekly handsome replica of a black foxen with upright ears and an intelligent face. "If you had nothing to do with it, why do I have to go as an oort? I want to wear your head instead."

"No," he said flatly. He'd selected the foxen head for himself because the creature was so highly regarded, and he knew many others would choose it as well. There was safety to be found in anonymity. As for the oort head, he did feel a twinge of guilt about that, but the choice assured that all eyes would be upon her, not him. Besides, the costumer hadn't had many left to choose from at the last minute. "You'll wear your own head. End of subject."

She gave him a sharp look ripe with resentment. *Very clever.* His choice of an oort head for her was her husband's way of getting back at her, subtle vengeance for what she'd done to him. It was common knowledge that oorts were feckless creatures, graceful and beautiful in appearance, but foul tempered and treacherous in nature. The females were even worse. They were wanton creatures with no fidelity, even to their own kind, and would often gore or maim any male oort fool enough to try to mate with them.

"Fine," Alexandra snapped at him. If she arrived at the ball clad in the tall blue oort head, she'd be the butt of a thousand scurrilous jibes.

She could almost hear the whispers and laughter already—vile, malicious comparisons between the behavior of oorts and what she'd done to him on their wedding night. Of course, that was the entire point, she reminded herself. At least for a few hours, she would bear the brunt of the jokes and public derision, not her husband. "If you insist."

"I insist."

She muttered a curse beneath her breath, then jammed the heavy thing down over her head, pushing it this way and that until it settled comfortably against her shoulders and the base of her neck. She tilted her head back to glare at him through the narrow eye slit, then silently mouthed a particularly choice curse and stuck out her tongue. If he thought the embarrassment of wearing an oort head would lay her low, he'd better think again.

"Satisfied?" Her voice came out muted and thin, muffled by the layers of plastic and fur enveloping her face.

Lucien choked back a laugh as she struggled to master the cumbersome horns. "Exceedingly." He could only guess at the look she was giving him behind the safety of the mask. "You look quite fetching, actually."

He snugged the dark foxen head down on his shoulders, then turned toward her and preened. "What about me? How do I look?"

Her mouth turned down in disgust. He was clad in his elegant wedding robe, the golden concoction with voluminous sleeves and a line of jeweled fasteners running from his collar to the floor—the very same gems she'd given him back the day before. "Oh, you look absolutely fabulous," she told him in a honeyed voice. The pea-

Jan Zimlich

cock had already bought more jewels to replace the ones she'd sold, including replicas of the diamond and ruby she'd used to pay Damion Flynn.

His brows rose. "Do I detect a trace of sarcasm in your voice?"

She rolled her eyes behind the mask. "Whyever would you think that?" she asked innocently, but was saved from his reply when the lift-tube glided to a gut-wrenching stop and the doors slid aside.

"After you, my dear." His hand swept toward the open doors in a fluid arc.

Alexandra took a deep breath and stepped into the fortress's great hall, her eyes widening with disbelief when she saw the setting for the archduke's ball. The hall was immense, with ornate columns carved from cool white marble curving outward from the walls every ten feet or so in an unbroken line. Above, a concave ceiling soared upward for hundreds of feet, so high she could barely see the elaborate frescoes painted on the domed surface. Beneath her feet, pale marble floors inlaid with jet onyx gleamed under the shimmery glow cast by thousands of golden hoverlights, robotic ornaments loosed at parties to drift and weave above the heads of the crowd.

She gaped at the drifting hoverlights in silent wonder as the soothing sounds of eolins and flutes filled the air, the golden orbs appearing to move and weave in perfect harmony with the music. Laughter and the steady hum of conversation filled the hall as well, swelling in volume until the sound almost overpowered the soft strains of the unseen orchestra. In the bright glow of the hoverlights, scores of gold-clad nobles wearing heads of various shapes danced or milled about, the combination of the lights, polished marble, and their golden attire throwing a hazy aura about the entire great hall. The haze itself seemed to eerily distort and magnify the shifting sea of animal heads, giving the costumed nobles the appearance of real creatures with bodies swathed in gold.

A foxen, newt, and elk danced through her line of vision, followed by an odd assortment of exotic beasts native to Old Earth and the Dominion alike. She spotted more sleek foxen weaving through the crowd of nobles, at least a dozen that she could see moving about.

Alexandra shook herself mentally, her senses overwhelmed by the cacophony of sounds and peculiar sights. To her wondering eyes, the ball looked like some scene risen to life from a fantastic dream.

"Beautiful, isn't it?" Lucien said.

She glanced at up him through the eye slit. "Strange is more like it." The scene was indeed beautiful in a peculiar sort of way, but she wasn't about to agree with him.

A high-pitched peal of sudden laughter warned her that someone had finally spotted her head.

"I don't believe it!" A woman squealed in astonishment. "She's actually wearing an oort head!"

Others joined in, laughing uproariously at the sight of the creature's tall blue head. Loud conversations and gesturing followed as the nobles speculated on the identity of the hapless wearer. A crowd began to gather, forming a glee-filled circle around them. The names Charbonneau and Fallon slipped from a tongue, then spread like wildfire to a dozen more. The talk and ribald laughter turned malicious, a cruel contagion that infected dozens of listeners.

Alexandra gritted her teeth and tilted the heavy head back as far as she could, holding it at an angle that she hoped appeared indifferent.

"That's it, love," Lucien whispered beside her.

"Hold that head up and show them you don't care."

She gave an unseen frown. *How odd.* First he'd forced her to wear the embarrassing head; now he was encouraging her to keep up a brave front, as if he actually cared how she felt.

Lucien clasped her hand in his and led her toward the fringes of the crowd, easing through the gathering throng with grace and aplomb.

Alexandra threw her husband a puzzled look and glanced at the elegant hand that was clutching hers in a way that could only be termed possessive. Even odder was the fact that as soon as his flesh touched hers she'd felt a tiny flush of pleasure sweep through her blood.

An imposing figure clad in a simple gold robe and a menacing snow-bear head suddenly stepped in their path, blocking their passage with his immense body. The man placed his hands on his hips, the white bear face seeming to glower as he pointed the snout and fangs toward Alexandra.

"An oort head suits you well, girl," the bear said gruffly.

Dread curdled the insides of her stomach. She'd know that voice anywhere. "Hello, Uncle Theodore."

The huge bear snout emitted a disparaging noise, an angry, growllike sound. "You little witch. If I had my druthers, I'd turn you over my knee right now and flay the skin from your treacherous backside."

Instinctively, Alexandra inched closer to her husband. "I'm a married woman now," she said tightly. "You haven't the right."

His hands curled into huge fists. "Just watch me. . . . I'm sure your husband would like to have his pound of flesh as well."

Lucien interposed his body between Alexandra and her brawny uncle. "Why, Lord Fallon, is that really you behind that immense head?" he said in a gushing, falsetto voice. "How good it is to see you again! I've so hoped for this day to come, when we could all be together once more." Out of the corner of his eye slit, he saw another figure sidling toward them—stiff, prim, and wearing a dour-faced bird head. Lucien's arms swept outward in a graceful gesture that encompassed his somber father. "Now that all of the unpleasantness is done with and Alexandra and I have been reunited, I know we shall all become dear, dear friends." He angled his head in the direction of Baron Charbonneau. "Isn't that right, Father?"

Theodore's bear head shuddered slightly, and he blew out a loud snort of disgust. *Friends indeed.* "Of course we shall," he said in a saccharine tone. A show of temper in the baron's presence might undermine the alliance even further. "The baron and I are already allies. True friendship can't be far behind."

Renaud Charbonneau's chilly silence spoke for itself. His gaze fixed on his son with unswerving intensity, his scornful look somehow penetrating the feathered face mask. "If you had been any sort of man on your wedding night, none of this would have occurred to begin with," he told his son icily. "Instead I have been publicly humiliated by your inability to control your own wife."

Theodore emitted a short bark of laughter, then clapped the baron across the back, thanking the gods that Charbonneau seemed to be laying the blame for this sordid business at the feet of his son, not the Fallon clan. "I concur with that! If you two hadn't botched things so badly, Alexandra would be breeding by now, and the baron and

I wouldn't have spent the past few weeks dealing with the scandal." His hoard of chits wouldn't be threatened either.

The sting of their words made Alexandra wince, not for herself but for her husband, who bore no responsibility for what she'd done. She glared at both of them. "How dare either of you say such a thing! Lucien bears no responsibility for my actions," she said angrily, wondering what had possessed her to come to his defense. "And who are you to point fingers at either of us? You arranged this marriage without our knowledge or consent, just so you could have your precious alliance and make a few measly chits. What about us? What about how *we* feel? The law doesn't give you the right to destroy our lives!"

Behind his mask, Lucien grinned. His impassioned wife was defending him to her uncle and his own father. But he had to put an end to the confrontation soon. Time was short, and he had to make his move as soon as the archduke made his appearance.

"The law gives us the right to do whatever we will, girl," Theodore said stonily.

She threw up her hands and glared up at him. "Then that law needs to be overturned. I am not your chattel, Uncle, to barter or sell when the mood strikes. I think the rebels are absolutely right—if the government refuses to change with the times, then it needs to be overthrown."

Baron Charbonneau gasped and glanced around to see if anyone had overheard his daughter-in-law's treasonous talk. His face heated beneath his mask. Several ball guests turned, and he was sure he read shock in their eyes. "Cease such talk immediately!" he said quietly. By marrying Lucien off, he had hoped to free himself from potential embarrassment, but now it appeared that he had simply weighted his neck with a second albatross. "Haven't you brought enough shame to our clans already?"

She gazed back at him coolly. "No . . . I don't think so. Not yet."

"Alexandra," Lucien warned quietly. "Don't bother. They're mired in the past, in the way things were done a thousand years ago. Nothing you can say will ever change their minds." A curious crowd had begun to gather around them, including several of the archduke's entourage. "But it may change the archduke's mind," he said even more quietly.

As the meaning of his hushed words sank in, Alexandra forced herself to calm down. The archduke could revoke her parole as easily as he'd given it, and she didn't want to become one of Thigg's guests again.

She stared at her uncle and the baron in disgust. "Well, it seems the two of you got exactly what you wanted in the end. Lucien and I are together, so I suppose you'll have your damn alliance. Be satisfied with that and leave us alone."

She grasped Lucien by the arm and tried to walk away, but Theodore blocked their path again.

"What about my chits?" Theodore grated, eyeing his niece's husband appraisingly. The peacock had probably spent enough on his buttons alone to refund his chits. "Someone has to pay me back."

"What chits?" Alexandra snapped.

"The reward that miserable little general is demanding for your return."

For the first time all evening Alexandra actually smiled. Her greedy uncle had gotten just what he deserved. She lifted her shoulders in an exaggerated shrug. "Sorry, Uncle. You should have known better than to put a price on my head. There's no telling what sort of vermin you'll unearth when you do something like that, and you unearthed a particularly nasty one. I suggest you pay up before he tosses *you* into one of his prisons."

Her heart pounding, she sidestepped him and continued on her way, smiling in satisfaction beneath her mask. After all these years, she'd finally managed to best her uncle in an argument. And despite his blustering threats, there was really nothing that he could do to her, nothing that wouldn't cause him further scandal. Perhaps this marriage thing wouldn't be so bad after all.

Lucien stopped abruptly amid a group of costumed dancers, forcing her to stop as well. "I suddenly have the urge to dance with my wife." He held out his hands. "Would you mind very much? I promise I won't step on your feet."

She gazed at him for a moment, considering, then clasped his outstretched hands. "If you want."

Lucien swept her into a graceful Andwillian waltz, eager for an excuse to hold her close for a short while. The archduke would be making his formal entrance soon, and that was when he'd have to slip away. "You were magnificent," he told her proudly. "Few people have ever spoken to my father as you did. I'm sure he's still reeling from the shock."

"My uncle, too." She smiled to herself as the crowd's robes and the hoverlights spun past in a rush of gold. "I must admit it felt good. They're both such pompous asses."

He laughed and pulled her closer as they danced past Lord Fallon and his father, who were standing shoulder to shoulder watching from the sidelines, the bird and bear an unlikely duo. "They're watching us, you know, probably gleeful that we're dancing together, and wondering if it's safe to move forward with the alliance."

"Let them wonder," Alexandra said harshly, maneuvering the oort horns so she wouldn't gouge the side of his head.

Lucien peered at her intently. "What about us, Alexandra? They may have arranged our marriage, but we can't put aside the fact that we are husband and wife. Would a life with me be such a terrible thing?"

Before answering, she gazed up into his foxen face, trying to gauge the man hidden behind the all-encompassing mask. A haze of golden light suddenly spilled through the narrow slit cut in his mask, illuminating the cool gray eyes secreted beneath. A tiny gasp slipped free of her throat. For a moment, all she could see were those silvery eyes, a sight so hauntingly familiar that her heart skipped a startled beat.

Damion's eyes.

There was no mistaking what she saw, what she *felt* in response to the sight of those stormy gray eyes. And then she remembered the sense of déjà vu that had plagued her whenever Vash was near, how his eyes had given her that same eerie feeling.

A tiny flame of comprehension suddenly slid through her body, flaring like wildfire when it spread to the chaos in her mind. The cool gray eyes staring into hers weren't just similar to Damion's and Vash's, no mere coincidence that she could calmly brush aside. They belonged to three different men, as diverse from each other as night to day. Different, yet somehow the same. But how could such a thing be possible?

Lucien felt her stiffen beneath his arms. "Is

something wrong?" he asked, concerned by her abrupt change in demeanor.

For once Alexandra was glad that her face was hidden beneath the oort head. "Nothing," she said in a shaky voice. Her hands and voice were trembling, and she knew her skin had turned a ghostly shade of white.

He frowned in concern and danced her toward the edge of the crowd. She had yet to answer his question. "Are you sure?"

"Yes." She touched a hand to the heavy head to adjust its position. "I'm just tired, and this thing weighs a ton."

The waltz ended, and the rousing strains of the Dominion anthem suddenly filled the hall, ending any hope of conversation. The hoverlights dimmed to pinpoints of gold, and the crowd surged forward, eager to find vantage points in order to watch Luc Davies make his grand entrance. Around them, the press of costumed nobles thickened.

A rush of adrenaline pounded through Lucien's bloodstream as a stream of flag bearers and courtiers began spilling through an arched doorway, lead elements in the archduke's lengthy procession. He had to slip away now, while all eyes—including Alexandra's—were focused on the pomp and ceremony of the formal procession. If fortune favored him, he would be back near the time the fanfare ended, with no one the wiser about his absence. He would demand an answer from her then.

He eased his hand free of Alexandra's and moved back a step as a drum corps joined the orchestra's stirring rendition of the patriotic anthem. Her back was to him now, and her attention was focused on the procession, not on him.

Nearby, another noble wearing a foxen head shouldered his way forward until he was almost even with Alexandra. Lucien grinned in relief. A stand-in had appeared, just as he'd hoped. He moved back several more steps, then stole away, slipping toward the entrance to a corridor that would lead him to the ground-floor suite Thigg used as an office.

Alexandra felt rather than saw him move away and turned her head instinctively, watching her husband covertly as he slipped through the crowd. She watched his progress through eyes newly opened to the strangest of possibilities, eyes that now searched for the tiniest of flaws in his public persona. She frowned. One oddity she noticed was her husband's fluidly graceful gait. Before she'd simply dismissed it in her mind as mincing and annoyingly effete. Now she realized that there was something exaggerated about the way he moved. Something *feigned*.

She set off after him, wending her way through the preoccupied nobles on a swift path that closely resembled his, careful to keep the top of his foxen head in sight at all times. If she lost him now, she'd never be able to find him again, not in such a thick crowd, and certainly not with so many other similar masks around.

He disappeared into a wide corridor, and Alexandra followed, stealing through the deep shadows that ran along the marble walls.

Lucien paused near a tiny alcove and peered down the long corridor, cursing silently when he spotted the security guards. A group of soldiers was visible in the distance, stationed at the juncture to a secondary hallway, where the fortress's public areas ended and General Thigg's headquarters began. He hadn't counted on there being quite so many guards at this time of night, far too many to try to slip past.

He frowned in consternation. The guise and identicard he'd planned to use might pass muster with a guard or two, but not with a crowd of them. There would be too many questions. Too many chances for something to go wrong. What he needed was a completely new identity, one that would assure him of instant access to the heavily guarded wing. A face no one would dare to question.

It came to him, then. Working swiftly, he checked the corridor and alcove to make sure no security lenses were roaming about, then pulled the suffocating animal head off and stashed it in the shadows. Then he removed his robe and turned it inside out, glancing down in satisfaction after he'd redressed in his new attire. His golden robe was reversible. It was now simple and unadorned, not the sort of garment worn by the fashionable Charbonneau, but so utterly ordinary that there was nothing to distinguish it from scores of others being worn at the ball.

Before he stepped from the shadowy alcove, he closed his eyes for a short moment and concentrated on his appearance. His hair suddenly shifted, turning darker, shorter, his complexion darkening as well. A mustache appeared where none had been, and features that had been slender and aristocratic a second before became coarser and less defined.

Lucien swept the black hair straight back and tilted his new squarish chin to an inflexible angle, then folded his hands tightly behind his back. He marched confidently toward Thigg's office. A moment later he turned down the secondary corridor and nodded curtly to the startled guards.

The uniformed guards snapped to full attention, clicking their heels smartly when they recognized the man marching toward them. "General, sir!" a young officer stammered, eyeing his superior's robe in amazement. "We didn't know you were attending the ball!"

"Obviously," Lucien said and threw the officer an arrogant look. He ground to a halt at the door to Thigg's private office and glared at the young man impatiently. "Well? I don't have all night. Open the doors, Lieutenant. I need to retrieve some papers before I meet with the archduke."

For several seconds, the officer simply stared at him, frowning in confusion; then he rushed to the privacy lock and nervously punched in the proper code. "Right away, sir!" As he entered the final sequence and the armored door swung inward, he saluted and stepped aside. "Is there something else we can do for you tonight, General?"

"No, thank you. You've done more than enough already." Lucien walked swiftly through the office door and closed it tight.

The young guard officer stared at the closed door in astonishment. In all his years of service, General Thigg had never said thank-you for anything.

Down the corridor, Alexandra still stood frozen in a shadow, gaping at the entrance to the empty alcove in utter disbelief. What she'd witnessed wasn't possible. Her husband's face had metamorphosed before her eyes, his features shifting and reshaping into an entirely new face, one that she knew all too well. And then he'd simply walked away, nonchalantly heading toward a different corridor wearing the face of General Thigg.

She took a deep breath to steady herself and clutched at the wall for support, unnerved by the enormity of what she'd seen. Like a chameleon, her husband had changed his appearance in the blink of an eye, seemingly with no more effort required than an ordinary person used to comb their hair. No human had the preternatural ability to do such a thing.

She gasped. Suddenly she knew, understood it all with perfect clarity. Lucien Charbonneau *wasn't* human, couldn't be. At least not entirely human. Her heart rate accelerated to a frenzied pace, and for a second she felt the urge to laugh aloud. She'd spent years searching for evidence of an alien race, when for the past few weeks living proof of its existence had been walking around right before her eyes.

She closed her lids for a moment and rested her head against the cool stone wall, dizzied by the flood of conclusions sweeping through her brain. So many things she hadn't understood, so many clues she'd missed completely. Everything made sense now. Better sense, at least. Like the figures carved onto her bowl and other artifacts, the multiple stone faces that were all different, yet somehow the same. And of course that explained why Damion, Vash, and Lucien had the same silvery eyes—obviously the only feature he couldn't change completely—because all three men were one and the same.

She shook her head in disbelief. Damion alone wasn't the Black Rose—all three of them were, and maybe a dozen other guises as well. Hundreds, maybe, and she was married to one of them. Her husband was the perfect spy, able to change his looks at will, to become someone else entirely when the need arose.

A sudden frown rippled across her face. Which man was actually real, and which was a false persona created by the Black Rose to further his goals? Her husband, her lover, or her friend? Or was he in truth none of those men? She was in love with Damion Flynn, but in reality he might not even exist. Or Damion might actually be the real Lucien Charbonneau. It was all too confusing to contemplate.

Her emotions vacillated wildly, swinging from stunned glee one second to fist-pounding fury the next. The husband she'd scorned had lied, connived, and deceived her in every way imaginable, then stolen her heart under false pretenses. But stolen her heart he had—whoever he truly was. And in the end, that was the only truth that really mattered.

She glanced down the empty corridor, her heart beginning to pound with fear for his safety instead of shock and disbelief. There'd been no sign of him since he rounded the corner and vanished.

She slipped through the shadows the way she'd come, making her way back to the great hall for her own safety as well as his. If he felt compelled to masquerade as the general, it meant that whatever he was doing was very dangerous to his health; he didn't need the added complication of her being spotted lurking about.

Chapter Eighteen

Helford Thigg strode past a guard, then turned down a narrow corridor that ended near his office, going out of his way to avoid the fortress's public areas and the horde of nobles attending the archduke's ball. He was tired, frustrated, and out of sorts. The last thing he needed was to be surrounded by a gaggle of arrogant boors.

His day had been bad enough already, flying about Primus on one goose chase after another in search of the elusive Damion Flynn. In the past three days, black roses had been found at or near Security Force installations all over the entire planet—so many roses he could make a bouquet out of them. The ends of his mustache turned downward. There were so many that one man couldn't possibly have deposited them all. Either that or the flowers had been left as diversions, a gambit devised to keep him and his agents thoroughly occupied. But to what purpose?

A frustrated scowl marred his forehead as he

rounded a turn and entered the main corridor outside his office. A single guard jumped to attention, but the others simply gaped at him, throwing each other befuddled glances as well.

The young lieutenant in command blinked several times and frowned at him curiously, then glanced down the corridor that led to the great hall. "General?" he said in a questioning voice.

Thigg ground to an immediate halt and glared at them all. He'd been gone from the fortress for only a day. Had the fools already forgotten how to salute? "What is going on here, Lieutenant?"

Still frowning, the officer shook his head slightly and stared at the general's crisp black uniform and polished boots. "I . . . I don't understand, sir."

"What don't you understand?" Thigg demanded. "Speak up, man!"

A very bad feeling settled in the pit of the guard's stomach. "You just left here a few seconds ago, sir." He pointed nervously to the adjoining corridor. "You were dressed in a robe and said you were going back to the ball! We thought it was you, sir, I swear it!"

"Fools!" Thigg's face reddened with cold fury when he saw his office door standing open; then he swiveled his angry gaze in the direction the lieutenant had indicated. In the distance, he could indeed see a man clad in a robe, walking swiftly toward the great hall, wearing what looked to be a foxen head. *Flynn.* It had to be.

"Stop that man immediately!" the general screamed. "Lock down every entrance to the great hall! No one leaves! No one!"

As the guards pounded after the imposter, Thigg raced into his office, fearing the worst. A knifelike stab of dread sliced through his gut when he glanced at the top of his desk. A single black rose lay atop the gleaming wood, right next to the square desk vault where he stored his data crystals, including the battle plans for his push against the rebels.

Thigg howled in outrage, his angry shout echoing down the stone corridor. The vault was empty.

Alexandra expelled a shaky breath when she finally spotted Lucien making his way through the crowd, his head back on and the jeweled buttons plainly in view. Whatever he'd been up to, he had seemingly emerged unscathed.

As he approached, she clenched her hands tight to stop them from trembling. Maybe now her limbs would quit quivering. She'd been terrified since she returned to the ball, worried that he'd been captured, or worse. One thing was certain—she wasn't cut out for the life of a spy—or that of a spy's wife.

"There you are, my dear," Lucien said smoothly. "I've been looking all over for you since the procession ended." In truth, he'd walked straight to her. It wasn't hard to find her when she was wearing the only oort head in the crowd.

She stared at him in amazement as the orchestra began playing a hauntingly beautiful Old Earth tune. How could he possibly sound so casual? She'd been nearly mad with fear these past few minutes. "Lucien . . ." she said weakly.

The foxen head cocked to one side. "Yes, love?" He took her hand in his and pulled her against his chest for another dance.

The oort horns bumped his snout as she lifted her face toward his. "I know who you are. . . ." she whispered near his ear.

Years of experience enabled him to keep dancing without missing a single step. "Of course you know who I am," he said lightly. "I'm your husband." A knot of apprehension wedged in the base of his throat, threatening to cut off his breathing.

She gazed at him silently for a long second. "You're my husband, and a few other men as well. Do you want me to name them all for you?"

He stepped on her foot and struggled to clear the knot from his throat. "Why, whatever do you mean?"

"I saw you . . . in the corridor. It's time for truth between us, Lucien—if that's really your name."

He froze in midstep and cleared his throat again. She'd seen him transform. She *knew*—maybe not everything, but enough to know that he couldn't be entirely human, and was a wanted man.

"And?" he said. A weighted question, that, one that could very well decide his future.

Her heart was beating so fast now she thought it might leap from her chest. "I just found out that the man I love is a fantasy. He doesn't even exist. But I know he's there inside my husband . . . somewhere. So I guess that means I love my husband, too . . . whoever he is."

For the space of a single heartbeat Lucien did nothing; then he gripped her hands tighter. "I'm nobody, Alexandra. Nobody but a man who's madly in love with his wife."

The orchestra stopped playing abruptly, and a woman screamed somewhere on the fringes of the crowd. There was another shout, followed by a chorus of angry voices, and the nobles began milling and shifting about, craning to see what was going on.

Alexandra stood on her tiptoes but couldn't see anything over a group of animal-head masks. Fear gripped her. "What's happened?" she said hoarsely.

Behind the mask, Lucien paled, and his body went completely still. A double line of Security Force guards had begun marching into the hall, streaming out along the walls to block the exits and surround the room. He touched the pocket where he'd hidden the data crystals. Somehow, some way, the Security Force had already discovered what he'd done, and now there would be hell to pay.

He grabbed Alexandra roughly and pulled her into his arms, drawing her close to his mouth. There was a very real possibility that he wouldn't leave the room alive. "Listen to me carefully, Alexandra, and do exactly what I say!" he whispered urgently. "Tay has landed the ship at the spaceport by now, and Loran's with him. If I'm taken prisoner, or if anything goes wrong at all, I want you to make a run for the ship. Don't dare wait for me! The three of you have to get off this planet and never look back. Those guards are after me, not you." His grip on her arms tightened. There was no telling what Thigg would do if he got his hands on her again. "Promise me you'll make a run for it!"

She stared up at him in shock. She couldn't lose him now. Wouldn't. Not when she'd finally discovered the truth. "No, Lucien, I can't—"

"Don't argue with me, Alexandra!" His fingers dug into her shoulders ruthlessly. "Not about this! It's too important!"

"I'm not leaving you!" she whispered back, and clung to his hand tightly, refusing to let go.

General Thigg strolled through an arched doorway, and the crowd fell utterly silent, shifting and moving backward to get out of his way. He tapped a hand against his thigh impatiently, his dark gaze sweeping over the frightened nobles. The doors were sealed shut, and armed guards were stationed every few feet around the edges of the room. He had Flynn this time. An insect couldn't escape the hall now, much less the Black Rose.

"Gather up everyone wearing a foxen mask!" he shouted to the guards. "Place them in the center of the room and remove their heads!"

Several nobles screamed in terror, and Thigg rolled his eyes toward the domed ceiling. Dealing with these foolish people was trying under the most ordinary of circumstances. "Remove their costume heads!" he amended, which caused sighs of relief to ripple through the crowd.

As the guards herded the costumed suspects into the center of the room, Thigg paced back and forth, growing more impatient with each second that passed. The cluster of dark foxen heads continued to grow in size, swelling until nearly fifty nobles had been forced to join the unfortunate group.

He scrutinized them intently, still tapping his thigh. "One of you is a man named Damion Flynn, better known as the Black Rose, and I intend to find out who it is!"

A veritable herd of black foxen stared back at him, the gold-clad bodies beneath those heads either short or tall, thin or overweight. Thigg's gaze suddenly stilled on an unexpected splotch of blue amid the gold and black.

He walked toward it curiously, lifting a bemused brow when he spotted an oort head peering at him from the back of the group. "I said foxen, not oorts," Thigg snapped in a commanding voice, but the wearer didn't move. The woman was clinging tightly to the hand of a tall noble, a gesture that looked almost desperate to Thigg's eyes. His suspicion aroused, he reached out and grabbed the curved horns and snatched off the head.

Alexandra gasped, her unbound hair tumbling around her shoulders in a dark torrent.

Thigg grinned in delight. "Ah, Lady Fallon! Why am I not surprised to find you here? I should have known it was you beneath that oort mask. How appropriate."

His gaze thinned and moved to the costumed man standing next to her. It was Flynn hiding beneath that head, undoubtedly wearing a second mask made to look like the general. A very clever ploy, one that had fooled an entire squadron of guards. "And this must be your lover. . . . I've been most anxious to meet you, Captain Flynn. Or should I say, the Black Rose."

The general snapped his fingers and a guard jerked off the foxen head.

Thigg's jaw fell and his body stiffened in shock. "No . . ." he whispered to himself. It was that simpering wastrel Charbonneau, not his quarry.

Lucien lifted his chin to an outraged angle and glared back. "What is the meaning of this, General?" he said in an arrogant huff. "How dare you treat my wife and I like common street thugs." He sniffed delicately. "I demand an immediate apology!"

Thigg's eyes narrowed with a blend of suspicion and bewilderment. Something was very wrong here. He'd been positive that it was Damion Flynn hiding beneath that head. He nodded to the guards. "Get everyone's mask off and search their robes! Flynn is here and he has my data crystals. I want them found!"

A sudden flurry of awed whispers rolled through the crowd, spreading from one aristocrat to the next. Nobles fell back to open a path through their midst as a small, glittering figure pushed through the press, his immense train carried by four breathless pages.

The archduke came to an abrupt stop a few feet shy of General Thigg. His pages halted behind him. Luc Davies glared at his general, his eyes crackling with blue fire. "You will cease this insanity at once, General!" His mouth set in a flat, inflexible line. "These people are our guests! They will not be treated in such a fashion by the general of our troops! Remove the guards immediately!"

Thigg glowered back. "One of your *guests* is the Black Rose, and no one is going to leave this hall until I find him!"

The archduke stiffened, his round face turning a hot, angry red. "Are you refusing our orders again, General?" He waved a hand toward the gathered nobles. "The entire High Council is here tonight, more than enough for the quorum needed to remove you as head of the Security Force! We shall call for a vote at once!"

Thigg's eyes widened. He didn't have the slightest doubt that the archduke would carry out his threat.

"Withdraw the guards, General!" The archduke's fiery gaze touched Lucien and Alexandra, then moved over the gathering of nobles. "The ball is over! Everyone leave!"

Hundreds of aristocrats followed the order without hesitation, whispering and shuffling as they hurriedly made their way to the doors.

The archduke glared at his general. "We shall deal with you later, General."

Thigg pulled in a long, slow breath to calm himself as his suspects began to scatter, moving toward the nearest exits with undignified haste. He steeled his shoulders and nodded to the captain of the guards, signaling for his troops to withdraw as well.

His chilly gaze rested on Alexandra Fallon and

her husband for a long second. "Another time, perhaps." Then he straightened a crease in his tunic and followed the retreating guards, his boot heels clacking loudly against the marble floor.

As the hall began to empty, Lucien tugged on Alexandra's hand, surreptitiously urging her into motion. They turned slowly and crept toward the nearest door.

"Lucien!" The single word echoed over them like the crack of a whip.

They froze in unison and turned back to face the archduke.

Luc Davies dismissed the young pages with an angry flick of his hand. "We would have a word with you, Lucien."

Within seconds, the great hall was completely deserted. A door slammed at the far end of the cavernous room, the sound echoing over and over in the ominous silence. Lucien gave her hand a reassuring squeeze. Only the three of them were left, standing alone in the center of the opulent room.

"Yes, your grace?" Lucien said calmly, though he felt anything but calm. His pocket was filled with stolen data crystals.

The archduke glowered. "We are very annoyed, Lucien. You and your wife have forced us to take a stand against our own general, but your recent activities left us with little choice. We could not allow you to be taken into custody."

A guileless expression settled over Lucien's features. "Me, your grace? I don't understand."

Luc Davies took an angry step forward, dragging the heavy gold train in his wake. "Do not attempt to play word games with us, Lucien. Your protestations of innocence fall on deafened ears. We know what you are.... We have always known what you are."

Alexandra paled, and Lucien stared back at him in shock.

"All those who've ever borne the title of Dominion archduke have known of the existence of your people, and toiled diligently to keep that knowledge secret. We have also allowed the remainder of your race to live and move freely among us without retribution, even intermarry with us when they so choose, as long as your existence remained secret from the public at large."

A shadow moved through his pale eyes. "It's our penance for the shame of what the first humans did to the Arulians, how we stole your worlds and warred with your people, all because we were terrified of beings different from us. But also because we feared that you would use your abilities to gain an advantage over us, destroy us as we sought to destroy you."

Lucien stared at him silently, dumbstruck by the archduke's unexpected admission.

The archduke's pale gaze settled on Alexandra. "Do you understand now, Lady Fallon? With the title of archduke comes many responsibilities. The confiscation of your artifacts was not an arbitrary act. Among the few who know the truth, there are still those whose fear is so great that they would foment bloodshed in order to rid the Dominion of the remnants of the Arulians. As with your father, we could not allow you to bring your evidence to light, because such knowledge might trigger a renewal of hostilities."

Alexandra's eyes widened. "You had my father's research stolen?"

He dipped his head in a regretful nod. "Some bones are best left buried in anonymous graves." He studied her for a long moment. "Let those bones rest in peace, Lady Fallon, for all our sakes. The time will eventually come when the truth can

Jan Zimlich

be known and accepted. But that time is not now. Not yet."

Luc Davies turned his attention back to his not-quite-human friend—the friend he was about to lose forever. "You and your wife cannot remain here, Lucien. General Thigg is an inquisitive man. Sooner or later he will unearth the truth about everything, and when he does, we won't be willing—or able—to protect you." A brief flash of amusement flickered in his eyes. "Thigg and the High Council would not look kindly on an arch-duke who had consorted with the Black Rose spy."

Lucien stared at him in amazement. He knew about that, too?

A corner of the archduke's mouth lifted. "Although the possibility had crossed our mind on more than one occasion, we weren't entirely certain until we were told that an impostor had stolen into General Thigg's office and made off with classified data crystals—an impostor who was physically perfect in every way. Only an Arulian could have ever hoped to accomplish such a remarkable feat. It *was* you."

Lucien shrugged and shifted uncomfortably but said nothing in his defense.

The archduke wagged an admonishing finger, then held out his palm. "The data crystals, if you please."

Lucien sighed. All his efforts had been for naught. "If you insist." He reached inside his pocket and removed the small crystal cubes, dropping them into the archduke's palm one by one. "This changes nothing, your grace. The rebels won't rest until lasting reform occurs within the Dominion. If it takes a war to achieve our goals, then we'll fight."

Luc Davies nodded slowly and closed his hand

around the crystals. "Change will come, Lucien, even without a war. Perhaps not in our lifetimes, but it will come, whether we want it to or not. Change is the only true constant in the universe. We cannot escape it, no matter how hard we try."

"A lifetime is too long to wait," Lucien said quietly.

"Perhaps it is." The archduke frowned and pursed his lips, mulling over the consequences of what he was about to do. But he saw no help for it now, not if he were to keep hiding the truth. "Tell your rebel leaders that we will agree to formally meet with them in thirty days' time. We shall attend that meeting with an open mind, but promise no more than that."

A relieved smile touched Lucien's features. "Thank you, your grace." He hadn't offered much, but it was a start. Now he just had to wait and see what the archduke demanded in exchange for the favor.

"Do not be among those leaders, Lucien." The archduke caught and held his gaze for an endless second. "In exchange for meeting with your rebel cohorts, we ask that you both leave now, and not return. Too much knowledge often carries a very steep price, and the price you will pay is banishment from the Dominion. We shall concoct a likely tale to explain your absence to your families, but under no circumstances are you to return without our express permission." He motioned toward the hall's main doors with an annoyed wave of his hand. "You had best leave quickly before we forget our friendship and turn you over to General Thigg instead."

Lucien bent forward in a formal bow, slower and deeper than normal to show his gratitude and respect. The archduke could have ordered them both killed with a flick of his elegant hand.

Instead he'd given them their lives—and a future. Together. "Good-bye, your grace."

Luc Davies watched in silence as they hurried to the doors and safety. He touched the glittering crystals nestled in his palm, wondering how many of them were still secreted in Lucien's pocket. One, two? The gods only knew. Lucien might be his friend, but he was still a spy, and no self-respecting spy would have returned them all. He would have certainly kept the most damning of the crystals, the one containing Helford Thigg's plan of battle. Of course now, if Lucien was in possession of those plans, there could be no war. At least not in the near future. He would inform Thigg of that to assure there would be no bloodshed.

The archduke suppressed an amused smile and started walking toward a different set of doors, the heavy train sliding along the marble behind him. He wasn't in the mood for a war anyway. Maybe next year.

Chapter Nineteen

A dense spiral of stars glittered like fiery jewels set against the velvety darkness, pinpoints of blue and red and gold that merged into a brilliant white closer to the chaotic swirl of the galactic core. Alexandra draw in an awed breath and continued to stare, mesmerized by the breathtaking vista shimmering outside the cabin's viewing window. *So many stars. So many possibilities.*

In the near distance, a small green world turned slowly through the cosmic night, sunlight rippling across the surface of an inland sea: Tay and Loran's new home. Within hours the couple planned to leave the *Nightwind* together, determined to forge new lives as colonists on the planet below.

Alexandra's eyes darkened with a touch of sadness. She'd miss Loran dearly, but they would see each other again. Someday she'd be able to return to the Dominion and visit her friend. A few years, Lucien had said, five at the most, long enough for the archduke to forgive and forget. Until that time, they wouldn't tempt fate.

She turned toward her sleeping husband, the silky bedsheet twisting and tangling down the length of her bare legs. One good thing had come from their banishment—his days as the Black Rose had been put to an unexpected end, and for that she would always be grateful. She didn't particularly relish the notion of being the widow of a spy any more than she wanted to be the wife of one.

Alexandra studied his chiseled face curiously, her gaze roaming over the strong line of his jaw and aquiline nose, the firm yet sensual lips that drove her wild with desire. The husband who lay sleeping beside her was and wasn't Lucien Charbonneau. All trace of the callow aristocrat she'd married had vanished in the past few days, and a slightly altered man had taken his place, one with boldly sculpted features and a well-muscled body reminiscent of Damion Flynn's.

A sudden frown danced across her features. For some reason, she couldn't quite lay to rest the stubborn niggle of doubt that kept surfacing in her mind. Was this in fact the real Lucien Charbonneau, or just another impostor?

"Lucien?" she said quietly, her eyes narrowing with a small glint of suspicion.

He stretched slowly and opened his lids, not surprised to find his seductive wife peering at him so dubiously. His brows lifted in amusement. He'd caught her watching him at the oddest times these past few days. "Yes, love?" he answered softly, and drew her into his arms, pulling her lithe body tight against him. The touch of her satiny flesh to his caused a renewed rush of desire to sweep through his blood.

She propped her elbows atop his chest and

gazed into his silvery eyes. "Have I finally met the real you? Or am I going to wake up tomorrow with a total stranger in bed beside me?"

Lucien gave her a lazy grin, his hands beginning a slow downward course, sliding past the curve of her waist to catch and hold her hips. "Don't tell me you're still pining away for Damion Flynn. I told you I wouldn't share my wife with another man."

She nipped his ear in retaliation, then teased her lips along the side of his neck, eliciting a low groan of pleasure from her chameleon husband. "You still haven't answered my question, Lucien." She wound her hands through his thick blond hair and pressed herself against him.

The hue of his eyes darkened to a deep, passion-filled gray as he folded his arms about her, his lips tracing a heated course that would take him to the base of her throat, then much lower. "Does it really matter?" he murmured against her flesh.

She stared into his face for long seconds, smiling softly, then slowly shook her head. "Not in the least."

HEART'S Prey
JAN ZIMLICH

She is a wild woman with flowing coppery tresses and luminous emerald eyes. Yet Rayna Syn is so much more to Dax Vahnti: She is his assassin. The savage beauty's attempt on his life fails, but the Warlord cannot let his guard down for a moment, not even when the lovely creature with wild russet hair enchants his very being. His need to possess the wondrous beauty is overpowering, yet the danger she presents cannot be denied.

___52277-2 $4.99 US/$5.99 CAN

Dorchester Publishing Co., Inc.
P.O. Box 6640
Wayne, PA 19087-8640

Please add $1.75 for shipping and handling for the first book and $.50 for each book thereafter. NY, NYC, and PA residents, please add appropriate sales tax. No cash, stamps, or C.O.D.s. All orders shipped within 6 weeks via postal service book rate. Canadian orders require $2.00 extra postage and must be paid in U.S. dollars through a U.S. banking facility.

Name_____
Address_____
City_____State_____Zip_____
I have enclosed $_____ in payment for the checked book(s).
Payment <u>must</u> accompany all orders. ☐ Please send a free catalog.
CHECK OUT OUR WEBSITE! www.dorchesterpub.com

BODY & SOUL
JENNIFER ARCHER

Overworked, underappreciated housewife and mother Lisa O'Conner gazes at the young driver in the red car next to her. Tory Beecham's manicured nails keep time with the radio and her smile radiates youthful vitality. For a moment, Lisa imagines switching places with the carefree college student. But when Lisa looks in the rearview mirror and sees Tory's hazel eyes peering back at her, she discovers her daydream has become astonishing reality. Fortune has granted Lisa every woman's fantasy. But as the goggle-eyed, would-be young suitors line up at Lisa's door, only one man piques her interest. But he is married—to her, or rather, the woman she used to be. And he seems intent on being faithful. Unsure how to woo her husband, Lisa knows one thing: No matter what else comes of the madcap, mix-matched mayhem, she will be reunited body and soul with her only true love.

___52334-5 $5.50 US/$6.50 CAN

Romeo & Julia
Annie Kimberlin

Liz Hadley is a cat person, and since she doesn't currently own a kitten, there is nothing that she wants more. The stray that was found in the snowy library parking lot is perfect; she can't wait to go home and cuddle. Still, the arms that hold the cat aren't so bad, either. The man her co-workers call Romeo apparently also has a soft spot for all things furry, though it appears to be the only soft spot on his entire body. The man has the build of a Greek god and his eyes are something altogether more heavenly. And in the poetry of his kisses, the lovely librarian finds something more profound than she's ever read and something sweeter than she's ever known.

___52341-8 $5.50 US/$6.50 CAN

ParadiseBay

Victoria Alexander

In the early seventeenth century, a group of women were transported to an uncharted island as punishment for crimes ranging from poor housekeeping to promiscuity. Within several years of their arrival, a British ship, under the command of mutineers, stumbled onto the island to be greeted enthusiastically by the marooned females. Thus was born Paradise Bay.

Today, its pristine golden beaches and sweet tropic climes are the perfect place to ring in the new millennium. For four hundred years the magic of the island has brought people together with a fiery sunset, the scent of coconut sweetening the evening breeze. Who can resist the passion? Not Trish and Jack, and certainly not you. Come to where the day begins. Give yourself to Paradise Bay.

___52350-7 $5.99 US/$6.99 CAN

An Original Sin
Nina Bangs

Fortune MacDonald listens to women's fantasies on a daily basis as she takes their orders for customized men. In a time when the male species is extinct, she is a valued man-maker. So when she awakes to find herself sharing a bed with the most lifelike, virile man she has ever laid eyes or hands on, she lets her gaze inventory his assets. From his long dark hair, to his knife-edged cheekbones, to his broad shoulders, to his jutting—well, all in the name of research, right?—it doesn't take an expert any time at all to realize that he is the genuine article, a bona fide man. And when Leith Campbell takes her in his arms, she knows real passion for the first time . . . but has she found true love?

___52324-8 $5.99 US/$6.99 CAN

Something Wild

Kimberly Raye

Dependent only upon twentieth-century conveniences, Tara Martin seeks to make a name for herself as a top-notch photojournalist. But when a plea from her best friend sends her off into the Smoky Mountains to snap a sasquatch, a twisted ankle leaves her in a precarious position—and when she looks up, she sees the biggest foot she's ever seen. Tara learns that the big foot belongs to an even bigger man—with a colossal heart and a body to die for. And that man, who was raised alone in the wilds of Appalachia, will teach Tara that what she needs is something wild.

___52272-1 $5.50 US/$6.50 CAN